BEYOND AZARA
A UNIVERSAL LOVE STORY

MARTIN W. BALL

BEYOND AZARA:
A UNIVERSAL LOVE STORY

by Martin W. Ball

©2012 Martin W. Ball
Kyandara Publishing
/CreateSpace

ISBN: 978-1470031954

Dedicated to all those willing to undergo the rigors of genuine self-discovery and find the courage to be themselves.

Special thanks to my wife, Jessalynn Jones, and my good friend, David Wolske, for the assistance with editing. I greatly appreciate your input and help in bringing this book into its final form.

Martin Ball
Spring, 2012

About *Beyond Azara*:

"A combination of *Brave New World, 1984,* and *The Teachings of Don Juan.* A recommended read for those interested in 'after Armageddon' and the survival of the human spirit in spite of war, despots, and religious philosophies out of touch with human needs."

- John A. Rush, Ph.D., author of *The Mushroom in Christian Art,* and *Failed God*

"With his latest work of fiction, Martin Ball continues to astound us with his prolific output and his on-going conversation about all things entheogenic"

- James Oroc, author of *Tryptamine Palace: 5-MeO-DMT and the Sonoran Desert Toad*

"If you thought the sex, drugs and rock and roll of the '60s was something, wait until the seductive sexual and entheogenic juices role right off of the pages of this post-apocalyptic magnum opus, right into your neither region, sending you into a world where you'll cum to understand yourself. And the best part is, this book's details of experience and methods are the real deal."

- Jan Irvin, author of *The Holy Mushroom*

I am Water
And I am Everywhere
∞
I can fill any shape
Take any form
∞
I can reflect you
As long as you like,
For I am You
∞
Remember:
What you do to water,
You do to yourself
∞
I am Water
And I am Thirsty . . .

Chapter 1

SLIPPING INTO
INFINITY

"Do not fight what you feel," came the old man's voice, deeply resonant, vibrating richly with otherworldly tones. It was almost inhuman in quality. "Just breathe and allow."

Jendru felt himself falling back, slipping into infinity. *Whose voice is that?* He struggled for an instant to recall his mentor's name, but it was like trying to pull a single thread of information out of an endless, rapidly expanding vortex. There was nothing stable, no ground, no foundation: only infinitely pulsing waves of ever-expanding energy.

"Let your mind go. Let all your thoughts drop away."

That voice? Who is that?

Details. Why couldn't he recall them? They seemed to be important to someone, but to whom? Who was it that wanted to know who was speaking?

"Understanding is irrelevant. Just feel."

There it was again - that deep, profound voice. It was unrecognizable. It almost sounded artificial. Was someone trying to trick him?

Chaos enveloped Jendru. Absolutely nothing made sense. He couldn't even think of his own name. Where did reality go? What was this? He felt nauseous. Everything was endless geometry, turning inside out, like belts of infinitely repeating shapes cycling through the vortex of a torus passing right through the center of his being. How long had this been going on? It felt eternal. Somehow, *this was reality.*

This is what is real.

"Yes," he heard the voice say again, as though in answer to his private thoughts.

Suddenly, the nausea was overwhelming. He was

turning inside out. *This is impossible.* Frantically, he sought after something, anything that would bring the tumult to a peaceful stillness. But there was nothing there - only endless fluctuations of pulsing energy.

"You can let that go, if you want."

He's right. I can.

With the dawning of that simple understanding, Jendru's body began vibrating violently. Impossible waves of energy danced along his central column. His body undulated in resonance with the endless flow. He distinctly felt a line running down the middle of his being, dividing reality into two mirrored, symmetrical sides.

It was coming now. It threatened to annihilate the young man. He could tell that he was fighting against it. He felt himself twisting in the energy, trying to find a place of serenity, away from the overwhelming nausea.

If I let this out, it will destroy me.

He couldn't fight it any more. There was no point. If it were to kill him, then so be it.

Jendru suddenly sat up as the geometric flow focused in on the upsurge and turmoil that he could only assume was his belly. He felt the decision of *yes* flow through him as the torrent unleashed. Bitter, acidic fluid poured out of his mouth, expelling into the gap between his open and bent legs.

"Yes," he heard the deep voice say again. "Beautiful, my love."

More and more came, each retch digging deeper into his being. Mucous, bile, and bits of half-digested food spilled onto the mat and covered his bare chest and stomach. Strangely, he found that he loved it. Absolutely loved it. The filth was glorious. And he somehow knew that in loving the vomit, he was loving himself, accepting himself. More and more came. With each heave, the intensity only seemed to grow, climbing towards some infinite apex.

This is everything I ever thought I was . . . I'm full of shit, just like everyone else.

The final heave propelled him backwards, once again sinking into infinite oblivion. But this time it was different. This time he wasn't afraid. This time the nausea was gone, and in its place was pure, distilled ecstasy. Nothing mattered anymore . . . only this . . .

What am I doing?

Suddenly Jendru was aware of himself once more. His hands were poised in front of him, thumbs and middle fingers touching at the tips, with both hands brought together forming something of the image of a mask, his other fingers pointing upwards. Jendru had the distinct impression that he had been moving, making gestures with his hands and arms. But as he looked at his hands, he found he had no idea what had taken place. The last thing he could remember was the terrible, ecstatic vomiting that had felt as though all of reality were turning inside out with him at the very center, the eye of some cosmic maelstrom. And then infinite ecstasy . . .

Looking beyond his hands, he saw his mentor sitting opposite him with his hands out in front of him in what appeared to be a mirror image of himself. Jendru could tell that the effects of the drug were still extraordinarily strong. Geometry flowed out of the image of his teacher. His skin was luminescent, with creeping subtle flows of intricate geometric shapes and forms swirling about the surface of his body. Jendru caught his teacher's eye, and suddenly found it almost impossible to look him directly in the face, which was shifting and changing rapidly, appearing beatific one moment, demonic the next. He sucked in a deep breath, the sound of which made him feel oddly self-conscious and exposed.

"Yes, hello again, *Jendru.*"

Seyloq - that's Seyloq, but why does he sound so strange?

"Why does your voice sound like that?" Jendru asked, marveling at the artificiality of the sound of his own voice, again acutely self-conscious. He could feel his heart beating and the pressure of his blood in his veins. There was the distinct impression that panic could well up at any moment. He took another deep and disturbingly self-conscious breath.

I want to understand what's going on here . . .

"This is my voice," answered Seyloq simply.

Jendru looked hard at the old man, trying to focus and bring the riot of flowing geometry into some kind of order. Here before him was clearly the man that Jendru knew as

Seyloq - of that there was no doubt. But still, there was something different about the man, something about the way he held his face. It was subtle, yet also undeniable; this man both looked, and didn't look, like Seyloq.

"Then why do you sound so different?" asked Jendru, feeling nervousness rise in his chest as he asked the question, realizing he was fearful of what the answer might be. Instantly he thought back to the lessons of his official teachers; all the discourses on possession came flooding back to him along with all the dire warnings, exhortations, and derision of the kind of path that Seyloq represented to them.

Maybe he's really a demon after all . . .

Jendru tried to look the old man in the eyes, but could not.

"The voice you are familiar with is the voice of Seyloq, and it will return in a short while, after the medicine has run its course. *This*, however, is *my voice.*"

Jendru glanced up again. Seyloq, or at least, the body of Seyloq, smiled kindly at him. The worn wrinkles of his face from his smile were accented by the slowly diminishing waves of flowing geometric forms that filled the space between them.

"But *you are* Seyloq," said Jendru, still acutely self-conscious of the sound of his own voice. Why did it sound so artificial, so contrived? It was like he was an actor playing a part, even though it was distinctly his voice. There was nothing different about it, but for no reason that Jendru could understand, it sounded fake. Where was *himself* in this voice?

"Yes," responded Seyloq. "I am. But Seyloq is not me."

Jendru let out an uncomfortable laugh. Was this some kind of test? What had he gotten himself into? Again, the threat of panic. Maybe his teachers were right. He shouldn't be here.

"I have to go," said Jendru abruptly, attempting to get up from the mat.

"You might want to get cleaned up first," said the old man, pulling a towel out from behind him. "Here, you are covered in beauty," he said with another sly smile as he brought the towel up to Jendru's face.

That's right. I purged. I'm covered in it.

"Thank you," said Jendru, bowing slightly as he took the proffered towel. Even that slight gesture made him self-conscious. Seyloq never bowed - something his official teachers had been sure to point out. Seyloq didn't follow any of the customary or ritual procedures. Jendru looked up and caught Seyloq's eye. Yes, he had seen the bow and only looked at Jendru quizzically. He looked amused.

"You're covered in puke in my living room," said the old man, sounding distinctly more like "Seyloq." "There's no need to follow the proper forms. Do you think I give a shit?"

That was another thing. You weren't supposed to use language that way.

"No," said Jendru meekly as he wiped away at the bile and mucous covering his chest.

"There's more in your hair," said Seyloq. "You can use my shower, if you want. Go get cleaned up, and I'll get some fresh clothes for you. I'll deal with the mess out here."

"That's okay," responded Jendru, handing back the soiled towel. "I'll take care of myself," he said, adjusting so that he was sitting on his knees, inches from where he had vacated the contents of his stomach onto the mat. He was suddenly hit by the smell and he recoiled back, momentarily panicking that the nausea might return.

"Suit yourself," said the old man. "*You're* the one covered in puke, not *me*." Seyloq stood up, opened up his arms and stretched out as far as he could, letting his eyes roll up into his head as a long, slow breath purred out of his throat. "The door is that way. I trust you can let yourself out."

The old man gathered up the tools of their session together. Fiddling with one of his machines, the music that was playing changed to something lighter and the lights went up a few notches. Jendru took the opportunity to watch the old man for a few moments. There was still something odd about him, something that was, well, *different*.

"The medicine is still flowing," Seyloq commented, looking back over his shoulder at Jendru before walking down the hall to put his tools away.

He's reading my mind, thought Jendru, feeling more uncomfortable than ever.

"No, I'm not reading your mind," said Seyloq loudly, from further down the hall. "I'm reading your body - your energy. Mind readers are charlatans and fakes - not to mention deluded. I don't deal with that kind of nonsense."

Jendru grabbed his shirt, hastily put on his shoes, and quietly slipped out the door into the early afternoon.

Chapter 2

JUST IN TIME FOR TEA

High Maegin Chondrasil Sojan sipped at his lukewarm tea between twirls of the spice stick. He looked out the open window to the forest and pyramids in the valley between the two semi-dormant volcano ranges of Ladjup and Nadrasuli, the Twin Fire Dragons. From here, he could see that everything was busily underway with preparations for the upcoming *momentous event. I did not think it would be us . . . me.* He took another sip of his tea. He removed the spice stick and set it down on the window sill after shaking several drops of tea off of the dark brown stick out the open window and onto the leaves of the spice tree growing from the level below in the terrace garden. It was the proper form, after all. The tea tasted too spicy now, and he sucked in a little air to cool his lips, followed by an almost imperceptible bow toward the spice tree below him.

The sun was starting to sink low in the sky, casting golden light across the valley and highlighting the deep red and brown bricks of the pyramids and streets of Azar. The gold embroidery on the Maegin's jacket flashed enticingly in the slanting light as he reached up with one hand and brushed his fingers over his smooth scalp. He could feel the lines of the symmetrical tattoo that decorated his head in the place of hair. As with other monks, the tattoo was a stylized rendition of Azar, the Twins, and the sun, running from his brow down the back of his head and ending at the top of his spine. He remembered the pain, feeling the tattoo. It was something that one had to endure. A long time ago, it seemed, he had needed to shave his head daily to not obscure the sacred design. No longer. How many years had it been since he had needed to shave? He couldn't recall, precisely.

The sound of rustling fabric behind him brought

Chondrasil back into the room. Turning, he saw Maegin-Lu Pirfiro Nult standing patiently at the open archway to the study. He wasn't alone.

"Maegin," said Pirfiro with a deep bow (for him, anyway - for years his belly had increasingly gotten in the way).

"Brother," said Chondrasil with more of a nod than a bow.

The Maegin-Lu stepped further into the room. He was wearing formal attire of heavy gold-threaded robe. The light slanting in through the open window caused bright flashes to ripple about Pirfiro in his shimmering, plump form. *He must be hot in that*, thought Chondrasil, and then, realizing he couldn't see who had come with the lesser brother, shielded his eyes so that he could look beyond the glittering monk.

"Alcian Jor Alesh Merva has paid us an early visit, Maegin," said the lesser monk, turning and gesturing grandly to the woman standing behind him. She was dressed plainly, in stark contrast to Pirfiro, who always had a taste for flair, in a simple outfit of cream white linen. Her deep red hair was pulled back into a braided bun, held in place by a silver ring, inlaid with green stone that matched her necklace and earrings. Gold, after all, was for the monks, not the civilian population, even if she were from Jurnda. That, at least, was good. The cut of her shirt was a bit much, though. Life in Azar required more modesty for the women than this city girl displayed.

Chondrasil looked her up and down. She was younger than both the monks, by far, and had only been serving as Alcian for the past six months. *Still green.* Even so, people seemed to like her, and she'd shown respect to the Maegins and the temple city. It was a bit strange of her to show up early like this. As this was her first visit to Azar since her ascension, Chondrasil was surprised that he hadn't been informed. That was Pirfiro's decision, no doubt - too eager to be in the center of the action with the delegate from Jurnda to bother with the details of making sure the High Maegin learned of her presence before the end of the day.

"High Maegin Chondrasil," said the woman, stepping forward and holding out a gold scarf, which she offered to the

older monk with a respectful bow. Chondrasil accepted the
gift, taking it in his hands and then draping it over the
shoulders of the Alcian, making sure to let the ends fall across
her chest and deep neckline.

"I hope you don't mind my coming early," said Jor
Alesh, absent-mindedly fanning herself with the ends of the
scarf. "I've come to spend some time in your city prior to the
event to familiarize myself a bit more with your ways. As you
can see, I've dressed inconspicuously in order to blend in, but
Maegin-Lu Pirfiro insisted that any tour of the city for
someone such as myself required at least a formal escort."

Chondrasil ignored the obvious irony of her comment
and gave a quick glance at Pirfiro, who nodded in agreement
and smiled, pleased with himself. "I was down at the docks
when the Alcian arrived," explained Pirfiro, "and took it upon
myself to guide our illustrious guest about."

"Well, it's lovely to have you here, though I was not
expecting you for a couple more days," Chondrasil said
graciously. "I was just having some tea. Would you like
some?"

"Yes, please," said Jor Alesh. Turning to the lesser
monk, "And you, Pirfiro, will you join us?"

"If that is acceptable to the Maegin . . ." said Pirfiro,
looking expectantly to his superior.

"Come," said Chondrasil, "Let's step outside onto the
balcony and we can all have tea."

Pirfiro took the lead and guided Jor Alesh outside while
Chondrasil gathered two more cups for his guests and met
them out on the balcony. The sun was setting and the clouds
along the mountain ridges were lit up with vivid hues of
orange, yellow, and hints of purple and magenta. The evening
lights were coming on throughout the temple city and along
the terraced levels of the various pyramids. Bells and chanting
could be heard in the distance along with the sounds of
children playing somewhere not far off.

Jor Alesh stirred her spice stick in her tea and made an
obvious gesture of flicking a few drops toward the terrace
garden below where the spice tree grew before setting it down
and taking a sip. Pirfiro did the same, glancing to see if

Chondrasil was watching. He was. Pirfiro smiled with a slight raise of his eyebrows.

"It truly is beautiful here," said the woman.

"Yes," said Chondrasil.

"I wonder what it is like at Darsul," she said in return.

"I suppose we are soon to learn."

"I can't imagine it's very nice," said Pirfiro derisively. "At least, not from what I've heard."

Chondrasil shook his head. "It's been hundreds of years, Pirfiro. Speculation and rumor; that's all we know."

"Things could have changed," added Jor Alesh.

"I'd say so," said Chondrasil. "If they hadn't, why would they be coming?"

"Good point, Maegin," said Jor Alesh, giving her spice stick another twirl, complete with ceremonial flinging of the clinging drops of tea.

"I've been pondering this for most of the day," said Chondrasil, "and I'm no closer to understanding. Patience. We'll know soon enough." *I never thought it would be us.*

"I didn't imagine when I took the position of Alcian that this would be my first real challenge."

"That's one way to put it," said Chondrasil. Jor Alesh and the other monk looked at him. "On the other hand, it could be precisely what we've been waiting for."

Jor Alesh nodded and tilted her head slightly to one side, catching a glimpse of a flock of birds heading in for the night, returning to their roosts in the cliffs along the river Qya that ran through the valley of Azar. As the civilian leader of the city of Jurnda, these religious issues were a bit beyond her. She was curious, and had been sure to accept the invitation to attend the reunion with the wayward Darsulans. Jor Alesh was naturally inquisitive, and she also saw maintaining good relationships with all the communities of Lur as one of the primary responsibilities of the Alcian, even if the Darsulans had been isolated for the past two hundred years or so. Something was bringing them back, and she wanted to know what it was and what it would mean, if anything, for Jurnda.

It was half a millennia ago that Azar had been established as a unique religious community on the micro continent of Lur, completely isolated from the mainland, or *The World*, as it was commonly called. Over time, as the population expanded, Jurnda grew as its own city with its own secular society, distinct from Azar, though still nearby. The Darsulans lived *somewhere* on Lur, though reportedly, no one knew where, or even how many of them there were now.

Azar had been established as a refuge in the aftermath of the *Great War* that had devastated human society back in *The World*, and here on Lur as well. Due to numerous causes - climate and environmental changes, competing political and national factions, radical inequalities and financial collapses - a vast and complex holy war had raged across the face of the globe, with fervent believers on every side, all vying for their god's favor and victory against the infidels and followers of false prophets. The war had lasted several generations, and in the end, human society stood on the brink of total collapse. In the aftermath, most religions had been outlawed by the few surviving groups that sought reconciliation and the rebuilding of human society free from the passions of religious belief and identities that had been so central in fanning the flames of war.

Originally, Azar had been a religious retreat and colony for those who refused to give up the teachings of Azara in the post-war world. Azarans had not been involved in the religious wars, but when the peace accords had been signed, all religions had been subject to severe regulation, mostly by popular consent. The vast majority of religionists had effectively wiped each other off the face of the planet, so there weren't many defenders left to speak up for the various traditions, particularly those that had been most culpable in the outrageous, apocalyptic violence. The traditions that had survived, reeling in the shock of horrific violence and the vast brutality of believers, had mostly morphed into social and political philosophies with a secular bent, though occasionally harking back to their religious roots. Religious doctrine had been effectively outlawed and careful pains were taken to show that what remained was philosophical in nature and not something that individuals could use to develop dangerous beliefs that might lead to future violence. How this was working for those back in *The World*, Jor Alesh couldn't say, nor could anyone else on Lur. It was a big planet, after all, and the Azarans had removed themselves as far as possible from all that had occurred.

The original population of the tropical landmass of Lur had been wiped out in the various "cleansing" campaigns perpetrated by various sides of the terrible conflict. By the time the war was over, Lur had been free of humans for several generations, and the devastation that had been wrought on the island continent had healed with the natural re-growth of the forest, reclaiming all that humans had once called their own. Ruins still dotted the landscape, mostly hidden in vines and overgrowth with remnants of machinery and ancient technology scattered here and there.

What was now known as the valley of Azar provided the ideal place for a new beginning for the followers of Azara. They had come here to regroup, rebuild, and start again. When the pilgrims found the Twin Dragons, they knew that this was the place for the Flower of Azara to blossom and the colossal project of the construction of the city had begun.

Divided between the official Church hierarchy and the laity, the population of Azar grew until the sacred valley could no longer accommodate everyone. The city of Jurnda was established downriver,. along the coast where the river Qya emptied into the Sea of Loa Neshi. Over time, Jurnda became the seat of secular power on Lur, while Azar remained the holdfast for the followers of the esoteric Azaran religion. Thus, despite having originally been founded as a homogeneous religious and spiritual community, Lur had developed into a society with secular and religious distinctions. Originally, fewer than seven thousand followers had made the crossing of the Sea of Loa Neshi to found Azar. Now, the population of Lur was estimated to be several million. Azar remained relatively small, however, with around 20,000 individuals living in and around the sacred valley.

As the ascended secular ruler of Jurnda, Jor Alesh's world was largely divorced from the realities of life in Azar. For many in Jurnda, the Azaran religion was considered a curious relic of the past. For believers, it was the crowning jewel of life on Lur. Secular life in the city ran much as they supposed life back in *The World* must be like, though there had been no communication with the restructured societies back on the mainland since the original exodus of those early Azaran pilgrims. *The World* was effectively a world away and the Azarans, or Lurans, as they more inclusively called themselves, had led a fruitful and isolated existence for 500 years in their post-war paradise.

Jor Alesh knew some of the doctrine, at a general level, and had even participated in several sacramental ceremonies over the years. But the deepest esoteric secrets and philosophies of Araza were almost as foreign to her as the little she knew of religion back in *The World* before the war. The Azarans had brought their teachings with them and had supposedly "purified" the tradition before the exodus, purging it of what had been deemed "foreign" influences and borrowings, so only fragments of the pre-war world were known on Lur. This attempt at consolidation and doctrinal purity hadn't prevented new outgrowths and breakaway groups that challenged the doctrine, in one way or another. One such group, the Darsulans, had attempted to establish a new sect within Azar. But as tensions began to increase, it was decided that it was best for the Darsulans to have an exodus of their own. As a result, the Darsulans moved to the far side of Lur in an agreement that mirrored the Azarans' original exodus from *The World*. That was almost two hundred years ago, and there had been no contact between Azarans and Darsulans in the intervening centuries.

But now, all of that was about to change. A message had arrived requesting that a delegation of Darsulans be permitted to enter the city of Azar. Though it was deemed to be a religious issue, Jor Alesh had been invited to attend their visit. Jor Alesh wasn't sure what High Maegin Chondrasil's motives in this decision were, but she had no intention of not attending. The fear back in Jurnda was that history might be on the verge of repeating itself. That was the last thing anyone wanted. Though the Azarans were almost militantly peaceful, it was unknown how the breakaway group of the Darsulans may have developed over centuries apart. Given the violent history of religions, it had been assumed that a life lived apart was best for all. If history were any indicator, religious practitioners didn't seem to get along with each other, and they had the potential to instigate the most horrific of terrors. Thus Jor Alesh found herself here, sitting on the balcony sipping spice tea with the High Maegin of Azar, awaiting the return of the wayward Darsulans.

"How do you mean? – *'Precisely what we've been waiting for,'*" Jor Alesh asked the senior monk. She took a sip of tea and turned to look at the older man in the fading colors of the sunset. "Aren't you a bit nervous? After all, we isolated ourselves here for a reason, correct?" Pirfiro seemed as eager to hear Chondrasil's answer as she was.

The senior monk took a few moments, his eyes closed, taking a long, slow breath.

"Wayward souls always seek reincorporation," he answered, at last. "Though the gods are many, there is only One, and all souls ultimately seek reincorporation into the body of the One. Like an adventurous adolescent, the Darsulans explored their need for independence and self-expression, but now that they have matured and grown wiser, perhaps they have seen the error of their misguided doctrines. It is my belief that the time for reincorporation has come. And beyond that, depending on how all this goes, maybe it is time for us to return as well."

Jor Alesh's eyebrows shot up. Pirfiro gave a little cough. *Did he just say what I think he said?* They both shifted uncomfortably as Chondrasil stood up and placed his hands on the railing of the balcony, looking out over the well-lit pyramids of Azar.

"It was never our goal to abandon humanity, Alcian," said the monk. "The human family is one. Like the gods, there are many expressions of humanity, but our differences are only conventions, artifice. Our founders created this sanctuary here to promote and preserve the ancient teachings of our tradition, the Revealed Truth. *The World* has existed without our guidance for 500 years. Perhaps the return of the Darsulans is a sign that the time has come for the human family to reunite and begin a new epoch."

"You are wise, High Maegin," said Pirfiro with a deep

bow as he stood up to face his superior.

Jor Alesh rose too, feeling that it was expected, or that things were about to shift.

"Speculation," said Chondrasil, turning to face the two others, a light smile on his face. "We'll know soon enough what brings these Darsulans to our sanctuary. But I'm not the only one who feels the winds of change. Many other Maegins have been receiving messages in their visions and holy raptures. Whatever the case, *something* is happening, and I intend to do my part according to the will of the One. Though you are a secular ruler, Alcian, aware or not, you too will play your part. It is the will of the One."

Jor Alesh was about to give a response, but Chondrasil didn't give her a chance.

"Come," he said, "it is almost time for tonight's service. Will you do us the honor of joining us for communion, Alcian?"

How long had it been since she last had communion? Certainly not since her ascension. *Has it been two years, already?* she thought. *No, longer, actually.* It had been five years. She had gone to a communion two years previous, but hadn't partaken. She was deep into her political career by then, and over the centuries, the civilian population of Jurnda had grown increasingly distant from the esoteric practices of the monks, their devotees, and novitiates. Drinking communion was increasingly rare in the general population and especially among the civic leaders. Attending communion was one thing; drinking was another thing entirely.

Jor Alesh felt into the question. She could feel the tightness in her gut, the distinct tension in her back. She remembered how it had been that last time. It was a strange thing, the communion with Azara. Grueling was something of an understatement, at least for Jor Alesh. They said it became easier with experience. At the time, it had seemed like a miracle that Jor Alesh had come out the other side unscathed. In fact, she had felt refreshed and invigorated - like someone who had faced death and prevailed. In retrospect, she had been glad that she had done it. But at the time, when in the grips of the communion drink, it had seemed like torture and she had found herself on the brink of madness. She couldn't say that it was an experience she was eager to repeat, despite her gratitude at having survived it previously. She looked to Chondrasil and Pirfiro, both of whom had shared communion hundreds, if not thousands, of times. *If they can do it, so can I,* said Jor Alesh to herself.

"Yes," she said, looking at the two monks. "I think if any occasion suggests that I partake of the communion, this would be it. I would be honored to join you."

"Excellent," said Chondrasil, clearly pleased that the secular ruler of Jurnda would be submitting to his ritual authority, and the power of their tradition. Once, it had been an expectation that the Alcian would come and share communion upon his or her ascension, but that practice had ceased long before Chondrasil had become High Maegin. Though he'd have to check the temple records, he guessed that this would probably be the first attendance by an actual sitting Alcian in several generations. Many retired Alcians had come after their term of service was complete, but a current Alcian? *Another sign,* Chondrasil said to himself. "Pirfiro will have an escort find you and bring you to the Obsidian Temple within the hour. Though you may be hungry, it's best to fast before communion . . ."

Chondrasil broke off, suddenly conscious of a sensitive issue. He personally knew little about the private life of Jor Alesh. Everyone in Azar knew the rules, and for monks such as himself, proper adherence was never a problem. Who knew what the case might be for Jor Alesh, however.

"Forgive me, Alcian, but I must also mention . . ."

Jor Alesh cut right in to save Chondrasil any embarrassment. "Don't worry, High Maegin," she said, feeling herself flush slightly. "The life of a public servant doesn't leave a lot of time or opportunity for that sort of thing. Well, maybe if I were married, but no, I haven't had intercourse since my ascension."

"Ah, yes," said Chondrasil, clearing his throat. "Well, three days abstinence is all that is required, Alcian. No need to go into further details."

"Of course," said Jor Alesh.

"Very well.   Pirfiro will see you out, and I'll see you shortly at the ceremony."

With that, Chondrasil excused himself and made his way to his private quarters where he would don his ceremonial attire and call the monks to order.

Chapter 3

LIFE ON LUR

The city of Azar was laid out in a fractal grid alongside the Qya River. In the center was the Obsidian Temple, made of a mixture of red and black obsidian stone. The Obsidian Temple was the largest of the grand pyramids of Azar, and the only one made of obsidian. The rest were a dark red color, made from less prestigious, though still highly valued, lava rock that had come from the Twin Fire Dragons. According to geologists, the entire island continent of Lur was slowly moving west, making the easternmost volcanoes the most likely to cause problems as the land slowly passed west of the hot spot and the necessary pressure would build up, birthing new volcanoes. For now, the Twins were dormant. It had been generations since anyone had seen the Dragons breathe their smoke and ash into the blue tropical skies.

From the Obsidian Temple, the lesser pyramids were laid out along the spiraling fractal grid of red stone streets. The further one moved from the Obsidian Temple, the smaller the pyramids became, so by the time one reached the outskirts of the city, the pyramids were no taller than a human and more ornamental than functional, aside from completing the larger fractal pattern. Though they were often lost to the forest, if one followed the suggestions of the city grid, one could wander off into the jungle and find increasingly small pyramids in the dense undergrowth with the smallest said to be no larger than several inches tall.

While the Obsidian Temple had flat, smooth sides, most of the larger pyramids were stacked and terraced, allowing for various gardens, apartments, walkways, and even arching bridges that spanned between the upper reaches of some of the pyramids. They had different functions: housing monks, learning and study, ceremony and initiations, performances, lectures, or other such public gatherings of a non-ceremonial nature. They all had their own names, which were used to find one's way about the city. Aside from the monks' quarters, and the residences of laypeople, the pyramids were all open and permitted free access, though the Obsidian Temple would be closed to non-initiates during advanced communion ceremonies to protect the sacred secrets of the religion.

Back in *The World*, Azaran temples and ceremonial centers had tended to be isolated and removed from the rest of society. An ancient mendicant order, the Azarans had never been highly integrated into society. They found their isolation to be conducive to the performance of their spiritual and religious work. Most of what the monks performed was understood to take place on an energetic/spiritual level, and therefore was most effectively performed when removed from the distractions and temptations of everyday life.

The Azarans hadn't become directly involved in the *Great War*, though they were eventually drawn into the chaotic maelstrom, as was true for everyone else. The raging fire of the war had simply burned too brightly, and there was nowhere that was spared the searing flames and the terrible destruction that had passed across the face of the planet. Still, they had fared better than the majority of religions that had both perpetrated and become swept up in the war. Azara was always a minority religion, practiced by a select group of highly dedicated devotees. When the legions of faithful rose up to slaughter each other in a holy sacrifice of mutual bloodletting, the Azarans simply moved further into the mountains. By the time the armistice was finally reached, the followers of other religions had died by the millions, even billions. Disbanding and reeducating the remainder was seen as the best option by those left struggling to rebuild society. No longer being welcome, even as hermits in the hills, the Azarans had left *The World* entirely.

Jendru Amdin had never been to the mainland, never seen *The World*. No one on Lur ever had, as far as he knew. The few surviving Azarans who fled *The World* turned their back on it in mutual agreement with those they had left behind. Here on Lur, they could practice as they saw fit and there was no authority who could say otherwise.

That was the world Jendru knew. The idea that religions could turn on each other and fight it out to the bitter end had seemed a strange, even impossible, reality. How could any group that claimed knowledge of the divine turn against their fellow humans? Maybe the world had become too small, thought Jendru.

Growing up in the metropolis of Jurnda, Jendru had always looked to Azar with awe and wonder. Life was "normal" in the city, but everything Jendru learned about Azar led him to believe that life in the pyramid city was anything but normal, at least as he understood it. The Azarans kept their own ritual calendar, and when appropriate, the Maegins would come to Jurnda and officiate public ceremonies where small portions of the communion would be made available to the populace. This practice allowed the curious to literally and figuratively get a taste of what Azara was all about, and it kept the largely-ignorant in awe of the Maegins' power and access to the sacred. It was a fact that was difficult to dispute: whatever else one might think of the Azarans, communion was nothing to scoff at. Though difficult to understand, even a mild experience generated by the communion drink (which was often simply called *Azara*) was enough to convince most that *something* was definitely going on here, even if the average person wasn't keen enough to understand or appreciate it.

It was at fifteen that Jendru first tasted the reality of the spiritual world. It was the spring festival of Oldrup. Upon his request, his parents brought him to the Zantor pyramid in central Jurnda, along with several hundred other communion seekers. "This medicine will never violate your free will," the attending Maegin had said, "and therefore this must be your choice. If you are not here by your own decision, then leave now and no disgrace will come to you. But if you take this communion under coercion or undue influence, you will have to suffer for your own errors. All we ask is that you take this medicine with a clean and open heart."

Jendru hadn't needed any convincing. Even as a small child, he had spent hours dreaming of the secrets held within the Azarans' pyramids and their mysterious drink. The world of spirits, gods, and the One, Azara, seemed too fanciful to be true. Yet the Maegins all appeared to be intelligent, thoughtful, and truly compassionate and dedicated individuals. So there had to be *something* to all of this, even if that reality was remote to the ordinary workings of life in Jurnda. So when the opportunity for him to drink finally arrived, Jendru eagerly participated, excited to see what it was all about.

He knew now that what he had experienced then was merely a taste, the bare surface of the spiritual world that the Maegins served. He also knew that he had only consumed a relatively small dose of the communion drink. By comparison, his experience then was almost nothing to what he would later encounter. Still, it had made a deep and abiding impression on him. He had made up his mind then and there that he would one day move to Azar, and if it were the will of Azara, he would become a Maegin, or at least a Maegin-Lu, and would dedicate himself to the mysteries.

But now, all that paled in comparison to what he had just experienced. Jendru wandered down the twisting, angular streets of Azar in the fading light of the sunset, having made his way back to the ceremonial city from Seyloq Surya's home in the mountains of Ladjup. Several hours had passed since his amazing experience with the old man. While Jendru had initially felt that he had gained some clarity, that seemed to be gone now and a fuzzy, distinctly uncomfortable confusion firmly settled in its place. Though the Maegins had been training it out of him, he couldn't help but think as he did. *What the fuck was that? Holy shit that was crazy! This is insane!*

The Maegins never spoke like that, and would be very displeased to hear Jendru use such language. Still, these were his private thoughts, and at least they were genuine. As a five-year novice, he had assumed that he had seen and experienced what there was to see and experience. It had seemed laughable that any medicine could possibly be stronger or more profound than Azara. Yet that was precisely what he had experienced. And not only that, the man who provided him with this experience had knowingly rejected virtually *all* of Azaran doctrine.

He didn't know what to think, though he suspected that

either Seyloq was truly crazy and deluded, and perhaps possessed, as some of the Maegins claimed, or he was onto something that not even the Maegins understood, which in itself seemed crazy and impossible.   Compared to the Maegins, Seyloq was rude, selfish, without scruples, unethical (or, at least, which was about the same thing, unconcerned about ethics and proper conduct), and to top it off, he was an apostate (and not to mention he was not celibate)! Seyloq was worse than the Darsulans.   At least they had founded a doctrine, albeit an erroneous one.   Seyloq pissed on all doctrine - literally! Before he left Azar, he had reportedly urinated on a stack of Azaran hymnals. And this was to whom Jendru was turning for alternate teachings before taking his vows? What the fuck was he thinking, indeed!

Jendru muttered his thoughts to himself as he made his way through the streets, heading toward the novitiates' pyramid. The Maegins always counseled a calm, demure demeanor, something Jendru had been cultivating for the past five years and now found to be easily broken by the overwhelming experience that he had just undergone. Maegins weren't supposed to mumble to themselves. They were supposed to appear calm and behave impeccably at all times, especially when under stress. This was an extension of their ritual practices: when consuming Azara, the communion drink, fierce and uncomfortable energies could be released. While laypersons often had a difficult and challenging time through their experiences (as well as acted out and openly expressed those difficulties), the Maegins were famous for their cool, calm, unwavering presence (with the exception of reincorporation ceremonies - those could be quite lively - but that was on pre-planned occasions).   Otherwise, strength, fortitude, determination and poise were the rule. Jendru felt as though he were the complete opposite, stumbling down the street half in a daze, remains of vomit on his clothing and the smell of it lingering in his hair, muttering to himself about how confused and conflicted he felt. It was not the proper image of a novice who had almost completed his required five-year apprenticeship before taking his formal vows.

You're jeopardizing everything you've worked for! If the Maegins find out - if Chondrasil finds out - they won't let you take your vows. Then what? You'll go and apprentice yourself to the crazy old man and live up in the hills like him? Your future is with Azara, not this demonic lunatic!

The sound of hurried footsteps coming from an adjoining pathway brought Jendru out of his self-critical thoughts. It was a fellow novice, Khalanto. Khalanto Tordin, unlike Jendru, had been born and raised here in Azar. He was a bit younger than Jendru, and as a result, was only two years into his apprenticeship. His parents were laypersons in the religion of Azara, and, like many such dedicated laypersons, had lived all their lives in Azar. As the religion was more a system of practice than anything else, it didn't garner many lay followers, though there were enough to populate Azar as well as provide new youth to take their place in the ranks of the Maegins. Azara was a religion of practitioners, not believers. The Maegins always claimed that their practices were not about belief. Jendru had thought likewise, until he started listening to Seyloq. According to Seyloq, Azara was a religion of beliefs, like all religions, regardless of its experiential basis. While glimpsing the truth, it was largely illusion wrapped in self-generated fantasy. According to the Maegins, Seyloq Surya was a mad old man who bitterly looked down on everyone and everything. They dismissed his words easily like they were nothing. They were perfectly happy to ignore him and pretend that he didn't exist.

Khalanto panted as he caught up with Jendru, pulling his robes about himself and smoothing out the woven fabric. His eyes were wide and he had a clear look of anticipation about him, practically energetically leaning into Jendru.

"You did it, didn't you?" Khalanto asked excitedly. He stopped Jendru, moving in front of him and holding him with his outstretched hands, taking a moment to look him up and down. He completed his inspection with a deep inhale through his nose.

"You did!" he exclaimed as Jendru attempted to brush past and continue on his way back to his quarters. It was getting late and neither of them had much time.

"Oh, don't deny it," said Khalanto. "I can smell you

from here. Look - you still have vomit in your hair! You're a
mess! I can't believe that you went today, of all days! What
was it like?"

Jendru shook his head. "I don't want to talk about it
now," he said, attempting to continue his walk. *It's all your
fault,* he thought to himself, giving Khalanto a hard look.

"Whoa there," said Khalanto, stopping Jendru once
more, grabbing at his elbow. "I see what you're thinking. I
may be a few years behind you in my training, but I know
what a look like that says."

"What?" asked Jendru, knowing he sounded defensive.
It was as though all his careful years of training were simply
evaporating. He was exhibiting almost none of the careful
control that he was supposedly close to mastering. If his
mentors could see him now, they'd all agree that he'd taken
several steps back and would refuse to allow him to take his
vows. *This is all wrong!*

"Lighten up!" said Khalanto.

"I don't know why I ever listened to you," said Jendru,
once more attempting to brush past him, jerking his arm away
from the grip of his younger friend.

"So it's my fault then, eh?"

"Yes."

Khalanto shook his head. "I didn't make you go
anywhere - that was your choice."

"Who encouraged me?"

"What does that matter? You make your own choices. I
didn't make you do anything."

Jendru sighed. "You're right," he said apologetically.
"I'm just shaken up. It was a lot stronger than I anticipated,
and I'm having trouble keeping myself together, that's all. I
only blame you a little," he added with a meager smile.

"Yeah, yeah . . . can't hold your medicine . . . I get it."

Jendru gave his friend a hard look. "You have no idea."

Khalanto was one to talk. His nickname among the
other novices was "Bucket," given his propensity to vomit with
virtually every round of medicine. Jendru had only purged
once with Azara - something the Maegins had taken note of.
They had said it indicated that in a past life Jendru had

already done his preparatory work of cleansing and purifying himself. Even High Maegin Chondrasil had claimed that Jendru showed "great promise" and had taken a special interest in him. When Jendru had relayed that sentiment to Seyloq, his modest pride had been quickly dismissed by a characteristic proclamation that, "The High Maegin's full of shit. Feel free to ignore his nonsensical statements. Take them personally at your own peril."

Jendru had been shocked. "But the High Maegin is a realized being," he protested.

"No he's not," responded Seyloq. "He only thinks he's a 'realized being.' Being the real thing is quite different from what they teach you over there in Azar. Granted, they fully believe what they teach, but what they don't realize is that it's all an act. Would you call a great actor a 'realized being' if he played one on the stage, or would you call him a 'great actor' who can convincingly play the role of someone who's supposedly enlightened? 'Chondrasil' is an actor on the stage of reality. Sure, the 'character' of 'Chondrasil' is all realized and all that great and mystical stuff, but so what? Performances are always more enjoyable when they're believable. But no performance, no matter how well executed, should be mistaken for reality. So go ahead and let his character praise your character. Just don't confuse this for anything truly meaningful or significant. Besides, I'm sure you've got plenty of purging left to do, so don't flatter yourself by repeating their delusions and fantasies. Past life - bullshit!"

"Then tell me about it," said Khalanto, pleadingly. "Enlighten me."

"I'm not even sure I know what that means anymore," said Jendru, more to himself than to Khalanto, reflecting on the word in its more absolute terms than the younger novice had perhaps consciously intended.

No one had mentioned Seyloq directly to Jendru until Khalanto had entered as a novice two years ago, three years into Jendru's own apprenticeship. The Maegins never talked about Seyloq until Jendru had decided to directly ask them, curious about this heretical man that Khalanto had told him of. Apparently, Seyloq was something of an embarrassment.

Khalanto had grown up knowing mostly rumors and speculations about the odd man. As a youth, he had imagined that Seyloq was something of a beast, half-human, half-animal, at best. It wasn't until an unexpected day when Seyloq came to Azar that Khalanto realized that he was an actual person. Khalanto had gone from childhood belief to skepticism (having concluded, like other children, that Seyloq was merely a fictional character their parents created) and then to curiosity about the real thing - this strange man going about his enigmatic business.

Khalanto's curiosity had rubbed off on Jendru. "They say he works with a medicine that's far stronger than Azara," he had told Jendru, on more than one occasion. Of course, no one seemed to believe that - especially anyone who had received a full dose of the potent drink. Jendru was incredulous, having already undergone three years of novice training with the Maegins. His early twenties had been one amazingly profound experience after another. The thought that there could be a stronger and more powerful medicine out there strained the bounds of rational belief. How could it be? And if there was, then why didn't the Maegins themselves use it? What made this Seyloq so special (and, it would seem, dangerous)?

Unlike the other novices, Khalanto didn't treat the subject of Seyloq as taboo. The more Jendru learned from Khalanto, the more he realized that his views were widely shared by others - the difference being that they never talked about it, whereas Khalanto did, especially as he seemed to have found a willing ear with Jendru. It was the drink, Azara, that had brought Jendru to Azar, and rumors of something stronger intrigued him. If there was someone with more knowledge and power than the Maegins, then Jendru wanted to meet him. What was taboo for others had become something of a fascination and almost obsession with Jendru. Though rationally, virtually everything seemed to indicate that he should stay away and not jeopardize his position in Azar. Against his supposedly better judgment, Jendru couldn't get Seyloq and the mysteries he represented out of his mind.

So he had done it. Of course, Khalanto had prodded

him all along the way. If Khalanto had more determination and courage, he might have joined him. Instead, Khalanto was vicariously seeking to experience Seyloq and his wonders through Jendru, and apparently had succeeded. Now, if only Jendru would open up and tell him what he wanted to hear.

"It's strong, okay?" said Jendru. "It's really, really, really strong."

Khalanto's eyes lit up with a look that said, "I always knew it was true!"

"Stronger than Azara?" the younger novice asked.

Jendru shook his head, struggling with how to communicate the reality he had just experienced. "The medicines are similar, in some ways, but Seyloq's medicine is so far beyond Azara that it's hard to explain. It's like if you took your strongest, most powerful work with Azara, and then tried to compress it into a much shorter time frame . . ." Jendru faded off, suddenly realizing that he couldn't say with any certainty how long he had been under the effects of the medicine. There was a big blank in his memory of the experience. He could recall something of an initial struggle, followed by truly cosmic purging, but then what? The next memory he had was of seeing his hands out in front of him with no idea of what had transpired in the meantime, or even how long that time period had been. Though it seemed it was not too much later when he left the old man's home, there was a definite sense of the timeless, of infinity, that lingered in his being - a profound sense of eternity. So how long had it been?

Shaking his head, he continued. "I don't know . . . thinking about it now, it doesn't seem like it was very long. It's hard to tell. He doesn't do any ceremony or prayers or anything like that - the usual structures that we use to mark time and keep everything within the ritual container. He gave me some instructions. And then we jumped right into it. And then . . . Well, anyway, imagine taking your strongest Azara experience and compressing the fullness of it into something that only lasts a matter of minutes - certainly less than an hour - and also amp it up a few notches (*now there's an understatement*), and maybe you'll have something of an idea. But how do you contain the infinite in an idea? In a word? In a concept? I don't know what to tell you. It was infinite. You'd have to try for yourself, I suppose."

"I'm not as brave as you," said Khalanto quickly, shaking his head for emphasis. "But was it good? Did you learn anything? Did you see Azara?"

Jendru looked at his friend. "I don't know, Khalanto," he said. "All I feel right now is confused. I think I may have made a mistake in going there and taking that medicine."

Mixing medicines. The Maegins always counseled against this. They used Azara because that was their holy medicine, given to their ancient progenitors in a supreme act of divine revelation. It was said that Azara had come directly to the original sages, those who eventually became known as the first Maegins. In the form of the Mother/Father and the Flower of Azara, God had spoken to the Maegins directly, personally, and had instructed them in the use and purpose of the sacred communion: the saving of lost souls through reincorporation, and the path that led from life to life in the long journey of returning to source, to the All Being that was Azara. Mixing medicines was not part of that program. According to the Maegins, it was an affront to the grace that Azara had deemed worthy to grant those early sages. As they put it, an energetic connection, a direct pathway to the divine fullness of God, had been revealed. To stray from that narrow path was to wander the jungle of infinite incarnations with no hope of final release, no welcoming back into the arms of Azara. Mixing medicines was something that wasn't done. That had been one of the primary reasons the Darsulans had left, and the fact that they fully initiated women. Among Azarans, women could be laypersons, but only men could become Maegins and Maegin-Lus. The best hope, according to the masters, was that a woman, through her dedication and good work as a layperson, would be born a man in her next life, benefitting from her preparatory work in her previous life. "We don't make the rules of life," the High Maegin had explained to Jendru when he had asked about this particular subject, "but we do enforce the laws as revealed by Azara. To do any less would be to defy God."

"Like I said, Chondrasil is full of shit," Seyloq had said

when Jendru brought this to his attention. "'Don't blame us - we're just enforcing God's rules!' People like Chondrasil don't have the faintest idea who or what God is, despite all the time they spend nursing from the tit of the so-called 'Mother/Father'. It's stupid thinking like this that fueled the fire of the war in the first place. If these people were as enlightened as they think they are, they would have left that archaic thinking behind generations ago. Delusion tends to beget delusion. Now that's a rule God has no problem enforcing - no ritual, shaved and tattooed heads, or special robes required!" he had concluded with a great laugh.

"Well that's new," said Khalanto with a chuckle. "Maybe his medicine is stronger than you think! I haven't known you to second-guess yourself before. 'The lowly Seyloq has brought down mighty Chondrasil's chosen pet!' - I can see the news brief now! Let's put that one in the temple circulars!"

"Just drop it, okay," said Jendru. He'd had enough of this. Besides, they were going to be late. Time was clearly running out. Other novices, monks, and laypersons were emerging from the pyramids, all making their way to central Azar, to the Obsidian Temple. Tonight was to be a prayer meeting to mark the questionably auspicious return of the Darsulans. As always, Azara was on the menu and Jendru still had to clean himself, don the proper attire, and get to the pyramid before his absence was noticed. Ceremonies like these were always optional, but given Jendru's propensity for never missing an opportunity to drink Azara, he didn't want to have to explain his conspicuous absence to anyone, especially not Chondrasil. *That* was the last thing he wanted to deal with now.

"I'll see you at the temple," Jendru said, indicating that he was done discussing Seyloq and his mysterious medicine.

"Fine," said Khalanto resignedly. "But tell me one thing," he said, still refusing to leave.

"What?"

"Well . . . what was Seyloq's medicine? Was it a drink, like Azara? Or was it one of those mushrooms or cacti the Darsulans are said to use?"

"None of those," answered Jendru. "It was a crystal."

"What?" asked Khalanto, clearly disbelieving. "How do you take a crystal?"

"You smoke it," answered Jendru. "He took a large crystal, shaved some off, crushed it up, and then put it in a pipe and had me smoke it."

"Really? You're serious?"

"Yes," said Jendru. "Two hits from the pipe - that's all I had."

Khalanto's eyes grew large. "Really?" he asked again.

"Yes, really," said Jendru, feeling the pressure of time reaching in on him. He could hear the exasperation in his voice. "Now go. We can talk more, later. I'll see you at the temple."

Taking a quick look around, Jendru oriented himself and branched off down a side path leading to the pyramid that contained his novice quarters, leaving Khalanto to make his own way to the Obsidian Temple with the other novitiates, whom he quickly and discretely joined. Jendru stopped and turned, feeling tempted to shout out, "Don't tell anyone!" but quickly thought better of it and only quietly mumbled his concerns to himself, shaking his head and hoping for the best, somewhat disappointed to find that he was in the same confused state in which Khalanto had originally found him. It was going to be a long night.

Chapter 4

THE OBSIDIAN TEMPLE

The Obsidian Temple was the centerpiece of the fractal grid that was Azar. Its sheer, glossy sides reached up into the night, reflecting the lights from the surrounding pyramids, but having none of its own. Like a mirror, the temple reflected everything back to its source, itself a dark void, mysterious, a numinous monolith, towering over everything else within its domain.

Steps led up to four immense thresholds that then turned back down into the open center of the black pyramid. At the apex of each stairway, two Maegin-Lus waited to greet all those who would come to share the holy communion. They were dressed in the elaborate gold robes that Jor Alesh recognized from Pirfiro's attire earlier that day. She was still dressed in the linen outfit from earlier, not having changed as it appeared nearly everyone else had. *Everyone looks so splendid,* she thought to herself, realizing how relatively informal her communions in Jurnda had been.

There was the monumentally impressive Obsidian Temple, for one thing. In Jurnda, the temples were made from more local materials. Though all were relatively similar pyramids in shape and structure, they were generally much smaller and weren't nearly as physically and aesthetically imposing. The services were run by small groups of monks, but nothing like the vast collection of holy men gathered here in the heart of the sacred city. In Jurnda, people wore the simple light clothing like Jor Alesh was wearing. Here at the Obsidian Temple, Jor Alesh looked plain, even provincial, in comparison to the riot of color that was about her.

Jor Alesh pushed into the crowd of people lining up to enter the dark pyramid. Light from within danced in the tall doorways, creating a soft yellow-orange glow with the people slowly and methodically shuffling their way up and in. Looking around, Jor Alesh could see clear distinctions between the people. There were of course the Maegins and the Maegin-Lus, all dressed in their ritual finery with gold robes, the Maegins distinguished by an outer sash of deep crimson, inlaid with intricate geometric designs. Then there were the acolytes, those who had taken their vows but were not yet full monks. They were dressed in a wide variety of colored robes, all with rainbow patterns of fine thread crisscrossing in various symmetrical patches, making them appear to be wearing some kind of light, rainbow armor. Their heads were shaved, but they would not receive their tattoos until their final initiation. Next there were the novices, those who had not yet completed their initial five-year training and taken their vows or a mentor. They were dressed in the same colored robes as the acolytes, but without the intricate rainbow patterning. And they still had their hair. Then there were also the laypersons, dressed in various clothes, all colorful, all patterned, and all quite fine. A few wore the simple cotton robes, dresses, or tunics as worn in Jurnda, but not many. Among such finery, the Alcian looked simple and almost out of place.

Despite the fact that Jor Alesh was Alcian of Jurnda, here, she was no one special - merely a very plain person in a sea of ritual color, form, and celebration. Though the hierarchy of Azar recognized her authority in Jurnda, the Alcian had no direct power here. At times like this, the arrangement was made spatially clear by the fact that Jor Alesh would be far away from those who were running the show at the center of the pyramid. Her place would be at the outside of the gathering within the temple at the farthest edges from the sacred center. Specifically, she'd be with the laypersons - the only place where women were allowed in the ceremony, given that the highest position for a woman within the religion of Azara was that of layperson. Only the men could move up from novice to acolyte to Maegin-Lu and eventually Maegin, or even High Maegin, such as Chondrasil Sojan.

Pirfiro had offered to escort Jor Alesh within, but she saw no point and declined, choosing instead to take this opportunity to mingle among the people as had been her intention earlier that day. Pirfiro had made sure to ruin that possibility, insisting that he don his gold robe and parade her about the city, thereby insuring that she'd have no anonymity. She wondered if it had been his idea, or if his superiors had insisted upon it. She had come early, and unannounced, to get a feel for the thoughts and feelings of Azar outside of any official functions or channels. It wasn't that she mistrusted the Maegins, but she knew of their power and influence. She thought it might be enlightening to see what people were talking about when the Maegins weren't looking, or when they didn't know to whom they were speaking.

Most of the people of Azar didn't spend any time in Jurnda, and she'd only been Alcian for six months, so the chances of her being recognized outright were slim. Jurnda was big enough so that she could go many places and not be immediately recognized. Here, she was just another city person to these devotees. Even with her escort from Pirfiro, most had probably assumed she was simply a dignitary from the city and hadn't guessed her true identity. She was fairly young to be the Alcian - in her early thirties - and she carried herself with a quiet grace that didn't speak glaringly as one with power and authority. She could "put it on" (as she liked to call it) if needed, but otherwise, she more enjoyed being Jor Alesh than some idealized authority figure.

Here, slowly moving toward the towering entrance to the pyramid, Jor Alesh appeared anything but a figure of authority. Here, she was no one. She knew as much about Azara as the average person, but no one here was average. These were devotees - every last one of them. These people lived, breathed, and died (and, according to their teachings, were reborn) in Azara. For many of them, ceremonies such as this were a weekly event. For some, it was practically daily, though that was largely confined to the Maegin-Lus and their acolytes - at least that's how Jor Alesh understood it from what Pirfiro had explained as he escorted her around the city.

"Novices should drink communion at least once a month for their first four years, and then are encouraged to drink weekly for their final year, though it is still up to them. They don't have Maegin-Lu mentors yet, so they do not yet have full personal guidance, though we do, of course, go to great pains to take care of them and see to their growth and development," he had explained, almost didactically. "The real training begins for the acolytes who have established a personal relationship with their chosen Maegin-Lu. During those first five years, the novices are instructed to observe all the Maegin-Lus carefully to see with whom they are most energetically and spiritually attuned. When the time comes to take their vows, they chose their mentor and take their vows under him. They and their mentor then drink weekly, or even daily, if that is appropriate for the student. When the Maegin-Lu feels that the acolyte has learned the ways of Azara and is fully immersed in the mystery, he may be advanced to Maegin-Lu, if he wishes to become a mentor himself and take on more of a ceremonial role within the tradition."

"Does anyone ever not complete the process?" Jor Alesh had asked.

"It is rare, though it does happen. Usually, that will occur at the earlier stages of being a novice. The rigors of regular consumption of Azara is not for everyone, as I'm sure you are aware, Alcian," said Pirfiro with a hint of smugness, as though that were intended for Jor Alesh personally. *He must not think too highly of us in Jurnda*, she thought to herself.

"Being a novice is demanding, but being an acolyte, much more so. If a man cannot make it as a novice, becoming an acolyte is impossible. We stretch this time period out to five years for a good reason: to weed out those who don't have the stomach for it," he said with a little laugh, causing his own ample girth to rumble. "It's an energetic thing," he said, more seriously now. "Not everyone can attune themselves to the higher vibrations of Azara due to the evolution of their soul - surely this you know," he said, looking directly at Jor Alesh, subtly changing the subject.

"Yes," she answered quickly, remembering her lessons from school as well as her briefings prior to departing for Azar. "With each incarnation the soul has the opportunity to either grow and evolve, thereby attaining a higher vibration, or devolve and lower his or her vibration, making communion an agonizing and disturbing experience," she said, almost as though reading from a textbook.

Pirfiro smiled widely. "Very good, Alcian," he said. "Clearly, our ways are not a complete mystery to you."

"No," she said, "though there is still so much I need to learn."

"And I'm sure you will."

Whatever it was that people truly thought around here, Pirfiro hadn't revealed it, nor had the High Maegin in his brief meeting with her. They had met once before - at her ascension, though the pomp and circumstance had largely prevented their getting to know one another in any real depth. Minor ascensions for lesser positions were never attended by the High Maegin, though the Maegins who served Jurndan communities usually did make a formal show of seeing to the changes in the political structures of the city. The ascension of the Alcian only happened every five years and the High Maegin always graced the ceremonies with his presence and blessing. Chondrasil Sojan had been High Maegin long enough to have overseen the two previous ascensions, as well as her own. Soon, perhaps by the time Jor Alesh stepped down, it would be time for a new High Maegin. There came a point when the rigors of performing as High Maegin simply became too much, and a younger Maegin would be chosen by his brothers. Chondrasil was approaching such an age. He clearly had no ambition to step down, though, and in fact, still had some surprises left.

Jor Alesh had certainly been surprised when Chondrasil suggested the idea of returning to *The World*. No one in Jurnda had imagined that this would be the Azaran response to the coming of the Darsulans. But it seemed to Jor Alesh that this was primarily Chondrasil's idea, and not necessarily something that was reflected in others. Standing in the crowd, moving up into the pyramid, she overheard people talking about the Darsulans, their disagreements in doctrine and practice, speculations over why they were coming, what they intended, and how this all fit into Azara's plans for humanity and the cosmos, but nothing about returning to *The World*. Jor Alesh detected a mixture of excitement, anticipation, and caution.

Some worried that nothing good could come of this, but more seemed optimistic. All seemed to agree that whatever would be, would be, and only Azara knew the true purpose behind the plays of life and death on this side of the veil of illusion. Though many also hoped that the Maegins knew more than they and trusted that all was in their compassionate and wise hands. Tonight's prayer ceremony, regardless of what was to come, would insure that the people of Azar had done what they could to raise the vibration, both individually and collectively, and would pave the way for whatever plan Azara had for them. It was the unique mixture of fatalism and proactive spirituality that was the religion of Azara. Fate might be written in the fabric of the universe, but that didn't mean that there was nothing to do, because there was always communion, always the drink. There was always access to Azara, as mysterious and enigmatically personal as it was.

One particular conversation caught Jor Alesh's attention, and with the slow progress of the mass of people bottlenecking into the pyramid, she let her ears settle in on two novices behind her. What drew her attention was, in contrast to everyone else, these two were not talking about the coming of the Darsulans. Though relatively low in the church hierarchy, being only novices still with full heads of hair, they were discussing something that was obviously very important, and by their tones, potentially dangerous as well.

"Seyloq Surya," said one to the other, his voice colored in a tone of awe and wonder. "I still can't believe that you did it! You have to tell me more about it. How could his medicine possibly be stronger than Azara?"

The second novice looked to his friend, but in turning his head, noticed Jor Alesh listening in. "Quiet," he said, sounding angry, though attempting to keep his volume under control. "I don't want to talk about this. Not here. Not now."

"Are you going to go back? I mean, do you think you'll do it again?" asked the first novice, ignoring his friend's discomfort.

"I don't know," said the second novice. "He scares me. I think he's far more dangerous than the Darsulans, and look what happened to them. They've been exiled for what, two hundred years?"

"They're not going to do anything about Seyloq," said the first novice dismissively. "He's just an old coot up in the hills. So what if the occasional curious novice, such as yourself, chooses to go and commune with the guy? I think they're waiting for him to die so they can go about ignoring him without any more trouble."

"You don't get it. The Darsulans merely have doctrinal differences - this guy is off the map. I don't even know if he counts as human anymore. I think he may have a demon possessing him."

"A demon!" blurted out the first novice, a bit too loud to pretend that Jor Alesh didn't hear. He gave her a nervous smile and tried to turn his attention back to his friend.

"I thought that was something you gentlemen were supposed to be good at reincorporating," interrupted Jor Alesh, seeing an opportunity to break in and possibly get more details.

"Excuse me?" said the second novice.

"Demons," said Jor Alesh. "I thought that part of your training was reincorporating demons. Isn't that true?"

They were on the steps now, with Jor Alesh above the two novices. Soon they'd be inside the pyramid.

"I'm sorry," said the novice she had just addressed. "I don't believe we've met. My name is Jendru Amdin, novice of Azara. Are you a visitor?" It wasn't a question, as the answer was more than obvious.

Jor Alesh nodded. "I came in from Jurnda today. My name is Jor. And your friend is?"

"Khalanto, at your service."

"So what's this about demons? I'm curious," explained Jor Alesh, "as all anyone else seems to be talking about around here is the Darsulans. Should I be expecting demons in the ceremony tonight?"

It was one of those things that people like Jor Alesh just didn't know what to make of. She'd never met a demon herself, and wasn't even sure what the concept referred to, other than what seemed to be fanciful stories of lost and tormented souls bent on doing harm and wreaking havoc at any opportunity. For Azarans, it was clearly something real. She had heard the disquiet in Jendru's voice. Whatever she might think of demons, there was no doubt that Jendru meant what he said.

"No, not tonight," said Khalanto. "This isn't a reincorporation tonight - only a prayer meeting. The Maegins won't be inviting those kinds of energies into the temple. But hey," he added, "you never know. That's the thing - you gotta be prepared for whatever happens, stay in the flow, and keep your vibration high. You never know when some dark energy, spirit, or even demon is going to try and get in there and make you his."

"He's just trying to scare you," added in Jendru. "It can happen, but it's rare. Azara looks over us. For a prayer meeting such as this, chances are it will all be love and light. You needn't be concerned."

"But what about your friend?" asked Jor Alesh. "The one you were talking about earlier - Seyloq Surya? He was taken by a demon."

"I don't know," said Jendru, "but I do know you'd be better off not mentioning him again. He's not very popular around here. And he's not my friend," he added. "I don't even know him."

"But you think he's possessed by a demon?"

"Look, I don't know him and there's nothing I can tell you about him. There are rumors, that's all. It would be best if you didn't mention him again. In fact, you'd do best to put him out of your mind entirely."

Clearly this was the end of the conversation. They had reached the top of the stairs. Jor Alesh couldn't help herself gasping with awe upon looking into the interior of the Obsidian Temple for the first time. Though made from black and dark red volcanic glass, which made the pyramid look exceedingly imposing and mysterious from outside, the inside was literally covered in gold and shone with the light of thousands of candles. It made Jor Alesh dizzy, and she found herself steadied by the novice, Jendru.

"Beautiful, isn't it?" he asked.

"Astounding," she answered.

From where they stood, the stairs descended to the floor of the pyramid, fanning out to either side of the entrance. All four sides of the interior looked identical, with each face of the walls decorated in symmetrical architecture, all gilded in gold. In the center of the floor was a series of elevated platforms, culminating in a central altar. There, Jor Alesh could see the High Maegin, Chondrasil Sojan, turning about and surveying the gathering crowd. Below him were the Maegins. Just beyond and below them, but still raised above the crowd, were the Maegin-Lus, numbering more than the Maegins. More numerous still were the acolytes, and then the novices, extending out from the center, eventually mixing with the laypersons and guests, such as herself. It immediately struck Jor Alesh how this was a perfect representation of the Azaran hierarchy. The High Maegin was the direct link to Azara and therefore had placed himself in the center, above everyone else. Then in descending order, the rest of the religious fanned out from that central point of focus. Directly above the High Maegin, though at a considerable distance, was a three-dimensional construct of the geometric form known as the "Flower of Azara," a complex design most often seen in two-dimensional art, here rendered in full form. Given its size and complexity, Jor Alesh found herself staring at the ceiling, trying to take in all the detail.

"The Flower of Azara," said Jendru. "You know it?"

"Yes," said Jor Alesh, "but I've never seen anything like this - only pictures of the design."

"This is how it is meant to be seen - and experienced," said Jendru. "Here in this temple, we use our bodies, our minds, our voices, and our souls to conduct the flow of divine energy, and Azara's flower is the universal conduit. Sometimes, we call the High Maegin 'the conductor,' as it is his responsibility to insure that connection is never disrupted or broken during our ceremonies. That's why he's in the middle, directly under the central star of the Flower of Azara. Without the High Maegin, the energy wouldn't be able to ground properly, especially during a large ceremony such as this."

"What would happen if he weren't there?" asked Jor Alesh.

"Demons," said Khalanto, raising his eyebrows and letting his eyes go wide in mock fear.

"Well, that, or chaos," said Jendru. "With this many supplicants, you need a conductor - someone to keep things focused and hold it all together. Watch the High Maegin tonight and maybe you'll see."

"Or maybe you won't," chimed in Khalanto. "I heard that they're serving a special batch tonight - because of the Darsulans coming and all. A city woman like you - well, the buckets will be behind you, if you know what I mean."

Jendru sighed. Though he was only a few years older than Khalanto, it sure felt like more. It wasn't that he was overly cautious or serious (at least, so he liked to think), but so often Khalanto acted like a child, always teasing, always trying to get a reaction out of people, as he was doing to this woman, Jor.

"There will be guardians there to assist you, if you need it," said Jendru, wanting to be helpful. "In fact, during the second round, I'll be serving as a guardian. I'll keep an eye on you, in case you need anything. Look," he said, pointing to a group of individuals lined up against one of the pyramid's interior walls. "Those are guardians. See - they're wearing the white sashes. You can always go to one of them. They're all novices and acolytes, so they know what they're doing. We've seen it all here. You've got nothing to worry about, no matter how strong the Azara may be. You're safe here."

"Thank you," said Jor Alesh. "I'll be sure to make use of your services, should it come to that."

"You can probably count on it," said Khalanto with a wink. He then dashed off, making his way down the stairs briskly, miming drinking a gulp of something fowl tasting and then grabbing his gut with a laugh.

Jendru shrugged and looked at Jor Alesh. It was brief, but the Alcian could tell that this novice (who hadn't yet taken his vows!) stole a glance at her in the reflected golden candlelight. It had been dark ascending the stairs up into the temple, but here, everything was bright, clear, pure. Her red hair and green eyes glimmered in the light. *She's beautiful,* Jendru realized with a slight blush, quickly turning away, but not fast enough for her not to notice. She was smiling when he glanced back.

"Have a good ceremony," he said, somewhat awkwardly.

"Thanks," said the woman. "You too."

"Like I said, I'll keep an eye on you."

She smiled and he turned, taking big steps down the stairs and making his way to the other novices who were all busy finding their places.

Best not to even think about it, Jor Alesh told herself. *Of all times and places to be turned on, and of all people! Just put it out of your mind.*

Regardless, she felt herself moisten down below, a realization that came with a ruddy flush to her face. She took a deep breath, raised one eyebrow in commentary on her inner state with a slight shake of her head and proceeded down the stairs. *Well, there's at least one demon I'd like to reincorporate . . .* That made her laugh. *Why is it that when attempting to put something out of your mind, it inevitably comes roaring in with full force? It's like a game you just can't win. Oh well, let's get this show on the road. (God, it's been a long time since I've had a good fuck.)*

Chapter 5

CHONDRASIL'S PET

Jendru caught up with Khalanto, who was mingling with the other novices on the floor of the great pyramid temple. Davon, Treland, Vico, Sumra and all the others were there. These were Jendru's five closest friends, and with the exception of Khalanto, had all originally joined as novices at the same time. A young man could become a novice upon turning twenty because "Azara is not for children," as the Maegins said, and one had to wait until officially reaching adulthood before formally joining. Of course, one could always participate as a layperson, and even children were given very small sips of Azara, if their parents brought them to a ceremony. Fifteen was the earliest anyone could receive a full serving. Most novices joined at the age of twenty, but some, like Treland, had waited a few years, though it was rare to find anyone over thirty "putting on the robes," as they said. Of the five, Khalanto was the youngest and Jendru, Davon, Vico and Sumra were all the same age − twenty-five. At the end of this season, they would all be eligible to take their vows, shave their heads, and take on a Maegin-Lu as a direct mentor and spiritual guide.

"It's too bad Chondrasil is High Maegin," Jendru heard Sumra saying as he joined his friends. "Look at him up there," he said with obvious admiration. "I'd take him as my Maegin-Lu in a heartbeat."

Treland, always the "wise elder" of the group, commented in his characteristic fashion: "Wishing for that which one cannot have is a sure path to discontent, and ultimately, suffering."

"Look who's the High Maegin now!" burst Khalanto. "Someone's been studying up on his doctrine!"

"You don't have to always be so ironic, Khalanto," said

the older novice. "The truths of our tradition are profound and we should always seek to drink from the well of wisdom."

"Dammit, Treland, can't you ever say anything that isn't a proverb or saying or bit of wisdom?" chidded Khalanto.

"Isn't this what we're here for: to learn and soak up that which has been poured out for us?"

"See, that's exactly what I mean, Treland," said Khalanto. "Where are *you* in there? You sound like a holy book."

Vico looked agitated by the exchange. "He's right, Khalanto," he said. "This is what we're here for. Who *we* are and what *we* think is meaningless. We're here to become conduits for our tradition. A conduit that is filled with its own thoughts and desires cannot allow the divine to pass through."

"Oh, trust me," said Khalanto. "I had a monumental 'passing through' just before coming here - take a deep breath and you're sure to smell it!"

"You're such a child," said Davon. Sumra and Vico nodded in agreement.

"Relax, all of you," said Jendru. For whatever reason, they listened to him. They always did. In their gang of six, the others had always looked to Jendru for common sense direction and guidance. Jendru wondered if it was something about him, or merely his connection.

"Okay, Chondrasil's pet," taunted Khalanto.

The truth was Khalanto was correct. Though mysterious to him, Chondrasil had taken an immediate liking to Jendru, and the novice always had welcome access to the High Maegin. It was something that Sumra was jealous of, given the awe and reverence with which he looked upon the High Maegin. Not that that was anything unusual - the High Maegin was a great man, and everyone revered him. But Chondrasil Sojan didn't deign to make personal relationships with many novices; yet for Jendru, he had made an exception. Jendru hadn't understood the uniqueness of their relationship at first, but by the time Khalanto had joined as a novice, their bond had become quite obvious. No other novice could go directly up to the High Maegin and say hello, or stop by his private quarters for illumination on a tricky axiom of Azaran doctrine and practice. So here, Jendru couldn't complain about Khalanto's taunting.

"Jendru - Whom are you going to choose as your Maegin-Lu?" asked Sumra, returning to his earlier thought. "I know you'd choose Chondrasil too, but since he's out of the running, what do you think?"

"Oh, that's an easy one," blurted Khalanto. "Seyloq Surya, no doubt!"

Silence. Stares and silence.

"Will you shut up?" said Jendru after a long pause.

"Watering your roots with poison will only bear sour fruit," added in Treland.

"How is that even relevant?" protested Khalanto. "Besides, I was just kidding, right Jendru? Weren't you saying something about Mordoc, or even Tilvash?"

"I haven't made up my mind yet," said Jendru. *Well, at least that was honest,* he thought.

"Tilvash - he's the one for me," said Davon. "But Mordoq, he'd be a good choice too, Jendru. Either would serve you well. But not *you*, Khalanto. For you, the laywomen would be appropriate. Who else would put up with your stunning wit?"

"Ha ha," replied Khalanto. Then, the mischief building back up in his eyes, he said, "If you want to know about laywomen, ask Jendru." Khalanto took a moment to look around, eventually spotting the woman who had introduced herself as Jor when they were on the steps. "There's your beauty," he said, attempting to gesture in her direction with his head in a manner that was discreet, but ultimately lacked subtlety, thereby catching her attention. She waved and smiled from a distance. Khalanto waved back with a broad smile.

"See," he said to the others. "She's something, isn't she? And she likes our Jendru here."

"What do you mean?" said Jendru defensively, put on the spot and increasingly uncomfortable. Was there no button that Khalanto wouldn't push? It was like constantly dealing with a small child.

"I see more than you think, *brother*," he said.

"That one there?" asked Vico.

"I met her on the steps," said Jendru. "She said she's from Jurnda and her name's Jor, but I don't know anything else about her. Well, I do know she doesn't know much about Azara."

"She's the Alcian," said Vico, as though stating the obvious. "I saw her walking around with Maegin-Lu Pirfiro earlier today. She's come for the arrival of the Darsulans, though I understand she showed up earlier than Chondrasil was expecting her, unannounced and unescorted. I was there when Pirfiro caught sight of her. He was surprised, to say the least. He had to rush off to get his gold cloak and made me keep an eye on her while he was gone. He said that Maegin Vorta was supposed to bring her up from Jurnda, but she showed up here on her own, and so that's that. She is beautiful," he added. "Not that it matters to any of us."

"All temptation leads away from the One," said Treland. And then he added, for good measure; "Azara created women and demons to tempt the true of heart and test the strength of the faithful, for only a true man is fit for ultimate reincorporation; firm, steadfast, and filled with resolve, like a cup of the divine nectar."

"Yes, Treland, we know," said Davon.

That was unexpected . . . the Alcian of Jurnda . . . , thought Jendru. He looked back to the red-haired and green-eyed woman. She noticed and gave him a personal smile.

"Khalanto's right, you know," said Davon to Jendru. "That one there is trouble."

"Trouble. That's Jendru's middle name. Nothing like walking the edge, is there?" said Khalanto.

"Enough!" said Jendru. "It's time. The Maegins are all ready. Everyone go to his place. It's time to drink."

Chapter 6
DRINKING AZARA

Being a prayer meeting, the retractable chairs that could disappear into the floor were all out and those still standing began to take their seats, each according to their position within the church hierarchy. Everyone had his place, no exceptions. Communion carriers mingled about the seated groups of devotees and monks, handing each person a small glass of ruddy brown liquid, which would be the first of three servings for the ceremony. Though one could acquire a taste for the communion drink of Azara, first reactions were often gagging and automatic retching. On some occasions chocolate was mixed into the drink to make it more palatable, but tonight it was raw Azara, undiluted and strong.

Azara was always a combination of two plants, though exact species could vary. The important thing was that the two plants had to work in synergistic combination to provide the necessary catalyst for the unfolding visionary and energetic experiences. Once one took his vows as an acolyte, instructions were given about the various plant combinations and mixture ratios. The first vow of acolytes was the oath of not revealing to non-initiates what the exact plants were, thereby keeping the knowledge secured within the tradition and preventing possible secular desecration of the sacred drink.

An important part of Azaran practice was the recognition that the drink made the ceremonial work possible, and not the other way around. Though prayers were said and rituals were performed to prepare the sacred drink, here in ceremony, the first act was to insure that everyone who wanted to consumed the drink. Only then was it possible to begin the ceremony proper with all prayers, hymns, and functions following. As the Maegins described it, this was the act of "opening the flow" - the flow of divine energy that was unleashed and made palpable and present by the communion drink. Though the full effects wouldn't fully manifest for another thirty to forty minutes, most practioners could feel a subtle shift in energy almost immediately upon getting the bitter drink down. The initial onset period was the time for opening prayers and benedictions. Petitions to Azara and the celestial hierarchy could be made by the Maegins, essentially bringing everyone into a highly synchronized state of being and awareness, known as "tuning up the congregation." Once everyone was tuned up, the energy could flow and the real work could be done. Eventually, the energy would die down as the effects of the drink ebbed away. Once that cycle had been completed, everything would start over again with another round of Azara, and the flow would be reopened. There'd be another tuning up, then more work and gradual winding down. This would be repeated from three to five times in a night. Tonight, the ceremony called for drinking communion three times and would be a relatively "short" ceremony, though it would last until the early hours of the morning.

Despite her high position back in Jurnda, here among the faithful and the dedicated, Jor Alesh was at the bottom of the pyramid and therefore among the last group to be served communion. By the time the servers (who were all acolytes and Maegin-Lus) got to her, she could tell that they were already beginning to feel the effects of communion themselves. They all had very serious and concentrated looks with slightly glazed eyes. They seemed almost luminous in their countenances. Their movements were fluid and smooth without any sense of urgency. As was their role, they never spoke, and aside from briefly and intensely looking each supplicant in the eye before pouring, never made direct eye contact. For the rest of the ceremony, this was to be the way of things: no direct eye contact with others and no speaking. All conversations would need to wait until morning as "normal" social interactions were considered a disruption to the flow of divine energy. It was a time to center, concentrate, and go within.

Jor Alesh had always thought of the Azara drink as impossible to describe, but unmistakable in flavor. She got her serving down in three gulps, instantly fighting the urge to spit it back up. Before she was able to rinse her mouth out with a sip of water, she fought through a series of energetic gags and releases, but fortunately, nothing came back up. Anyone who spat up their drink right away was considered to have been rejected by Azara and would be asked to sit at the outer edge of the gathering to wait until the next serving of the drink later in the ceremony. Such a reaction was taken as a sure sign that the individual's current energy state was incompatible with the requirements of the ceremony. Anyone who was able to keep the drink down beyond those first few moments was deemed to be energetically fit for the work, even if they purged everything out fifteen minutes later. It was that first reaction that counted, and not what followed.

Jor Alesh managed to keep hers down. *Looks like I'm in for the full ride,* she told herself, settling into her seat. It was cushioned and comfortable. Underneath was a small tray that held an Azaran hymnal. She reached down and took it out, flipping through its pages. She recognized many of the themes of the hymns from her previous communions, though she couldn't be sure if she knew any of the hymns specifically. There were many references to energy, flow, celestial beings of the divine hierarchy, praise for the Mother/Father, Azara, exhortations to demons and lost souls to reincorporate into the divine light, etc. For laypersons such as herself, taking communion was more about simply making it through the ordeal than doing any of the "work" that the monks performed. While they were tasked with their own spiritual evolution and the divine work of reincorporating lost and wandering souls, or even channelling spirit entities and proclaiming divine revelations, for Jor Alesh and others of her rank, it was a time for personal reflection, going within, and as was often the case, simply making it through to the other end of the experience.

Not being a religious expert or devotee, Jor Alesh liked the sound of Azaran music more than any specific appreciation for the content of the songs. Now that everyone had been served, the Maegins and Maegin-Lus began their chants in the center of the scared space. Accompanying their chants were atonal flutes, chimes, and gongs, all sounding off at what she presumed was the appropriate times, though she had never been able to divine the sequence or timing of the apparent cacophony. Maybe it was as random as it sounded, she pondered, and there was no over-arching score that they were following.

Already she could feel the energy starting to rise within her and respond to the deep chanting of the monks, the clashing sounds of the gongs, and ethereal call of the flutes. Suddenly nervous, she felt distracted and unfocused by the open hymnal. She closed it up and put it under her seat, also noticing that no one else had their hymn books out, making her feel all the more self-conscious. Looking about, she noted that she was in one of the few places that were designated for women. Like all the men, the women were mostly sitting with their hands placed up, either on their laps or above their knees, as though waiting patiently to receive some divine gift. Most had closed eyes and virtually everyone appeared to be quietly praying. Some people were even crying.

Listening to the sounds about her, she noticed that despite the randomness, the various sounds all seemed to fit together in some strange and inexplicable way. She had never experienced anything like this before. The communions she had attended back in Jurnda hadn't been nearly as large as this, including only a handful of Maegin-Lus and Maegins and smaller groups of laypersons. There were probably several thousand people here and the number of monks and their young apprentices far outnumbered the laypeople. The inner circle of musicians numbered a couple hundred.

The acoustics of the temple chamber were such that she found she could distinctly hear what was happening virtually anywhere in the chamber, especially if she focused on it. Looking up to the central altar, she could clearly hear Chondrasil's voice among the others. She liked the sound of his voice. It was rich and warm, though also commanding and firm. There was something paternal about it that gave her comfort and reassurance. Though soon to be in the full grip of the Azara, they were all in the conductor's hands, as well.

Jor Alesh closed her eyes and listened. The cacophony continued, but so did the strange sense of everything somehow congealing together, with every unique sound finding its place in the chaotic whole, where it was resolved into perfect symmetry and balance. In a world of random events, everything was perfectly ordered, perfectly in place. Somehow, everything simply fit.

A warm wave of energy came up from somewhere down below. At first it was just the intimation of energy, barely registering in Jor Alesh's mind. As it crept up on her, she became aware that her body was extremely relaxed - much more than she had experienced previously when drinking communion. She smiled to herself. It was almost unreal. She was warm and fuzzy, perfectly comfortable with herself and her experience.

With her eyes closed, she realized that she could not only feel the warm, rising energy, but could see it as well. Bursts of dazzling color started to form behind her closed eyelids, radiating out in complex geometric forms. The visions weren't strong yet, so whenever she tried to "look" at them, they would disappear like ephemeral phantoms, leaving a black, blank canvas, only to be filled a moment later by some new colorful display that would quickly melt away into nothingness. It took her some time before realizing that she was watching a synchronized flow of light that simultaneously coincided with the rise and fall of her breath, which had become entrained with sounds of the chanting and instruments, which itself seemed to be expressing the slow build-up of energy that was emanating up through her from somewhere below. Though there were many distinct "parts" to the experience, it was clearly one unified and orchestrated event. It was as though each distinct part were a reflection from somewhere else, with reality being parceled out into mutually reflecting surfaces of an intricate crystal matrix. *It's so beautiful*, she felt herself commenting privately within.

Suddenly a loud crash of gongs and cymbals exploded into Jor Alesh's awareness. It was as though any structure that had been holding her being together suddenly and unexpectedly shattered. The energy that had been rising from below now had a very distinct point of origin - her genitals. It was no longer merely a warm, fuzzy energy, but raw, pulsating, sexual energy of a kind Jor Alesh could not recall having experienced before in her thirty-two years of life. Whatever happened next in the ceremony, Jor Alesh couldn't say, as her awareness of everything external to her immediate experience flew away in one instant. A riot of colors and geometric forms burst full-force into her awareness behind her closed eyes. Earlier, if asked, she would have said she was watching the play of light with her closed eyes. This was beyond watching. For all she knew, this explosion of geometry and color was simply all there was and any notion of her observing something was meaningless and without reference. She was the energy of her experience, and it felt *good*.

Really, good was too mild, too neutral a term. Jor Alesh was ecstatic with pleasure. Wave after impossible wave swept up from where she remotely assumed her genitals must be, exploding into her heart (wherever that was), and shattering any remaining rigidity in her mind (in her head? *Where* was the mind?). For a split second, a wave of self-consciousness caught her and she thought to herself that what she was experiencing wasn't proper, wasn't fitting for the solemnity of the occasion, with her vague recollection of being somewhere doing something important. But the truth was that she didn't care. *Fuck it*, she thought. Then again, *Fuck it . . . yes, fuck it, fuck me, yes, yes, fuck me, Fuck Me, FUCK ME!*

Whatever inhibitions she may have had, they were long gone now. A spasm shuddered through her vagina, sending rippling waves of pleasure throughout her entire being. The colors and geometric forms were coming fast, always pulsing, growing ever brighter, ever more impossibly complex. There were so many planes of detail, so many receding and paradoxically expanding and approaching patterns, that she couldn't keep track. *Oh God, yes, yes, fuck me, fuck me to oblivion, infinite, infinite, infinite . . .*

Then there it was - the Flower of Azara. It looked exactly like the three dimensional representation at the apex of the interior of the temple, but rather than a static, human-made object, it was breathing, pulsing, vibrating. Every surface and plane appeared to expand and contract organically as faces turned in on themselves, only to reveal other, more complex, more fantastical images. The symmetrical, geometric form filled all of Jor Alesh's awareness - it was her entire universe. Though abstract, she found herself wildly erotically attracted to the pulsating geometric mass of light, color, and form.

The shape began turning inside out, which only served to bring her erotic energy to a frenzy. Suddenly, the entire form was comprised of endless ecstatic fucking with human forms madly making love to each other in a wild orgy of no restraint. Throbbing erect penises dove into yearning vaginas as their owners reeled in ecstasy. Everyone was making love to everyone and there were no boundaries. Within it all, Jor Alesh couldn't tell if she were a man or a woman. In fact, she had no idea who or what she was, only that she was lost in this endless sea of wild fucking. Fucking for life. Fucking for death. Fucking simply to fuck. It was all one vast exchange of energy where any boundary was merely a membrane, a surface allowing sensual contact, a place to meet, to exchange, to transform from one into the other. *This is all there is . . .*

And everything blurred into one, infinite, eternal, and endless white light.

With a shock, Jor Alesh opened her eyes. The first thing that she noticed was that her crotch was wet. Discretely, she reached between her legs and then subtly brought her finger up to her nose, rolling the mucous against her thumb as she sampled the scent. *My God, I've completely creamed myself,* she thought, taking a quick moment to look around to see if anyone noticed. It didn't seem so. From what she could see, everyone was peaceful. The chanting and cymbal and gong crashing had stopped. The light was about at half the level of when she had first closed her eyes. She could hear a few people crying, and in the distance, several people were purging; otherwise all was calm, and no one was paying her any attention. She felt a little nauseous and weak, but otherwise she was okay.

She did an internal check. Everything felt relatively

normal. She could hardly feel the medicine anymore. Closing her eyes, there were vague impressions of color, but no more than normal. *Looks like round one is done,* she said to herself. She tried to recall what she had just been through. It must have been an hour or more. She couldn't tell. She blushed as the full erotic nature of what she had experienced came back into memory, but there was a clear point beyond which she could recall nothing. *Pure white light . . . then . . . nothing?*

People were beginning to stir. Others were coming out of their prayers and meditations. Someone handed Jor Alesh a tray. On it were a variety of differently hued chocolates ranging from light to dark. She suddenly realized that she was quite hungry and took a couple squares before passing the tray along. *Oh my God, that is so good!* The chocolate melted in her mouth in a subtle echo of her earlier ecstasy. She licked her fingertips to be sure and get every last bit of the delicious treat.

Well, if that was round one, what will rounds two and three bring? she asked with a private laugh.

Chapter 7
CONFRONTING TRUTH

The one thing that seemed clear to Jendru was that whatever was happening here was happening not because of everyone's best efforts, but despite them. It was a most peculiar revelation, and one that didn't sit well with the novice. For almost five years he had dedicated himself to this path. Until now, he had held the religion of Azara and those who participated in it in the highest possible esteem. The Maegins were great men doing great work. And Jendru had wanted to be part of that, integral to it all, thick in the heat of reincorporation, bringing lost beings into the light, and all else that they did. He had spent years picturing himself in his Maegin robes, singing the songs, chanting the chants, and all the responsibility that went with such important tasks. People such as Chondrasil were like living gods for Jendru, though of course that was hyperbole. The one true God was the Mother/Father. On the etheric plane, there were multiple manifestations and guises for the Mother/Father, who could take on any form and appear in multitudes of ways. The Maegins were not gods. They were conduits, workers of the divine light, conductors of divine energy. They were Azara's human representatives, but not to be deified. And it wasn't as though he worshiped Chondrasil and his brothers, but their power and skill astounded Jendru. He wanted to be like them.

Becoming a Maegin would mean doing his part in the divine work. It was that simple. Yes, it came with various forms of social power and prestige, and though these trappings appealed to Jendru, it wasn't what had drawn him to the order, and it wasn't what had kept him here over the past five years. It was the work itself, and its significance. According to Azaran doctrine, the etheric plane was filled with lost souls, who, without the assistance of the Maegins, would be forever separated from Azara. It was only the Azarans, through their practices of reincorporation, who could bring the lost souls to resolution. It was the same with demons (though the process was somewhat different). These practices (in addition to raising one's individual vibration level and evolving through lifetimes of spiritual work, thereby being a personal path to liberation and reunion with the divine) were the ultimate project of Azaran religion. Azarans didn't seek converts. They didn't try to change the world. Individually and collectively, they evolved towards union and worked for the liberation of lost souls - of which there were billions. Even five hundred years later, reincorporating the lost souls of those who died in the war was still a major feature of regular Azaran practice. Jendru himself had guided countless souls back into the light in numerous sessions with the medicine. He *knew* the work was genuine and he *knew* that everything the Maegins taught him was true and correct.

Only now, it didn't feel that way. There was a distinct disconnect between what Jendru thought he *knew,* and what he, for the first time, *felt.* He didn't like it. He blamed Seyloq. *It's the demon that's inside him,* Jendru told himself. *He's trying to convince me to abandon this work, to abandon the divine, to abandon Azara.*

What was worse, he didn't truly believe what he was telling himself. He wanted to blame Seyloq. The argument fit perfectly. In fact, it was exactly what the Maegins would say if he told them about visiting the apostate - but that was it - he knew he *wanted* to believe this. If he could, everything would fall back into place, everything would make sense, and this would be another spiritual test along his path to becoming a Maegin, and he'd grow stronger because of it. But Jendru couldn't shake the nagging feeling that there was a fundamental difference between what one *wanted* to believe and *wanted* to be true and what *was* true. Saying that Seyloq was possessed by a demon was too convenient. It didn't *feel* genuine, despite how much his fears wanted to make it so. When he was honest with himself, he didn't feel there was anything incorrect or dangerous in anything Seyloq had thus far shared with him, despite his reputation as a heretic, lunatic, and apostate. The opposite was closer to his genuine feeling on the matter - when he was honest with himself.

Life would be easier if he could brush off his session with Seyloq and everything he had said, but he couldn't. Somehow, Seyloq had breached his doctrinal defenses and was undermining his confidence in what he was doing here. It seemed unlikely that any amount of external reassurance would change this shift that had occurred within him. And it wasn't anything that he could pinpoint. When he recalled various things Seyloq had said to him, he found himself arguing back and largely disagreeing - sometimes even passionately so. The problem was that his feelings no longer matched up with his rational and doctrinal mind. Things no longer fit, and he didn't like it.

I'm becoming a non-believer . . .

But that was precisely the problem! A primary tenent of Azara was that it required no belief, it being based on experience - direct and immediate experience of the truth of the doctrine and divine revelation through the medium of the drink. Demons, past lives, lost souls, reincorporation. Jendru might only be a novice, but he'd had his share of experiences. None of this was simply doctrine or a matter of belief for him. He had *experienced* all of these things. So where was belief in all of this? No belief required! The Maegins would describe *other* religions as being based on belief, but theirs was a *practice*, a practice that was grounded in the reality revealed by the Azara drink, and that reality was simply undeniable. Rationally, it seemed to him that he had to accept the doctrines as true because that was what he experienced. Yes, he had been told about it, instructed, trained, and prepared for the work, but even then it had surprised him when it all started to happen for him exactly as he had been taught. This was the way things were. No more arguments.

But now . . . Jendru wasn't so sure. Maybe it was something Seyloq said about everyone being characters - how Chondrasil was a character playing the role of an enlightened being, but that didn't make him enlightened. Something about that hit home and dug its way under Jendru's rationalizations. Whatever the case, this was what he *saw*. He *believed* Chondrasil and the other Maegins and Maegin-Lus to be truly liberated beings, soon to be reincorporated into Azara, but that's not what he saw.

There had been no profound inner insights or radical visions for Jendru with round one of the medicine. Instead, almost comically, he just sat there and watched. Something had changed for him. Instead of seeing immensely important light workers serving the greater good of the cosmos, he saw a bunch of actors, all acting out roles. And what was worse, the actors didn't know they were acting. Everything they did was invested with a heavy dose of overly sincere realism and commitment. Because they believed this to be the ultimate reality, they were all heavily invested in it. They were like actors who had forgotten that they were playing roles and had become convinced that they truly were the characters they were playing. At the height of his realization, Jendru laughed out loud, something he now felt quite self-conscious and critical of - though in the moment, it had felt like the most genuine thing he'd ever done in a ceremony.

Jendru simply didn't find the show convincing anymore. It was strange, the way he seemed to be able to see through everyone's disguises. Chondrasil was a fervent believer. Pirfiro was a pompous and self-important ass. Most of the Maegins and Maegin-Lus dripped with sincerity, constipated by their own sense of spiritual purpose. Jendru's friends were all characters too. Khalanto was the scared clown, always joking, but secretly frightened of the things he joked about. Treland was the intrepid student, devoted to his learning, but overly-reliant on repeating the tried and true wisdom of the ages. No one seemed immune from Jendru's critical gaze. And worst of all, Jendru simply didn't care! His reaction at the height of the medicine was, "Of course - this is the way things are!" and he found it hilarious that no one else seemed to notice. He had been made privy to some private, cosmic joke that went over everyone else's head.

With the medicine having subsided, he found himself deep in the grip of an existential quandary. He no longer believed in the reality of what they were doing here, and he didn't like how that made him feel.

He came to a conclusion: whatever it was they were accomplishing here, it was despite their best efforts, not because of them. Their "best efforts" were merely the antics of characters in some cosmic tragedy or comedy, or some ironic mix of the two. His prior experiences with Azara and all that he had come to personally know of the doctrine no longer seemed like anything to him. Another aspect to his realization was that whoever he thought *he was,* and whatever he thought *he had been accomplishing,* was as much the antics of a character as anyone else. He could find no reason to exclude himself from this powerful realization. It applied to all, equally. In the midst of the medicine, all of this had made him laugh, filling him with joy and a sense of surrender and peace. Not anymore. Jendru's realization was like an invisible sliver caught under a fingernail, and it was digging away at him. Because it was true: he didn't believe any more. And with that absence of belief, he found that he had no idea what he was doing. He was an actor who had forgotten his lines, or at least no longer felt their power, but he didn't know who the director was and didn't know where to turn. The easy thing to do would be to talk to Chondrasil (which couldn't happen until tomorrow at the earliest), but his confidence was shaken. How could he take Chondrasil's counsel seriously? Where was his faith?

Fortunately, thought Jendru, he'd drunk enough times to know that realizations that came with one round could easily be drowned out or washed away by new revelations of subsequent rounds. Since he had to perform his duty as a guardian, he doubted he would be relieved of his existential worry, but he held out hope for what round three might bring. At the moment, he needed to deal with his discomfort, focus on the ritual, and continue on. There was nothing more he could do.

Chapter 8

ROUND TWO

Round two was nothing like round one. Jor Alesh could feel the nausea welling up within her almost instantly upon getting the drink down. She gagged a little at first, but there was no immediate threat of purging. She could tell; it was coming.

Everything had a glazed, glassy look to it, accented with subtle geometric forms that casually breathed and flowed into one another. The music and chanting had resumed when they had come around to serve up the next round of drink. Many of the devotees had taken out their hymn books and were singing along - Jor Alesh presumed that they must have moved on to a different set of songs as she recalled that during round one, no one had a hymn book out. If the songs were stylistically different, she couldn't tell, aside from the fact that the gongs and cymbals didn't seem to be joining in this time. She couldn't tell which way she preferred it - sacred cacophony or group sing-along. Either way, it didn't matter much. She was going to vomit and vomit big, and she knew it.

She had always heard that you weren't supposed to fight against it, so why was she resisting? Was it because round one had been so pleasurable? Had she created an expectation that needed to be challenged? Or maybe it had more to do with the fact that she simply didn't want to purge here in front of all these people. She knew it was silly, but as Alcian, she'd hoped to present a stronger image, one more like the steadfast Maegins. It wasn't a competition, she knew, but still; these were important times and leaders needed to be strong. Maybe she was thinking too much. She was willing to go into full ecstatic sexual bliss here, but not vomit? How silly was that? Of course, as far as she could tell, that ecstasy had all been internal. She didn't *think* she had been writhing about in her chair, moaning and groaning. There wasn't any evidence that she had done so. In fact, she suspected that no one had any idea of what she had just gone through - the most profound cosmic fucking of her life. If only every round could be that much fun!

But purging was another matter. No way to hide that. No way to keep that under wraps, personal, secret, concealed from others. Vomiting was, by definition, public (at least in this context). She knew there was no shame in it. According to the Maegins, it was a good thing. It provided health benefits, cleared out the system, and readied the body for higher-level vibrations. It was all supposedly part of the process, and reportedly, everyone purged at least sometimes. But none of this changed the fact that Jor Alesh didn't *want* to do it. She wanted more of what she got before, though she'd settle for pretty colors and interesting shapes. She wasn't, after all, looking for anything in particular here. She wasn't trying to find God, or anything else that the followers of Azara might be seeking in the sacred drink. She was only a visitor here, doing her best to fit in, gain some deeper insight into Azara, and prepare herself for whatever was going to happen when the Darsulans arrived. Was it too much to ask not to feel so profoundly nauseous?

Apparently so.

She tried taking deep breaths and squirming into a more comfortable position in her seat, but these attempts only made her feel more self-conscious. It wasn't as though anyone was watching her (she thought), but every little rustle, every sigh seemed to shout out, "I'm going to puke everywhere and I don't want to!" She felt like her own enemy. The harder she tried to be inconspicuous, the more conspicuous she felt. It was like she was caught in some kind of loop where every time she tried to gain the upper hand on her experience, she found herself pushed back down. It was both frustrating and confusing. She wanted to relax, to trust, to let go, but found that she didn't know how. How had she managed it last time? What a bizarre mystery. It was so strange to her how every time she drank Azara, it was a fundamentally different experience.

Yet paradoxically, it wasn't. It was always clearly Azara, and nothing else in her life had ever come close to the fundamental experience of the drink. As far as she knew, this drink was unique and unparalleled. She supposed that the Maegins would define it by its vibration, its energy. That made sense to her. It had a signature, of sorts, and that signature always clearly identified it. It could take on many forms and come in many guises, thereby *appearing* to be different every time. Underneath the wild diversity, the signature was always there. Was that what they meant when the Maegins said that the manifestations of God were many, but that ultimately God was One? What did they call it? A polytheistic monotheism? Did that make any sense? At the moment, it seemed to. *Am I turning into a theologian?* she wondered.

Oh God, it's coming.

Evidently, her pondering of the deep questions would have to wait. Urgently, she stood up from her chair, clumsily turned, and stumbled past the other women sitting next to her. She found an isle and started walking to the rear of the ritual hall where Jendru had told her she'd find a guardian and a receptacle to receive whatever offering she felt certain she was going to make at any moment.

It felt as if the floor kept moving beneath her as she tried to walk. It was like she was losing control of her limbs, or that she had forgotten how to use her body. She seemed to sway along with the rhythm of the hymns, the sounds echoing all about her and phasing through odd metallic waves that she faintly recognized as distortions caused by the Azara, affecting how she was able to hear the music. There was a riot of geometry, as though she were walking through a translucent corridor that shifted with every step. *God, this stuff is crazy,* she thought to herself as she stumbled along.

What's that?

Something in the geometric matrix of her sight caught her attention. She couldn't have said what it was - a glimmer, a shift in the patterns, almost, she thought, a wink. *The damn thing's winking at me! Is this some kind of joke?*

A series of subtly blinking flashes started to move

through the matrix. *It knows it has my attention*, she thought to herself, simultaneously a little frightened and amused. The little flash darted back and forth, made a few quick turns, circled around her, then shot off down the translucent corridor. She followed it with her eyes. It was like a fairy or sprite, she thought, suddenly thinking of childhood stories of children being led off into the forest to discover a magical land, trailing after some mischievous pixie. It made her smile. And then there it was again, rushing right up, coming directly in front of her face. She let out a little gasp. *It even looks like a fairy!* she realized with a start. It was a little figure made of light with luminescent wings that were reminiscent of a butterfly or moth. *This is too ridiculous*, she thought. *I'm having the strangest night!*

And then it was off again, zinging down the translucent corridor through which Jor Alesh was still stumbling along. It whizzed up high and circled around her again, making her dizzy (suddenly realizing that she didn't feel so nauseous anymore, but following the little fairy with her eyes was giving her a bit of vertigo). It shot over her head, flew around her back, and then seemed to move directly through her, piercing her between the shoulder blades (which didn't hurt, but was quite distinct). It then shot out of the center of her chest and slammed into what looked remarkably like the Flower of Azara she had seen in the apex of the previous round of medicine, sending shards of crystallized rainbow light flying in every direction. When the pixie dust settled, Jor Alesh realized she was standing directly in front of the novice, Jendru, who had changed out of his novice robes and was wearing the guardian outfit, clearly identifying him as someone who could help those who were in distress or in need of assistance.

For a moment, Jor Alesh stood there, dumfounded. For the life of her, she couldn't remember why she had come here to the outer edge of the ritual gathering. She looked at Jendru. *God, he's so beautiful*, she caught herself thinking. She could tell that the medicine was strong. The novice looked like he was full of light, standing there shimmering, almost glistening. She wanted to look him in the eye, but remembering proper ritual decorum, looked him up and down instead (though that wasn't much better, she thought). She found herself staring as an image started to form. She glanced away and then looked back. The image was still there. In fact, it was three distinct images. There, on his forehead, on his chest, and down at his crotch, were more representations of the Flower of Azara. They were pulsing and breathing, like in her earlier vision. She glanced at herself and saw the same images, as though they were mirroring each other. Not being able to help herself, her mouth fell open a bit in a state of awe, and rules be damned, looked him in the eye. Though he was still a man, and she a woman, she had the uncanny sense that she was looking into a mirror. Somehow, impossibly, she *knew* that *this man was herself.* The thought registered with an echo of confusion: *that doesn't make any sense!* But looking into his eyes, she could clearly see that the same realization had occurred to him.

This is impossible . . .

Something clicked. Somewhere deep inside her, something shifted. The nausea was back, but this time, with a vengeance. Everything was spinning - no, not spinning, turning inside out! *Oh God, this is crazy! I'm going to go insane!* She could feel herself fighting it. She started to swoon and could see the floor rising up to meet her. Strong arms reached out to her and held her in steady hands prior to her making a special, personal visit to the shimmering gold floor. "You're okay," she heard a voice say. She was down on her knees, still holding on to whoever was steadying her with one hand, the other holding her up from the floor. Someone pushed a bowl in front of her face. *Yes.* And then it all started coming out.

She tried to scream. Screaming and vomiting didn't exactly go together, however, so it all came out as a guttural retch. It rocketed out of her mouth, splashing up the sides of the bowl and ricocheting back onto her face. She didn't care. This was only the beginning. More was coming. *No time to think. Just get it out. Let it go, let it go . . .*

Again and again she retched. Chunks of food clogged her nostrils. So much was heaving out of her that she was temporarily afraid she wouldn't be able to breathe. It was like swimming up from a deep pool of water with her lungs burning, aching for air, but the stream of vomit kept coming, one vicious wave after another. She finally took a deep breath, and then more came. It was spilling everywhere. She could taste it, smell it. *God, will this ever end?*

Finally, at long last, it seemed like she was done. The medicine didn't feel as strong now, but it was still working on her. Strangely, she felt expansive, almost jubilant. Her face was buried in the bowl, her hair tangled in the vomit. She laughed. The whole sequence of events was ridiculous. The thought of anyone making a religion of this seemed absurd to her in that moment. Cosmic sex, fairies, fun house mirrors, and bucketfuls of puke. Could it get any more bizarre than this?

Someone was offering her assistance to get up from the floor. *Oh yes, how could I forget - the beautiful young man.* She looked up and pulled her puke-filled hair away from her face and gave a weak smile to no one in particular, trying to communicate that despite her appearance, she was okay. "Can you sit?" the man asked. She nodded her head, almost drunkenly. She plopped down on the chair and rubbed her hands down her face, only to pull them away and remember that she was still covered in puke, which was all over her hands. The man handed her a damp towel. It felt so nice and cool, so refreshing. She cleaned her hands and face and swabbed it about her chest with a still-clean corner. The man didn't say anything, standing silently to her side and slightly back. She looked around. The singing had stopped and there were many people milling about. She followed them with her gaze to see what was happening. It was only then that she became aware that restrooms were available at various locations around the temple room. She made a mental note that she'd be sure to visit one as soon as she felt able to walk. But, in looking down at herself, she realized she'd need more than a washroom. Vomit had spilled out of the bowl and had gotten on her front and legs. What she really needed was a warm bath and the silk sheets of her bed (*And this beautiful creature to share them with!*).

She looked up at him. Noticing his thick dark hair, it suddenly occurred to her how she didn't find the shaved head look attractive. She wondered if she'd find this one here as beautiful if he had already taken his vows and shaved his head. What would he look like when he had his tattoo? By then, he'd be older, too. By the look of him, she judged he was probably around five years younger than herself. But why was she even thinking of these things? The man was a monk in training! Well, not yet officially, as he wasn't an acolyte, but from her perspective, a novice was essentially the same thing. *Just my luck,* she sighed silently to herself.

"Um . . ." she said.

"Yes?" He looked concerned, compassionate.

"Do you think it's okay if I don't stick around for the final round of the medicine - I mean, I'm a mess."

He smiled. "Yes, you are. That was some pretty epic purging. I'm impressed."

"What can I say? I guess I'm a natural."

"Do you want to get cleaned up?"

"Very much so. I don't want to offend the Maegins, but I'd like to return to my quarters, and at the very least, change my clothes. My room is pretty far away, though, so I don't think I could make it there and back before they serve the next round. In fact, I'm not even sure if I can make it there, considering the state I'm in," she said with a laugh.

"I think they'd understand if you didn't stay," he said. "The High Maegin noticed you back here, so he knows you've been having a rough time. If you like, I can escort you through the city. Where is your room?"

"Uh . . . Loazranji pyramid . . . I think."

"Ah," said Jendru. "That's a pretty good walk from here. You said you were from Jurnda. Are you familiar with the city? Do you know how to find your way around?"

"Um, not really, no," said Jor Alesh.

Jendru nodded. "Then when you're ready, I'll escort you. Take your time, though."

"Thanks," said Jor Alesh. "I *think* I can walk. Are you sure *you* can leave, though? Shouldn't you be *here*?"

"I'm only a novice," he answered with a slight shrug. "I'm not required to be here, especially now that I've fulfilled my guardianship for the night. It's up to me to stay or go."

"Well then, yes, please. I'd very much appreciate your assistance finding my way."

"Whenever you're ready."

Chapter 9

ALL THINGS AZARAN

It was well past midnight by the time they exited the pyramid. Scattered clouds brought a warm rain. Lightning and thunder peeled through the night sky, lighting up the dark pyramid city. The sound of songs from the temple grew fainter as they made their way, eventually replaced by the metallic trills of insects and haunting calls of the night creatures of the jungle.

Jendru had been sure to grab them a parasol at the exit of the Obsidian Temple. A pedestrian city, Azara was filled with parasols that didn't belong to anyone in particular. The rain was most often warm and so not necessarily uncomfortable, but anyone who wanted to stay dry could easily grab a parasol and deposit it in a receptacle outside of wherever their destination might be. Many of the main streets were covered in glass archways, but most of the side streets weren't. Personally, Jendru didn't mind the rain and rarely took a parasol for himself. But it wasn't often that he walked a woman through the streets of Azara and thought that she might appreciate not getting soaking wet, especially after her ordeal during the last round of medicine.

The city was mostly dark, with the exception of some accent lighting on the various stepped pyramids. The streets and walkways were softly lit by bioluminescent fungi and mushrooms that grew symbiotically on the various fruit trees and plants that lined the paths; mango, guava, passionfruit, starfruit, and more. It was a little tricky finding ripe fruit in the otherworldly blue-green light of the glowing mushrooms, but Jendru eventually settled on a ripe mango and bit into it, removing some of skin with his teeth and then offering it to Jor Alesh. Sweet mango juice ran down the sides of her mouth as she dove into the tantalizing offering, suddenly realizing that after all that purging, she was quite hungry.

"Are you sure you won't be missed?" she asked, handing the fruit back to Jendru.

"Oh, they'll notice," he said, "but they'll understand. The real work of the night is done," he added. "Rounds one and two were the powerful ones. For this last round, it will be singing and dancing, and they're probably only giving out half-servings of Azara. It's mostly a celebratory prayer meeting - not doing the real heavy work. If it weren't, my absence would be a bit more noteworthy."

They walked on in silence as Jor Alesh finished off the mango. When she was done, Jendru tore off a soft, velvety leaf from a low growing plant and offered it to her to clean her hands with.

"Thanks," she said. "I needed that."

"You certainly had a go at purging tonight," commented Jendru.

She nodded. "I haven't been through something like that before."

"So this wasn't your first time?"

"No - I've been to communion a few times before, though only in Jurnda. It's been a few years since I participated, though."

"And?"

"What do you mean?"

"How was it tonight?"

Lightning crackled nearby and she got a good look at Jendru, suddenly flushing with the memory of what occurred earlier. "Pretty amazing . . ." was all she said. She decided to change the subject. "Do you know who I am?"

"Yes," said Jendru. "You're the Alcian - Jor Alesh Melva - youngest Alcian in several generations, and the first woman Alcian since Tenda Altriand Olash."

"You know your Jurnda politics?"

"I was raised in Jurnda. My parents are artists there. I only came to Azara when I turned twenty and could start as a novice."

"I always wondered," said Jor Alesh, "why do they make you wait until you're twenty? Why not earlier? And even then, you have to wait five more years before taking your vows. It seems like they start you off late in life. I mean, it's not that you're old, but still, it seems a little late."

Jendru smiled. "Well, do you want the official doctrine, or what Chondrasil told me?"

Jor Alesh was curious. "Both," she said.

"Okay - official doctrine: The real work of Azara is not so much a religion as it is a form of spiritual/energetic technology for reincorporating lost souls. Sure, laypersons are allowed to practice, and it is understood to have great benefits for them both spiritually and physically, but the real work is about maintaining the flow of the energy and bringing lost souls back into the embrace of Azara. This is work, and it takes real commitment. It's not a form of worship, however - which is what your average layperson often wants. And the youth aren't wise enough to understand the deep rigors of this practice. It is something that initiates must come to with commitment. The requirements of the practice supersede all other allegiances, including work, family, and even politics.

"Thus the Maegins decided that at twenty, one is ready to begin such a commitment. At twenty-five, after five years of experience, one can know if this work is truly for him and if he can devote himself to it fully. Though it's rare, some novitiates do drop out after a period of time and don't go on to take their vows. However, making individuals wait until they're twenty before beginning the process reduces that possibility tremendously. What we do here is a service to the cosmos. We gain immeasurable benefit from it, and we all individually raise our vibration level and make our own eventual reincorporation all the more likely and inevitable through our work, but the work itself is selfless. We are to set aside all of our own personal concerns for evolution and redemption and focus exclusively on how we may use our energies and abilities for the benefit of others on the etheric plane. Trying to get young people to understand that can be difficult."

This all made sense for Jor Alesh. She wondered what the unofficial explanation might be. She looked at Jendru expectantly and he continued.

"Chondrasil enlightened me about some other important

factors," he added. "According to him, back in *The World*, in the old form of Azara, novices could begin as early as twelve. After the war, and our exodus, we were few in number and there were only so many laypersons who were able to make the journey here to Lur. At that time, new births were a priority: a religion that doesn't seek converts and only has celibate male monks only works if the religion functions within a larger society where there is a sufficient portion of the population that is ready to leave secular life behind to join the ranks of the spiritually chosen. So changes had to be made.

"Given the necessity of celibacy for monks, something had to be done to insure that there would still be a lay population. According to Chondrasil, it was a practical matter that became encoded as part of Azaran doctrine - in fact, many things changed when we began our new life here. But anyway, I think you get the point. The Maegins decided that they needed more young men available to procreate, so they established the later age for becoming a novice. Once you take your vows as an acolyte, all sexual activity is forbidden. It also used to be the case that novices took celibacy vows, but when you're getting boys as young as twelve, chances are they've never had sex and don't know what they're missing, so it's, in some sense, easier that way. Now, noivces have to practice for five years before taking their vows. They're not forbidden from having sex during that time, though it is highly discouraged. It's harder for many to give up and the five years of training is something of a test. They keep us pretty busy drinking Azara, and you have to be celibate for three days prior to any ceremony, even laypersons. Anyway, it all came down to the Maegins' realization that if they maintained the traditional practices, the religion would die off within a few generations. If they hadn't made this change, it's doubtful that Jurnda would exist today. In a way, both you and I, as citizens of Jurnda, have this change to thank for our being here at all."

"That's funny," commented Jor Alesh, "how something so practical becomes a part of doctrine. And here I thought the doctrine was divinely revealed, yet the Maegins make their own changes."

Jendru had thought as much himself and said so to

Chondrasil. Here, the High Maegin's response served him. "The doctrine wasn't changed," he said, "merely aspects of its application. Doctrinal consistency is highly valued in Azara. It is what makes everything that we do here meaningful. If we change the doctrine, then what are we doing? The doctrine is that sexual activity contaminates an individual's energy stream. Those who practice reincorporation need to be free from all potentially polluting energies in the body. Reincorporation, and all that goes with it, is fundamentally a *spiritual* activity, and only disembodied souls can be fully reincorporated. For those of us doing the work, we need to do all that we can to effectively leave the body behind. This is what purging does: it removes earthly contaminating energies so that we can function more fully within the etheric. In helping lost souls reincorporate into Azara, we are also removing our remaining earthly energies so that when we die, we might be saved from another incarnation and simply return to Azara. Or, if there are still energies that need further working out, we are reborn, ideally to a family of laypersons, so that we may continue our work within the Church. But it's our willful attachment to things of this world that prevents us from returning to the infinite embrace of Azara, so we need to commit to forgoing the pleasures of the body and workings of the world in order to fully devote ourselves to the spiritual work. While the practice of Azara shifted, the doctrine is fundamentally unchanged and the tradition is still pure. We are still doing the holy work we've always done."

"What happens if all the lost souls become reincorporated and there's nothing left for the Azarans to do? What then?"

Jendru looked at the woman, dumbfounded. "There are billions of lost souls," he said. "The work will last until the end of time. The war alone created countless lost souls. And that's only our planet. According to the revelations of Azara, the universe is populated with countless sentient beings and they are all subject to the same spiritual laws. We Azarans are the gatekeepers of the divine. Our work benefits the entire universe. It will never be done."

"Well, that's one way to insure job security," said Jor

Alesh.

"You think it's a joke?"

Jor Alesh shrugged her shoulders. "I don't know," she said. "It all sounds fine and noble, but remember, I'm the Alcian. I've spent my entire adult life tending to the needs and issues of living people, not the dead. For many of us in Jurnda, what you do here in Azara is esoteric and highly removed from the daily tasks of living. Most people simply want to live happy, meaningful lives where they feel that they are able to express themselves, explore their possibilities, and contribute to human society in some way, especially in the aftermath of the war. In Jurnda, our focus is to make the best possible world out of what we've been given right here - not in some other life or some other realm. For most people, spirits and demons and unincorporated entities sound like fantasy, to be honest. As I'm sure you're aware, having grown up in Jurnda, most of us feel that Azara is somewhat archaic, or at least so far removed from ordinary life that we don't understand it."

"So is that what brings you here?" asked Jendru. "You want to understand?"

"Yes," said Jor Alesh. "Now that the Darsulans are paying you a visit, I wanted to learn more about your ways and beliefs. Who knows why they're coming, or what repercussions that will bring. Some worry about the possibility of violence or other forms of social disruption. We like the life we have in Jurnda and don't want to go back to how things were back in *The World*. People are worried - that's all. People are skeptical about all this talk of doctrine and competing beliefs."

"According to Chondrasil, our practice isn't about beliefs at all. It is the accurate enactment of divine revelation."

"Well, that's Chondrasil's interpretation," said Jor Alesh. "As a relative outsider, I may be wrong, but I'd have to say that there's a great deal about what you Azarans do that strikes me as belief. Take women, for instance," she said.

"What do you mean?"

"Why can't women practice as Maegins? Why is it only

men?"

"Women, as the bearers of children, are energetically bound to the physical world," answered Jendru. "It is quite literally through them that souls are unincorporated from Azara. Birth binds us to the physical plane and the cycles of reincarnation; wandering, lost, separated from Azara."

Jor Alesh shook her head. "But that only holds true if you buy into your whole doctrine!" she protested. "And that, from my perspective, is *belief*."

"That's only because you don't know what the real work is - you don't have the experience."

She was getting frustrated. "And that's because you men won't let us women into your inner circle! You say I can't understand how your beliefs aren't beliefs because I don't have the necessary experience, but your entire system is set up to prevent people like me - *women* - from advancing far enough where our interpretation would be given any credit. Honestly, it just sounds like a bunch of self-fulfilling bullshit to me. It sure is convenient, anyway. If everyone thought women were as useless as you Azarans seem to think, then I'd never be what I am. In Jurnda, we let all people excel according to their innate abilities. We don't put structural barriers in people's way. It's about honoring reality, rather than doctrine. People succeed or fail based on what they're actually capable of, not what someone else decides for them. As a woman, I find your religion insulting and demeaning. I'm sorry, but I don't see that men are any more spiritually gifted or 'energetically pure' than women. It's a load of crap."

Jendru knew that he should be offended and should be inspired to defend his faith and practice, but he didn't feel it. In fact, he felt himself agreeing with her and heard echos of Seyloq in her opinions.

Jor Alesh stopped along the path and looked directly at Jendru. She seemed to be scrutinizing him in the dim blue-green mushroom light haze. After a moment, she said, "It's interesting, but you're not offended, are you? Is it that you simply don't care what a woman thinks, or maybe you have a mind of your own, after all?"

Jendru continued walking, requiring her to catch up with

him. "As I said, I'm still a novice. I haven't taken my vows yet."

She could tell this was only a superficial answer. *He's hiding something.* Suddenly a name from earlier popped into her awareness. It was almost like there was another voice in her head. *Ask him about Seyloq,* it said.

"What about Seyloq?" she asked. "What does he think?"

Jendru gave her an uneasy look.

"I can see there's something going on here - something going on with you and this man, Seyloq," she said. "You can trust me, if you want to talk about it. I may be a critic, but I won't go telling your superiors what you share with me."

Instead of answering her directly, Jendru decided to change the subject. "If you want to talk differences of doctrine and interpretation, I'm sure you'll have much to discuss with the Darsulans. In fact, from what you say, I think you'll get along with them just fine. They let women become Maegins, you know."

Now this was interesting. Knowledge of Darsulan doctrine and practice was virtually unknown, especially in Jurnda. All that was known was that doctrinal differences had led to the breakaway group migrating away from Azar. The histories that had been recorded in Azar only mentioned the doctrinal split, not what it concerned, as though those who had written the histories were so offended by the heretical doctrine they couldn't even bring themselves to say what it was - at least in the histories made available to the secular public of Jurnda.

"Really?" she said. "Is that all?"

Jendru overlooked her ironic tone. "No, that's not all, but it's a big part of it. I'm sure they'll tell you all about it when they get here. Or you can ask Chondrasil. He knows more about it than he lets on."

"I'll be sure and do that," she said.

Jendru came to a stop and turned to face Jor Alesh. "We're here," he said, indicating the pyramid behind him. "This is Loazranji."

Looking around, Jor Alesh recognized the pyramid as

the one she had been assigned to for her visitor's quarters. "I trust you can find your way to your room," said Jendru. "It wouldn't be appropriate for me to escort you in at this hour."

"Of course," said Jor Alesh. "Thank you for bringing me, and for the conversation. I hope we can talk more over the coming days."

Jendru shrugged. "Maybe," he said. "I'm only a novice, as I've said, and I'm sure you'll have plenty of important people to talk to and meet with."

"Yes," said Jor Alesh, "but I get the feeling that none of them are going to tell me about this Seyloq, and I'd like to know more. As Alcian, it's my job to rely on a variety of sources, and not just the official ones. I know you don't want to tell me about this man, but I'm not naïve, and I can tell that there's something going on here. I'd like to know more. I'd ask your friend I met earlier as we were ascending into the temple, but he seems a bit immature. I'd much rather get it from you. Though I have no real authority over you, I hope you understand that I'm inquiring not only for myself, but as Alcian. This visit of the Darsulans is sensitive and everyone is a bit nervous. It's my job to determine what's happening here and understand how it might affect us back in Jurnda. I don't know what this Seyloq fellow is all about, but I can tell that there's something to it, and I want to know more. There are still a few days before the Darsulans arrive. I hope we can talk more before then."

"If Azara wills it," said Jendru, falling back into a pre-set saying.

She gave him one last hard look and then followed it with a smile. "Good," she said. "I'll look forward to it."

Back in her room, after a refreshing shower, Jor Alesh masturbated herself to sleep, finding herself not reliving the cosmic fucking she had received back in the temple, but rather visualizing the novice Jendru sliding into her and pressing deep into her sex, almost feeling the pulse of his organ releasing into her.

Back in his room in the novice quarters, Jendru lay restless, awake, confused, and determined to return to Seyloq Surya in the morning, if only he could wait that long.

Chapter 10

DECONSTRUCTING DOCTRINE

The valley of Azar lay east to west between the twin volcanic ranges of Ladjup to the north and Nadrasuli to the south. Beyond the volcanoes and lava fields to the east, the river Qya, which flowed between the ridges, curved to the north and made its way to the Sea of Loa Neshi, the tropical turquoise waters that separated the small continent of Lur from the mainland and thereby *The World*. The metropolis of Jurnda had grown up around the Qya delta along the edge of the sea among the wetlands, tidal flats, and sand dunes.

Between Azar and Jurnda, rich agricultural fields served both the reclusive temple city and the burgeoning metropolis and surrounding communities. At the other end of the valley of Azar were mines and quarries that originally supplied the necessary building materials to create the elaborate temple city. When the Azarans first arrived some five hundred years ago, they had found the mines already developed, though far from exhausted.

Coming to Lur had essentially meant starting over for the refugees from the *Great War*. The island continent was chosen by those pioneering followers of Azara for its ecology and climate. It was the right environmental zone for growing the necessary plants for the communion drink, and several varieties were indigenous to the island. The area also had fertile lands for farming as a result of the millennia of volcanic activity. The pre-established mines and quarries settled the choice of the valley of Azar as the religion's new home. Though the original population of Lur had been completely decimated by the war, the ruins and half-functioning technology and tools they had left behind served to give the Azarans a new start, and human society had begun anew on this small continent to the south of the mainland. The war lasted so long, and with the human population removed, everything was completely overgrown when the first Azaran explorers reached this far south. The environment itself was in nearly ideal conditions: the perfect place for humanity to start again.

The *Great War* had numerous causes, and many factors had coalesced together to bring humanity to the brink of total disaster. A major driving force had been battles over increasingly scarce resources and access to good land, fresh water, and other necessities for life. Not wanting to repeat the tragic and disastrous mistakes of their progenitors, the early refugees on Lur instituted sustainable harvesting and land management programs that continued to be a guiding factor of life on Lur. Rather than dominating the environment, people on Lur made every effort to live in balance with their surroundings and leave as little impact on the land and its lifeforms as possible. Though originally something of a religious value, the practices had been continued by the secular culture of Jurnda, and were a matter of pride. The last thing anyone wanted on Lur, whether Jurndans or Azarans, was to repeat the tragedies that had driven their ancestors to this land.

A few once-wide roads wound through the tropical forest from Azar to the mines and quarries. Although vehicles were forbidden in Azar itself, because the city was uniquely designed for human habitation with only pedestrian walk ways, ancient roads had been cut through the forest to the mines and quarries. Though the valley of Azar had no evidence of prior human habitation, the old roads cut directly through the valley and passed out into the alluvial plains from the volcanoes where ruins could still be found in the over-grown forest. These roads had been cleared and brought back to life, seeing heavy traffic during the founding and construction of the temple city. The work was slow and the technology limited, so it took two hundred years for the temple city to be completed and reach the form that it currently had, three hundred years later. Now the forest was reclaiming many of the roads, and only the most well traveled were still open to the sky, the rest being more like tunnels through the forest than proper roads.

Not too many people lived out at mines' end of the valley, though there were enough to keep foot traffic flowing from Azar to the outskirts. With the completion of the construction of Azar, all vehicles and machines had been dismantled and shipped downriver to the growing city of Jurnda, where they were put to work once more. There, with the founding of new centers of learning and industry, secular human society flourished with new sciences, technologies, and inventions. By comparison, Azar was quaint and conservative, almost pastoral. The Church leadership had intentionally kept technology to a minimum in the temple city, instead choosing to focus their energies on their sacred work. Most Azarans saw the trappings of secular and material society as distractions and diversions. They weren't against technology and progress outright. It was only that the Azarans had a different focus and purpose that separated them from the rest of humanity. It was probably this sense of self-isolation that had originally spared the Azarans from the fate of so many in the *Great War* back in *The World*.

Overall, the people of Lur were about as free and independent as humans could be. Though the Azarans ruled life within their valley, they exercised no control or direct influence beyond their temple city, and this was exactly how they wanted it to be. Their work was focused on the etheric, after all, and what happened on the material plane, as they put it, was not their concern. In Jurnda, most governance occurred at the very local level, and in essence, there were no laws. People like Jor Alesh Melva, the ascended Alcian, served in an advisory capacity. While her views were considered vital in any community decision-making process, she had no outright authority to enforce her will. Furthermore, there was no military or police force. People were expected to be responsible for themselves, and problems resolved through local solutions. In many respects, people could do what they wanted within the bounds of what others would tolerate or support.

Though it was rare, there wasn't anyone to stop people from choosing to make their homes out in the forest beyond Azar. Sometimes they were families of laypersons who wanted to work the forest and spend their time harvesting its various gifts of fruits, mushrooms, animals, or even medicinal plants or other raw materials. They could often been seen in Azar with their goods, and though choosing to live somewhat remotely, were still considered to be parts of Azaran society and were included in any self-assessment of the size and breadth of the community. There were others who had withdrawn from life in both Jurnda and Azar, but who still desired some close access to the benefits of society and thus made their homes out in the wilderness just beyond the city. What these people were doing out here was anyone's guess, but it was a free society, so no one made it an issue.

And then there was Seyloq Surya. Like other recluses, he lived out past the mines and quarries well outside the bounds of Azar proper, though close enough to be only a few hours' walk from the outskirts of the temple city. Though he wasn't alone in living out this way, as far as Jendru knew, he was in a category all by himself. Seyloq didn't have any immediate neighbors, though his modest home wasn't too far off of one of the main roads through the jungle. Apparently he had lived out this way for over two decades, having abandoned Azar long before Jendru joined the ranks of novices, or even tasted his first sample of the communion drink. As he understood it, the Maegins would prefer Seyloq to live further way ("He should have taken a clue from the Darsulans!" Chondrasil had once said to Jendru), but for his own reasons, he had chosen this as his place of permanent residence, and there was nothing anyone could do about it. Thus his presence was tolerated, though not enjoyed, by the hierarchy within the Church.

Jendru set out from Azar for Seyloq's early that morning. He had only managed a few fitful hours of sleep, and when the raucous sounds of macaws and parrots roused him in the morning with the rising sun, he decided to get up, despite his desire to try and get another hour of sleep, and make his way to see the enigmatic apostate. He enjoyed the walk and appreciated having time to himself, making a concerted effort to keep his mind under control and enjoy the scenery, the humid air, and the life around him. He was only partially successful in keeping his mind quiet, however - there were too many questions rattling around in there. He wanted to talk to Seyloq, and he wouldn't be satisfied until the old man answered some of his questions.

When he came upon Seyloq's house, Jendru found the peculiar man out front in the grass, wearing nothing but cream-white linen pants. His body was tanned and wrinkled, though in fairly good shape. His long wavy grey hair was a bit wild on his head, despite being pulled back into a tight bun. Upon first seeing him there, Jendru thought that Seyloq must be meditating, but he quickly rolled onto his back as his bare feet shot up into the air. It was an odd posture, Jendru thought. Seyloq seemed to be balancing on a point at the top of his spine and bracing himself on the ground with the back of his head. His arms were out to his sides and his legs sticking straight up in the air. He held the position for a few moments, but then started flowing through a series of movements where his arms and legs were always in synch with each other as his body rolled forward and back along the ridge of his spine.

Watching him, there was something distinctly familiar about these fluid, symmetrical movements that Jendru couldn't place. He couldn't recall ever having seen anyone move quite like this. There was something about the movements, especially when Seyloq was balanced on the top of his spine, that seemed almost to defy gravity. Seyloq was perfectly balanced. He looked as though he could hold the position indefinitely without ever having to steady himself with his shoulders, arms, or hands. The movements struck Jendru as both beautiful and disturbingly uncanny. There was just something *unnatural* about it.

Jendru conspicuously cleared his throat to announce his approach as Seyloq rolled into a sitting position with his legs bent in a diamond shape out before him, the soles of his feet pressed together. In reaching the sitting-up position, his arms flowed fluidly along the sides of his body, turning over in place several times, eventually resolving in a prayer position out in front of his body with palms pressed together, mirroring the placement of his feet. Hearing Jendru, Seyloq gave a quick glance his way, then brought his gaze back into focus along the midline of his sight. Not looking directly at Jendru, he asked, "Back so soon?"

"Yes," said Jendru, somewhat meekly. He suddenly felt uneasy again because there it was: that voice. It didn't sound like Seyloq. Not that Jendru knew Seyloq all that well, but it was that strange, almost artificial sounding, deep voice that Seyloq had spoken in when he was here taking medicine with the old man the day before.

"I see," said Seyloq, rolling up on his spine and then returning to a seated position once again. "Are you ready for more medicine?" He looked directly at Jendru, causing the young novice to turn away, finding the old man's direct gaze too intense.

"Uh . . . I was hoping we could talk."

"Oh." He was sitting on his knees now, hands placed on his lap. "Then what can I help you with today?" He gestured for Jendru to come and sit, which he did. He sounded slightly more like Seyloq.

There were so many questions in Jendru's mind that he wasn't sure where to start. Not finding anything else better to begin with, he decided to ask about the voice issue.

"Well, there's a lot," he said, "but maybe we can start by you telling me about your voice. I'll be honest with you: I think maybe you're possessed by a demon."

"And what makes you think that?" said Seyloq, suddenly firm and serious. His back arched a little, and though there wasn't anything obvious, it felt to Jendru that the old man was leaning into him. Jendru cringed a little, but tried to keep it imperceptible. Like throwing some kind of switch, there the voice was again in all its uncanny fullness and richness. Jendru wanted to squirm in his seat, but resisted the urge.

"That, right there," he said. "That voice. Why do you talk like that?"

"I told you yesterday. What is it that you do not understand?"

Jendru tried to recall what Seyloq had said. The medicine had been so strong. Something about this being his voice and that he was Seyloq, but Seyloq wasn't him. It sure sounded like possession, if it made any sense at all. "I don't understand how you can say that you are Seyloq, but Seyloq isn't you. It's like a riddle, and it sounds to me like you're possessed by a demon. No one else talks, or sounds, that way."

The old man laughed. "So who do you think I am, then?" he asked.

Jendru could feel himself getting frustrated. "I don't know! That's why I'm asking. The evidence tells me you're possessed, or crazy, or both."

Seyloq laughed again. "But you are not able to shake the feeling that I know what I am doing."

Jendru nodded. "I'm confused. Nothing makes sense. My mind tells me that I should stay far away from you, and certainly not listen to you, but here I am. I can't sleep, and all I want to do is talk to you, and I don't even know why. Nothing you say makes sense, but then again, it does. In fact, last night at the prayer ceremony, it was exactly like you said: everyone was a character, myself included. I used to think I knew what we were doing in our ceremonies, but now I'm not so sure. Maybe it's like you say and it's all an act. I don't know! I want to understand, but I don't. And if it is an act, then what's real? Who am I? Who is anyone? Ugh . . . what's going on here?!" He tore up a lump of grass and threw it away in exasperation. "And why do you sound like this now, in this big voice? Can't you talk to me like a normal person?!"

"Okay," said Seyloq. "I will tell you as plainly and directly as I can: I am you. I am not a demon and I am not possessed. For all practical purposes, I am a mirror. When you look at me, you are looking at yourself. When you listen to me speak, you are listening to yourself speak. I am you."

All Jendru could do was squish up his face. "Gee - thanks. That makes a whole lot of sense. Now everything is clear." Though used as protection, the sarcasm only made Jendru all the more self-conscious. *Why does this man make me so uncomfortable all the time?!*

"It's quite simple," said Seyloq, oddly sounding more like himself in this moment (Jendru just realized that it was only at these times that "Seyloq" spoke with contractions - when speaking in the strange voice, never). "But accepting reality is its own challenge. Truth is what it is, regardless of what we think about it, or whether we understand it or not. In the end, it's best to accept reality. You'll have an easier time of it if you do."

"That's too cryptic. You're not helping me."

Seyloq held out his hands in a gesture that said, "This is what I have to offer."

"I'm not one of your Maegins," he said. "If you ask me a question, I'm going to give you my answer based on what I know. I'm not going to speak to you in pre-set aphorisms or in snippets of doctrine or philosophy. I'm going to tell you directly and clearly. If you want to learn, then it's your task to find your clarity within yourself. When you do, everything I say will make perfect sense. You'll be able to see that I've been speaking truthfully all along. You're not there yet. In the meantime, listen, pay attention, and go easy on yourself. You're an eager young man and you want to understand. That's good. It's also clear that you don't understand, and that's good too. If you continue to choose to learn from me, you'll find that what you have learned from the Maegins makes less and less sense. Eventually, you'll leave all that behind entirely, as did I. If you're able to do that, you'll be free. In the meantime, you'll have to struggle to identify that prison you've created for yourself. Learn how to take responsibility to dismantle it and simply walk away, if you like. If you're willing, I can help you with that, because, as I said, I am you." His voice was getting deep again. "I am a version of you who has already let himself out of his prison. As such, you can trust me, though I understand that you find this difficult."

Now it was Jendru's turn to laugh. "You're like talking to a self-contradicting riddle. You make sense, but you don't."

"I am only speaking the truth. It is up to you to recognize it. If you do: congratulations. Then it will be your responsibility to act on it. If not, so what? It is your life. I am already out of my prison. I am done. From over here, you are already perfectly free. There are countless versions of myself that are lost in their own illusions, like you. But they are their own problems, not mine. From over here, you are free and clear. From over there, where you sit in your immediate body, you are not. If you want to do something about it, then do it. If not, stop worrying, go back to the feet of your Maegin-Lu, take your vows, and carry on. It does not make a difference to me, though personally, I do want to help you. I do not impose my desires on others, however, so it is up to you. I am not attached to whether you wake the fuck up, or remain an ignorant and deluded sleepwalker. I want to help you though, because I can see that you do genuinely want to wake up. And that you have the potential to do it. Everyone has the potential, but there needs to be the desire and willingness. Without that, the potential is forever potential and never actual. It takes will."

"Okay, okay!" said Jendru. "Just help me understand. Explain to me more how you are me and how this voice of yours that comes and goes is really you, which I guess means me, and how the 'you' that sounds like you isn't you. Can't you see that this doesn't make any sense?"

Seyloq laughed. "It confused me too, when it happened to me. I had my own trials to go through to reach this state of clarity - everyone does, and there are no short cuts. The ego works the same in everyone, though in each version of the self, the ego develops its own patterns, issues, projections, and attachments. The basic function is the same, however, no matter how unique anyone is. I will admit, the process *is* confusing. It is not impossible to understand, if you are able to find the understanding within yourself. To that extent, it does not matter what I say or do. All that matters is that you find the understanding within yourself. This is not like your precious doctrine: you cannot truly learn it by reading about it, or even getting direct instructions from another. You have to discover it yourself; and once you discover it, you have to accept it; and once you accept it, then you can begin to take responsibility for it. That is the way it works. It is up to you -

no one and nothing else. Like I said, I can help you, but I cannot do it for you. I cannot make you understand. That is your responsibility from over there, just as it was my responsibility from over here, for we are one and the same.

"So, to help you understand, let me ask you a question: what is the ego?"

"According to Azaran doctrine?" Jendru asked, which was the only way he knew how to answer the question.

"Sure, if you like." His voice was sounding more casual now.

"The ego is the false sense of self," said Jendru, "that is attached to the body and the current life of the individual. The true nature of the self is a soul, which is not corporeal in form - it is an energetic essence that has its source in Azara, the Mother/Father. The ego is created by souls breaking off and separating themselves from Source. As long as a soul is identified with the ego, it will continually be reincarnated in physical form, as its limited and dense vibration is unable to resonate with the infinite vibration of Azara. This is what makes our practice of reincorporation necessary."

"And how does one overcome the ego?" asked Seyloq.

"You overcome the ego by initiation into Azara," Jendru answered. "By drinking the communion, we raise our vibration level. This allows us to venture into the etheric where, by reincorporating lost souls, we learn to attune our own personal vibration to that of Azara. Through this process, we come to learn of ourselves as transmigrating souls and of our pure, energetic, incorporeal essence that is the true nature of the self. We learn of past lives, and how we have chosen to become attached to the physical. Through our practices, we cleanse ourselves of all of these dense vibrations, bringing us more and more into the etheric light, eventually fully releasing our souls to return to their divine source, beyond the physical and beyond the realm of reincarnation. We are then freed and live forever in union with Azara. It is the inevitable path of all life as all things are in a process of returning to source. Our religion, our practice, is to devote ourselves selflessly to this divine process. We serve as agents of Azara in both the world and in the etheric. It is our holy mission. Through it, we are liberated from our egos and learn to live selflessly and in compassion for others."

"Very good," said Seyloq. "You have proven yourself a good student of Azaran doctrine. I'm sure you'd make a fine Maegin. The problem is that you're starting to have doubts about this, and are finding it harder and harder to believe, despite the fact that you've been trained to believe that this is not about belief at all and is merely the way things are. However, I can tell you from personal experience that out of all that you told me, only the very first was true. This is the problem with religion and belief in general: essentially worthless doctrines *do* contain nuggets of genuine insight, but egos dress them up in all kinds of fancy outfits, to the point where it becomes a challenge to find those original, fundamentally true insights among all the glamour and fantasy."

"So you're saying that Azaran doctrine is all fantasy?" demanded Jendru.

"Essentially. Yes."

"You don't believe that Azaran doctrine is divinely revealed?"

"No."

"And you don't believe that what we experience when we drink communion is real?"

"Um . . . parts of it are. Most of it isn't. Most of it is merely the ego trying to make sense out of things and run the show. When you understand what the ego is and how it works, this is pretty clear. And you cannot fool me, Jendru," said Seyloq. "I know you do not understand all this yet, but I can see that you are starting to see some of this for yourself. That is clear enough simply by looking at you."

"Then why use medicine at all, if it's all fantasy and illusion? You use your medicine. So what makes you special? Why is it that when you use medicine, you're learning truth, but when we Azarans do it, we're playing some fantasy game?"

"Because I am committed to truth - the truth about myself," answered Seyloq. "I do not use medicine to enact some archaic doctrine, or to do anything even remotely 'spiritual' at all. I use it to learn the truth about myself through the exploration of my energy. Nothing more, nothing less. And because I have used the medicine this way, I have learned the true nature of the ego and the true nature of being. I do not have any doctrine to protect and no beliefs to hold onto. In fact, in coming to this truth, I had to let go all of my beliefs and ideas. All I have is the truth, and I know it is true because it is about me."

"That sounds pretty ego-centered, if you ask me."

"I know."

"So you're just more ego illusion and you're no different from anyone else."

"Are you hungry?"

"What? Why?"

"Doesn't matter. Are you hungry?"

"Yeah, a little. I ate some fruit on the way here, but not much. Since that you mention it, I guess so."

"Well, which is it: are you hungry or not?"

"Okay - yes, I'm hungry. So what?"

"How do you know?"

"Um . . . I feel it."

"Well, there you go."

"What do you mean?"

"You know you are hungry because it is a truth you can feel. Hunger, like all things, is a form of energy. Your body, as a collection of interrelated energetic processes, needs periodic intake of biological substances in order to continue to function. This is reality. It is not a belief, or an idea - it is the way things are. It is how biological beings like ourselves function. Energy is real, as are the demands and requirements of energy. If you want to live, you need to eat. The experience of hunger is an energetic way you have of monitoring your vehicle so that you can exercise your will to fulfill what is necessary or desired. Given that you are self-aware, your hunger is not something that is open to debate by others - it is your immediate experience. You know it is there because you feel it."

"So what? I don't see what this has to do with what we're talking about."

"Well, it is a bit more complicated, but that is how things are with me. I know myself. I know my energy and how it functions. Because I know myself, I know when others are saying things that are either fundamentally true about me, or fundamentally incorrect. In that sense, it is pretty simple."

"I could be wrong about my hunger."

"You could," agreed Seyloq. "That is very true. That's why it is important to learn about yourself, so that you can be sure that you are reading yourself correctly. To accurately learn about yourself requires careful observation and truly paying attention. This is especially true given that the ego is a liar and a deceiver. It will always work to cloud your judgment about whatever it is that you experience or think at any given moment. Genuine self-knowledge does not come naturally to most people. It takes considerable effort to make progress. That, not some glorified spiritual ideal, is what the medicines are for. They help tremendously in the process of uncovering truth about the nature of the self, if you choose to use them in this way. It is always a matter of free will. Merely using medicines will not necessarily bring anyone any closer to the truth. It may, but it is not a given, by any means. There is nothing necessarily automatic about any of this.

"Anyway, to return to the matter at hand, you're hungry, yes?"

"Yes."

"And just who is it that is hungry?"

"I am."

"That I know. But *who* are you?"

"I'm Jendru."

"That's your name. Who is Jendru?"

"Me."

"You're moving in a circle."

"I am myself."

"True. What is yourself, then?"

"My soul, I guess."

"So you're a soul? I thought you said the soul was an etheric energy that was non-corporeal that was only attached to a body through an ego?"

"Yes. That is what I truly am."

"So your soul is hungry?"

"No. My body is hungry."

"Oh - then *you* aren't truly hungry. When I asked you if you were hungry, what you really meant to say was that you, the genuine you that truly is you, isn't hungry, because the real you is an immaterial soul, but that the body your soul is attached to through your ego, which is only a false sense of self and thereby an illusion, is hungry, but since that's an illusion, you aren't *really* hungry in any fundamental sense."

"Uh, I guess so. That sounds confusing, though. It's easier to simply say 'I'm hungry.'"

"Yes, it is easier, and probably more truthful as well. You see, once you try to start speaking clearly and truthfully through your doctrine and belief system, things start to get confusing and complicated fairly quickly. You can't even answer a simple question like whether you're hungry or not! Your ideas get in the way of the very simple task of observing the energetic state of your being and commenting truthfully about it. Belief! It is a muddled morass of confusion!"

"But ordinary speaking, ordinary conversation is only a convention. Azara teaches us that truth is beyond the form of the material and the words that we use. That's why we rely on the medicine - to take us beyond the traps of convention."

"So then all ordinary conversations are pure nonsense, no one ever says anything true to one another, and only by participating in your silly rituals can anyone come to glimpse the profound esoteric truths as revealed by your tradition. Is that it? It's no wonder that religion became so embroiled in the *Great War* back in *The World!*"

"I didn't mean it that way."

"So what? – That is essentially what you said. I am merely extrapolating. You want to know how I can claim to know the truth, which I am speaking very plainly to you. Yet you are caught in so many ideas, you cannot even tell me if you are actually hungry or not, or who the one experiencing or not experiencing hunger even is. You have ideas upon ideas piled up between you and reality. What I am telling you is that I do not. I have done the work. I am finished. Complete. I know who and what I am. And because I know, because I have uncovered the truth in myself, by myself, and for myself, I know how to speak truthfully and clearly. It is that simple. I am the real deal. I know exactly who and what I am. You do not. So you rely on metaphysics and philosophy and doctrine and 'spiritual experience' and all the rest they fill your head with down there in the valley. While you will make a great Maegin, you do not have a clue as to who or what you genuinely are. So you are in no position to make reliable statements about what is or is not true. You are in your own way of perceiving and accepting the obvious. If you care about this, then you have an opportunity to do something about it, and I am more than happy to help you with it. If you do not care, then so what? Go take your vows, drink your communion, and go about your holy business. Your only loss will be that, eventually, I will get tired of watching you chase your tail in circles. Then you will have to find someone else to talk over your questions and confusions with. It is your life, after all."

"Fine. If you know who and what you are, and if, as you say, you are me, but I can't answer this question, then why don't you tell me? Who am I, Seyloq?"

Seloq looked squarely at the young novice. "You are God, for lack of a better term."

Jendru stared at the old man. *He is insane,* he thought to himself. *He's not possessed by a demon - he's insane. He thinks* I'm *Azara.*

Seyloq laughed and once again pulled one of his seeming mind-reading tricks. "Mind you, I did not say you were Azara, which I can tell is what you think I am saying. I said that you were God. There is a big difference; namely, the fact that God is real, and Azara is an invention of the ego. One of these genuiney exists. The other is an artifact from a relatively minor religion in human history. But you, my friend, my *love,* are the real deal. You are the real thing, even if your ego is attempting to convince you otherwise; probably by projecting ideas about me and marshaling a little fear to aid its cause. Egos are *very* predictable, and even easier to read - once you learn how to pay attention. If you commit yourself to truth, stick with it, and are honest with yourself, you will reach a point where you are genuinely able to see that I am telling you what you have essentially known all along but have been reluctant to accept, merely because your ego had other plans and other ideas. If you can go beyond them, truth is fairly obvious: and if you are honest, undeniable. That is up to you, however."

Now Jendru was squirming in his seat. He had managed to keep his discomfort in check up until this point, but this was too much. Seyloq smiled. "Lots of egos are squirmers. No need to be too hard on yourself about that," he remarked.

"Look," said Jendru, firmly, "so I may not know who or what I am, but I think if I were God, I'd certainly know it. Now it sounds like you're trying to tell me that I don't really know if I'm hungry or not, but you said I could know it by how I feel, and no one else could tell me what I truly feel. Well, I'm telling you that I don't feel like I'm God, and you can't tell me what I'm feeling, so you don't know any more about me than I do. You're contradicting yourself!"

"Oh, it is quite obvious that you do not feel that you are God. On the contrary, you feel angry, confused, uncomfortable, and all the rest. These are all reactions of your ego, which has convinced you that it *is you*. Like I said; that is all very obvious. You have the potential, like everyone else, to know that what I am saying is true. But it is clear that you are not able to accept it yet, and that is a good thing. If you simply believed me, or took my word for it, then you would have another set of silly beliefs at your ego's disposal. Right now, what you are experiencing is resistance and doubt. If you are willing, these can be overcome, and then maybe you can begin to get to know yourself. There are already cracks in your armor. It is possible that your self-realization is inevitable. For what it is worth, you are on your way. If you were not, you would not have come here yesterday, or be here now. These are all good indications, though you still have a long way to go, so do not fool yourself on that one. But in the end, the truth is that *you do know that you are God* - it is just that your ego has convinced you otherwise. Egos are sly. You are not even aware of how you are willfully deceiving yourself and subsequently choosing to believe in your deceptions. That is the ego for you - it goes around making shit up, and then behaving as though that made-up shit were true - and does it all very convincingly, too. It is a very subtle self-generated prison, and a tricky one to get out of. Once you understand how the ego works, however, it is not all that difficult."

At this point, Seyloq stood up and moved out of the direct sunlight to find a new place in the shade. Jendru watched him and then looked away as Seyloq turned his attention back to him.

"Look," said Seyloq, sounding more casual. "I'm getting a bit tired of chasing tails with you today, so let me say a few more things and then you can run along on your way. As always, I'm going to tell you very plainly. There is only One being. For conversation's sake, we'll call that being 'God,' but that doesn't mean *Azara,* or any of the other names that have been invented by humans over the millennia. This being, this 'God,' is a being of energy, and everything that you will ever experience *is a direct expression of this one being.* This *includes* you: everything you've ever experienced, thought, felt, sensed, or anything else, including your very mind and being. So when asked about your true identity, the only accurate answer possible is that you are, in fact, God. There's a problem if you are attached to some idea that God is a transcendent or all-powerful master of the universe, or some etheric entity, or anything else that you might conceive as existing exterior to or counter to you. These are only ideas, and in our conventional conversation here, I'm urging you to simply set these notions aside. Understand that everything that exists is the expression of one unified energetic being and I'm calling that being God, because I can't think of a better term.

"Now, understand that literally *nothing else exists. The One being is All that there is.* All of reality is fundamentally and literally the self. You, as a human being who is identified as 'Jendru,' are also a direct expression and embodiment of this one being. You are not some soul trapped in a body yearning to return to its divine source in a world of illusion and attachment. You are God experiencing itself from the perspective of a human being in a world/universe that is also fundamentally the self. It is *only* the ego that thinks otherwise.

As you yourself said, the ego is the false sense of self. It is comprised of various patterns of expression and mobilization of energy. Through these patterns, it creates a sense of self that works very hard to distinguish itself from what it chooses to identify as 'not self.' As such, the business of the ego is the business of creating illusions around conventional dualisitic distinctions, and then enacting personal and communal commitment to those illusions and distinctions.

"To bring us back to an earlier point, one of these areas of ego manipulation and use of energy is through the voice. Every ego develops its own personal style of communication and expression. When people speak, they are speaking from their egos. This goes back to the idea that egos serve to shape individuals into what are essentially characters - people play their parts and speak from their respective roles. I, however, am someone who knows who and what he truly is, and I do not have any ego resistance to that. For this reason, my voice often does not sound like 'Seyloq's' voice because *'Seyloq' is merely the ego that developed in this body here, but is not fundamentally me.* And not only do I know this, I live this truth in my energy. So, depending on the situation, or depending on how much medicine I've had, my voice changes and the 'real me' comes out to play. Often, there's no reason for me to need to do that, and attempting to speak in that voice would only be the play of my ego. So I don't ever try to sound either like Seyloq or myself - I speak and my voice reflects my energy accurately. Mainly, it's an indication of the fact that I know who I am and I don't let my ego get in the way of expressing myself. My ego is a part of me, but it doesn't control me, and it will never again be able to convince me that it is me, because I know the truth and live that responsibility in every moment of every day. My one and only goal is to be myself, always.

"Now, when I say that I am you, this is because I know that I am God, and that God is the only being that exists. So whether we like it or not, we are all one. This isn't some feel-good spiritual axiom or positive affirmation. This is reality. Despite all the diversity that we see and experience, all of this, everything, without exception, is all one being. This also means that all of reality is a mirror. No matter what you are experiencing, it is *always and forever an expression of yourself.* There are no exceptions. You can believe me or not, if you like, but it's irrelevant. Reality has nothing to do with belief. It's only peoples' beliefs that convince them otherwise! Truth just is."

"You sound like a nihilistic egomaniac," said Jendru.

"Who the fuck cares?!" exclaimed Seyloq, clearly amused. "What I sound like is completely and totally irrelevant. Truth and clarity, if you care about living freely and responsibly in reality, are the only things that matter. And the only reason they matter is because they affect *you.* If you are living in delusion and illusion, the only one it truly matters to is you. Granted, there's a good chance that your delusions and illusions will affect others, but living in truth and clarity is as much their responsibility as it is yours. All versions of the self are equally responsible for themselves. In that sense, the only one I'm responsible for is me, right here, right now, from this perspective. This holds true for everyone, from his or her perspective. If everyone understood and accepted that, then no one would ever project their delusions and illusions onto others, and we'd all be better off. But the only one you can ever do anything meaningful about or for is yourself, because the truth is, there is no one else. There is only and forever *just you. You are the only being that exists.* True, there are many versions of you running around, and the vast majority of them haven't got a clue, but so what? *Be responsible for yourself.*"

"You're the most maddeningly confounding person I've ever met, Seyloq."

"Good. Someone's got to be, if you're ever going to figure all this out for yourself. Now get out of here. Come back when you're ready to do some real work, and not just make me talk at you. Come back when you're ready for more medicine, and maybe after we can have a good chat and get you a little more clarity. Just remember - it's a process, and you still have a way to go."

Jendru wanted to talk more and share more of what he had experienced in the communion ceremony last night, but he could tell that Seyloq was done. He had enough to think over anyway, so he let it rest. It was well past midday. He was sure there were responsibilities back in Azar he was neglecting by being here, so he got up, said goodbye to the crazy old man, and began the long walk back through the hot and humid jungle to the world that was admittedly making less and less sense to him. It just didn't exert the same pull on him that it once had.

Chapter 11
THE DARSULAN PROBLEM

High Maegin Chondrasil looked up from his writing desk upon hearing a knock at the open doorway. Standing there was a fresh-looking Jor Alesh Melva, the young Alcian from Jurnda. Despite their common heritage and ancestry, the concerns and responsibilities of the two respective leaders were worlds apart. Jor Alesh represented a world of high learning, intricate and expressive arts, technological innovation, and all that life in the city brought with it. There, the focus of society was human flourishing and contentment, living in balance with the surrounding nature and resources, always mindful of not repeating the mistakes of the past. Seemingly content that the Azarans had spiritual matters under control, Jurndan society had always been secular, concerned with how things were here in this world, with no thought of what came next or what lay beyond. And from what Chondrasil had observed, they seemed content and satisfied with this, happy with their comfortable and material lives. Though by Chondrasil's standards, much of their activity in Jurnda was spiritually pointless and only served to trap souls even more effectively into the dense realm of matter and flesh. It would be easy for Chondrasil and others like him to be critics of society, but this wasn't the focus of Azaran practice. It was a practice set apart, and the balance appeared to serve everyone according to his or her own needs and interests.

In the five hundred year history of life on Lur, the only major kink in this arrangement had been the Darsulans and their "new revelations" that fragmented the once uniform religious community. And now, for some as-yet-unknown reason, they were returning. If it weren't for this momentous event, Chondrasil doubted that Jor Alesh would be here at his door, or drinking communion with them in their sacred temple.

"Alcian Melva," said Chondrasil, standing up from his desk and coming out to greet the younger woman. "You look well this afternoon," he said. "Come in."

"Thank you," she said, stepping further into his office. Taking a clue from Chondrasil, she followed him out onto the balcony where she had sat with him the night before as they watched the sunset with Pirfiro. "Please, call me Jor Alesh," she said, taking her seat beside the High Maegin. It was a warm and humid afternoon. Large grey and white clouds drifted through the blue sky with occasional scatterings of light rain. The seasons here weren't that distinct and today was fairly typical for almost any day out of the year in Azar. Looking to the sky, Jor Alesh thought of how pretty the sunrise must have been that morning. She had slept in late, missing it, and had only gotten out of bed when she heard the bells indicating lunch was being served in the Loazranji pyramid dining hall. After dressing and a quick meal, she had found her way here to Chondrasil's office in the Zusil pyramid.

"You look well today," said the High Maegin. "Your second round was a bit difficult for you last night, yes?"

"Yes," she said. "It wasn't the most graceful purging I've ever done, so I had to leave before the end to get cleaned up."

"Yes, that can happen," said Chondrasil reflectively. "I trust that our novice, Jendru, was able to provide you with the necessary assistance."

"Oh, definitely," she said. "As I am mostly unfamiliar with Azar, I requested that he escort me back to my quarters. I apologize for any inconvenience that may have caused the proceedings. I know it's a bit unorthodox for communion recipients to leave before the ceremony is closed."

"Rare, but not unheard of," said Chondrasil with a smile, "especially for laypersons, such as yourself. We'll be drinking again in a few days, after the Darsulans arrive," he added. "I hope that you'll be able to join us."

"I hope so, too." With pleasantries out of the way, Jor Alesh took the opportunity to shift the subject. "I'd like to talk to you about the Darsulans."

"How can I help you?" responded Chondrasil. He took a moment to adjust his robes about him and settled his hands down on his lap, as though making a small ritual preparation for the discussion he was anticipating they were about to have.

"Well," said Jor Alesh, "I'd like to know more about this group: what defines them, why they left, how their practices are different from yours. Here we have a situation that I know virtually nothing about. For us in Jurnda, the Darsulans are a curious footnote in our more recent history. But that's about all, as this was an event that was largely confined to you here in Azar. I know that you cannot tell me why the Darsulans are coming, or even what they think and believe these days, but I was hoping that you could fill me in on any insights that you think might be relevant for understanding them and their motives. Ultimately, I'm on a fact-finding mission. When I return to Jurnda, I hope to inform others clearly about the dynamics at work here so that we can make informed decisions about whatever comes next, if it even involves us in Jurnda. Regardless, it would be careless of me to forgo what is perhaps the most significant cultural and religious event of our lifetimes."

Chondrasil nodded and closed his eyes, bobbing back and forth slightly as he went rummaging through his memories. Eventually, he spoke.

"This is something I've been studying extensively, as you can imagine," Chondrasil began. "Who the Darsulans are today, I have no idea. However, I can tell you of their origins and what caused the split between us. I wouldn't be surprised if they are different from what I'm able to tell you. They weren't known for being conservative in their doctrine or practice - something that originally drove us apart - so who knows how far they may have strayed from our original revelations by now.

"First, it is important to understand that the practices of Azara are divinely revealed - given to us directly by the Mother/Father. It happened so long ago that not even we know when it was in human history that the truth was fully revealed. At first, all of this was passed on orally among key initiates. Only much later were our doctrines written down and codified as we currently know them. Regardless of when or how it happened, the important thing is that it did happen: God revealed to us the nature of the beyond and how those of us trapped in the material world could use the divine sacrament to transcend our earthly perceptions and desires and participate fully in the divine work of reincorporation. This was revealed not as a favor or as a gift - it was given as a divine responsibility and a revelation of the true course of life. Through these revelations, we learned of the divine plan and the part that we were chosen to play in it.

"This practice is work. Though it brings us personal rewards, this is not why we undertake this holy task. We do it because this is what Azara has asked of us, and we do it in the way that Azara originally revealed. We understand that our doctrine is fundamentally unchanging. It is eternal and it is complete. It wasn't as though Azara gave us incomplete instructions. We were never given a divine invitation to make changes or alterations to the doctrine. It was revealed fully and completely. It is our role to enact the truth, not tamper with it or change it.

"Of course, necessity has required that we make occasional adjustments, but these are done with full consultation of all the Maegins and Maegin-Lus to determine that whatever changes are instituted are in full conformity with our doctrine. For example, back in *The World*, there were no large temple cities like we have created here in Azar, and our order was not as highly organized as it is these days. However, the fundamental work, those things that we do within our ceremonies, has remained the same. Long ago, this was only practiced by small groups of isolated devotees. Today, we are several thousand strong in number of Maegins and Maegin-Lus, so the efficacy of our work has increased, but the work itself is unchanged and is perfectly congruent with what has come before us.

"I know by your standards, we appear conservative, maybe even backwards or superstitious. Here you are, Jor

Alesh, a young woman, chosen as Alcian for her people. In Jurnda, there are no barriers. Men and women follow their hearts and desires and make the life they want for themselves, and your society bends over backwards to make everything possible for them. This is not the way of things for us. We have taken our vows and we live a selfless life, a life lived beyond the ego, a life of pure service. We take no wives, and once we take our vows, we keep ourselves pure and celibate, ready to take the communion whenever it is required of us. We forgo our pleasures and desires, for we know that true happiness can only be found through service. The only true goal for any life is reincorporation into Azara. Reincorporation is the end of all life and is the journey that we all must take. Yet confusion and false understanding and belief abound, so our work is long and ongoing.

"Though I know that you are probably loath to hear it, there really is no place for women in this work. This was revealed by Azara long ago at the founding of our order. Women are of the material world. They are the vehicles through which new life is brought into the world. Even when chaste, women still bleed. They still flow with the force of incarnation. By their very nature, they are not fit for this work. It is the egos of women that take offense at this, but we are not concerned with the vagaries and whims of the ego. We are only interested in truth and fulfilling the divine doctrine. The work we do is men's work. There is little more to say on the matter.

"So I suppose this brings us to the point where we can discuss the Darsulans. Obviously, all this happened well before my time, and it remains to be seen whether Darsulans still follow their original doctrine, or if they have instituted even more changes. Whatever the case may be, it all started here in Azar.

"Darsul was a Maegin-Lu, charged with the task of instructing acolytes. As you are probably aware, after five years of practice as a novice, men can take their vows and become acolytes and full practitioners in our order. It is the role of a Maegin-Lu to serve as a direct mentor to the acolytes. Other than this distinction, there really isn't much difference between a Maegin and a Maegin-Lu. As Maegins do not have the responsibility to teach acolytes directly, they have more time and energy to conduct our ceremonies, fulfill administrative duties, and also oversee the Maegin-Lus to insure that all are correctly teaching the doctrine. We recognize that one of the best ways to learn is to be a teacher, so Maegin-Lus are often recently dedicated monks, having just completed their studies as acolytes. There is no set time for being an acolyte, and as soon as your Maegin-Lu suggests to the Maegins that you become fully anointed, the Maegins call a council and then orally test the acolyte on doctrine, followed by a special communion ceremony. If a majority approve, the acolyte is officially made a Maegin-Lu and he can then begin to take on students of his own and share what he has learned. Though there are no formal prohibitions, novices and acolytes are strongly discouraged from sharing doctrine with those outside of our order, even laypersons. Our ways are subtle, and they take years to master. And since they are divinely revealed, we must insure purity and conformity of doctrine.

"Anyway, I've gotten away from our purpose: the Darsulans. As I was saying, some two hundred years ago, there was a Maegin-Lu named Darsul Omdidran. From what I understand, he was bright and charismatic. He was extremely popular among the acolytes as a mentor, and in fact had to turn down requests for his instructions; so much so that some chose to stay novices until a spot opened up in his schedule and they could begin studying with this man directly. I suppose that there may have been some jealousies among the other Maegin-Lus, at the time, though there is nothing specific in the records. These days, the Maegins may make suggestions to noivces who are ready to take their vows to study with Maegin-Lus who have open spots to try and balance out mentor/acolyte ratios and keep social tensions to a minimum, though of course it is always the acolyte's choice. This is a relationship that must be entered into of one's own free will.

"But as for Darsul, he was in high demand as a Maegin-Lu, and everything seemed promising for both him and his students. Darsul also regularly volunteered to bring communion to outlying communities and Jurnda, along with his students, apparently with a great deal of success. Many spoke of Darsul being High Maegin someday.

"Then the rumors started. Darsul and his group of followers became more isolated from others here in Azar. They spent more time away than here. And when they were here, the Maegins and Maegin-Lus started becoming aware of what at first seemed like minor deviations from doctrine, but it only grew worse over time rather than being corrected. At some point, it became known that in addition to holding formal communion ceremonies in outlying communities, Darsul was having private communion ceremonies. When these were investigated, it became clear that Darsul was not following doctrine. He and his students were confronted by the High Maegin, who at the time was Vendana Ilpo Dundrup. A hearing was held, and there the full nature of Darsul's deviation from the doctrine became clear. In short, he was busy creating his own unique tradition.

"Darsul insisted that the two traditions could co-exist and could even fulfill different purposes. He claimed that he did not teach his own doctrine in his Azara ceremonies or classes, only teaching his own inspired doctrine on separate occasions. While this is perhaps somewhat defensible, many of his acolytes were regular attendees of his private ceremonies and lectures. Whatever divide he was pretending to enforce was mere illusion. His teachings were clearly bleeding over into Azara and were having a direct impact on his initiated acolytes."

"So what was wrong with his teachings?" asked Jor Alesh, breaking into Chondrasil's soliloquy.

Chondrasil sighed. "Oh," he said. "There were so many things. For one, Darsul tried to defend his practices by claiming that he had received a new revelation from Azara. This, in and of itself, goes against our doctrine. In our understanding, the truth that Azara revealed to our ancestors is the full and complete truth, and in our enactment and preservation of that doctrine, we are fulfilling the will of God as it was revealed to mankind. This is not open for debate or reinterpretation. The will of God is not some whim that changes with the times or circumstances. It is eternal and unchanging, like God itself. It is the manifested world and the egos that are attached to it that are changing. Our tradition is like an anchor, a pillar of eternity. What was true will always be true. It is only the human ego that wishes for things to be otherwise.

"Well, according to Darsul, the revelation he had received was that, while the practice of our religion was right and proper for the salvation and reincorporation of lost souls, it was incomplete when it came to the living. His revelation, he claimed, was that the medicines were for the living, and the growth and healing of all humans, not exclusively those who were willing to undertake the holy task of reincorporation. The energy of the flow, as we call it, was open and inviting to all, he said. He also rejected the requirements of celibacy, saying that, while this might serve the work of the Church and our duties of reincorporation, it wasn't necessary for individuals who did not want to devote themselves to this work. As he saw it, Azara is concerned with the etheric and the afterlife, whereas he wanted to apply the medicines to life in this world, for everyone who wanted it, without putting requirements and restrictions on them. He felt that the medicines could play a role in anyone's life, regardless of one's religious or spiritual dedication. Individuals could benefit from the medicines for their own sake in this life and world. Men, women, young people - whomever. He said they were for healing, personal growth, creativity, personal insight, and all manner of things. In fact, he didn't see his practices as creating a church - maybe more a lifestyle that was grounded in a philosophy of personal exploration through the use of the medicines.

"As you know," Chondrasil continued, "We keep the ingredients of the communion, and how to prepare them, secret. This is considered esoteric knowledge within our order. Not even our devoted laypeople or novitiates know precisely what goes into the drink, or how we go about preparing it. And even those who do know still don't know the proper prayers, rituals, and symbols that must be used in order to render the drink holy in the eyes of Azara. Mind you, the drink itself, without all that we do for it, is just a drink, albeit a powerful one. At a chemical level, it will do what it will do. Yet it is our prayers and rituals, and following the proper forms, that make the drink holy - that attune it to the infinite vibration of Azara. Without this, it is an invitation to demons and delusions. The drink is dangerous, and its knowledge must be carefully guarded and protected from those who would seek to abuse it.

"While Darsul claimed to respect this, he also claimed to have received revelations that were not as strict, revelations that would be open to all, vows or no vows, commitment to the order or not. Though he was gracious enough not to desecrate our holy sacrament, he had apparently discovered other medicines that grew in the local flora, and these he and others used freely in his own ceremonies. These were things like the blue-staining mushrooms, and cacti of various shapes and sizes that grow more in the interior of Lur. Darsul claimed that all these medicines had their own powers and provided access to the divine energy that is Azara. And many of these did not require any special preparation - anyone could go out into the fields or forest and find them. Darsul felt that all of this should be common knowledge. He saw no reason for this to be kept securely in the hands of an initiated elite.

"When all this first came to light, we had no idea of the extent of Darsul's influence. It was hoped that only a small few had been infected by his delusions and false teachings. But the more it was investigated, the more it became clear that Darsul had been cultivating these teachings and practices for years with anyone who was interested by the time he was fully discovered. Many, Vendana Ilpo Dundrup included, realized then that the signs had been present for years, but they had all willingly overlooked them. And despite whatever claims Darsul made of keeping the traditions separate, not only were his students infected, but what was perhaps even worse was that he had forgone his vow of celibacy. He had violated his vows as a monk and thereby contaminated any Azara ceremony he participated in. I cannot stress enough how important it is that the flow of divine energy be channeled by pure vehicles. This is why, when we have our ceremonies, it is the Maegins and Maegin-Lus who are at the center and highest up. We are the ones who are most fully committed to the necessary purity. For us, purity means upholding the doctrine, refraining from sex and all sexual activities, including masturbation, and never, ever mixing medicines, for it is the Azara communion drink alone that has been sanctioned by Azara. Of course, there is more to it than these things, but these are where the greatest potential for egregious transgressions lie. And Darsul violated all of them.

"It was a horrible shock to Vendana and the others at that time. It meant that virtually all of the ceremonies Darsul had participated in over the years were effectively contaminated by his impurity. As Alcian, I don't know if you can imagine the horror of this revelation. It sent shock waves throughout Azar, though Vendana took great pains to insure that they did not reach as far as Jurnda. It was an internal matter, after all, and we took precautions to keep the information from getting out. Darsul was immediately suspended from all ritual and teaching duties. The hearings held during the investigation were closed to all but the Maegins and Maegin-Lus, with strict orders that information was not to reach either the laypersons or Jurnda. Of course, Darsul already had many followers outside of the fold, so we couldn't control everything. But at least we were able to maintain some privacy and decorum throughout the wrenching ordeal.

"I'm sure it must have felt to those involved as though all of this was threatening to break apart the clear unity of purpose and resolve that had been built here in the aftermath of the *Great War*. The founding of Jurnda, a secular society outside of our direct control or influence, was itself something of a concern, but as Azaran doctrine has always been to let society go its own way, we have lived in a happy relationship with you in Jurnda, and in many ways our societies and communities compliment each other. This was very different. This was a religious and doctrinal break that threatened to undermine everything we'd built here, and our very relationship to Azara and the eternal divine doctrine. It was clear: if enough people adopted Darsul's views, Azara would be no more.

"So as you can see, this was no minor disturbance or some mere disagreement over the interpretation of doctrine. This was a potential revolution. Azara hadn't faced a threat like this since the war, and it has probably been the single most significant event since our founding of Azar five hundred years ago.

"Thus, the banishment. In Jurnda, perhaps you know a slightly different story of mutually agreed-upon isolation and separation. This is only half true. Those who were not officially part of the Azaran church were not under our jurisdiction, but of those who were, they were all excommunicated and banished from Azar. As we had the ear of the Alcian in Jurnda, they were not welcomed there either, though we did not make it known to the Alcian the extent of influence Darsul already had there, or here. It was perhaps a surprise when several thousand people suddenly left, traveling with Darsul and his apostates to the far side of Lur. It was known as 'The Purge,' and we lost many promising acolytes and novices, including a few other Maegin-Lus that Darsul had corrupted. Mostly the church hierarchy remained intact, and we carried on as though nothing had happened. Since then, we have only lost one other Maegin-Lu, though on occasion novices do not take their vows, or acolytes drop out before becoming full monks, mainly due to the rigors and demands of our practice, but not because of doctrinal issues."

"And the one Maegin-Lu you just mentioned, was that also doctrinal?" asked Jor Alesh.

Chondrasil shook his head and seemed to wince slightly. "No, not exactly," said the High Maegin. "That individual was not trying to implement a new doctrine, or claim a new revelation, as was the case with Darsul. No. That individual rejected *all* doctrine. One day, without any explanation, he got up in the middle of a communion ceremony and simply walked out. There is no record of anyone having done anything like that before. I was there at the time. He was a colleague and friend of mine. We had entered as novices in the same year and even had the same Maegin-Lu, Shoralindi Vitmra."

"Would this be Seyloq Surya?"

Chondrasil looked at the Alcian directly for the first time in quite a while. "You've heard of him?"

"Yes," she answered. "I heard some novices mention his name and it caught my attention."

Chondrasil looked concerned, and Jor Alesh noticed an almost imperceptible hardening of his usually pleasant demeanor. "Who?" he asked sternly.

"I don't know," she said casually, as though she didn't notice the change. "Just some novices. They caught my attention as they were saying something about Seyloq being possessed by a demon, or something like that. It struck me as an unusual thing to say about someone."

"A demon . . . that I don't know," said Chondrasil, "but he's one that you'd do best to stay away from, regardless."

"Thank you for your concern," said Jor Alesh, "but I have an inclination to talk to him. As Alcian, it's my responsibility to consider as many perspectives as possible when faced with a sensitive issue. It might be interesting to hear from a living apostate, when here we have the descendants of past apostates coming for a visit. Maybe there's something in his experience that could shed some additional light on what we're all about to go through."

"Hmm . . . maybe," said Chondrasil, clearly displeased but also restrained by his lack of authority over the Alcian. "Don't expect much," he said dismissively. "From what I hear, he's quite crazy. But if you want to waste your time speaking with a madman, that's your prerogative, I suppose, and there's nothing I can do about it. Just be careful. I can have Pirfiro escort you to see him, if you like."

"Oh, thank you, but no," said Jor Alesh. "I think having someone as unsympathetic as Pirfiro present would lessen my chances of getting Seyloq's honest opinion."

Chondrasil laughed. "You clearly don't know Seyloq Surya," he said. "He's not known for being reticent to speak his mind, regardless of the company. He'd probably enjoy it - too much, in fact - if you were to bring Pirfiro along. They never got along before Seyloq left, and it certainly isn't any better now."

"Thank you, but I'll find my own way, just the same. I think I've taken more than enough of your time today, but I'd like to ask one more - well, two more, questions before I go."

"Yes?"

"One - do you know why the Darsulans are coming? And two - how were you informed of their impending arrival, since no one has heard from them in two hundred years?"

"In answer to your first question, Alcian, I don't know. What they want is as much a mystery to me as it is to you. As for the second question, I suppose you ought to know the answer: someone from Jurnda delivered a letter to us here in Azar, though we haven't been able to determine whom. It would seem that the Darsulans haven't been as isolated as we thought."

Chapter 12

SOMETHING MORE

"Since we have some time, why don't you tell me more about yourself?"

Jor Alesh had found Jendru tending a garden on one of the pyramid terraces along with several other novices. Though she saw Jendru's peers give him a hard time when she called up to him, she pretended not to notice. At her insistence, he disappeared into the pyramid and emerged from a doorway at its base a few minutes later. "I'm ready to go meet Seyloq Surya," she had said, not giving him the opportunity to protest. She had no real authority over Jendru, but she used the weight of her position to let him know that this was not a request. Reluctantly, he agreed.

As a minor act of protest, he had started off quickly through the forest without speaking. She had to run to catch up to him. He was a strange fellow, she decided. He wasn't volunteering much, but it was clear to her that something was going on with Jendru that he wasn't talking about. In truth, Jor Alesh was quite enjoying this little game they were playing. Most of her duties as Alcian were rather mundane, but here in Azar, she had become something of a detective, prying into arcane religious secrets and mysteries, and Jendru was another intriguing part of the puzzle.

It helped that she found him terribly attractive. Last night, after spending the day speaking with more Maegins and Maegin-Lus in Azar, and her long conversation with Chondrasil, she had excused herself early from a banquet dinner with the Church hierarchy to seclude herself in her room and "relax," as she had put it to her hosts. Lying naked on her bed with the lights out and the windows open, she had let her hands move down to her sex, slowing rolling one finger over her clitoris while using the other hand to penetrate herself. All the while, she had pictured Jendru pressing himself into her, imagining what his penis must feel like and the strength of his body. It was absurd, she knew - he was a novice, soon to take his vows and live in celibacy for the remainder of his life. *What a waste,* she had concluded.

If things were otherwise, she'd take him into the forest right now and demand that he fuck her to oblivion. It would be so sweet, she thought; her back pressed into the moist earth, the sounds of birds and jungle insects and the faint rumbles of thunder in the distance. She flushed just to think of it and could feel the moistness between her legs. Yes, she wanted to fuck this man, and his inner turmoil and secrets just made her want him all the more. So reserved, but so powerful. She could picture what his face would look like, releasing into her, letting himself explode and dissolve that cool, detached persona he worked so hard to maintain in her presence. That was the real thrill of it - she could tell that no matter what he was telling himself, he wanted it too.

Walking along beside him, she imagined what his reaction would be if she were to stop him, reach down, and take his penis into her hand and massage it into erect vibrancy. She wanted to stroke it, kiss it, take it into her mouth. Yes - that's what she wanted. She wanted to feel his hardness on her tongue, wanted to pull his seed right out of him as though it would nourish her, let it seep from her mouth and taste the salty mix as it slid down her throat. It's true - she wanted to devour him.

God, when was I ever this hungry for a man?

Masturbating herself to sleep the previous night, she had needed to muffle her cries and moans of pleasure while imagining Jendru inside her. It had been so wild, so passionate. And psychedelic too! It was almost like going for a round of medicine. Behind closed eyes, visualizing the beautiful young man, it was like he was the Flower of Azara come to life, personalized, humanized, just for her. It had felt . . . transcendent. It was as though all of reality was making love through them. Of course, it had all been a fantasy. But it brought her to wild ecstasy, and she caught herself moaning in pleasure as her fingers worked harder and deeper at her sex.

At the climax, everything exploded into white light and sexual fluids gushed from her aching vagina as wild quivers of energy vibrated from deep within her, shivering up and down her spine. Reminding herself to be quiet, lest the Maegins become concerned, she pulled her fingers from her vagina, stopped at her breasts to give her erect nipples a firm squeeze, and then licked the pungent juices from her fingers, wishing it had been Jendru's cock and not merely her hands. If there had been any semen left, she would have pulled the fluid from the head of his cock and rolled it on her tongue, sucking it from its chamber, letting her tongue follow the shape of the head of his member, encompassing it with her lips and engulfing it deep into her throat.

It was true. She'd take him right here, if he were open to it. So what if he was in training to be a Maegin? He hadn't taken his vows yet. They wouldn't be breaking any explicit rules, though no doubt his superiors wouldn't look too kindly on it, were they to find out. But that was the thrill. And despite Jendru's reserved and formal demeanor, she could tell that he was a risk-taker, and someone who followed his own mind. This had become increasingly obvious the more Jor Alesh learned about this mysterious Seyloq Surya. If Jendru was willing to associate with a known heretic and apostate, what else would he be willing to do? It was a fantasy, she knew, but by God, she wanted to fuck this man, and fuck him hard.

It would be a delicious secret, but oh, what a scandal it would be if anyone found out! The Maegins would think twice before inviting any more female dignitaries from Jurnda, that was certain! She could see the news headlines now: "Alcian Seduces Azaran Monk, Bringing Scandal and Shame at Delicate Time of Return of Darsulans." Wouldn't that be an interesting twist in the mix?

"Why are you so interested in me?" Jendru asked her, finally responding to her question. "I'm just a novice, and I don't have anything to do with the Darsulans, or whatever it is that brought you here. Yet here we are again, me escorting you, and you've got more questions. Are all the Alcians like you?"

Jor Alesh felt a little thrill. Jendru was suspicious of her and her motives. She liked that.

"I'm trying to pass the time," she responded. "You said this walk would take a while, so why not use the opportunity to get to know you a little better? You mentioned before that you were from Jurnda. I'm curious about what brought you here to Azara. What made you want to be a monk?"

"Looking for something more," said Jendru, "looking for deeper meaning."

"Like what?" asked Jor Alesh. "You found life in Jurnda unsatisfying? It wasn't deep enough for you?"

"No, it wasn't," he said as a matter-of-fact. "Life is great in Jurnda. From what I've learned of history, it seems like Jurnda is one of the better iterations of human society, so I'll give it that. People are happy, free to do what they want, pursue their own interests in a social mix that supports and nourishes them. In many ways, I think life in Jurnda is probably about as close to a human ideal as any society could get. It was enough for my parents. Maybe you've heard of them? Sila and Jeresh Amdin? They're artists, and their works are fairly popular. They've never had trouble getting commissions or public showings of their art."

Jor Alesh was a little surprised. She had never been too closely associated with the art world in Jurnda, but she did know these two artists. She had seen their work recently - in one of the prominent art museums in central Jurnda. "Those are your parents? Really?" she asked. "And you never wanted to follow in their footsteps and become an artist as well?"

"I like it well enough," said Jendru, "but not enough to want to be an artist. I dabbled in music for a while, too. Really, creative activity is great and I enjoy it, but it was that sense of wanting or seeking more that left me unsatisfied with those endeavors. With my parents being celebrities, I probably could have had it easy had I chosen to follow after them. But that's just it - it would have been too easy. I wanted something to challenge myself, something I could really devote myself to. And maybe do something great, something that genuinely matters."

"You think art doesn't matter?"

"Not really, no. Not in any kind of cosmic sense."

"So you think your parents have wasted their lives?"

"I don't know - maybe. Here, in Azar, we make all kinds of art, but it all serves a purpose, a higher purpose. Everything we do is dedicated to Azara and following our holy mission. What we do here really matters, and that matters to me."

"Sure - if you say so," said Jor Alesh. Her tone indicated clearly that she thought otherwise. And there was still the nagging suspicion that Jendru agreed with her more than he was letting on. He was busy playing the role of dedicated novice, yet his heart wasn't really in it.

"What do you mean?"

"Well," she said, "look; I'm not a member of your religion, and I don't share your beliefs. And I know, we already had this talk, so I know that from your perspective, it's not about beliefs, but from my perspective it is. What if, just what if, Jendru, none of this were real? Consider that possibility. What if everything you and the Maegins think you are accomplishing in your work is all illusion and fantasy? Can you really be sure that you're doing something *real*? Maybe, just maybe, this life here is all we have, and the participation in human culture and expression is the only real meaning that there is. What if there is no 'beyond' or 'out there'? If so, that would make your parents' work far more meaningful than what you think you are doing here. They are making positive contributions to human society in a way that gives them and other people pleasure and happiness. On the other hand, you monks are secluded up here in the mountains and jungle performing these oh-so-serious ceremonies to no real end whatsoever. Where is the grand *meaning* in that?"

"You sound like Seyloq," said Jendru, shaking his head. After a few moments of walking in silence, he added, "The truth is, I don't know if I've found the meaning I've been looking for. I thought I had. I was so excited to begin my work as a novice, and for the first few years, it seemed to provide everything that I felt had been missing in my life. I had purpose, meaning, and *real work* to do - work that made a difference - not just here, but in eternity. It was the complete opposite of how things are for you as Alcian. Your concern is the reality of human society. Mine hasn't been. My concern has been the eternal, the transcendent, the etheric. We're taught to divorce ourselves from normal human concerns and interactions and dedicate everything we have, all of our energy, to doing the work on the etheric.

"When I first joined, I felt as though I were one of the few, the elect, the chosen. I felt I had a divine purpose and a sacred calling. Before I turned twenty, it was all I could think about. It was all that I wanted."

"And now?"

Jendru looked at her. "I don't know."

"Seyloq?"

He sighed. "Yes, Seyloq. Admittedly, I don't understand him. He tends to confuse me more than anything else. Still, I'm drawn to him. In some ways, you remind me of him. There's something fresh and direct about him. He casts aside doctrine like he's taking off a pair of shoes. He's just so . . . I don't know . . . free. But he's bizarre, too. You'll see - half the time, he talks in this strange voice. And he often uses his body symmetrically. He's really intense, but there's a playfulness about him that feels oddly refreshing, like he doesn't care. But paradoxically, underneath it all, it's also perfectly clear that he does care. And cares in a way that other people don't seem capable of. There's something, I don't know, universal about him."

"He sounds fascinating."

Jendru laughed. "You have no idea. He claims to be God, you know."

Jor Alesh stopped in her tracks, a disbelieving look on her face. "He says he's Azara?"

Jendru shook his head. "Definitely not. He has no love for things Azaran. He says we're all God - that God is the only being that truly exists and everything is a manifestation of this one, universal being. When I was with him yesterday, he said that I was God. I'm sure he'll tell you the same thing, if you talk to him long enough."

"You saw him yesterday?"

"Yes."

"Why?"

Jendru thought for a moment. "Because everything is breaking apart for me, and even though I can't really understand him, he's the only one who seems to make any sense or really knows what he's talking about. It's maddening. Everything I've learned, everything I've been trained in, tells me to stay away from him. Most of the time he makes me uncomfortable and nervous. But here I am, heading back to his house for the third day in a row. Yesterday, he told me to come back when I was ready for more medicine. He's probably going to make me take some. He'll probably want you to, as well. He doesn't really like to talk to people who haven't taken the medicine. He says it's all just words, despite his willingness to talk as long as you might like. For Seyloq, working with his medicine is the thing."

"Is this one of the medicines that the Darsulans use?"

"I don't think so," said Jendru. "Not that I would really know, but I haven't heard of anything like this."

"But it's not Azara?"

Jendru shook his head. "Definitely not," he said. "It's some kind of crystal, and you smoke it, not drink it. In some ways it's like Azara, but much, much stronger, and faster, and less visual as well. I've only tried it once. It was amazing . . ." Jendru drifted off, temporarily returning to the overwhelming feeling produced by Seyloq's medicine. He felt his heart rate increase, but it wasn't frightening. It was more like the excitement of being on the verge of something awesome, something profound. Jendru knew it was true - working with Seyloq and his medicine was providing something that he was not getting in Azar. The questions and desires that had brought him to Azar were now leading him to Seyloq. It was time he admitted that to himself.

The couple passed over one of the many bridges that dotted the path, crossing over a waterfall that flowed down into the Qya River below. Jor Alesh stopped a moment to look up and down the green canyon, taking in the view. The mist from the spray of the waterfall felt nice. The day was getting hot and humid. She stood there in the spray for a few moments, letting it soak her clothes and mist her face and hair. She caught Jendru glancing at her breasts and nipples, perky under her wet clothing. When she turned to face him, he quickly averted his eyes. "We should keep going," he said. "There's still a long way to go."

She refused to budge.

"So why do you want to be a Maegin?" she asked, facing Jendru squarely with her hands on her hips, signaling a challenge to the novice.

He didn't answer.

"It sounds to me like you'd be happier studying with Seyloq. Is it really so important for you to take your vows and follow that life in Azar?"

"I don't know," Jendru admitted. "Taking my vows, officially becoming part of the Church . . . for so long, I envisioned this as my life. Back in Jurnda, it seemed like the only possible choice, but now . . . What would I do with myself if I didn't take my vows? Live in the backcountry like Seyloq, a reclusive hermit? What would be my purpose?"

Jor Alesh smiled. "And you need to know that? Do you have to have a plan, a purpose? Why not follow your heart and see where it leads you? Sure, taking your vows and working to become a Maegin plans out your life for you, but maybe that's too safe, too secure. To be blunt, maybe that's not what you really want. It seems to me that you have a sharp mind and a big heart, but there's a conflict inside you. Part of you wants to play it safe. The other part wants to embrace the unknown. You'll need to decide which is more important to you. It's great to have a purpose, but if that gets in the way of your own happiness . . ."

Jendru could feel the reaction of his learning inside him. "The Maegins say that Azara and the work is the only true purpose. Everything else is the false truth of the ego leading one astray, leading one to further incarnations and separation from Azara. It is only the selfless work of the followers of Azara that can redeem us from the follies of our egos."

Jor Alesh gave him a friendly smile. She wanted to reach out and take his hand and reassure him, but he kept himself distant. "I don't know much about the ego and selflessness and redemption," she said. "All I know is that life is short and uncertain. Maybe the Maegins really do know the secrets of the universe. Maybe not. If your heart isn't fully in it, though, I would think that committing yourself out of a sense of duty or responsibility sounds like ego to me. Doing something because you feel you *should* sounds like a trap."

"Maybe," was all that Jendru said as he turned and continued on the path to Seyloq's with Jor Alesh following close behind.

Chapter 13

TROUBLEMAKER

"Back again so soon? And with a woman! Loosening up, I see. Excellent. Things are looking up for you, love."

After several hours of walking, they had finally made it to Seyloq's. It had taken longer that it would have if Jendru were coming by himself. Jor Alesh revealed herself as a city woman at almost every turn, taking her time to survey the jungle and take in the sights as they meandered along the path. What for him was ordinary and everyday was for her a novel excursion into wonder and discovery. Every flower, every plant, insect, or bird was something new and fascinating. It was midday and the warm morning rains had ceased, leaving a sticky, hot humidity in their place.

The view from Seyloq's was impressive, Jor Alesh thought. From here, he could look out over the entire valley of Azar and the surrounding mountains. The Qya River was far below them, unseen, but still heard. This far up, it was impassable by boat with too many falls and rapids. Small boats could only go as far up the river as the eastern edge of Azar, which could been seen in the distance, the tops of the pyramids rising above the sea of green trees and foliage. Colorful birds, mostly parrots and macaws, swooped above the treetops, squawking and chattering with each other. Many of the trees were in bloom, dotting the green sea with bursts of color. Jor Alesh thought back to what Jendru had said - how Seyloq claimed to be God. He had apparently found a suitable location for himself here, overlooking the world below from his perch in an idyllic garden paradise.

Looking at his house, Jor Alesh wondered how he had it built. For being so isolated, it was anything but rustic. Large glass windows opened to the scene about them with a front deck and comfortable chairs. A stream ran through the grounds and wove its way past the deck and through a garden that was decorated with large volcanic rocks; dark sentinels in the green. A small pond echoed with the sounds of frogs or toads - Jor Alesh couldn't be sure which. Large mushroom-shaped trees dotted the grounds with the bulk of the forest cut back to allow maximum sunlight and unobstructed views. But at the edge of the grounds, the forest loomed large and wild. All Seyloq needed to do to disappear into it was to step off his deck and vanish into the endless green. Glancing around, Jor Alesh could see a number of trails heading off in various directions, indicating that Seyloq made good use of this feature of his location.

Seyloq was an older man. He had long, slightly wavy, grey hair, which he wore tied back in a bun. Beneath the slightly thinning hair, she could see the dulled remains of the tattoo that all the Maegins and Maegin-Lus wore, clearly marking Seyloq as an apostate. You'd never notice unless you were close. She wondered if anyone in Jurnda would recognize what this meant. Here in the valley of Azar, nestled between Ladjup and Nadrasuli, she was sure it stuck out like a pyramid in the jungle – no doubt everyone who encountered Seyloq here instantly recognized him as the one who had forsaken his vows and abandoned his holy work in the Church. Strange, she thought, that he would leave the Church but still remain within its orbit, like a thorn in its paw, on the outskirts, living a life that mocked so much of what they held sacred. Only one conclusion was possible: he was a troublemaker.

"Master Seyloq," said Jendru, "let me introduce . . ."

Seyloq cut him off. "First of all, don't call me 'master.' Seyloq will do. And secondly, I know who this is: Jor Alesh Melva, Alcian of Jurnda. The youngest Alcian in who knows how long, and a woman, too. And, from what I understand, something of a child prodigy, which explains her early ascension and success as a public servant."

Seyloq looked the woman up and down, still standing in the doorway, not yet having invited his visitors in. "And quite attractive, too, don't you think, Jendru?" he added with a subtle wink.

Jendru didn't respond. He felt himself blush slightly, awkwardly clearing his throat.

Seyloq laughed. "You see!" he said emphatically to Jor Alesh. "These would-be monks don't know what to do with a woman! I was like that once. Happy to say I got over it. This one here is so hard up, he'd probably blow his wad before he ever got it in you. But give him time, and I'm sure he'd keep you satisfied.

"So, what brings you here to my door, Alcian?" he asked Jor Alesh directly. "Let me guess; you want to talk to the apostate about the Darsulans? I assume that's why you're in Azar in the first place; coming to scout about, gain some info, get an overview of our little mess, and then return to Jurnda to share the wisdom of what you've learned."

"Yes," said Jor Alesh. "That is why I came. But oddly, everywhere I go, conversation seems to always come back around to you, quite unexpectedly. So I thought I would get to know this crazy God-man for myself," she said with a smile. She liked him already. Seyloq turned to Jendru. "I like her," he said. "Come in." Seyloq opened the door wider and moved aside, gesturing for the couple to enter.

Jendru motioned with his hand that Jor Alesh should go first. Stepping inside, she immediately noticed that the air was cooler within than without. Climate control was an everyday feature of buildings in Jurnda, but this was the first she had encountered it out here in the forest where open windows were the norm. Technological development in Jurnda had long since surpassed the rudimentary technology used by the Azarans, who chose to live with a minimum of physical comfort or technological gadgetry. The Maegins called such things crutches and attachments and shunned all but the minimum that was necessary to keep their pyramid city lit and functioning. Clearly Seyloq didn't share their views on this. No surprise there.

She could also hear music playing that she recognized from Jurnda, which could only mean that Seyloq had a media player, something that was effectively banned in Azar as a secular distraction. Though she didn't recognize the artist specifically, she knew it was relatively new as stylistically, the music was very much in fashion at the moment in Jurnda, where musical and artistic styles came and went with the tides of public interest.

"You like Jurndan music?" she asked after they were all inside and Seyloq had closed the door.

"Some of it," Seyloq answered, walking them into the main section of the house where he had a comfortable living room. The decor was eclectic, with a mixture of different art and decorative items, all from Jurnda. Noticing Jor Alesh taking everything in, Seyloq commented, "As you can see, Jurnda is not foreign to me. Though I was born and raised out here, after I left the Church, I decided that there was no need for me to live as though Jurnda were a different world. Just because I like it out here doesn't mean that I can't enjoy the riches of the secular world."

They moved further in, taking seats on plush chairs in Seyloq's living room. In the middle, there was an open space. Against the far wall, a rolled up mat. Placed next to the mat was a large eagle feather and a small wooden box carved with intricate geometric designs. Jor Alesh felt she had a good idea of what she was looking at. Seyloq didn't fail to notice her observation. "Yesterday, I told Jendru not to return until he was ready for another session, and here he is today with the beautiful and exotic Jor Alesh. Perhaps things will get interesting today - we'll see," he said. "But, I imagine that's not why you've come, Ms. Melva," he added. Then, "Or maybe it was."

Jor Alesh decided to ignore this, for now. "I've heard a lot about you," she said. "Many curious things. You're something of an enigma, I gather."

Seyloq laughed. "I suppose you could say that. I'm not an enigma to myself, if that means anything to you."

"Yes," she said. "Jendru tells me that you say you're God."

"What about it?"

"Is this true?"

"Yes."

Jor Alesh looked at the older man. Everything about him told her that he was being sincere. "You don't look it," she said.

Seyloq laughed again and Jendru moved about in his seat uncomfortably. "I like her!" he said again to Jendru, clapping his hands. "And what, pray tell, is God *supposed* to look like?" he said in a deeply resonate voice, his body suddenly taking on a dramatic posture with arms outstretched, as though displaying himself.

Jor Alesh thought for a moment. Images of Chondrasil and the other Maegins came into her mind with their careful attention to appearance, symbolism, and from. Everything about Seyloq spoke of a confident casualness. He was clearly a man who was comfortable in his own being. There was no pretense or formality about him. By outward appearances, he was just another human being. Yet there was a calmness about him that was balanced with a subtle dynamism that seemed to infuse his entire being. There was neither pride nor carefully cultivated humility about him - something Jor Alesh had noticed in abundance among the Maegins. His very being seemed to say, "I am myself." He wasn't trying to be anyone or anything, from what she could see. He simply was.

"Maybe I should shave my head and wear fancy robes," he suggested. "Or perhaps I should go get myself some worshipers and have them build a temple with a big throne in the center where everyone can come and worship me and pay homage. I could surround myself with sacred symbols and have my followers carry me about on an ornate chair so that I might never need to demean myself by touching the corrupted earth. And when I get angry, lightning can flash from my eyes and I can command the elements to rain destruction down on those who would fail to believe and accept my divinity. Would that be more appropriate?"

Now it was Jor Alesh's turn to laugh. "Well, that would seem to fit the part," she said.

"Seyloq doesn't play a part," said Jendru.

"Ah, the novice speaks words of wisdom!" joked Seyloq.

"Seyloq says that only egos seek to play a part or a role. The true nature of being is free and unconditioned by egoic expectations."

Jor Alesh looked at them both. "But you do claim to be

God?" she asked again.

"Yes," said Seyloq as a matter-of-fact, his voice very deep. "I am. So are you. So is Jendru. So is the sound system and media player. So is the air, the light, the earth we walk upon and the stars that swing in the sky above our heads." Saying this, he opened his arms and held out his hands as though taking all of the cosmos into his universal embrace. "There is only one being, and everything that we can experience is that one being. When you strip away all the artifice of the ego, this fundamental truth reveals itself as obviously as recognizing that the forest is green or that the sky is blue. It is simply the way things are, and to pretend otherwise is illusion.

"I have learned this by exploring myself, and when I could no longer pretend that things were otherwise, I accepted the truth that I was God. This fact only makes me special and unique because I know this is true. I have liberated myself from the confines of my ego, while others have not. My ego still exists and is still a part of me, but it does not get in my way - I do not listen to its lies and delusions and it does not prevent me from being myself at all times. So my energy is centered and open, unlike the energy of one who is still trapped in his or her ego with blocked and suppressed energy that leaks out in inappropriate ways. I say that I am God not because I believe it, but because I know it. I have no interest in belief, only truth. And the truth is that there is only one being and that one being is everything; you and me and Jendru included. Many bodies, many manifestations, but at heart, and in reality, only one being."

"Who taught you that?" Jor Alesh asked.

"No one," answered Seyloq. "I was taught everything *but* this fundamental, simple truth. I was taught that God was Azara, the Mother/Father, the source of being and holy light that transcends and redeems the fallen material world. I was taught that we are all souls, flowing from life to life, incarnation to incarnation, forever seeking and simultaneously avoiding our eventual return and reincorporation into the holy light of Azara. I was taught that souls are deluded by eogs, lost, corrupted by the body, corrupted by women, corrupted by demons. I was taught that our role as humans was to serve as vehicles and conduits for the energy of Azara, and that we should set aside our personal concerns to devote ourselves to the holy and selfless work of reincorporation and devotion to Azara. I was taught that we are, at best, servants of the One, representatives of the One, fragments of the One, and that only those who are ready to completely abandon the body and incarnation can be one with the One. Life, I was taught, was separation, suffering, illusion, and pain. Life was to be transcended for the holy arts. I was taught that through the communion drink, our souls could lift free from the confines of the body and its heavy, ego-based energy. I was taught to believe in the etheric realms, disembodied spirits, pure energy, unencumbered by the clumsy crudity of the body. I, like so many others, was taught to believe in the doctrine.

"And I did, for a time - for many years," said Seyloq. "I was a Maegin-Lu, as I am sure you are aware. I drank communion. I said the prayers, recited the hymns, and reincorporated countless lost souls back into the flow of Azara. I had many acolytes and the praise and respect of my peers and seniors. According to some, I was destined to be High Maegin, someday."

"So what changed for you?" Jor Alesh asked, truly curious.

"A vision. At least, that's how it started."

Jor Alesh didn't say anything, only looking at the older man attentively, indicating he should continue.

"It was in a major work," Seyloq went on. "Despite my concentration and my best efforts, there was something I kept seeing that just didn't fit or make any sense. It was a toad. No matter how hard I tried to elevate my spirit and do the work, this toad kept coming into my vision. It was large, and on its forehead was a jewel that resembled the Flower of Azara. I recognized the toad as a kind that lives out here in the jungle, mostly in the falls and streams that flow into the Qya River." Seyloq laughed. "Do you know what the toad represents in Azaran symbology?" he asked.

"No," said Jor Alesh.

"Ignorance and the ego," said Jendru. "The toad lives

in the muck and slime of the world," he continued, reciting Azaran doctrine. "It is said that all who renounce their vows, ones such as Seyloq, will be reincarnated as toads, that much further from their reincorporation with Azara. The toad is a lowly, disgusting animal with warts and poisons. But out of the same muck and filth in which the toad lives grows the Flower of Azara, showing the holy promise that even the lowest of the low may eventually be redeemed and taken back into the arms of the Mother/Father."

Seyloq clapped his hands and laughed. "Excellent!" he exclaimed. "Couldn't be more ironic, could it?" he asked Jor Alesh. "No one suspects the toad! Vile, rejected, forlorn. What could be more perfect?"

Jor Alesh didn't get it. "So this vision of the lowly toad convinced you to leave the Church?" she asked, feeling like she was missing the joke.

"No," answered Seyloq. "Not right away. The vision puzzled me, however, and that puzzlement drew me out here into the jungle. It took some searching, but before too long I was able to locate some of these toads, the kind that I saw in my vision. They were a bit more ordinary looking, mind you, but for the most part, what I had seen in my vision was a fairly accurate representation of the toads. I had, of course, seen them before, having lived my whole life out here. I contemplated what it all might mean - what it meant about myself, primarily. Was I the toad? Was I trying to tell myself something? Was I a toad in monk's robes, pretending to be something that I was not? Despite my divine service, maybe I was a fraud, a fake: a toad parading around as a servant of Azara.

"These weren't comfortable meditations. My urge was to deny it, push it aside, and devote myself even more fervently to my work as a Maegin-Lu. But it nagged at me, pulled on me. I found myself coming out here to sit with the toads, to listen to their chirping, as though half expecting some divine revelation to carry itself to my ear from their throaty exhortations. Nothing came: merely the sounds of toads calling to each other, marking territory and seeking mates. Just the business of life. I prayed to Azara, but no resolution came. No transcendent epiphany presented itself.

"Even back in Azar, I could hear the toads from my quarters in the pyramids. And at night, when I tried to sleep, there it was, staring at me out of the darkness, imprinted in my mind. It never spoke. It never did anything. It only sat there, looking at me, the Flower of Azara on its forehead, like a jewel between its eyes. Then one night, it came to me: *milk the toad.*

"Oh, what a fool and degenerate I felt myself to be, wandering out here into the jungle, seeking after these toads and collecting their venom. Mind you, this was about the most lowly thing a Maegin-Lu could be doing, and there was no lack of inner conflict within me. I did it anyway, though I had no idea what I was doing. I caught and milked the toads. I amassed a collection of their crystallized venom. But I didn't know what to do with it, or how to use it. I tried making a drink of it, and nothing happened. I tried anointing myself with it in oil, but again, nothing happened. What a fool I felt like, stumbling around with my toads and venom, secretly trying to follow this nagging vision and command from within, but not knowing what to do or why.

"Then one day, in desperation, I decided to put some of the dried, crystallized venom into a pipe and smoke it the way the forest people sometimes smoke dried herbs. And that was it! I'll spare you the details, other than to say it immediately became obvious to me that all the work I thought I had accomplished as a Maegin-Lu, and the many souls I had reincorporated into Azara, were not anything that existed independently or externally from me. It was perfectly clear: all of this was *me*. And it was also clear that I had, essentially, been playing a game with myself. The entire foundation of Azaran religion came crashing down around me as a delusion of the ego. It was *all* a reflection of myself. It's hard to describe how laughingly obvious this was. This truth was as obvious to me as the illusion had formerly seemed real. It's similar to dreaming: in most dreams, we are convinced that what we are experiencing is fundamentally real and exterior to ourselves - we are subjects experiencing an independent and objective reality. The lie, the illusion, is revealed for what it is when we wake up *within* our dreams. We become aware that everything we experience within the dream is a product of our own minds and has no reality independent from ourselves - the dream is, in fact, ourself. We are not just a character in the dream - we *are* the dream, in totality. Once you know that, you cannot, except under conditions of willful self-deceit, pretend that the dream is real or separate from yourself. It's a revelation from which there is no going back, if you choose to live in truth.

"And that has been my primary commitment: truth. I joined the Azaran church because I believed it to be true. This revelation shattered that illusion for me. It was the first of many of my personal illusions to be shattered - the most significant of which was my illusion that I was a soul or a spirit that had been separated from source, separated from Azara, separated from God. Working with this new medicine, it became clear to me all talk of souls and spirits and reincarnating and reincorporating entities was a complete fabrication of the ego and had no more reality than dreams. Like dreams, they may *seem* very real, but there is often a drastic difference between appearances and reality, and this conclusion was unavoidable. For with this new medicine, I found that I was infinite, despite my apparent limitation to this perspective in this body, in this life. When all artifice and conventional constructs of my ego had been stripped away, I revealed myself in all my fullness - an infinite being of energy that is all things. Put simply, I discovered that I was God, and it wasn't anything that I had been taught or formally believed. It also became clear to me that *this,* this world we live in and the bodies we find ourselves in, *is it.* There is no *beyond.* There is no grander purpose. There is no divine plan. There is simply *this, here, now.* I know this to be true because I know myself. I know who and what I am. I am no longer deceived by my ego. So yes, absolutely, I am God. The difference between me and everyone else, apparently, is that I know what this means and have accepted the truth of it."

"That's a pretty strong claim," said Jor Alesh, "and one that would be taken by most as a profoundly egotistical view."

"I know," said Seyloq. "But that does not make it untrue. I am in the business of telling the truth. It does not matter to me how it sounds to other people. It is only egos that care what other people think - primarily, what other *egos* think. I do not care because I am not bound by my ego, so I say it like I see it, come what may. By telling you I am God, I am not looking to fulfill my ego. I do not want your worship, your praise, your devotion, or anything that an ego making such a claim would most likely desire. I am just telling you, for one, because you asked, and secondly, because it is true. Ultimately, what I want is to share this truth with others, because it is true. It is liberating."

"So, according to you, Azaran religion is a sham?" asked Jor Alesh.

"Fundamentally, yes," said Seyloq.

"And the Darsulans? They're deluded too?"

"Perhaps less so than the Azarans, but essentially, yes. *All* religion and spirituality is delusion. *Any* doctrine or belief system is an imposition of the ego onto the energy of reality. All of it is a game, an act. Imagine what it was like for me, participating in Azaran ritual, knowing what I know! There I was, in the Obsidian Temple, and it was the most profound joke - a whole group of people fervently devoting themselves to God and some grand purpose, but the truth - the truth! The truth is that every last one of them is God pretending to be something other than what they are, failing to recognize themselves, failing to know who they are. It was a joke, a game, a self-created and imposed charade. So I left."

"Why leave?" asked Jor Alesh. "Why not tell them the truth, as you're telling Jendru and me? If they're ignorant, as you claim, why not enlighten them?"

"Well, for one, you see how well that went for Darsul - not that the cases are really that comparable. He, after all, tried to introduce a *new* doctrine, whereas I have rejected all doctrine completely. But the main issue is desire. You cannot enlighten someone who does not *want* to be enlightened. That is part of the truth of being God - your free will is never violated, and all of reality is a system that continually conspires to enact your *genuine* free will and desire. Nothing can ever force you to wake up and become enlightened to your true nature. Only a commitment to truth is sufficient. This is also why people can participate in a religious program such as Azara for their entire lives and never really get any closer to the truth, even with the aid of the communion drink, which, I will add, is a sufficiently powerful tool, so the possibility is there. You have to want it, though. Most people reach a certain level of personal realization and then stop progressing. They essentially become stuck, and it matters not how much medicine they take, or how hard they meditate or pray or anything else. You have to be committed to being honest and genuine with yourself at the deepest, most intimate levels. If you do not have that commitment, then there is no point to talking to you about these things, because it all becomes more fodder for the ego.

"Let's take you, for example," Seyloq continued, slipping back into a more normal, conversational tone that wasn't quite so authoritative and intimidating. "I'm talking to you because you see your job as exploring truth and sharing what you've learned with others. Ideally, this is the definition of your role as Alcian. You probably see yourself as an impartial observer and gatherer of facts. According to your ego and your sense of self, this is what defines your activity and purpose as Alcian. So energetically, you're open, and nothing I've been saying here personally challenges you or threatens your identity. Thus, you're a good candidate for me to potentially get through to.

"Jendru here is another matter. He's not on a governmental fact-finding mission, like you, but in his own way, he is on a fact-finding mission. That's what drew him to Azara, originally. And it is what drew him to me, and what keeps bringing him back. Unlike you, Ms. Melva, Jendru has a bigger leap to make, however. His identity has been shaped by his commitment to Azaran religion, doctrine, and practice. Therefore his ego has a great deal invested in these particular energetic constructs that he has been taught to take on as his own. Underneath it all, Jendru is more committed to truth than he is to Azara, so I can help him. But as you can see, it's one person at a time, and only those who are open and willing. Because we all, as embodied versions of the One, have unlimited free will. We can choose to resist and ignore the truth for as long as we want, up to and including our final passing, our death. That's how much we love ourselves. Our free will is always inviolate. It cannot be compromised, ever.

"So, back to your question: why not share what I've learned with other Azarans? Understand that Azaran religion is nothing other than ego writ large, as is also the case with all religion, politics, or any cultural or ethnic identity. Despite their heady and grand claims, followers of Azara are *not* actually accomplishing anything that they think they are accomplishing - it is *all* illusion. But you see, that doesn't matter to the ego. All the ego wants is tools and patterns that will help it define itself, and the more people it can enlist to that end, the better. Above all, religion is a form of identity. Sure, the Azarans can give you all kinds of reasons why Darsulan doctrine is wrong and incorrect, and they could point to numerous examples of such. But that's not the real problem with the Darsulans, is it? The real problem is that they are a challenge to Azaran identity. As a competing identity, it says to the Azarans: maybe some of those 'truths' you've committed yourself to aren't as fundamental as you've chosen to believe, and if so, what does that mean about you who choose to believe them?

"You see, their very existence provides something for the ego to react against - something to use to define itself and protect itself from the fissures in its illusory constructs of self and world, self and other. The conflict is especially tense between two groups such as these because both claim to be revealed by God as fundamentally true. Well, they can't both be true - either that or God's schizophrenic. Either God thinks women can be Maegins or not, it would seem to me. The real question is whether either position is true. From my enlightened perspective, they're only disagreements about an illusion anyway, so neither has any real truth-value - they're just competing systems of identity. One is more inclusive of women and a bit more lax in its rules, and the other is more conservative. They're two expressions of the same fundamental delusion, so they're both far more similar than they are dissimilar. Quibbles over doctrine are different ego sets playing off of each other. And it's all making an issue over what is, quite literally, nothing."

"So you walked away and came out here . . . to do what?" asked Jor Alesh.

"To be myself," answered Seyloq. "There's nothing else to do, really. That's the real joke for the ego - always looking for some purpose, something to define it, to give its existence meaning and value. But there's no greater purpose in life than to simply be yourself. If you're deluded by your ego, trapped in its energetic constructs, you'll have endless challenges to the task of simply being yourself. To truly be yourself, you need to liberate yourself from your ego. That's not your purpose, though. That is an enactment of will, of personal desire. Your purpose is to be: it is your choice *how* you are going to be - deluded or enlightened.

"Once I realized my true nature and identity, there was no place for me in Azar. You can't reform an identity that doesn't want to be reformed. If I were to stay there, it would have been endless conflict, and that's not much fun. I probably could have helped to liberate a few, but overall, the collective ego would have only become more defensive, more deliberately wrapped in defiant illusion, so why bother? Here on the outskirts, I can do what I want, live my life the way I want. And I'm also close enough that I can share what I've learned with individuals who are truly ready, especially the ones who manage to fall through the cracks of the carefully constructed illusion of Azaran religion - ones such as Jendru here.

"Being honest with myself means recognizing that I *do* want others – other versions of myself - to wake up. Living a liberated life is something worth sharing with others, but it has to be done authentically, one person at a time. There is no path, no doctrine, no system - just one person at a time coming to the truth and discovering it within him or herself. And because this is the truth, it has the potential to change the world."

"How?"

"What brought our ancestors here?"

"The *Great War*."

"And what was that about?"

Jor Alesh thought for a moment. "I suppose you'd say it was competing identities, competing egos struggling with each other over their chosen delusions, exacerbated by deteriorating environmental and social conditions."

Seyloq smiled. "You're a fast learner, Ms. Melva," he said. "And why haven't we gone back to *The World?* Why keep ourselves isolated here on Lur?"

"Because our ancestors wanted to find a place where they could determine their own fates and practice freely. Everyone was wary of religions back in *The World.* So the Azarans, if they wanted to practice, had to find a place that was isolated and removed."

"Exactly - they needed a place where they could fulfill the delusions of their egos unchallenged by others who feared and rejected them. But did the Azarans found a uniform society? No! They didn't, because the human ego is always reformulating itself. First it was the growth of Jurnda and your secular culture, and then it was the Darsulans with their challenging doctrine. You see, the very causes that contributed to the *Great War* are repeating themselves here on Lur, despite everyone's supposedly best attempts not to repeat the mistakes of the past. Understand, the ego can't help itself - this is its nature as a function of consciousness: it must, to satisfy itself, create identities and then hold onto the false constructs it has made in order to maintain the illusion of that identity.

"When I say that the knowledge I hold that we are all God, and that the ultimate purpose of existence is for us to be ourselves can change the world, it should be obvious that I'm telling the truth. The entire trajectory of human societiy has been dictated by the illusions and attachments of the ego. What the world would be like if human societies were directed by self-realized truth, we can only imagine. We can only imagine it because, by all indications, it has never genuinely happened in human history. We've never seen what a liberated society would look like, or how it would function, or what it would produce. It is a mystery and a complete unknown."

"So you think that we here on Lur are living out an ego

fantasy and are destined for conflict, strife, and suffering?"

"Sure," said Seyloq. "Granted, we all seem pretty well off, but all the makings for trouble are present and accounted for. In my understanding, things back in *The World* were going fine until the climate started changing - sea levels rose, weather patterns changed, floods and droughts . . . nature swept in and revealed that human society and prosperity was far more precarious than anyone thought. All the different religions had their own view of why these disasters were happening. When the ego is challenged, it tends to look to what it can hold onto, how it can defend its identity in the face of change and uncertainty. The ego is primarily reactive, and when confronted, it brings all that it has to the fore. So that's all it took - challenge the ego and the world was at war, and everyone vied for how effectively they could destroy others. Here on Lur, we currently do not face any such threats, but who knows what the future will bring? The ego, if left unchecked, is bound to cause trouble for humanity, and all that we come in contact with.

"Given that we all are God, that everything is God, in the final analysis, it really doesn't matter. But from our individual perspectives as living embodiments of the One, it matters a great deal, because we are the ones who have to live with the realities we create for ourselves. Everything is always perfect, but that doesn't mean that we can't express our will to make things the best they can be for us. Genuine self-knowledge translates into genuine self-love, and that means making your happiness and fulfillment a priority because your life is your life, no one else's. Collectively, through individual awakening and self-responsibility, we could transform the world and bring humanity into a future the likes of which it has never seen, or even conceived – a society based on unconditional universal love, genuine self-knowledge, and responsibility."

"And this is how you accomplish this great change - by hiding out here in the jungle, giving toad medicine to those who come into your orbit?"

"Basically, yes," said Seyloq. "I serve those who come seeking, and share what I can. Keep in mind, it's not only those in Azar, like Jendru, who come to me." Seyloq glanced around his home, letting his eyes fall conspicuously on the various objects about them. Jor Alesh followed his lead.

"You work with people from Jurnda," she said. "You're not isolated out here at all, are you?"

"No," said Seyloq. "I have more connections with people in Jurnda than I do out here. They bring me things and have modernized my home. With the technology they've gifted me, I'm able to follow the Jurnda news and entertainment feeds. I keep a close eye on Jurndan culture, art, politics, all of it. In fact, I'd bet that I know more about certain aspects of life in Jurnda than you, Alcian."

"How do you mean?" Jor Alesh asked.

"Are you aware that there are groups in Jurnda that are in contact with the Darsulans?"

Jor Alesh wasn't, though from what she had learned from Chondrasil, she assumed there had to be some connection. This was the first independent confirmation of such.

"When I first left Azar, I spent time wandering about Jurnda. Remember, I was born and raised out here in the valley, so I wanted to see for myself what life beyond Azara was like. It didn't take me long to find underground groups of would-be Darsulans. Their connection with the exiled Darsulans is tentative, at best, and there are no real official ties, but human interest is human interest; it cannot be stopped. The Azarans did what they could two hundred years ago to simply remove the Darsulans and the doctrinal threat to their identity and grand purpose. But various currents and eddies slipped through the cracks, and some of the knowledge of Darsulan medicines made its way into Jurndan society. Though Darsulan teaching is still wrapped in doctrine and belief, their ways are looser and more relaxed than Azaran doctrine, and small groups of Jurndans have made use of their medicines and practices, mostly in a secular context, but still influenced by the Darsulans. Given the religious hegemony of Azara, they have practiced in secret and have established some unofficial ties to Darsul. So this breakaway group is not nearly as isolated as many have believed. And unlike Azarans, they have embraced the changes and developments in Jurndan society. Those in Jurnda have shared technology with them and even engage in trade to procure access to the medicines, which the Jurnda-based Darsulans have recently begun synthesizing. These are, I think, exciting developments, and I have personally benefited from them."

Seyloq got up and walked over to the wooden box next to the mat and eagle feather that Jor Alesh had noticed when they first entered the room. Seyloq opened the box and removed what appeared to be a large amber colored crystal. "This," he said, holding out the crystal in his hand, "is toad medicine, manufactured by Jurndan alchemists. It is pure, clean, and powerfully effective. Their science accomplished what I could not: isolating the active compound and making it accessible to anyone who wants it, regardless of natural sources. What is even more astounding is that the alchemists have determined that this very molecule is present inside each and every human being, and inside mammals in general. And even here about my home, I've had various plants and grasses tested, and it's in many of them, too. Apparently, the key to our awakening and liberation has been with us all along - we just didn't know it."

"So there are those in Jurnda who are using this medicine?" Jor Alesh asked, surprised that she had never heard of such a thing, though understanding that there were undercurrents in Jurnda that no one knew of - at least, not officially.

"Yes," said Seyloq, "thanks to me. I don't control them, nor have I provided them with a religion or a doctrine. I introduce them to the medicine, show them how I use it, work with them - but what they do beyond that is entirely up to them. Some have desired that I be their 'leader,' but that's entirely missing the point. I'm not going to play God for anyone. I'm not a monk. I'm not a priest. I'm not a prophet or a healer or any of those things. I am God, and I am myself. I'm responsible for myself, like every other version of me is completely responsible for him or herself. Personally, I want to help as many other versions of myself as possible liberate themselves from their egos and their attachments and illusions, but I refuse to be anything other than what I am. I will not compromise, not for anyone's sake."

"It all seems rather passive," said Jor Alesh. "If you really are in possession of the truth, why be so coy about it?"

"Personal choice," said Seyloq, putting the large crystal back in its box and returning to his seat. "And besides, I'm not as passive as I may appear."

"How so?"

"Who do you think invited the Darsulans to come pay us a visit?"

"What?" exclaimed Jendru and Jor Alesh simultaneously.

Seyloq laughed. "My love and compassion is universal and infinite," he said, "but my tolerance and patience for delusional games is short. All this sneaking around, underground traditions, self-imposed exile, doctrinal disputes; it's all a game, and personally, I'd like to see the confusion cleared up. I have the long-term interests of humanity in mind here, and sometimes that means making a little trouble. Someone's got to stir the pot, and it might as well be me. My only agenda is truth, and I'm willing to cause some trouble in order to expose it. I'm not some mastermind, however, so don't get me wrong. I have no delusions of grandeur. I don't have a plan. I felt like stirring things up, and that's all part of being myself - following my inspiration and trusting that in following my energy, I'm being authentic and true, and that's all I can really ask of myself. What comes from that is anyone's guess."

"So you invited the Darsulans? How?"

"I sent them a letter through the underground groups in Jurnda. It was simple. I told them that new revelations indicated that the time had come to resolve doctrinal differences, and that a new era of sharing and openness was upon us. To that end, they were invited to Azar to share sacraments, discuss doctrine, and begin talks to examine the question of open integration between the various societies on Lur."

"So you lied to them?"

Seyloq smiled. "Yes, and no. The letter was absolutely

genuine. I wrote the letter while I was still a Maegin-Lu and a member of Azara. It was a reflection of what I was going through during the process of my own awakening. At the time, it felt very important to me, but I was still unsure of myself and what was happening to me. Keep in mind, the process of coming to know myself wasn't easy, by any means. It challenged everything I ever thought or believed or held to be true. That's not exactly a recipe for a day at the park. Look at Jendru! He's going through it now - ask him if it's easy or if he feels comfortable or confident in himself! By the look of him, nothing is making sense and he feels he has nothing to hold onto, nothing and no one to look to outside of himself. Everything that once gave him meaning and purpose is washing away. To accept the reality that you are God is no small achievement, despite the fact that it's simply the way things are and it is what is it, regardless of what you think or believe. In the end, it's obvious, so admitting it to yourself is always a relief, eventually.

"But anyway, I wrote this letter as I was undergoing this process. It was a reflection of my personal struggle with Azaran doctrine, and I was drawn to the fact that Darsulan doctrine was a bit more relaxed and open. I had thought that the Azarans could learn some things from the Darsulans, if only they would be open to it. Yet they were anathema, so there was no one among the Azarans I could talk to about my desire for us to share and learn from each other, and possibly transcend our conventional doctrinal differences. So I wrote this letter, signed it as Maegin-Lu, and then sealed it and kept it hidden away. I didn't know where to take it or what to do with it - besides the fact that I didn't really have the official authority to make such an invitation. I wasn't yet completely ready to challenge the Church. And, as far as I knew at the time, no one was in contact with the Darsulans, or even knew where they were. It was an exercise in self-expression that I needed to do at the time - give myself permission to speak my true thoughts, even if it was to no one in particular and of no noticeable effect.

"But then, after I left and spent time wandering Jurnda, I learned that there were those who were in occasional contact with the Darsulans. It occurred to me that I still had the letter. I sat on it for a long time, but it kept coming back into my mind. Eventually, I passed it off to some people in Jurnda with the hope that it would find its way to the Darsulans, which it apparently has.

"As I said, I don't have an agenda here. It simply felt right to me, and that's what I follow. As God, we are all essentially beings of energy. An intuition or an inspiration is a movement of energy. The ego wants to analyze and plan and understand these movements, but often ends up co-opting, censoring, or second-guessing those inspirations. I've liberated myself from my ego, so it doesn't have the power to stop me from doing what I want. I wanted to send the letter and see what would happen, so I did. Beyond that, well, I suppose we'll all find out shortly. Already it's brought you to me, and that's no small accomplishment. You are the Alcian, after all, and by all appearances, you seem open, ready even. You've sat here and listened to me go on about things that many would find offensive, absurd, and sacrilegious, but you've taken it all in, and energetically, you've remained open. Not once have you attempted to put up a defense, or counter what I'm sharing with your own pre-set views or ideas. Granted, you've been trained for such as Alcian, but not every Alcian can actually fulfill the requirements of the role. In my estimation, you seem quite exceptional, Jor Alesh Melva, and I'm very pleased that events have conspired to bring you here. What you do with that is up to you."

"I'll try your medicine, if that's what you mean," said Jor Alesh. She was truly interested. She had never imagined that *this* was what being Alcian would mean, but here she was and she knew she wanted to try it. She still wasn't sure what to make of this man, Seyloq Surya. Despite his claims to be God, not something that most rational people would accept casually, he did make a great deal of sense to her, and at the very least, she found his perspective refreshing. Having drunk Azara, she knew that the only way to truly assess what such a substance makes possible was to experience it. If this toad medicine helped Seyloq break through his illusions and transcend his ego, then perhaps it could do the same for her. And maybe then she could truly understand where he was coming from and why he was making the claims he made. "I'd like to see it in action first, though," she added, turning to Jendru. He'd hardly said anything this whole time and she wondered what he was thinking. Had he heard all this before from Seyloq? She didn't think so.

"I'm ready," he said, facing Seyloq.

"Well then, let's get started."

Chapter 14
TAKING MEDICINE

It only took Seyloq a few minutes to rearrange his living room and get everything prepared. To make room for the mat, he moved a low table away from the chairs and then unrolled the padded mat directly in the center of the room. He went about closing the curtains and blinds and turned all the lights down to a dim glow. The music he changed so that it was instrumental and dreamy, rather than the lyrical and vocally driven music that had been playing throughout their conversation. From the large crystal, he shaved off some fragments and then cut them up with a sharp blade into a fine crystalline powder. Next, he took a small glass pipe, packed it with some plant material, and carefully placed the crystal powder on the top, ready for the flame. Through it all, Jor Alesh noticed that Seyloq didn't say any prayers, didn't make any ritual gestures or bows, and apparently treated the whole process in a very straightforward and practical manner. If there was anything special about this, it wasn't immediately obvious.

"You don't do any ritual?" Jor Alesh asked when Seyloq's attention turned back to his two guests.

"No."

"Why not?" She was curious.

"Because ritual is just the ego indulging in its fantasies and illusions. The only thing that ritual does is make people feel good about themselves, or maybe make them feel safe, or that the person in charge has got things under control. I don't traffic in illusion here - just reality. There's a big difference," he added with a smile.

"Jendru," he said, addressing the novice, "come and sit on the mat so I can explain to our guest here how this works." Jendru did as he was asked and positioned himself on the center of the mat, facing Seyloq. "Now, Jendru's heard all this before, but since you're new to this, I'll give you my standard opening explanation of what we are about to do here, how to get the most out of it, and what you might be able to expect of me and my role in the process."

Jor Alesh nodded and looked on.

"This medicine," Seyloq began, "is the most powerful energetic opener that exists. Even if you've tried Azara, you have no idea what to expect from this. The simplest way to put it is that this medicine can help you reveal to yourself that you are God. That sounds a bit religious, so I prefer to speak of things energetically. I like to call all medicines 'energens' in that what they are doing, at the most basic level, is opening you up to your energy. They amplify and intensify your natural energy, and when you allow it, they let you experience your energy in its truest form: infinite, unbound, and eternal.

"But to understand how this works, we have to address the ego. The ego is ultimately a function in human consciousness that seeks to distinguish between what it decides is 'self' in opposition to 'other,' or the dualistic divide between subject and object. The ego is not itself a thing - it is more a collection of energetic patterns and habits that have been willingly adopted by the individual, and as such, the ego expresses itself differently in each person, for each person has a unique and individual history. These energetic patterns are used by the ego to define its sense of self at every level of our being - what we think, how we think, what we believe, how we choose to express ourselves, the gestures we make, the tone of our voice, our speech and behavior patterns - all of these are manifestations of the ego. And as I've already stated, most of the time, the ego is busy censoring or trying to control our natural, infinite energy in ways that conform to its expectations of who we *should be* or how we *should* express ourselves. In other words, the ego is our primary adversary to behaving naturally and authentically in our being. The ego gets in the way of us naturally being ourselves.

"The ego is always reflected in and illustrated by the energy of the body. The body is the vehicle for the expression of your energy and is your medium of interface with yourself as an embodiment of the One. Internally, your relationship to yourself, to your energy, is mediated and controlled by your ego. These internal relationships are then mirrored through exterior reality and the relationships between your body and your surroundings and the others you interact with. A big part of working with this medicine - really, any medicine - is to become aware of how your ego is attempting to structure and control your natural energy and how this is reflected both internally and externally. It is a process of becoming ever more self-aware, and through such, becoming ever more responsible for yourself, your choices, and how you express and mobilize your energy. This is the essence of personal liberation and enlightenment: self-awareness and the resulting self-responsibility, actualized through personal choice and expression through the medium of your vehicle, your body.

"When dealing with the body, there is a basic energetic distinction that can be made: authentic, genuine energy, and ego, illusion-based energy. Authentic energy always expresses itself in the body symmetrically, whereas ego-controlled energy is generally, though not always, expressed asymmetrically. When working with medicine, this is an extremely important distinction to keep in mind. Jendru, can you show Jor Alesh the neutral position?"

At this request, Jendru laid back on the mat. His arms were open, at his sides, with palms facing up. His legs were open as well. To Jor Alesh, he looked like someone trying to embrace the universe while lying down.

"This," continued Seyloq, "is what I like to call the neutral position. Here, the body is relaxed, open, and in a position of complete surrender and allowing. This is absolutely vital for opening to the infinite nature of your energy. People who are struggling with their egos will almost always disrupt this natural, balanced posture by moving into various forms of asymmetry, such as curling up on their side, trying to turn over, shaking from side to side - really, there are too many examples. If, in your session, you become aware that you've broken this neutral, symmetrical posture, consciously bring yourself back to it.

"Most egos don't like feeling this vulnerable and

exposed. They want to hide, or find something to hold onto. Mostly that's accomplished by struggling to maintain some kind of dualistic, subject/object division. To avoid this, treat this event as your death, or as going to sleep. Let your ego know that there is nothing you need to do here, nothing to figure out, nothing to accomplish - just relax, and let go. Surrender to everything you're experiencing.

"That's really the first step – surrendering, relaxing fully, and letting yourself go. When this occurs, your ego will most likely interpret the experience as dying, or merging with the infinite, or transcending all of time and space. Don't fight with it - let it happen.

"Some people need to take many rounds of medicine, or even many sessions, to even reach this first step. Many, most, in fact, never really get there - the Azarans and Darsulans are a perfect case in point. It also helps to have access to the strongest of the strongest medicines, such as what I have here. You can do this with any medicine, or no medicine at all (though that is much harder) - always remember that *everything* you experience on the medicines is a reflection of yourself - nothing more, and nothing less. If your ego refuses to let go, then you'll have a dualistic experience, which might be filled with wonderful or terrifying visions, depending on what your ego is projecting and holding onto. In such experiences, it is a communication from the self to the self, and the ego does all it can to dress up the communication into identifiable objects, others, and concepts. These are all workings of the ego. *All* appearances of spirits, deities, demons, and the like fall into this category of ego projection. Again, there is *nothing* in the experience that is not yourself. It's *all* you. Once you find your center and achieve clarity, all this is laughingly obvious and you wonder how it was that you ever believed any of these charades. But as long as the ego is holding on and refusing to surrender, all of this can have a sense of hyper reality and is extraordinarily convincing - it all *seems* uniquely real. *Seems* is the operative word here, though. Appearances can be uniquely deceiving.

"Maintaining symmetry in the body is one of the primary tools at your disposal to minimize the potential disruptions and interferences by your ego. It's not a guarantee, because the ego is an extraordinarily fast learner and can quickly figure out how to fake open symmetry, but it is at least a good place to start, and a place to bring your attention to. Remember - you are the final arbiter of your own genuine expression. If you're being symmetrical but still in your ego, you'll know it, even if you don't want to admit it to yourself. Self-honesty is key in this work. Only you can delude and deceive yourself, and only you can be honest with yourself.

"In this process, I'll serve as something of a reality coach and energetic mirror. I'll be both observing and feeling you. When I see a break in symmetry within you, I'll bring it to your attention. When I feel you holding on or struggling, I'll do what I can to assist you to let go and open up. If you trust me, you'll find that I'm always responding to you and guiding you authentically. If your ego wants to project distrust, you'll find that I'm very difficult and challenging to work with. I might seem to you to be some kind of demon or alien or whatever. That is your projection, and not reality.

"So, our first step is to get you to open up, surrender, and let go. Ideally, what we are seeking is for you to experience yourself in your full, infinite, energetic state. This can only be experienced when the ego is transcended. By definition, the ego is a collection of limited energetic patterns and as such, cannot be present or active during a fully expansive energetic state, as it quite literally gets in the way. When the ego drops, when it surrenders and gives up, you are no longer bound by what you think or believe yourself to be, and the patterns you've amassed to maintain that illusion. You reveal yourself to yourself in your full, infinite nature. Experientially, you could describe this as ecstasy, union with God, infinite, eternal, beyond space and time, etc., etc. Realistically, it means that you are experiencing yourself as you truly are: God, the one being that is everything.

"You see, fundamental identity never goes away - only the false identity of the ego. Ego may drop, but the sense of 'I Am' continues, and in fact expands to embrace absolutely everything at a universal level. This is the nature of being

God, the identity at the heart of all things. The false energetic distinctions constructed by the ego have been overcome and you experience yourself as you are: infinite.

"Now, this sounds great, but for most people, this is pretty overwhelming. Keep in mind that your ego has effectively been working your entire life to prevent you from realizing this truth, and as such, it has found all kinds of ways to prevent your natural, infinite energy from expressing itself. From a practical perspective, we can describe most people as being radically twisted up internally, energetically. Their natural state is a spontaneous fountain of infinite energy, but their egos have spent their lives trying to keep this spontaneity under control and managed. This means that when the ego lets go, most people have large amounts of energy that they need to process in their bodies, and this can take on many forms. For some, it is purging and vomiting. For others, it takes the form of a radical sexual explosion. For still others, it is feeling as though their mind is falling apart and shattering – or any mix of these. It all depends on where people have been holding themselves back. Your central column of energy in your vehicle, your body, runs from your head to your genitals. The ego can get you stuck anywhere along that line. When the ego falls away, the energy that has been stored and censored along this line releases and expresses itself. Your job is to let that happen without getting in your own way or trying to control the process. Your job is to surrender and allow.

"Eventually, the ego will begin to reassert itself. It lets go when it feels it has no other option, but as soon as the energy release and expansion afforded by the medicine starts to collapse in on itself, the ego sees an opening and an opportunity and it rushes back in, usually by re-establishing dualistic patterns one at a time. It finds an area to get a foothold and rebuilds itself from there. Usually this begins to occur within fifteen minutes after first consuming the medicine. I'm watching for this transition - usually it's marked by a change in breathing, a slight appearance of asymmetry in the body, or any number of telling occurrences. When it does happen, I'll offer you more medicine. I like to offer clients up to three full rounds of medicine.

"We'll start with two hits each. I'll hold the pipe. First you take a hit, then I'll take a hit, then repeat. For most, two hits are enough to get started, but always be honest with yourself. Remember, what we're going for here is complete surrender and complete, infinite expansion. You will know if you've had enough medicine to reach this state - primarily by the fact that you won't be able to even ponder the question. You'll know - if you can ask yourself if you've had enough, or if you could handle more, then the answer is yes, you can have more. I'll know because I'll be feeling into you, and I always know when a client's ego drops. But you'll do yourself a favor if you're honest with yourself and readily admit when you can have more, no matter how intense, bizarre, or frightening it may all seem. Don't rely on me to tell you what to do.

"Throughout it all, go with what you feel. Trust yourself. Breathe into yourself and stay relaxed, even when things get intense or beyond your ability to understand.

"At its foundation, what we're doing here is working with energy. Though we are in different bodies, the reality is that we are all one being - there is nothing that exists that is not the One. At the practical level, what this means for our session is that when your ego drops, the energetic barrier that you've created to fashion yourself as a unique individual drops as well. When that occurs, I can use my body to help you process your energy. Remember that I am a clear and centered mirror. I don't have any more ego bullshit to process through, as I've liberated myself from my ego permanently. As a result, when I have clients, I can use my body, my energy, from over here to help you. More specifically, what that means is that I can be very much involved in your process as you work through the medicine. It of course varies with the individual, and I never know what is going to happen, or how I may be called to interact, but I am open and without resistance. So, I might growl, purr, click, whistle, tone, or anything else that might help move energy. Also, I might put my hands on you, or even use my body with yours to move energy. As long as you are trusting and allowing, I can do my work. If there is any resistance, I have to back off - that free will thing.

"I also use my feather to help move energy," said Seyloq, leaning over Jendru and picking up the large eagle feather placed by the medicine box. To demonstrate, Seyloq moved into position at the foot of the mat, standing over Jendru. "I always begin at the bottom and start moving the feather back and forth, like this," he said, moving the feather in a pattern that traced out the symbol of infinity. "It's kind of like a magnet," he explained. "I wave the feather, and I feel where the energy is." He demonstrated, moving back and forth over Jendru, sometimes touching him with the feather, sometimes not, always moving in the same rhythmic motion up and down Jendru's body. Even from this demonstration, Jor Alesh could see that Jendru was affected, his body responding to the waving feather and the shifting focus along the central column of his body. "And I usually end by grounding out the energy at the feet, like this," Seyloq said, tapping the feather over the tips of Jendru's toes. "As long as you stay open and trusting, I can keep moving energy with the feather and it can really help to clear things out and let your body open and reset. Just breathe with what you feel and go with it. You might feel large amounts of energy running through your body. Trust that you can manage it and let it work itself out.

"You can also expect that my voice will change - so don't be alarmed. The voice is largely an expression of the ego - tone, cadence, intonation, habits of expression. I use the 'Seyloq' voice in most everyday conversations, as we've been having here, but even now, I'm sure you've been able to detect fluctuations in my voice and manner of speaking. I use my ego like an outfit, or perhaps as a character I play. When I take the medicine, or when my energy expands on its own, due to circumstances, my voice changes so that I speak in my true voice. Some people react by projecting that I'm possessed by some demon, or putting on an act, or trying to be dramatic. Actually, I'm not trying at all. I'm just being myself, and that's what I sound like. In fact, that's what everyone sounds like because at heart, we are one. Sometimes it's funny - I can have complete conversations with people where we're both speaking in 'the voice,' but when their ego comes back in, they generally have no idea of the conversation they just had or how they sounded! People are so alienated from their true selves that the only way they can experience it is to check out completely. Later, they can only remember it as a whiteout - a time for which they have no specific recall. With practice and experience, this phenomenon fades away - ideally, to the point where there is no longer a distinction, as is the case for myself.

"Let's see . . . is there anything else? Jendru?"

"Eyesight."

"Yes," said Seyloq at Jendru's prompting. "Thank you. Eyesight is important for symmetry. Bilateral symmetry is what we're aiming for here - the natural expression of your infinite energy. Eyesight is important for this. It mostly doesn't matter if your eyes are open or closed, but it does matter where you look. The ego wants to look around, always looking *for something*. So even there, keep your eyes centered. Up, down, crossed - doesn't matter - as long as you keep your eyes centered and resist the urge to look around. Always remember that it's your ego that wants to take a look around, not you, not your genuine energy. If you're having trouble with this, I may ask you to look me in the eyes to help keep you centered and balanced."

"And don't forget purging," said Jendru.

"Ah, yes, purging. I have a bowl here, if we need it. It's important not to try and suppress any feelings of nausea - really, it's important not to suppress or edit anything you feel - let it out as you feel it. Don't hold back. If you can sit up to purge, I'll have the bowl ready for you. If you need to let it out while lying down, let it happen. You'll be okay. And on occasion, the purge works its way out through me, through my body. So sometimes I purge for people, or even on them - which sounds pretty horrible and undesirable, I know, but it's always perfect when it happens. Trust and allow. That's the name of the game."

"How long does the medicine last?" Jor Alesh asked, thinking that it was already well into the afternoon. There were still several hours of sunlight, and it wasn't as though she was in a rush to get back, but it did occur to her that Jendru was probably missed back in Azar, though she supposed that was his concern, not hers.

"You'll feel the effects of the medicine before you exhale your first hit. If you fully transcend your ego, it will only last for about fifteen minutes, after which your ego will begin to reassert itself. If you're willing, we'll take more medicine, at that point, up to two more times. Depending on how quickly you work through the medicine, it will take between an hour and two hours for the entire process. When we're done, the medicine will have completely processed through your body and there will be no lingering effects, aside from the refreshing and liberating energetic reset that the medicine provides. But you and Jendru will be able to make it back to Azar without any difficulty.

"Well, I think that's that!" exclaimed Seyloq, clapping his hands together once with a broad smile and raised eyebrows. "No time like the present! Shall we?"

Chapter 15

HERE WE GO AGAIN

Here we go again, Jendru thought as he situated himself on the mat. He could feel his pulse racing, making him feel slightly dizzy and shaky. He took a couple of deep breaths as Seyloq sat down directly in front of him. Jendru had his legs slightly open and Seyloq sat upon his knees, sliding up to Jendru to hold the pipe out for him. Jor Alesh sat to the side in one of the chairs at the periphery of Jendru's vision. Seyloq had added the extra instructions that during their sessions, Jendru and Jor Alesh should not try to interact with each other - or give any thought or care to what the other was thinking or perceiving. "This is your session, and what she thinks or sees does not matter. All that matters is that you allow yourself to feel what you feel, and express yourself authentically." Seyloq also explained that this tended to be more of an issue when couples came together ("Yes, couples come for work, but I always work with each person individually. Sometimes the relationships last, sometimes they don't. Plenty of people keep themselves in relationships that no longer serve them. When you start trafficking in truth, there's no place to hide.").

Jendru's hands were shaking now. He was thankful that Seyloq was in charge of the pipe, holding it out before him. He stared down at the bowl. The pipe was small, made of colored glass. The medicine was on top of a different base material than his previous session, Seyloq had explained. The last time Jendru was here, Seyloq had used an herb that he said had no psychoactive properties. This time, he was using one of the smoking plants that the "forest people," as Seyloq called them, used for relaxation and enjoyment (According to

Seyloq, there were more people living in the forest beyond Azar valley than most were aware of - they weren't exactly local laypeople of the Azaran faith and had developed their own minor, mirror traditions using this local plant - more mixing of medicines, Jendru noted, but he was so deep in at this point, why bother caring?). "This one goes really nicely with the medicine - with any medicine, really," Seyloq had said, "plus, it tastes better than the one we were using before and is definitely my preference. You'll see - I think you'll like it, though you won't really notice the difference until the medicine starts to wear off and you find that you still feel slightly and pleasantly altered."

Small grains of amber crystal dust made a layer on top of the plant material. Jendru marveled for a moment that something so small, so seemingly minor and insignificant, could harbor such profound power. *And it's already inside you,* Jendru recalled from Seyloq's lecture earlier. This simple crystal was present inside each and every human being. It was a marvel. And Seyloq had to discover it in the venom of a toad, of all creatures. No one suspects the toad! Jendru let out a little chuckle. He was feeling a little more relaxed now. He was ready.

He gave a slight nod of his head while looking Seyloq directly in the eye, indicating his readiness. Seyloq nodded back and without saying anything, held the pipe directly up to Jendru and activated his lighter, sending out a faint yellow-orange glow of burning light. Jendru could feel the anticipation rising within him and resolutely pushed past it, putting his lips to the pipe. He inhaled.

The medicine crackled on top of the plant material, sizzling and melting over its surface, quickly turning into boiling pools of liquid crystal. *He's right, this does taste better,* Jendru had time to think as he pulled in his first hit. The sweet floral taste of the crystal medicine was nicely complimented by the fruity, minty taste of the herb beneath it. Jendru drew deeply, pulling the mixed smoke deep into his lungs.

Jendru could feel the medicine going to work almost immediately. He watched Seyloq take a hit from the pipe, his eyes following his hands as they brought the pipe and lighter back to him. The medicine was already raging, but he knew: *I need more. Don't hold back. Take it all . . .* He took another deep hit, the smoke searing the back of his throat and burning down into his lungs. He knew instantly that this was enough. An infinite YES! unfolded and expanded within him.

"Yes . . . excellent, love," he heard Seyloq say in that deep, otherworldly voice. He could feel his eyes widening and his mouth falling open. It was all happening so fast. He could still see Seyloq sitting in front of him, slowly edging back from between his legs, taking up his place at the foot of the mat. Only seconds had passed and he could see the smoke from his second hit exiting his lungs and filling the space between them. *He knows I'm doing it,* Jendru had time to think to himself. *He really can feel what I'm experiencing . . .*

The image of Seyloq began to break apart into a hyper flow of fractal light forms. It was like looking through the most profoundly complex crystalline matrix where an infinitely pure white light had been refracted into endless rainbows. It all emanated from a stable point, somewhere in the infinite distance. There were so many layers, so much impossible depth to what he was seeing. It was as though from here, he could look out across the entirety of the universe. Everything was revealing itself to him in its purest, most energetic form. He was moving through it, faster and faster. There was structure to it, but it constantly shifted, moved, and turned in on itself, endlessly. Subtle forms seemed to rise up within the matrix of light, like beings, growing, changing, endlessly fucking, giving birth, eating each other, endless, endless, endless. It was the entire mass of life. It was creation, evolution, destruction, eternal change and transformation. It was all taking place right here. And it wasn't only in front of him. It wasn't something he was watching like a projection on a screen. He *was* this phantasmagoria of life, endlessly feeding off of itself, endlessly transforming. It was all energy, and it was all him.

"Yes, love." That deep voice again.

It was all coming so fast, so furiously that Jendru's mind couldn't hold on, couldn't make sense of it any more. The information was pouring through him faster than he could process it. He felt his mind struggling to make sense of what he was experiencing, what he was discovering within himself, and he couldn't. A flash of resistance: *It's too much!* . . . *So stop trying and just let go* . . . An inner knowing dawned. It was not the knowing of Jendru. It was just there. He felt a distinct duality within himself, a separation between the identity that believed itself to be Jendru and an identity that knew the truth. With this realization, everything fractaled out into infinity. He could feel his sense of false identity shattering, like so many shards of carefully constructed crystal. *The nature of being is a paradox . . . you cannot understand it . . . only accept and allow.* The knowledge resounded forcefully within him. He couldn't tell if he was hearing this in his head, or if Seyloq was speaking these words to him from outside. Regardless, it was the truth and whoever "Jendru" was, he knew it.

A wild torrent of energy exploded in Jendru's heart. He could feel it coming and knew that it was his acceptance of the paradox; being One and Many. He also knew that if he chose, he could shut it down, close it off. The sequence of events became instantly clear - he couldn't completely stop this process, but he could divert it. He could choose otherwise. If he did, he knew that violent body vibrations and overwhelming nausea would follow. But if he chose to allow . . . A tinge of fear. *This will destroy you . . . I don't care, let it come . . .* And it did.

"I just want to love!" Jendru cried out in a wild, passionate voice. He knew it was true, though he didn't understand what it really meant, for it was love with no object – simply infinite, universal love. Like a thousand super novas, the explosion of energy in his heart sent Jendru's body reeling back on the mat. It was love. The pure, infinite energy of love. Everything that Jendru ever thought he was shattered. There was no ground, no foundation, nothing to hold on to, nothing to identify; nothing, nothing, and nothing. Just an endless, eternal, infinite torrent of raging love. It was ruthless, uncompromising, fierce, horrific even, but in the horror of its absoluteness, it was the most profoundly beautiful thing possible. Beyond imagination, beyond conception, beyond everything. It was reality, and it was himself. Love. Infinite, raging love.

This was the truth that was beyond concerns of right or wrong, good or bad, just or unjust, sacred or profane. There was no separation in this love, no judgment, nothing to forgive and nothing to create shame. There was no humility, nor was there any arrogance. It was nothing like the concept of love or compassion in the conventional sense. It was absolute and universal. It was the love that knew that everything was the self and therefore everything was permissible. Everything that could be, would be, with no limits, no restrictions. It was the love that knew that all life feeds on life, and that birth and death and creation and destruction were reflections and manifestations of the process of the One. Absolute perfection. It was the only possible manner of being. Without this love, there would be nothing, nothing at all. It was clear: being was a case of everything or nothing. And love had chosen, yes *chosen*, everything.

Suddenly a wave of profound loneliness burst forth from his heart. *I am the only one that exists*, came the internal realization. *I am completely, utterly, and eternally alone . . .*

He knew it was true. He knew that it was this loneliness, this absolute isolation and uniqueness, that gave birth to everything. *Loneliness is the heart of infinite love. The self, God, I divide myself into infinite variation, for if I did not, then there would be nothing . . . all of reality is God. There is only One . . .*

"Thank you," he heard himself say out loud. Even in saying it, he wasn't sure who was thanking whom. Was God thanking Jendru? Was Jendru thanking God? Was Jendru thanking Seyloq for making this experience possible? Was Jendru thanking himself? Did it even matter, and was there any difference?

"Thank you!" he said again, and again, and again. He was laughing and crying ecstatically. Wave after wave of energy passed through him. His mind, his ego, wanted to know what it all was, but a deeper part of him knew it didn't matter - all that mattered was that he feel it, and that he speak it. It was true. He was profoundly, infinitely grateful, and it didn't matter who that self was, or whom it was speaking to, because it was simply true. "Thank you!"

Then something changed, something clicked. It was like some inner form that had been relaxed suddenly came back online, back into play. His energy had clearly shifted. There was no mistaking it. He was "Jendru" once again. He sat up. Seyloq was waiting for him. He already had the pipe in his hands, holding it out for Jendru to have another hit. "You can have more, Jendru," said the man he knew as Seyloq. There was something about the way that deep voice said "Jendru." There was a touch of irony in it, almost a placating tone that one would use with an obstinate child. It suddenly occurred to Jendru how different it was when Seyloq used his proper name versus calling him "love." *He's telling me he knows when Jendru is in play. He always knows when I'm in my ego, or when I'm out.*

Jendru looked hard at the man, Seyloq. He was still feeling the effects of the medicine, and it was quite powerful. It was bizarre that his ego could be operating when he felt so profoundly affected, but it was true; the ego was perhaps the most tenacious and pernicious "thing" in the universe. It took every opportunity to assert itself and maintain its hold on reality, neatly parsing experience into "self" and "other," "me" and "not me." It was like a disease, or a perpetual game of one-upmanship.

"Yes, the ego is relentless, is it not?" said Seyloq with that deep voice, staring Jendru directly in the eye.

"Yes," he answered in what he clearly identified as "Jendru's" voice. "I need more."

"Good - it is right here. Let us have some more together, shall we?" He was playful, almost seductive. Jendru pulled back for a moment, conflicted by what was obviously a feeling of love and trust for this man, but also a sense of suspicion and fear. He felt heat rise in his face and he had to look away. It was too intense to look Seyloq in the eye. It was like Seyloq could see right through him, like he was an obvious, open book to the confounding man. He was transparent. Utterly exposed and vulnerable.

"Come," said Seyloq, drawing Jendru's attention back to the pipe. "You are ready."

Jendru took one deep breath and then put his lips to the

pipe. Seyloq flicked the lighter and he drew in. He watched the fresh medicine that Seyloq had apparently applied to the bowl melt into the herb. It tasted so good, he thought as it sank into his lungs. He could feel the boost right away. He was slipping into infinity, but he wanted more. Seyloq took a hit and held out the pipe again. *It's happening,* he told himself. *Take another while you can.*

Time seemed to stand still. How long did he hold that second hit? It seemed like eternity before he exhaled. It was as though he had no conscious thought of breathing at all, completely unaware that he had been holding his breath or that he eventually needed to exhale. He stared wide-eyed at Seyloq. *Together . . . we're doing it together.* He knew, distinctly, that "Seyloq" was with him. He was right there in front of him, but in truth, they were one. In looking at the man he knew as Seyloq, he was looking into a mirror. There was no denying it. It was obvious. It was simply true. He *was* this man.

"Yes," said his reflection.

The torrent of infinitely expanding energy overtook him once more. He felt his body opening, crystallized fractal light flying out in every direction. It was as though he could distinctly feel every microscopic atom and particle of his body vibrating across all spectrums simultaneously. It was divine. It was true. He was God, and this was precisely what it felt like. *Ecstasy . . .*

"I am energy!" he belted out, his own voice deep, resonate, vibrating with the power of the infinite. He knew he sounded like the one known as Seyloq, but he also knew that it was him. It had been him all along. "Seyloq" was truly another version of himself. He was a reflection, nothing more.

"I am energy and I am infinite! I am the nature of all that is, for I AM!" He was bellowing. With every syllable, he felt waves of energy pass from his heart out to his extremities. He distinctly felt it in his hands, which were trembling out before him, fingers spread wide, rapidly vibrating back and forth. He knew in his heart that he had never spoken anything so true, so genuine. It was the most profound relief, to speak the truth like this. He knew that to claim anything less would be a deceit, a willful attachment to illusion and deception.

"I AM TRUTH, FOR I AM REALITY!"

"Yes!" said his reflection.

Suddenly he was falling back and his reflection was on him, as though he had drawn him down on top of him with some kind of magnetic field. His reflection had his hands at his heart. He was growling wildly and sucking at his chest. Something was rising up within him. He could tell that his ego wanted to fight it, but he chose otherwise. *Let it happen, whatever it is.* He could feel his reflection pulling this thing, this energy through his stomach, up to his heart. When he thought about it, it seemed impossible, or worse, like demon-craft. But he wasn't afraid. He knew it was necessary. He knew he could trust his reflection. *This reflection is clear. There are no obstructions within him. Trust, and allow.*

And then the energy popped. His reflection was on his feet, towering over him. Jendru's eyes had been rolled up into his head, but they came out now to look up at the man above him. He was straddling his mid-section, arms stretched out wide, face turned upward with a horrendous grimace. He was breathing rapidly and growling, sounding like a tiger ready to pounce. *He's passing the energy through him,* he told himself. *He's taken it on because he knows how to release it.*

And then he did. He could hear his reflection purge, but nothing came out, having caught the vomit in his mouth. He sucked in rapidly and then with a symmetrical flourish of his hands, spun out of place, moving to the bowl where he expelled the vomit in his mouth. "Now that is more like it!" he heard him say as he retook his place at the foot of the mat, sitting upon his knees and waiting.

Jendru realized he was "himself" again. It was okay. He had never felt so relaxed, so at peace, so profoundly calm. Yet even that wasn't really accurate, for he also felt energized in a way he had never experienced before. He realized it was a paradox. He was resting in the perfection of the infinite nature of being. It was simultaneously infinitely tranquil and endlessly explosive. It was then that he became aware that he was listening to music. It was so beautiful. So perfect. Everything was perfect. He felt himself cry once more. *It's so beautiful to be alive.*

"I have a little more," came that playful, deep voice.

"Okay," Jendru heard himself say. Was he dreaming? Was any of this really happening? Maybe this was all some wild fantasy. For a moment, Jendru considered the possibility that he was completely insane. He opened his eyes and turned his head to the left. There she was, Jor Alesh Melva. *No, this is real. She's the Alcian, and you're in Seyloq's living room. You're not crazy. This is real.* The woman smiled at him. She looked so beautiful. He smiled back. *I love her,* he said to himself, suddenly nervous at the realization. It made no sense. He didn't even know her. Not to mention, he was in training to be a monk, a Maegin. But he knew it was true. He did love her, and not in some neutral, compassionate, "spiritual" sense. He wanted to unite with her, to feel himself inside her, to become one with her like he felt himself as one with Seyloq, but as man and woman, as complimentary energies, completing and fulfilling each other. He wanted to make love with her. He could feel it in his sex, feel himself harden. Glancing at her again, it was obvious. *She knows. She knows and she feels it too. This is dangerous . . .*

He shook his head and sat up. He heard his ego speaking to him: *She's only a temptation, a test. Don't give in.* But his heart wasn't in it, so he ignored his ego and took the hit that Seyloq was offering. He took it, and then one more.

He fell back. Once more, everything expanded. It was all the self, all so profoundly beautiful. He felt himself crying and laughing again. It was all so ridiculous, so impossible, so incredibly beautiful. It was laughable that anyone could ever feel separated from God, ever feel fallen from the grace of infinite and universal love that was clearly the nature of all that was. It was a joke. A profound, cosmic joke. The love that was reality was so complete that it answered every desire, even the desire to create a sense of self that was lost, separated, worthless, unworthy, confused, blinded by belief, clouded by faith, seeking after illusory truths. The human quest for meaning was a joke. The only meaning was being: here, now, just this. The endless chain of choices that defined a person: it was all right here, right now. The choice of self was never ending, and there was the pure, infinite energy of love, ready to respond perfectly in every moment, in every ecstasy, in every horror beyond imagination, all right here, right now, perfectly perfect. Absolute perfection.

And it was clear. The most meaningful, satisfying, and pleasurable expression of this universal, absolute perfection and love was the sharing of being through the act of making love. Two bodies, one being, one heart, one love, one eternity. To be two and not two, to be one, to be both sides of the mirror, both sides of the reflection, united in perfect symmetry, perfect balance, perfect exchange of energy. *This* was the ultimate purpose. *This* was the reason for being: the enjoyment of the One, the simultaneous transcendence and recognition of the reality of being One, yet also being two, the One and Many. It was all bound by love. *This is why I divided myself. Only by being many can I reunite as one. Loneliness is the heart of love . . .*

The realization washed over him. He could feel "Jendru" struggling to regain control. Waves of energy passed through his body. The vibrations began in his belly and then radiated out to his extremities, causing his limbs to shake. His reflection, the one he identified as "Seyloq," was standing over him with the large eagle feather, moving it back in forth, making the shape of an infinity symbol, always crossing directly over the midline of his body. He let the vibrations work themselves out, feeling them become ever smoother and more fluid as Seyloq did his work with the feather. *Energy is never still . . . ever moving, ever changing, ever becoming . . . to be alive is to be this energy . . . it is the nature of the self.*

He wasn't sure how long he lay there as the older man did his work with his feather. He could feel him tapping at the tips of his toes with the feather, drawing the remaining vibrations of energy down his legs, grounding it through his feet. Shudders ran across his body, and he became aware that he was cold. He knew he was mostly Jendru now, his ego having reestablished. Still, he felt light, open, unwound and relaxed. Despite the acute awareness of the grip of his ego, there was knowledge in his heart that no matter what, he was free.

"The only limitations on your free will are the energetic limits of reality," he heard Seyloq say in that deep voice. "Choice is always with you. To choose authentically is to choose in clarity, in full recognition of both the limits and possibilities of reality. Living in reality is the purpose of your embodiment here, in this body, in this life. This is *you.*"

Jendru sat up. Seyloq was on his knees down by his feet, staring peculiarly at Jendru, an odd mix of intensity and playfulness on his weathered face. His grey hair was disheveled from all the activity. Seyloq stared a few moments longer, then removed his hair tie and pulled his loose hair back into place, regaining his composed look with a sly smile. "Excellent work today, love," he said, still with the deep voice that wasn't "Seyloq." "Now, if you would, it is time for our new friend to have her experience. When you are ready, you can take a seat to the side and let her take the mat."

Jendru looked up at Jor Alesh, turning his head to the side. She smiled at him. *We are two now,* Jendru told himself. Before, when he had looked at her with the medicine running wild within him, it had seemed that they shared a profound understanding and the veil of separation between them had been wiped away. He acutely felt himself as himself, and she was separate from him. *The illusion has reestablished, along with my ego,* he told himself. He smiled back at her with a slight shake of his head. *This is all too bizarre.*

"Wow," he said at last, sitting up and indicating that he wanted a sip of water.

"Take what you need, but do not indulge," said Seyloq, handing him a clear glass.

The water was divine - so clear, so pure. It tasted like juice, like sugar. He took several small sips, but resisted the urge to gulp it down. *My ego wants to hold onto the water, but I don't need to.* He understood what Seyloq had meant by not indulging. The ego was perpetually looking for something to hold onto, whether that was an object, a person, a relationship, an idea, a belief . . . they were all props, potential handholds for the ego. Jendru understood what Seyloq meant about living infinitely within the actual bounds of reality: be genuinely aware of the energy of your experience, but don't hold onto anything, don't let your ego run the show. Choose with clarity, with purpose, with awareness. It was all an awareness game. *Yes, it is all a game.* It was simultaneously liberating and terrifying. Nothing was what it seemed, yet somehow, everything was also exactly as it seemed. Reality was what it was, regardless of what the ego attempted to make it into. The only authentic mode was to choose clearly and consciously. He looked at Seyloq, who gave a subtle wink. He knew that Seyloq understood what he was realizing.

"You're getting the idea," said Seyloq, sounding more like Seyloq and less like the voice of the universe speaking through the body of the older man. "Now go sit over there and give this lovely young woman a turn."

Without saying anything, Jendru did as he was told and made room for Jor Alesh on the mat.

Chapter 16
NOTHING TO FEAR

"Are you scared?" asked Seyloq, holding the pipe out before him, indicating he was ready for Jor Alesh to begin.

"Yes," she admitted. She could feel her pulse racing within her. It made her dizzy. Her sense of anticipation was far beyond anything she had ever felt when waiting for the Azara drink to take effect. Though she had not yet tried Seyloq's toad medicine, she already knew that nothing she had previously experienced could have prepared her for this moment. She felt as though she were sitting with her executioner.

"Good," said Seyloq. "You will soon find that there is nothing to be frightened of, but it is good to be honest with yourself, and to recognize that this medicine is a monumental, and potentially life-altering, experience. Though there is never a need to be overly serious, it should be taken seriously. This is not just some prayer meeting - this is infinity."

"I don't even know what that means," said Jor Alesh.

"Of course you don't," responded Seyloq. "But you will."

He held the pipe out for her, indicating with his eyes and body language that it was time. "Take your hits, and let go," he said. She glanced at Jendru. He nodded, seeming to say that she could trust Seyloq, trust this medicine. She put her lips on the pipe as Seyloq held up the flame. She pulled it into her. She could hear the medicine sizzle as it melted into the bowl, a sweet, almost floral taste overtaking her. She knew right away that she liked this, maybe even loved it.

Things were already happening by the time Seyloq had

taken his first hit and brought the pipe back to Jor Alesh for her second. There was no doubt that the energy was rising and everything was expanding. Even then, she could tell that she needed, no, *wanted*, more. As strong as the feeling fovertaking her was, it wasn't enough. If she wanted, she could still fight against this, still hold on. The promise of infinity called to her. She put her lips to the pipe and took another, larger drag. Suddenly, there was no question. *This is it . . .*

From her ego's perspective, it seemed clear that she was dying. Absolutely everything was dissolving into pure, white light, refracted into fractal rainbows that stretched and vibrated across the universe. Her entire life and all her relationships flashed through her mind. She knew she was letting it all go. She could feel her body falling back as her awareness of her surroundings was breaking apart, along with everything else. Her mind couldn't hold on to anything, couldn't possibly make sense of what she was experiencing. *This is it . . . I'm dying . . .*

And she knew that she was okay with this fact. She was dying, and she was ready and willing. Everything she had ever thought, ever believed, ever related to was simply falling away, dissolving into infinite light, infinite patterns of energy. It was so clear, here, in these first few moments, that it was only her ego that wanted to hold on, and that whatever she was, it was most certainly not her ego. *She* was so much more. Infinitely more. Her entire life seemed meaningless from this exalted vantage. *Let yourself die*, she told herself. There was nothing left to hold onto and no reason to hold on. She was dying and it was the most beautiful thing she had ever experienced. *Infinite . . . infinite . . . infinite . . .*

There was no doubt: *This is God. God is the only reality. God is real! God is reality! Love! Infinite, inexhaustible love! Nothing else matters. Nothing else is real. God is love and I am that love! Infinite . . . infinite . . . infinite . . .*

Eternity . . .

I am the Alcian. This awareness burst into Jor Alesh's mind. Suddenly self-conscious, she opened her eyes and looked about her, instantly recalling where she was, what she was doing. She saw Seyloq down by her feet. It took her a few moments to realize that she was completely naked, lying on the mat with her fingers inside herself. Though she was lying still, there was the distinct impression that she had just been moving, as though she had been making love with someone or something. She could smell her womanly scent, wafting up from her moist crevice and her slick fingers. There was a rush of heat in her chest and face, suddenly embarrassed at this odd exposure. Taking a quick survey, she confirmed that she was completely naked, though she had no recollection of how this had come to be. She could see that her clothes were strewn about chaotically, as though they had been stripped off of her in some wild frenzy. There was an odd conflict within her. Part of her wanted to cover up in modesty. The other part, the stronger part, wanted to be fucked to absolute oblivion, and the fact that she was with these two men here mattered not at all. They were mere props on the stage that was herself, and modesty be damned, this was her true desire.

She sat up. "More," was all that she said, not feeling any need to interact with these two in any "normal" sense. Seyloq was obviously ready, having put more medicine on the bowl in anticipation of her desire and readiness. He held the pipe to her lips and once more she took a monumental hit. He did the same. "More," she said again to the questioning look on Seyloq's face. It was another massive hit, and she knew that it was sufficient.

Naked and exposed, she sat before the man she knew as Seyloq with her legs open before her, her sex completely exposed. Everything was expanding into infinity again, only this time it didn't send her back onto the mat. Still seated, her head dropped down toward her chest and her gaze fell upon her sex. Everything was exploding into infinite light, but she could still clearly see herself and her body. Her trimmed pubic hair allowed her a good look at her genitals. She could see that the pulse of energy emanating from her heart was swelling her lips, making her vagina appear as an open, yawning vertical mouth or a blossoming flower. There was something about the entire shape of her that was captivating, beautiful.

A revelation swept over her that she in fact was, in some essential sense, her sex. Her body was merely an extension of this organ, this fundamental interface of being. It was almost as though her vagina wore her appearance as a woman as a disguise. *This* was her actual self, in some fundamental, yet difficult to define, sense. It was a truth that was beyond sex, beyond desire, beyond modesty. It was just the way of things, and it was as true for any woman as it was true for a man. She was, in some fundamental sense, her own sex, her own organ. Strangely, she knew that it was universally true because it was true for her, and truth, she knew, was absolutely universal. *One self, one truth, infinite bodies . . .*

She looked up at the man sitting before her. His arms were open, his head turned up to the infinite, his eyes rolled back into his head. He was hissing in a way that resembled the sound of a rattlesnake. Without thinking, she shifted her position (momentarily shocked that she was able to move and control her body) and sat on her knees facing the open and expanding man before her. Looking at him, his heart was like a raging inferno of infinite power with radiating geometric patterns flowing outward, seeming to fill the entire universe. She felt overwhelmed by infinite love for this man, this one who was so clearly a conscious embodiment of God, of infinite being. Looking at him, he was profoundly beautiful, and she knew that she loved him. She felt her vagina open and moisten, her lower mouth gaping as though looking to swallow the man whole, to take him in and make him a physical part of herself. Yet simultaneously she knew that he already was a part of her and that physical separation meant nothing. *We are one. One being, many bodies.*

His eyes rolled down out of his head and he looked directly at her, bringing his head down so that he was peering out from beneath his brow, a powerfully intense look on his face. He growled out a liquid "Yes!" and snarled. God, it was so sexy. She felt penetrated by his gaze and knew that though their bodies were not touching, in some profound way they were making love. There was nothing present that could separate them. They were one.

She pressed her body into his, letting her naked breasts

press into his stomach and dangle over his sex, her face touching his chest at his heart as he leaned back on his knees. She could feel his relaxed breathing and his strong, yet steady, pulse. She let her eyes close and felt herself there, pressed into him, feeling his steadiness, his strength, his sheer force of presence. It was exhilarating to be so close to this beautiful being who knew who he was. It was clear: everything he had told her was true. He was God, and he knew it. His clarity and presence was profound. He knew exactly who and what he was. He was fully present with what was occurring here with her. There were no illusions, no projections, no judgments. Just infinite presence and being. She knew that she loved him as herself. He was a reflection, nothing more. He was herself.

And she also knew, as beautiful as he was, and as much as she loved him, the reflection she truly wanted for herself, here, in this body, in this life, was sitting to her left, watching this bizarre and surreal drama unfold in front of him.

She pulled herself back from the older man. He was still looking at her with that hyper intense look, peering out from beneath his angular brow. He snarled and purred like some enormous cat, bringing his hands up in front of him, pinching between his thumbs and forefingers, his other fingers spread out, the tips of his two middle fingers touching. His hands seemed to turn inside out a few times, each time returning to the same position. She felt herself wavering in her open connection to him, alternately completely relaxed and trusting, and then momentarily wondering what was happening or what she was supposed to do. She knew that this was the ever-present battle between her true self and her ego, this strange character that wanted to pretend that it was her. But she could feel the truth: she was *not* her ego. Her ego was only a part of her, a pattern within her sense of being with which she had perviously unquestioningly identified. But the truth was too obvious to ignore. She was not her ego, and she knew this was true.

"More," she said at last. She felt her ego question this decision. For a brief moment, she suddenly felt afraid. *What am I afraid of?* She knew the answer. She was afraid that if she smoked more, if she continued with this process, she was going to physically make love to this older man, right here in front of Jendru. There would be nothing to hold her back, nothing to prevent her from acting out what she was feeling within herself. Her ego reeled. This was so improper! Her ego ran with the thought of scandal - how the Alcian had gone to Azar on a fact-finding mission, only to be seduced and raped by some wild, drug-filled hermit in front of a novice monk out in the jungle. And worse, it seemed her whole sense of identity and purpose was threatened, as though if she were to make love to him, there would be no returning - somehow, he would steal her essence, and all that would be left would be a dead husk of a woman; comatose, purposeless, without identity, a lump of nothing.

Yet even these fears were not enough to stay her, for the truth was stronger. She knew, without a doubt, that she was perfectly safe, and that whatever happened here was ultimately what she wanted - even if that meant she was going to take another hit, lay back, spread open her legs, and let this man put his penis inside her and take whatever it was he desired. Ironically, even with this internal acceptance, she somehow knew that this was not what was occurring. This man, this one in front of her, didn't want her in this way. He was merely serving as a mirror for her to explore these desires and energies within herself. He was the perfect mirror. If *she* wanted it, he would enter her and fulfill her in every way that he could. But the truth was the one she wanted for this purpose was sitting patiently to her left, watching, wondering, uncertain in his own desires and choices. No, she would not make love to this mirror before her. Not in that way. For in truth, they already were making love. There was no need for the act to be physical and intimate in that way. This was, after all, a manifestation of *her* desire. In the truest sense, she was both of these men. As long as she was clear, and did not get in her own way, they would reflect her and her energy in their own unique ways. As a dualistic dance, they had different roles to fulfill for her. *This man here,* the older one, was not her lover. Not in that way. Nor was the younger man . . . not yet.

"This will be the last round," said the older man before

her. Without hesitating, she took a large hit, and after he had some, she took another. She felt herself slipping and expanding into an infinite eternity. She let herself fall. Not needing to think about anything, not needing to do anything, not needing to be anyone at all . . . just this. "Your journey is honored," she heard herself saying as she fell back on the mat while looking at the beautiful young man to her left, not knowing if she was saying it to him or herself - or if there truly was any meaningful difference. The voice that said this was both hers and not hers. Identity was pointless, she knew, and she made no attempt to make sense of it. Everything was expanding. It was ecstatic, orgasmic, infinite.

She exploded, and was gone. All that remained was pure, unbridled bliss.

Chapter 17

BACK TO AZAR

The sun was already sinking low in the sky by the time they began the journey back to Azar, sending orange, slanting light and long, sharp shadows dancing about them. Though the effects of the medicine had long since worn off, everything seemed more defined, more brilliant and colorful. The shape of everything appeared more distinct, more real.

The songs and chirps of the toads echoed about them as they made their way, almost casually, through the jungle. Neither felt any rush to get back to Azar, despite the time. Seyloq had sent them on their way, proclaiming that he was done for the day and didn't feel like talking. He was clearly tired and worn out by their afternoon activities. Given his age, he was holding up well, but it all took its toll physically and energetically. "The limits of the body are real," he had said, "and genuine living is always in recognition of this. Eat when you're hungry, shit when you gotta go, and rest when the body requires it. We may be God, but that doesn't exempt us from the reality of the physical - in fact, it demands that we respect it. That's the nature of the reality game. No point in living in wishful desire."

Thus the two had somewhat reluctantly left Seyloq, who saw them outside and then sat on his porch to take a smoke of some leafy material and watch them wander down the hillside. They had both turned back for one last look before disappearing into the thick jungle. The old man had smiled and waved. He looked so ordinary, so human, sitting there. The thought occurred to both Jendru and Jor Alesh that he was older than he seemed, and that, like Chondrasil Sojan back in Azar, his time was running out. Perhaps, just as Chondrasil was ultimately looking for the next High Maegin, Seyloq was similarly looking for someone to take the torch of truth from him and carry it into the future.

It was some time before either one spoke. It almost seemed a crime to them both, as though speaking would break whatever enchanted spell they felt themselves under. Living directly, immediately in one's energy, speaking appeared unnecessary - a distraction, even - removed from the pure present moment where no words were ever really needed. Truth was communicated through being, and one merely needed to be present to this fact, to be present with the energy of the moment, and therein all things were clear and perfectly infinite. No words were necessary to express or appreciate this - only awareness and presence. Thus they enjoyed the magic of the moment for some time, simply being there with each other, making their way back to a world that felt profoundly artificial and inconsequential, yet somehow still completely real.

After maybe an hour of walking, as the last rays of light of the setting sun filtered through the trees and foliage, it was Jor Alesh who broke their mutual silence and personal meditations.

"That was amazing," she said, letting the words fall from her mouth, simply stating the truth without a need or desire for confirmation from Jendru. He obliged anyway, at first silently nodding, and then turning to her and saying, "Yes."

They walked on a little further in silence, still accompanied by the song of the toads, now joined by the countless insects that sent their metallic trills through the night air. "How can you go back to Azar after that?" Jor Alesh asked at last, reaching out and pulling on Jendru's hand, bringing him to a stop. He didn't answer her at first, merely looking at her intensely in the dim light.

"Honestly?" he said rhetorically, "I don't know." He pulled his hand away and then almost absentmindedly brushed some of Jor Alesh's hair away from her face and tucked it behind one of her ears, letting his finger tips fall along the curve of her jaw.

"There was a time," he continued, "which was not so long ago – really, up until a few days ago - that my life made perfect sense, and I knew what my future held for me. From the very first time I encountered Azara and took communion, I knew that I wanted to be a Maegin. I wanted to be an integral part of the work that the holy men were doing. I wanted more than anything else to be one of them, to follow in their supposedly selfless footprints and become part of the holy work. And I was welcomed by the holy men, Chondrasil not least among them in his eager embrace. They told me that I was born for this - that my soul had chosen this as its life purpose, and that it was a clear indication of my own eventual reincorporation into Azara. This was to be my path, my purpose, my being. To be a monk, to drink communion, to be initiated into the mysteries - this was everything to me, and was to be my place until my own eventual death and return to source, or maybe even reincarnating again and again, always to return to the Church. They told me that I had done this before, and I believed it and found meaning in what they said. I've even had visions of myself as a monk and Maegin in past lives, ones that I interpreted as having been long ago, back in *The World*, from before the war. It cemented my belief that this was my destiny, that I had been born for this work and would be a great Maegin - maybe even one day becoming High Maegin, following in the wake of great ones like Chondrasil."

"And now?" asked Jor Alesh, already knowing the answer.

"Now . . . I don't know," said Jendru.

"You don't believe anymore, do you?" she asked.

"No."

She understood. Seyloq was correct. Despite the fact that the Maegins claimed to act selflessly and beyond the ego, doing the holy work of Azara, it was a sham - a sophisticated sham, but a sham, nonetheless. The Church and its workings may not be the everyday ego of an ordinary person, but it was still an expression of the ego. It was still a system of identity, still a dualistic divide between God and self, self and other, material and immaterial, body and spirit. In joining the Church, a man such as Jendru would have to give up his old ego, but in its place, he would take on another one that was more sophisticated, perhaps even more rigid, more closed off, more full of illusion and projection. It was all a training ground for perhaps *spiritual* egos, but egos nonetheless. It gave them purpose, identity, and meaning, but it was, at heart, a profound sham, and one that they thoroughly believed in. It was clear that Jendru's interactions with Seyloq were destroying his ability to believe this anymore.

"I feel like the rug has been pulled out from beneath me," said Jendru. "I had been working my way up the pyramid, but now it seems pointless, absurd even. It's only a show, and my heart isn't in it. And in its place, what? What do I do with myself? Who am I to be? What am I to do? I've committed everything to being a part of the Church, and now . . ."

"Not everything," said Jor Alesh. "You still have your hair," she joked. He ran his hand through his thick hair in response and felt the skin of his scalp, thinking of what it would be like to shave it all off and eventually receive his tattoo. What if he were wrong? What if, in following through with his formal initiation and taking his vows, the Maegin-Lus revealed more to him? What if, despite his five years of training, they hadn't really shared the deepest truths with him? All of this could be his test of will, of faith, of belief. If he went through with it, maybe he would learn that he was being a fool and would be forever grateful that he had not turned his back on the Church and their eternal truths.

He didn't believe this, however. Look at Seyloq, he thought. He had been a Maegin-Lu, charged with instructing new acolytes in the faith. His own realization, the same fundamental realization Jendru and Jor Alesh were undergoing, had sent him from the safe and known folds of the Church out into the jungle, into the unknown. He had left it all behind because he learned the truth. No, Jendru was fooling himself. It was merely wishful thinking that somehow full initiation would wash away his doubts. It was a ploy of his ego. A cloying attempt to maintain a hold on some illusion, a desire for meaning and purpose, for identity.

Jendru knew what was in his heart. His mind reeled with his newly accepted reality. His thoughts turned to Chondrasil. That would be the hardest. It was true that he had looked up to Chondrasil and had found something in the High Maegin that he had felt was missing in his own private, personal life. He loved his parents, but they were passionate artists, committed to living in the moment, pursuing their artistic inspirations, and ultimately driven by the desire to express themselves. While they respected the Church and the work of the Maegins, they had never really understood Jendru's desire to become a part of the Church. For them, life was about the dynamic pulse of the city, of Jurnda, and the ever-shifting mix of art, music, and culture that they thrived on. In their world, Azara was archaic, a leftover from *The World,* and though perhaps noble, a remnant from the war and all that had transpired then. A fulfilled life meant the flourishing of human creativity and living that was Jurnda. In the aftermath of the *Great War,* human civilization had been born anew and it was exciting and dynamic. Azara was the old. Jurnda and its flourishing was the now.

Compared to his parents, Jendru had felt himself conservative, regressive even. Yet that had not stopped him. He loved his parents, but he had turned his back on them to join the Church. At the time he had made his decision, it was as though he were dying to one life and beginning the process of gestating a new one. And in this, Chondrasil had been his guide and mentor, having taken a liking to him almost immediately. Jendru had never known another High Maegin, and for him, Chondrasil had represented all that was grand and profound about the Church. Unlike his own father, Jeresh Amdin, Chondrasil Sojan was someone Jendru wanted to be. Devoted, powerful, profound, selfless: serving the higher good and fulfilling the will of Azara. By comparison, his actual parents had seemed like dilettantes, hedonists. Chondrasil was transcendent. He was beyond the mundane workings of this world and the secular reality of Jurnda. He was a symbol of eternity for Jendru, a symbol of ultimate purpose, of the fulfillment of being.

Chondrasil had seen and sensed all of this in Jendru from the beginning. He had taken him in as a surrogate spiritual father, and guided and nurtured him in a way that his own father had never been able. Chondrasil had welcomed

Jendru home and made him feel wanted, even needed, within the Church. Jendru knew that turning his back on Chondrasil and what he represented would be harder than turning his back on the Church. And far more difficult than rejecting the ways of his true father and mother. If anything could keep him tied to Azara, it was Chondrasil, and Jendru's desire to make him proud and not offend this man who had meant so much to him. Not taking his vows would be like spitting in Chondrasil's face. Jendru feared that it would break both their hearts.

Part of him knew that this inner turmoil was pointless. According to Seyloq, Chondrasil was simply another version of himself, and any concern that Jendru had for Chondrasil's feelings was merely a projection. "Each version of the self is fully responsible for him or herself," Seyloq had told him. "Your responsibility begins and ends right here, in this body, in this life," he had said, tapping on Jendru's chest. "What the self thinks or feels in any other body, in any other life, is not your responsibility or concern. It is only your ego that thinks so. Your responsibility is *here.*"

How that so profoundly contradicted everything Chondrasil had taught Jendru! "Your divine purpose is to selflessly serve all other beings," Chondrasil had instructed him. "To think of yourself, of your desires, is to live in your ego. In transcending your ego, you become a servant of Azara. Your own will is nothing compared to the will of Azara. The highest act is to be a vehicle for the will of Azara. Only through this selfless work can the traps of the material world, of illusion, and of the ego be brought to an end. Only then can we be welcomed home as the beings of light and spirit that we truly are."

For Jendru, Seyloq represented the undoing of everything the Church stood for, everything they believed in. He was the complete antithesis of their practices in a way that the Darsulans could never be. In comparison, the Darsulans were merely a variation on the ego-generated themes of the Azaran religion. Despite their clashes of doctrine, they were trapped in many of the same ego-based delusions. Seyloq had thrown it all off, rejected all of it, for a radical and liberated freedom. "Why in the world would God attend *any* church?" Seyloq had challenged him. "Why would God think that there was *any* spiritual work to be done? God *is,* and *you are that.* Live your life! Be yourself! Everything else is illusion and the pathetic and pathological clinging of the ego. *You are free.* So live in freedom! Only you can hold yourself back. Only you can get in your own way. There is no one and nothing else that exists that you can blame. *This* is the heart of genuine responsibility: recognition that you are God, and that in the end, what you do with your life and how you choose to be is *completely and eternally up to you.* It doesn't matter what anyone else says or thinks. You are the one who has to live your life - no one else. You are your own responsibility. And this is true for *every* version of the self."

"I'm supposed to take on a Maegin-Lu as a formal mentor soon," said Jendru to Jor Alesh, again running his hand through his hair. "All of this is supposed to come off and I'm to take my vows and be reborn in the Church as a holy man. I've been here five years. They're expecting me to declare my intentions with a Maegin-Lu any day now. My friends expect it. Chondrasil expects it."

"Do you?" asked Jor Alesh. She took his hand in hers once more, rubbing her thumb lightly on the back of his hand, feeling his warmth and his turbulent internal energy.

"I did," he said, "but now . . . I'm lost."

"Maybe that's a good thing," she said. "I'm sure it's not easy, but taking vows, becoming celibate and committed for the rest of your life . . . my God, that's a big decision. If you have any doubt at all, I think you owe it to yourself to be clear about what you want. I know that Chondrasil would say that all those lost souls need your commitment, and that all of this is just a temptation - I mean, look! You're actually talking about all this with a *woman,* for God's sake! But think of yourself, Jendru. If anything, that's what Seyloq is trying to teach you. If your heart isn't in it, does it really serve anyone to pretend otherwise? Do you really think that Azara, God, or whoever, would really want that for you? Do you want that for yourself?"

He knew he didn't. What had drawn him to Azara

originally was its promise of truth and authenticity. Though esoteric, it was reality for him. Now, that was no longer the case. And he knew that it never would be again. Regardless of whether he was able to accept everything he was learning from Seyloq, it was fundamentally too late for him. His association with Seyloq had started some process in him, and though he didn't know where it was taking him, it was clear that it was beyond Azara. He didn't know when it had happened, but he had already passed the point of no return. In his heart, he had already left the Church. He just hadn't actually done it yet. Taking his vows would be a lie. It would be a lie that he could no longer participate in.

It was both a frightening and exhilarating realization - like suddenly becoming aware that he had been climbing a formidable mountain, but had been sleepwalking his way up. Now that he knew it, he could see that it was too treacherous to attempt to simply go back down. The only way forward was onward and upward to a summit that he could not yet see. Without even knowing it, he had committed himself to this course, and though his free will and personal choice still remained, the path was inevitable. There would be no turning back.

Jendru gave her hand a light squeeze. "I'm going to have to leave the Church," he said. Her hand returned the friendly squeeze. He could feel her desire in it, but was thankful that she was not pressing herself on him. He knew what he wanted. He knew what she wanted, too. He wasn't ready for that. Not yet. *One step at a time*, he told himself. Before taking that leap, he needed to clear things with the Church, with Chondrasil, with himself. Then, if she still wanted him . . .

"I know," she said, smiling. "For what it's worth, I think you're making the right decision. Admittedly, he's pretty strange, but I think it's clear that Seyloq has more to offer you - really, *you* have more to offer you - forget Seyloq! It's strange, isn't it?" she asked rhetorically. "Seyloq genuinely is who he says he is - God, I mean. But it really doesn't matter. He doesn't want our worship or anything else. He's a mirror. All he really wants is for other versions of himself to accept the same fundamental truth that he's found in himself. And it's just because it's true. It's simple, really. And refreshing. At least, that's what I think."

"And what about you?" asked Jendru, attempting to turn the tables on Jor Alesh. "Are you going to leave your position as Alcian and go sit at the feet of the master to suck the toad medicine from his pipe as you learn his wisdom?"

Jor Alesh laughed. "Oh, I'll go back to him, all right," she said, "and take more of his toad medicine, if I feel like it. I don't see any conflict with being the Alcian," she added. "In fact, I think I can do an even better job at being Alcian than ever before - maybe better than any Alcian before me. As Alcian, my job is to share the truth of what I learn with others and then let them decide what to do. If I understand Seyloq correctly, apprehension of truth is all about personal clarity. What could serve the Alcian better than this? Really, I feel empowered. As Alcian, I've been concerned about this issue with the Darsulans, but now, I feel like I can come at it with a truly fresh perspective - one that sees beyond their doctrinal divisions and disagreements. Admittedly, I've felt some pulls of loyalty to Azara as Alcian of Jurnda, given our intwined history, but not anymore. I feel more objective and dispassionate than ever. I feel like I can look at all of this with truly clear eyes, and for that I am grateful. If anything, all of this is going to help me be myself and fulfill my role even more effectively and genuinely than before. So no, I have no intention of changing my life or walking away from my commitments. Truthfully, whereas I was nervous about this Darsulan business before, now I'm excited - and kind of entertained, too. I know for Chondrasil and the others, all of this is of absolute importance. For me, it's more like some kind of play or drama that I'm able to simultaneously witness and participate in. Really, it's exciting. It's, well, it's *fun*."

"Well, I'm glad *you* think so," commented Jendru.

"I do," she said, "and I think you could too. You're looking at all this very personally, but I think part of what Seyloq is trying to teach you is that you can liberate yourself from that. Make up your own mind and make your choices, but don't take it all personally. If you don't take your vows,

Chondrasil will have his reactions and feelings about that, but so what? Why should it matter to you? Just relax and accept the fact that we're characters in a story that's ultimately larger than either of our limited lives and perspectives and go with it. Have the confidence to be yourself, no matter what comes of what others think. The important thing is to live your life the way you want to, and if you're doing that authentically, with clarity, like Seyloq does, then what comes, comes, and what goes, goes. Really, it's so refreshing. The more I think about it, the more I like Seyloq and his philosophy."

"He wouldn't call it a philosophy," said Jendru. "He'd call it reality."

"Whatever," said Jor Alesh. "I like it, and I like him. And," she added, "I like you. I know it's none of my business, but I'd like to see you happy and fulfilled. And if I could share some of that with you, well, I'd like that too. But it's your life, Jendru, and as your Alcian, all I can do is advise you based on what I know." She gave him a playful wink with that last comment.

Jendru laughed. "As if Seyloq and Chondrasil weren't enough, now I've got the Alcian after me too, eh?"

She smiled. "Lucky you," she said. "And I'm *much* prettier than either of those two old bags!" She was flirting and didn't mind showing it. "And apparently I don't have anything to hide from you, so you can trust me." Suddenly she thought again of his sex and what it would feel like inside her. God, she wanted this man. *Patience,* she told herself.

"It's late," he said, clearly not yet ready to go there. "We should get back. I'm sure our absence has been noted and it would look best if we weren't out all night together."

She rolled her eyes. They had such different perspectives, but she knew she had to respect the fact that as a novice, this was a very different experience for him. As they had discussed, she was feeling ever more confident and empowered in her chosen role as Alcian, and as a young woman with extremely obvious desires. But Jendru was contemplating changing his life completely, and she wanted to respect the fact that he had to do this for himself, if that was what he truly wanted. There was no point in pressuring him.

She wanted him. She wanted him right here and didn't care what Chondrasil or anyone else would think, despite the scandals that would inevitably arise. She could seduce him, she knew. She was a woman, and he was a man, after all, and what was transpiring between them was obvious, though still mostly unspoken. *Let him make up his own mind*, she told herself. For now, she'd have to wait and see how all this was going to play out. It was true. This was fun. All other concerns aside, she was having a good time.

"If you think so," she said playfully.

He looked stern. "I do," he said, turning from her and continuing down the dark path. "Keep up with me," he added. "You don't want to get lost out here."

"Certainly not," she said, hurrying after him, feeling like a little girl on a grand and exciting adventure.

Chapter 18

UNRAVELING

Despite his best attempts to slip in unnoticed, Khalanto was waiting for him in his room when Jendru returned to his pyramid quarters. The younger novice was relaxing on Jendru's bed, reading one of the many books of Azaran doctrine and practice that the novices were expected to study in the evenings when they didn't have other duties to perform, or when there wasn't a ceremony for them to attend. All Azaran ceremonies took place at night. It was a feature of their doctrine and yet another area where Seyloq clashed with his former church. From what Jendru had experienced, not only was Seyloq simply not interested in formal ceremony, he didn't have any regards for auspicious timing as well. Taking medicine seemed something he was willing to do at any time of day or night. Jendru had hoped that there might have been an impromptu ceremony this night, thereby allowing him to slip into his quarters unseen, giving him time to think of what he intended to tell his friends and fellow novices about his day with Seyloq and Jor Alesh, if anything. But those plans were dashed by Khalanto's presence and his obvious inquisitiveness.

"And where have *you* been?" Khalanto asked, an excited energy in his voice. "Pirfiro came looking for you today, you know."

"I was helping out the Alcian," Jendru answered. Then, taking the opportunity to change the subject, asked, "What did Pirfiro want?"

"You haven't heard?" Khalanto responded with a question.

"Heard what?"

"The Darsulans have arrived. They made their way up the Qya and have docked their boats at the riverfront. Chondrasil hasn't invited them into the city yet, though.

When Pirfiro came around looking for you, he said that Chondrasil wanted to make a show of our commitment. He wants to hold an oath-taking ceremony tomorrow when the Darsulans are allowed into the city. He wants them to see how strong we are in our commitment to our doctrine and practices."

Jendru didn't need Khalanto to explain any more. Pirfiro must be scouting out the novices to see who would be ready to take their vows tomorrow.

"So you need to make up your mind about your mentor," Khalanto went on. "Pirfiro said Chondrasil was especially hoping that *you* would be ready to take your vows - you're his favorite, after all. I think he wants to show you off to the Darsulans. You need to choose your Maegin-Lu."

Jendru could feel his heart racing and the sweat bead on his brow. This wasn't how he wanted things to go, and especially didn't want to reveal himself to his talkative friend. He didn't want to deceive him either. As Seyloq had said, this was about commitment to truth, after all, and being oneself, no matter what. Though he could tell Khalanto something convenient and keep the truth to himself, that wasn't really what he wanted.

"I'm excited for you," said Khalanto, oblivious to Jendru's inner turmoil. "But I'll miss having you as a friend, both in ceremony and here in our pyramid. I suppose you'll be moving out soon and getting your acolyte quarters in another pyramid, and then you'll be with them in ceremony, not with us mere novices. But," he said, cheering up a little, "at least my vows are only a couple years away. Maybe I'll choose the same Maegin-Lu as you and we can continue to study and practice together."

Jendru shook his head. "I don't think that will be happening, Khalanto," he said.

"Why not?" His friend looked concerned.

"I can't take my vows," said Jendru after taking a deep breath.

Khalanto stared at him.

"You're joking, right?" He forced a smile.

"No, I'm not." He sat down at the small desk next to his

bed. Khalanto, who had been lounging casually on the bed, sat up and set the study book down to focus fully on Jendru.

To clarify, Khalanto asked, "Do you mean you can't take your vows tomorrow because you haven't chosen a Maegin-Lu yet, or do you mean that you can't take your vows at all?"

"At all."

Khalanto couldn't believe what he was hearing. He stared wide-eyed at the older novice. "You're serious," he said, aghast. "It's Seyloq, isn't it!?" Then, forgetting himself, "Shit, Jendru. This is fucking serious!" he blurted out, then self-consciously covered his mouth as though to keep the swear words from being heard by others down the hall or elsewhere in the pyramid. It was too late, however, and Treland's head poked in the open doorway.

"What's the matter here?" asked Treland, obviously concerned.

"Jendru isn't going to take his vows!"

Treland looked at Jendru in silence, worry covering his face. All Jendru offered was a half-hearted shrug. "Is this true?" he asked. "Why?" Treland came fully into the room and sat down with his two fellow novices.

This wasn't the conversation that Jendru wanted to have at this moment. He looked down at his hands. How could he tell his friends that he no longer believed in Azara and all that they pretended to accomplish here? It was one thing for him to personally stop believing, but these were his friends. His rejection of Azara would likely be interpreted as a rejection of them. Jendru considered that it would be easiest for him to simply ignore his inner turmoil and awakening and continue along the path he had created for himself, living life as a monk, here in a world that he knew with friends who loved and supported him. That would certainly be the path of least effort, but what would that mean for him? How could he live a life that didn't bring him satisfaction and a sense of authenticity? Living a lie, even in comfort and surrounded by supporters and peers, is still a lie.

"I just can't," he said at last, without offering further explanation.

Treland nodded, as though in sympathy. Jendru imagined that the older novice was probably reciting some Azaran proverb in his head about tests of faith and fidelity, about commitment to the doctrine, and the dangers of falling by the wayside.

"It's Seyloq, and that woman, the Alcian," Khalanto volunteered. "Jendru has been corrupted by both of them."

Treland, attempting to avoid sounding judgmental, commented, "Whatever is the case, Jendru, you should speak with Chondrasil. Don't make any rash decisions. In the long history of our religion, surely you are not the first novice to encounter doubts when faced with the finality of taking his vows and truly committing to the process of becoming a monk. Doubt and skepticism can serve to strengthen your faith, if you have the will and determination to persevere. The Maegins claim that questioning the doctrine can be a vital step in learning its inner secrets. This is why it's so important to choose the right Maegin-Lu for yourself - someone who can understand what you're going through and provide you with the necessary guidance, challenges, and reassurance."

"No one here can understand what I'm going through," said Jendru. "Even you two, my good friends, have no idea."

"Try us," said Treland.

Jendru shook his head in defiance. "Go to Seyloq yourselves, if you want," he said. "His methods, his medicine, his entire outlook is radical. I'm not ready to explain it all to you, because I don't yet fully understand it myself. But I can feel the authenticity of what he's sharing with me. It's changing me - or freeing me - maybe that's a better way to put it. All I know is that before I started listening to him, Azara was everything for me. It was clearly *the path*. It was truth. Now . . ."

"So he really has corrupted you," said Khalanto, the usual joking tone of voice completely absent.

"No," said Jendru. "It's not corruption. That's just Azara talking. You don't know, Khalanto. Seyloq says that all of us are God, and that all religion is an illusion, a projection. And he makes sense. But it's not only that. He knows how to show you the truth by helping you to find it in yourself. He's not handing out another competing doctrine. He's showing the way beyond all doctrine and belief altogether. It's radical. Liberating."

"Forgive me, Jendru," said Treland, "but you don't seem liberated to me. You look like you're struggling with doubt and fear. Khalanto may be correct that you have been corrupted. Have you considered that Seyloq really is possessed by a demon? According to our doctrine . . ."

"I know all about our doctrine!" said Jendru dismissively, cutting Treland off. "I no longer believe in demons, so I don't accept that argument."

Khalanto and Treland looked stunned. "How can you not believe in demons?" asked Khalanto, incredulous. "We experience them all the time in ceremony. I know we're only novices, but the Maegin-Lus are there to teach the acolytes how to really work with the demons and reincorporate them back into the light of Azara. This is something that they do *all the time*. How can you say that you don't believe in what they're doing? It's not even about belief! It's *what they do*."

"I know," said Jendru, "but I'm beginning to understand things differently. I think that Seyloq is right when he says that these experiences are all expressions and projections of the ego. He says it's the difference of understanding the self dualistically or nondualistically. The ego's job is to create distinctions between what it chooses to identify as self and other. According to Seyloq, we are all God in physical form, so there really is no 'other,' especially at a 'spiritual' level. He completely rejects the idea of the reality of spirits and non-physical entities. He says that all experiences of these things are just projections of the ego that is refusing to recognize its true nature as God. So in this sense, a 'demon' is part of yourself, a projection of your own fears, judgments, unhappiness - whatever - but it comes from you. It's not 'out there' somewhere. It comes from within. When we find our inner clarity, these things disappear."

"And you've found your inner clarity?" asked Treland, skeptical.

Jendru held out his hands. "I'm finding it," he answered. "I wouldn't say I'm completely clear yet, but I am starting to understand, if that's even the right word. Really, this is beyond understanding. Everything that we would want to 'understand' is a finite expression, and our true nature is infinite. The infinite cannot be understood - it can only be accepted. It's a paradox. It cannot be mentally resolved. Azara has everything categorized, classified, identified, neatly sorted into different kinds of experiences, different practices, different entities . . . it's dualism through and through."

"It's a spiritual science!" countered Treland. "Of course it makes distinctions and provides categories. That is the nature of science, is it not?"

Jendru shook his head in protest. "It's not a science. You can't have a science of projections! The experiences may seem to be real, but they aren't. What's real is the energy underneath it all, and how it is an expression of your relationship to yourself. The way Seyloq explains it is this: your energy, your being, is infinite. However, the ego is constantly trying to cover over this fact, to obscure it from your awareness. The job of the ego is to create a sense of a separate, unique, individual self. So it separates everything it experiences into two basic categories of 'self' and 'not self,' or 'other.' This is an underlying habit of the ego, and it is like an energetic prison that we create for ourselves. When something threatens the imaginary construct of this prison, it is interpreted by the ego as something outside of itself and something potentially dangerous. The ego, ultimately, doesn't *want* to have its illusions shattered because it is continually using these illusions to maintain the fiction of its sense of self.

"Now, when we take the medicines, they generate heightened experiences of energy - this is something I'm sure both of you can agree with. Because of the heightened energy, it's an opportunity for the ego to let go of its limited energetic structures, and the individual can experience his infinite nature. Most aren't prepared to let go that completely, however. Then the medicine becomes an experience of projection and interaction with different energetic divisions within the self. When we do the work of 'reincorporation,' really all that we're doing is releasing different aspects of ourselves into our true infinite nature. But our doctrine, which is a manifestation of our egos, teaches us that all of this is somehow happening outside of ourselves and that we are genuinely accomplishing something spiritual. But it's all a play of the self. There's nothing really going on here - only the self playing with the self, and all along the ego refuses to give up the game, to step outside of the illusion and see it for what it is. Don't you see - everything we're doing here is a game, and ultimately, it's meaningless. None of us are actually accomplishing anything that we think we are. The religion of Azara, for all its power and all its fantastical experiences, is a waste of time. We're not doing anything *real*."

Jendru's friends were stunned. They had never heard anyone speak like this and challenge their doctrine, their religion, so directly.

"So you see nothing of value in what we do here?" asked Treland.

"Any value is merely incidental," said Jendru.

"What do you mean?" asked Khalanto.

"The doctrine and the practices hold people back. They trap us. They provide the ego with high-level structures and projections that are so convincing, you could spend your entire life working with them and never see past them. There's just so much *belief* involved, and there's a response for every person who sees beyond - you're deluded, possessed by a demon, being led astray - the list goes on. The doctrine has built-in answers and excuses for its own limitations, always finding a way to bring us back into dualistic relationship with ourselves, with Azara, with our visions. But the medicine, the communion drink, is *not* the doctrine. The doctrine must be taught, learned, enforced. We're taught that this is all for our spiritual safety. That we should trust in the wisdom of our ancestors. That we should trust in the authenticity of the divine revelations that were received at the founding of the religion. But the doctrine, the practices, the entire structure, just stands in the way. So individuals can get their benefits from taking communion, but the greater their commitment to the doctrine, the more lost and confused they become. It's the exact opposite of enlightenment! Really, it's probably the occasional layperson who benefits most, because they are the least invested in the doctrine. For those of us on the inside, we're trapped. We've become indoctrinated and can't see past the illusions we've created for ourselves."

Jendru knew that this was hard for Treland to hear. The older novice was steeped in doctrine - probably the most devoted of all the novices to learning every possible aspect and nuance of the doctrine - but he was thoughtful and philosophical as well. Jendru could see that he was carefully considering what Jendru was saying and mulling over possible responses - from the doctrine, no doubt - trying to find how the ancient texts might have anticipated such a critique. But Jendru had studied it all as well, and knew that Treland would come up empty. Philosophical debates on the doctrine presumed that the spirit world was real and genuine. Disagreements addressed different interpretations, different spiritual beliefs, and different practices and methods. But this was a case of radical skepticism, dismissing the entire spiritual program as illusory and without any substance. This was beyond what the doctrine was able to respond to. It was anathema. It was heresy. The only real response was to condemn it.

"So you've chosen to become an apostate," said Treland at last, not finding any other response to Jendru's accusations.

"No," said Jendru. "I've chosen to become a student of truth. I will not define myself by the standards of Azara or its doctrines. I'm only an apostate from your perspective. From mine, I'm liberating myself into truth and genuine freedom. That's not apostasy. That's enlightenment."

Treland stood up and shook his head disapprovingly at Jendru. It seemed to Jendru that he was taking all this personally, as he feared he would. He took Jendru's awakening as a personal affront to his own beliefs and his own chosen path in life. "You need to talk to Chondrasil," he said dispassionately, obviously covering over his more intense feelings – just as he'd been trained to do. "I'll pray for you." With that, he left.

"Whoa," said Khalanto when Treland was gone. "This is intense, Jendru." Though committed to Azara, Khalanto had never been the passionate student of doctrine the way that

Treland was, and therefore seemed to be having an easier time with Jendru's insights. His concern was for his friend, not for the doctrine or the religion.

"I know," said Jendru. "I can't help it. I have to stand up for what I'm learning. I'm not trying to offend anyone - especially my friends - but truth is too important to worry about whom you might offend, or even what others will think. Treland might find that he hates me for what I've said here, but I'm not going to let that stop me. It's too late for me. I've seen too much. Experienced too much. I'd be lying to myself if I said I could let it all go and simply return to the folds of the Church. It's like watching a play and listening to everyone insist that the play is real life when I know for a fact that it's a play. How can I be a part of that?"

"So what are you going to do?"

Jendru sighed and sank back in his chair, holding up his hands in front of him. "I don't know," he said. "It's not like I have some plan. This is just what's happening with me right now, and if I've learned anything from Seyloq, it's about being authentic with what I truly think and feel, and acting on that. He calls it 'being yourself.' That's my only plan - being myself. I don't know what that's going to mean. I suppose that Treland is right that the first thing I should do is talk to Chondrasil - get everything out in the open. There's certainly no point in hiding my feelings, and like I said, I can't continue to play along - not with what I've experienced and learned."

"And what have you experienced?"

"That Seyloq is telling the truth. As bizarre and unbelievable as it sounds, he really is God. Not in the sense of some all-powerful, all-knowing being that can create and destroy universes - nothing as dramatic as that. In fact, that's what's so fascinating - that being God really doesn't mean anything different from being a human being. It's just the clarity regarding the true nature of the self, the nondual nature of being. It clears up all the confusion, all the looking outside yourself, all the projection, the fear, the anxiety of being separate and alone. The truth frees you up to be yourself and live your life. There are no magical powers, no great spiritual works to do, no belief to spread among others. There's nothing to worship, nothing to pray to or for. Really, it's not much different from being secular - it's that you know who you are and your enlightenment frees you from your projections, attachments and illusions. It's liberation.

"So I don't know what I'm going to do. Plans are projections of the ego, and I think I'm done with those. I want to face what comes with authenticity and personal responsibility. That means addressing each event, each challenge, as it comes, and being open to whatever presents itself. Maintaining my clarity is my only real goal. So I'll go talk to Chondrasil, see what he has to say, and then make choices according to what's available."

Khalanto nodded. It was clear that he didn't really understand, but his love for his friend made him want the best for Jendru, even if this was all beyond him. "Chondrasil's not going to be happy," he said at last. "You couldn't have picked a better time, what with the Darsulans having arrived and all."

Jendru laughed. "You have no idea," he said. "That's Seyloq's doing too."

"What do you mean?"

"He was the one who invited them. Apparently, there are secret communities of Darsulan practitioners in Jurnda, and through them, Seyloq sent the exiled Darsulans a letter inviting them to come to Azar. Who knows what he was really thinking – just stirring up trouble, I think. As far as he's concerned, these are all ego games. and he doesn't see any point in treating them as anything more than that, so why not make trouble for them?"

Khalanto squished up his face. "He sure doesn't sound like an enlightened master. Where's his sense of respect and compassion?"

"Don't you see?" said Jendru. "He's *not* an 'enlightened master.' He's *God,* and he knows it. He doesn't share any human sense of ethics or propriety, as these are all products of the ego. It isn't that he's a bad man, but he isn't a good man, either. He's simply himself. From his perspective, here are two ultimately deluded religions that are afraid of each other, and neither really knows what it's doing. All he really cares about is truth. Bringing these two traditions together was a whim. For him, being true to himself, which is the most fundamental aspect of living in truth, meant stirring up some trouble and forcing a confrontation, of sorts. He's doing it because he can. I'm sure he hopes that there will be some positive resolution, but in the end, I don't think it *really* matters to him, personally. He certainly doesn't think that either doctrine or tradition is correct - neither is more true. Maybe he thinks that we'll all benefit from this in some way, but I'm sure he's not attached to any particular outcome. That's part of the tricky balancing act of being God in human form - recognizing your desires and choices, but not being attached to outcomes or results. Act without expectation. As long as you're acting on what you truly feel and know, and not your fears, projections and attachments, then you're being true to yourself, and that's all that really matters."

"Well, that doesn't sound like God to me either."

"That's the point, Khalanto. Our ideas of what we think God *should be* or *should act like* simply don't apply. They're merely ideas created by the ego that then becomes attached to those ideas. Don't you see? Seyloq is the most profoundly *unspiritual* man I've ever met, and in being so, he's completely genuine. Here in Azar, we're taught that God, Azara, is the Mother/Father, completely transcendent, the divine source of being and reality, but somehow removed from it. We're taught that God has a plan and a purpose for us, and that we can live in submission to that plan and purpose. God is the ultimate judge, the ultimate power. But if *we are that*, then all of our ideas about God are nonsense. *Our* nature is God's nature. *Our* plans are God's plans. It's simple, really. In reality, there is only one being that exists, and everything we ever experience is a direct manifestation of that being. There is no separation. There are no lost souls. There is no transcendent reality. There's not even an afterlife! It's all right here, right now, and it literally is you and me and everything we experience. *This,*" Jendru said while opening his arms with a grand sweeping gesture, "*is God. This is IT.*"

Khalanto was stunned. "How can there not be an afterlife?" he asked, clinging to this one point.

"Think about it," said Jendru. "Reality is God. You are

God. You have no personal identity beyond your physical body, which is essentially a vehicle for God to enjoy the reality of itself in. In other words, your life didn't come from anywhere or anything, and it's not going anywhere either. God is manifested in *physical* form. So right here, right now, *you*, the *real you*, not the ego that you think you are, is every living being and everything else that exists. When your personal body dies, life, reality, everything, still goes on. Life exists right here, right now, with or without your physical body. There is no 'personal' remainder. No body, no perspective, no vehicle with which to enjoy reality. The 'spirit world' simply does not exist. It's a projection of egos that are failing to recognize their true nature. It's all a product of the mind and ego. It has zero reality, other than as an experienced projection."

"But if I'm God, and I want to create an afterlife for myself, what's to prevent me from doing that?"

Jendru thought a moment, then said, "I think it's because you don't truly want an 'afterlife.' It would be completely purposeless and unnecessary. You already *are* reality. You've already evolved yourself into billions of life forms and a grand, unfathomable universe. You already are everything. The whole idea of preserving individual perspectives or identities would be a lie and self-deception of the highest order. It would be playing favorites, denying what you are by nature. God, at the most fundamental level, is truth, and only concerns itself with truth. And the truth is, reality, as we experience it right here, right now, is what is. Everything else is an illusion of the ego and its attachments and projections. By that logic, it is *only* your ego that *wants* there to be an afterlife. But when you accept that you are God, you immediately see what an absurd idea that is. An afterlife only has meaning from your personal, embodied perspective. From the God perspective, it's frivolous and unnecessary. You are all life. What does it matter to you, as God, whether this personal perspective that identifies itself as 'Khalanto' wants there to be an afterlife? It's like actors in a play demanding that their characters continue to exist after the play is over. The play itself is the thing, and outside of that, the characters have no existence or identity. That's reality. It doesn't matter if that's what they *want* or not. Reality is what it is."

Khalanto smiled meekly. "I'm not the philosopher that you are, Jendru," he said. "I suppose none of us really are - that's why you've always been Chondrasil's favorite. I think he's hoped that you'd be High Maegin someday. It takes a strong will and a sharp mind to be High Maegin, and you've got that in spades. Talk to him, Jendru. These are all just ideas for me, and I don't know how to respond. Chondrasil is learned, and he may have some good answers for you that neither you nor Seyloq have thought of. Talk to him."

"I will," Jendru reassured him, "but don't expect that it will change my mind. Seyloq and Chondrasil are contemporaries, you know. They both went through their training together. I doubt he knows anything that Seyloq hasn't already considered. Remember, he might not have been High Maegin, but he was a Maegin-Lu. He knows all this stuff inside and out, and when push comes to shove, I'd have to say that he's right. And besides, it's not about a philosophical argument. Seyloq would be the last person to say that he's promoting a philosophy. From what I've experienced, I'd have to agree. This is more a description of reality than anything else. It's not metaphysics. It's how things are. And I've seen and experienced it myself. I'm still coming to understand it intellectually, but that's secondary. When you've experienced yourself as God, you know it's true."

"So now you're God too, huh?" asked Khalanto, not believing.

"Yes, I am. And so are you. I'm not claiming anything special for myself; other than the fact that I've *experienced* this directly and, as a result, know it to be true. When you go beyond the ego, the workings of the ego and its projections and attachments become obvious. There's no genuine going back from that level of personal awareness, unless you choose to lie to yourself and willfully deceive yourself. I'm beyond that now. I don't *believe* Seyloq or his teachings. I accept them because I know that I *am that*. As a mirror, Seyloq is unparalleled, and in that respect, he is quite special. But he's also nothing special. He's another version of the universal self, as are you, as am I. We are all God. I'm learning to accept that reality and take responsibility for myself as a version of God, just as Seyloq has for himself."

"If you say so," said Khalanto, almost patronizingly. "I'm sorry I ever prodded you into talking to Seyloq. I shouldn't have done it. Now you're going to leave, I'm going to lose my best friend, and it's all my fault."

Jendru smiled sympathetically and reached out to his friend, placing his hand on his shoulder. "No one is at fault, Khalanto. I take responsibility for my choices and actions. Yes, you served as a catalyst, but that's how the self works - we inspire and guide each other in ways we can't even imagine. It's all one big self, inviting us to discover the truth of who and what we are. You've played an important part in my journey of self-discovery, as has everyone and everything here in Azar. I'm grateful and appreciative for all of it. But my primary commitment is to truth. That's what brought me to Azar in the first place. And that's what caught my attention when you first taunted me to go talk to Seyloq. You have served me. From our personal, ego-based perspectives, it seems sad, as this is definitely going to threaten our friendship, because I know where your commitment lies and it's different from mine. And that saddens me the same as it saddens you. But my commitment to truth is more important to me than any relationship, so I'm not going to back down or compromise. Know that I don't *blame* you, and I urge you not to do the same. Though you might experience this as a loss, if you truly love me as a friend, and ultimately as a version of yourself, then you can be happy for me - or not! Really, it doesn't matter. I know what I'd prefer, but it's up to you. You are God and therefore are your own master. You are your own responsibility, as am I."

Khalanto shook his head as he stood up from the bed, making it clear that he was ready to take his leave. "Promise me that you'll talk to Chondrasil before you make any rash decisions," he said.

Jendru stood to face him. "The only promises I make

are to myself, Khalanto. But I will go see Chondrasil."

With that, Khalanto exited Jendru's room, leaving him to himself and his thoughts of what he intended to say to the High Maegin come the new day.

Chapter 19

THE DARSULANS

The temple city of Azar was abuzz with activity even before the sun rose that morning. Jor Alesh awoke to the sounds of voices calling out to each other in the fresh morning air. There was a light rain, but the air was warm. Having slept naked, she pulled on a light robe and stepped out onto her private balcony. Monks and laypersons alike were bustling about, many dressed in their finest robes and ceremonial attire. She watched for a few moments, wondering what was happening. Then, when Pirfiro, looking extra large in his bulging outfit, shuffled past below her, she called out to him.

"Haven't you heard?" he asked, disbelieving. "The Darsulans arrived late yesterday. We'll be having an oath-taking ceremony for novices this afternoon when they are invited into the city, and there is much to prepare before then. I'm sorry. I'd love to stay and chat with you, but I have many duties and must be about my business. Until later!" he said with a smile and a polite bow. She gave a little bow in return and wandered back into her apartment.

Immediately her thoughts turned to Jendru. What would he choose? She knew what *she* wanted. Last night, as she had lain there in bed, thinking over all that had transpired, she had fantasized about Jendru renouncing his religion and coming with her to Jurnda. If he wanted, she could take him on as an advisor - he certainly would be valuable in that role. Or maybe he would go the way of his parents and become an artist. Really, it didn't matter. Either way, the fantasy was that he would share her bed, and they would freely express their love for each other. If there was one thing she was not in doubt about, it was this - they wanted each other. The energy between them was obvious, and no amount of pretending to be a monk could cover it over. They wanted to be together.

When she really felt into it, it seemed to her that it was not a question of if, only when. She was hopeful that this unexpected oath-taking ceremony might serendipitously work in her — *their* — favor.

But that was Jendru's decision to make, not hers. She knew and accepted that. *No attachments*, she told herself. She knew that this is what Seyloq would counsel. He'd make a great advisor too, though she doubted he wanted such a position. After leaving Azar, he could have done anything he wanted. He had gone to Jurnda. But for his own reasons, he chose to live in the mountains, away from everyone. It was a curious choice. If he had wanted to directly influence Jurndan society, he would have done so already. Now, late in life, he was looking - perhaps he'd been looking all along. He'd been patiently waiting for the right student or students. His teachings were radical and probably many who visited him didn't fully understand. How many had come to him over the years, and how successful had he been in helping others embrace their true nature? True, the medicine he worked with was powerful, but it was also clear to her that personal will was ultimately the deciding factor. Even the toad medicine couldn't convince someone who was unwilling - this much seemed obvious to her. It was magical, but it wasn't magic. There were no unseen forces at work here - only the self, only the commitment to truth.

He's been waiting for us, she concluded. It wasn't meant as a self-congratulatory realization, though it did give her a thrill of personal pleasure. It wasn't as though Seyloq had been waiting for her and Jendru *personally*. He had been waiting, watching, sharing what he could, and all the while, looking for those who would truly understand. He wasn't a Maegin or Maegin-Lu, and he certainly wasn't bothering with creating some new religion in his name or image. No. He was simply waiting for new versions of the self who were ready to embrace their infinite nature as God. And Jor Alesh was convinced that he had found two such versions of the self in Jendru and herself. When she let her ego get hold of the thought, it admittedly sounded grandiose. Yet in her heart, it felt true.

What she had learned from Seyloq in only one day was

the most profound event of her life. She had no doubts that he was simply sharing the truth. She had experienced it for herself. And she, like Seyloq, wanted to share it. It was time to set the truth free, and she would be a vehicle for it, as would Jendru, if he chose.

The first crucial choice for Jendru would happen today. Had Chondrasil been planning this oath-taking all along, or was it a sudden inspiration? Given that no one had mentioned it, she suspected it was an impulse. She laughed. If Jendru chose as she believed he would, as she desired him to choose, then Chondrasil would be serving the greater purpose without even realizing it. From his perspective, it would be the tragic loss of a promising and gifted student. From her perspective, it would open the possibility of her being with Jendru. From Seyloq's perspective, it would be an act of personal responsibility and exercise of will on Jendru's part. From God's perspective, if there even were such a thing, it would be one more dramatic moment in the ongoing play of reality, and one that might serve the spreading of genuine truth in this world. Thinking across levels in this way was exhilarating for Jor Alesh. She was giddy with excitement. Somehow, quite unexpectedly, she found herself in the very center of what was, in essence, a cosmic drama. And at the same time, it was intimately personal.

Hurriedly she took a quick shower and donned her clothes. Things were happening and she wanted to get out into the thick of it. It would be Chondrasil's show today, but that wasn't going to prevent her from doing her job as Alcian, or from being herself as Jor Alesh Melva. Indeed, it was an exciting day to be alive.

Moving through the temple city of Azar, everything struck Jor Alesh as over-the-top. It wasn't only the elaborate attire of its citizens, or the abundance of decorations they were setting about the city, but it was also the city itself. True, it was beautiful in its fractal layout and design, and the impressive sights of the towering pyramids. Really, the city was a testament to human tenacity, if nothing else. Out of the ruins of the *Great War*, humans had crossed over land and sea to found this sanctuary, and here built some of the most impressive examples of architecture ever conceived. It was brilliant, triumphant even. Yet it also seemed extravagant and unnecessary. It was an entire edifice built on top of nothing. Yes, there was the Azara communion drink, but so what? The real power of truth was that it didn't need anything to prop it up, like these towering pyramids. They were beautiful and attractive, but they all served an imaginary purpose, and therefore seemed hollow and empty. Extravagance built on extravagance, all for nothing. How much time and energy, how many lives dedicated to this grand illusion? It was almost as though the greater the illusion, the more required to maintain it.

Even the expulsion of the Darsulans two hundred years ago had been to maintain the illusion. Heaven forbid there be dissenting doctrine present in this perfect edifice of illusion! The very architecture was the doctrine itself - a pyramidal hierarchy, concentrating power and authority at the very top and center. The layout of the city was the same: in the center, the grand Obsidian Temple, to which all the streets and walkways flowed in their inevitable fractal pattern, with smaller pyramids receding into the outskirts. Everything focused inward and to the top and center. And there, in ceremony, stood the High Maegin, grand orchestrator of the illusion, maintaining the flow of the energetic current, insuring that everyone who participated was properly instructed in the doctrine and the prevailing belief system. It was almost too perfect, too obvious. No wonder Seyloq chose to live on the outskirts of this illusion. What better vantage from which to poke holes in its facade? Being the mirror that he was, he had positioned himself to let some light into the perfectly ordered universe of Azara and catch the willing fragments as they fell out into the beyond. How perfect! Whereas the Church was all about reintegration, Seyloq was about disintegration. They were complimentary mirror images. It really was *all* a game.

And she was excited to be a player.

The site where the Darsulans were encamped was well outside the temple city proper. The river Qya was impassible by large boat beyond this point, leaving Azar isolated in the valley between the two volcanic mountain ranges of Ladjup and Nadrasuli. Here at the docks and waterfront, laypersons regulated the flow of people and supplies into and out of Azar. It was a small community in its own right, but was still considered part of greater Azar. One would have to travel a good way downriver before encountering the first outskirts of Jurnda.

That the docks and waterfront were a meeting place was obvious by the mix of architecture, which wasn't nearly as uniform as in Azar, and by the people. Jor Alesh could see that there were Jurndans here, local laypersons, and perhaps even some of the people Seyloq had called the "forest people," whom he described as not really laypersons proper, though they shared in some of the religion of Azara. And there were also the Darsulans. A small tent community had been erected directly on the docks next to their boats. They were dressed somewhat similarly to the Azarans, but without the shaved heads and tattoos. From what she could see, discounting the occasional bald man among them, they all had full heads of hair and no visible tattoos on their scalps. Their clothing had similar colorful geometric designs, which Jor Alesh recognized as coming directly from the experience with the medicine. Yet even here there were some subtle differences, which she attributed to their incorporating mushrooms and cacti into their practices. She was curious about these and wondered if she'd have a chance to experience them, though intuition told her that they would likely seem mild in comparison to Seyloq's toad medicine - could anything truly compare? As intense and powerful as the Azara drink was, it wasn't anything like Seyloq's medicine. True, Azara had a stronger and more intense visual quality to it that was very beautiful and quite sophisticated, but having worked with Seyloq, these visual aspects seemed almost a distraction - more an artifact of the experience than anything essential to it. Doctrinally, she suspected that the Azarans would disagree - it was the visual quality that provided them with their valued visions, after all. But if the visions were essentially illusions, then so what? Beautiful, complex, sophisticated, and potentially meaningless, or worse, objects of attachment and ego grasping.

From what she could see, the Darsulan entourage was a

mix of ages and sexes. Neither men nor women appeared to dominate the group, and there were even several adolescents. No one appeared to be too old or infirm. She supposed that their elders had elected to stay behind due to the rigors of the journey. Where had they come from, she wondered, supposing that answers to such questions would most likely reveal themselves over the coming days. It crossed her mind that maybe they wanted to keep their place of origin a secret, at least from the Azarans. Someone was in contact with them and knew how to find them. Lur wasn't *that* big of an island continent, but it was big enough for these different communities to live in virtually complete isolation from one another. And now, here they were, with representatives from all the various factions. A new day was dawning for life on Lur, but what the new day would bring was anyone's guess.

Looking at the crowd of Darsulans, Jor Alesh didn't see anyone that struck her as being in charge. Unlike the Azarans, they didn't seem to distinguish various levels of authority by dress and decoration. Instead, they all looked similar. Walking into their camp, she was greeted by a young couple, male and female, who introduced themselves as Yoral and Desha Vot, an indication that things were different among this breakaway group. Jor Alesh explained to them who she was and they eagerly took her deeper into the camp to meet the woman they described as "The Mother." She was a plump older woman with peppered hair and a cane, seated among a collection of other women, mostly younger than herself. She watched Jor Alesh approach from a distance, and when she was close, said, "Forgive me for not getting up. As you can see, I'm a bit old and prefer to sit, but please, come and join me and introduce yourself."

Her accent sounded a little strange to Jor Alesh, as was the case with the rest of the Darsulans. In their time apart, they had developed different inflections and cadences to their speech, making them sound slightly foreign, though still mutually intelligible. The other women surrounding the Mother stood up and bowed politely to Jor Alesh, excusing themselves so that the two might have a private audience. Yoral excused himself as well, and the older woman instructed

Desha to bring Jor Alesh something to eat and drink, saying that they would share some of the unique foods from their part of Lur that were probably unknown here in Azar. Jor Alesh took a seat, thanking the older woman and happily received some bright pink fruit from Desha along with a cup of green tea. She got the impression that she was participating in something of a ritual greeting, or at least, a common custom among these people. Food first - introductions second. It was hospitable. She wondered what they thought of the Azarans keeping them here at the docks, not yet having welcomed them into the city proper, let alone offering them food.

"Thank you for the food and drink," said Jor Alesh after getting down a bite of the tasty pink fruit and having a sip of tea, following the older woman's lead, who had received the same from Desha.

"You are welcome," she said. "Now, tell me who you are. You don't look like an Azaran. Are you from Jurnda?"

Jor Alesh nodded. "My name is Jor Alesh Melva," she said, "ascended Alcian of Jurnda."

"Ah," said the old woman, smiling and clapping her hands together. "I've heard of you. What a great pleasure to meet you here at this momentous time. My name is Meridalthi Vitri, Mother of the Reformed Azaran tradition. You may call me Meri, if you like."

Jor Alesh was momentarily taken aback. "Reformed Azaran tradition?" she asked.

The older woman smiled. "Yes," she said. "That is what we call ourselves. It is my understanding that here we are known as 'Darsulans,' which, I suppose, is reasonable. Our order was founded by Darsul Omdidran many generations ago, and our community is also known as Darsul. However, we consider ourselves to be followers of Azara. Many of our practices are different, and our doctrine is reformed, but we are still Azarans."

"But you don't use the title of Maegin?" Jor Alesh asked.

"Oh yes," answered Meridalthi, "we do. I am High Maegin, along with my husband, Regolvan. Together, we are known as the Mother and Father, just as Azara is the Mother/Father."

"Is your husband here?" asked Jor Alesh, glancing about.

"No. He has stayed in Darsul for this visit. We thought it best that one come here and the other stay. I know that I do not look to be in the best shape myself, but my husband is yet older and more frail than I, so he chose to remain behind, though he did want to come."

"Did you travel far to get here?"

Meridalthi closed her eyes and nodded, as though reviewing their journey in her mind. "Yes, especially for an old woman like myself. For a young thing like you - no problem. Lur is not that big, after all. But for me, yes, I feel like I've traveled a world away, especially after seeing your city of Jurnda. Of course I had heard of it - the big buildings, the countless people, but we live very differently in Darsul and there are not so many of us. We like our life, but as you can see, many of our young people were eager to come on this trip and see the world for themselves, and they are all in awe of your beautiful city. Perhaps we can spend some time there before returning to our home."

"You would, of course, be welcome," said Jor Alesh. "I can arrange lodging and anything else you might need there. It would be our pleasure."

"And what would they think?" asked Meridalthi, her head nodding toward Azar.

Jor Alesh smiled. "I don't speak for the Azarans."

"No, I don't suppose you do. We all live in different worlds, don't we?" Not really expecting an answer, the old woman had another bite of fruit and a sip of tea, which Jor Alesh mirrored. Meridalthi watched her closely and then commented, "You're Alcian of Jurnda, but you've taken communion. You have the look about you."

"What look is that?" asked Jor Alesh.

"The look of someone who's seen, someone who knows. I may be an old woman, but I know what I see when I see it. You're something special, aren't you?"

Jor Alesh smiled. "I suppose you could say that." She was used to compliments and the admiration of others. Ever since she could remember, people had told her that she was special and gifted. This was a bit different, however. She wondered what the old woman saw in particular.

Seeing that Jor Alesh was pondering her comment, Meridalthi added, "It's your energy, dear. Very clear. Very strong. I usually only see this in people who have spent years working with the medicines. There's a relaxed confidence about you. I like it. But you're not an Azaran, you say?"

"No, I'm not. I've had communion a few times," she said. "And yesterday I did some work with a man who uses a different medicine, so yes, I have some experience there, but probably not as much as you think."

"Well, if that's true, then you truly are exceptional." She took another bite of fruit and sip of tea. "So, what can I do for you, Jor Alesh Melva, ascended Alcian of Jurnda? Did you come merely to chat with an old woman, or are you here on official business?"

"Both, really," said Jor Alesh. "Do you know much about the role of Alcian?" she asked. As Meridalthi didn't, she took a few moments to explain how she served Jurnda as an advisor and counselor. Though she had no direct authority here in Azar, part of her job was to maintain good and respectful relations with the Azarans and thus was invested in the outcome of this visit.

Meridalthi gave her a scrutinizing look. "You can't fool me, dear," she said, almost playfully. "There's more to you than that. Like I said, I know what I see, and you have the look. But that's fine - keep your secrets. There's no reason you should tell me everything at our first meeting. So tell me, what can I do for you?"

"I'd like to ask you a few things."

"Go ahead."

"I presume you are aware that there are underground groups in Jurnda practicing your traditions?"

The old woman nodded. "Yes," she said. "They're relatively new, if that's what you're wondering. We lived in complete isolation in Darsul for several generations until we were sought out by some of your citizens. They were young people who were interested in working with the medicines but were not drawn to the rigors and strict rules of practice here in

Azar. I suppose they thought of it as something of a quest. Regolvan and I had recently become the Mother and Father - oh, that was so many years ago! We were younger and fresher then! Ah, age gets us all, in the end. But they were nice young people and we welcomed them into our community. They were so excited and eager to learn. We taught them some of our ways, and gave them some of our medicine. Eventually, they left and returned to Jurnda. We get occasional visits from them, and others they have shared with. They've told us how they practice secretly in Jurnda, not wanting to cause trouble with the Azarans.

"Our reformed tradition is much more open and flexible than the conservative Azarans," she continued. "For us, the medicine is as much for personal healing and spiritual growth as it is for the work of reincorporation and the other noble ideals of our tradition. We don't require chastity and monasticism, for one, and while we have Maegins, our process is very different. The divide between the Maegins and the lay practitioners isn't as great. We believe that through the medicines a person can come to know him or herself, and that this is valuable. It does not require a person to commit to being a monk or a nun, or doing the work of reincorporation. From what I understand, this is the appeal for the followers in Jurnda. It's private, intimate, and not really involved with the higher calling of Azara. As we see it, every person can use the medicines to establish their own personal relationship with Azara, and for that, no doctrine is needed - just experience, practice, and a willingness to face the complexities of existence with an open heart."

"I can see how this would be appealing to Jurndans," said Jor Alesh. "For many of us, the Azaran religion seems complex, esoteric, and in some ways, foreign. As Alcian, my main concern is this tendency to practice in secret. We pride ourselves on having an open and free society, and this strikes me as the antithesis of that. That anyone feels they can't be open and transparent in their chosen activities or beliefs tells me that there are individuals who don't feel welcome or integrated into our society. That bothers me. It is my job to represent everyone impartially and equally, but I can't do that with secret underground groups. It undermines my ability to serve, and creates unspoken divisions within our society. I would much prefer things to be otherwise."

Meridalthi shrugged, indicating she thought the matter was out of her hands. "They're afraid of the conservative Azarans," she said flatly. "They don't want to be branded as heretics and infidels. They don't want to be social outcasts, as happened to us two hundred years ago. They like their lives in Jurnda. It's not so much religion that they want as a personal connection to the sacred that the medicines provide. They've found an answer in our traditions, but they are not of our tradition. They are Jurndan, first and foremost. And that is fine with us. We are happy to share our knowledge. We have no monopoly on the medicines. God created them for everyone, however one chooses to use them. The spiritual work still remains, but it is not exclusive. Each person must find his or her own path, and if the medicines can help, they should be available, along with the knowledge of how to use them. This is how we see things. We don't want to control things in the way these conservative Azarans do. But perhaps they are ready to change their ways and open their traditions as we have. They did invite us here for some reason, after all."

Jor Alesh sucked in her breath, recalling what Seyloq had told her of the invitation he had sent via the underground groups in Jurnda. "I wouldn't get my hopes up too high," she cautioned.

"You know something about Maegin-Lu Seyloq Surya that I do not?" inquired the old woman.

"The invitation you received," said Jor Alesh, "wasn't an official invitation from the Azarans. The man who sent it to you is a former Maegin-Lu, but he is no longer a member of the Church. In fact, he's viewed as something of a radical and heretic by the Church authorities. Understand that they don't know he's the one who sent you the invitation. They think you are coming on your own impetus. They won't be happy when they learn the truth. At any rate, I don't think you can expect them to be too open and welcoming. They probably hope that you're here to pledge your allegiance to their doctrine and admit the errors of your ways."

"Hmm . . . well, this is more interesting than I had thought. This Seyloq sounds like a curious fellow. Do you know him?"

"Yes, we met yesterday."

"And what do you think of him?"

Jor Alesh smiled. "He's unique, that's for sure. It's not much of a wonder why the Azarans don't like him. His views and practices are radical, probably even by your standards."

"So why do you think he invited us? Why the deception?"

"In his own way, I think it is his attempt to undermine the divide between your religions. He knows about the Darsulan groups in Jurnda, and I think he'd like everything to be brought to the surface. He says his greatest commitment is to truth, and I think he sees this as an issue that requires addressing. Not having any real authority or influence, he's doing what he can to bring the situation to a head. Given his disagreements with the Azarans, he'd probably enjoy seeing a doctrinal face-off as well, though to warn you, he doesn't think much of doctrine in general, so don't expect much sympathy there. And for what it's worth, he claims that he wrote the letter when he was still a Maegin-Lu, before he left the Church."

"And you trust his judgment?"

Jor Alesh nodded. "Like I said, he's unique. I've never met anyone like him. His insights . . . well, if you get a chance to meet him, I'm sure you'll see."

"I'm intrigued."

Jor Alesh considered whether she ought to tell Meridalthi more. "Are you familiar with a medicine that comes from the venom of toads?" she asked.

The old woman shook her head. "I've never heard of such a thing. We have several medicines that we use in our tradition, but not this toad medicine. Why do you ask?"

"Just curious," said Jor Alesh. "It's something new around here, and I wondered if it had reached you in Darsul. I guess not."

At that, the young couple, Yoral and Desha, reappeared. "They've come to tell us we can enter their city now. As soon as you're ready . . ."

Meridalthi clapped her hands and rubbed them together vigorously. "Well then, let's get started. You'll have to excuse me, Ms. Melva," she said to Jor Alesh. "It takes me a while to get going. There are many steps between here and there, and my children will have to carry me part of the way. I'm sure I'll see you in Azar, so until then." And then to Yoral, "Please tell whoever has come that we will begin to make our way into the city, but that it will take some time. And thank them, as well." The young man nodded and trotted off as Desha came over to help the old woman up from her seat.

"It's been a pleasure," said Jor Alesh, "and I look forward to spending more time with you in the coming days."

"As do I, dear."

Jor Alesh excused herself and quickly made her way back to Azar through the gathering crowds of people. From the look of things, the Darsulans were exotic specimens and everyone wanted to catch a glimpse. The route from the waterfront into the city was lined with onlookers. *Wait until they see who's leading these Reformed Azarans.* It was going to be an interesting day.

Chapter 20

APOSTASY

Jendru hadn't slept well. For most of the night, he had felt like he was on the medicine, with colorful fractals and multidimensional images continually transforming and flowing behind his closed eyes. Internally, he kept hearing himself saying, "I AM TRUTH, FOR I AM REALITY!" in that thundering, deep voice that sounded so much like Seyloq when he was speaking "as himself." *We really are the same being,* he mused. Whatever sense of separation and isolation Jendru had felt as "Jendru" was being dissolved. He could feel his energy opening up within himself, reformatting his body and being. It was like circuits that he never even realized had been crimped or shut off were straightening out and turning on, bringing him a completely new sense of himself. He could feel it at every level. It was empowering and profound. It didn't make for much sleep.

He arose early in the morning as the sun was rising, knowing that Chondrasil would no doubt already be up and making preparations for later that day, and his impromptu oath-taking ceremony. He knew what he had to do. He had to tell Chondrasil the truth, no matter how the High Maegin might take it. Attempting to sleep on the issue didn't change Jendru's mind at all. If anything, the night had left him even more resolved to do something about his situation *right now*. His patience for maintaining the charade of being a devoted novice had run out. He knew the truth in his heart: he was going to leave the Azaran religion. It was too late for him and there was no going back. The only way forward was to step fully into the truth he had discovered within himself and take complete responsibility for that. To stay would be to live a lie, and Jendru couldn't stomach the thought.

He felt the nervous, giddy energy of his impending

confrontation with Chondrasil pumping through him. Getting out of bed, he found his hands shaking. Taking a shower, he had to hold himself up as the fullness of his decision washed over him. He was going to refuse to take his vows. He was going to leave. And do what? That, he didn't know. *One step at a time, one decision at a time.* He'd figure the rest out later. For now, he had to make his truth known. He had to speak with Chondrasil and would deal with the repercussions as they came. Underneath it all, he felt liberation calling. He wanted to laugh and cry. It occurred to him that what he was experiencing might be similar to going mad, but he didn't care. If this was madness, then so be it. He had to follow his heart. The choice was his, and he knew what he had already chosen.

Chondrasil was busy with preparations and was not in his office when Jendru arrived to meet with him. An underling invited Jendru to wait and said that he'd find the High Maegin and let him know that he was needed. The nervous anticipation that had built up within Jendru in climbing up to the High Maegin's office (and had successfully been repressed with his gathered courage) spilled over now and caused him to vibrate in his chair. Once more, it was like he was on the medicine. He tried to stop it, but that only made him feel nauseous. Instead, he let his body relax and allowed the waves of energy to pass through him. Without even thinking about it, he found that his body was moving in undulating waves, causing his arms and hands to move about in fluid, symmetrical movements. "Yes!" he felt himself saying internally. "Just allow." Going fully into the energy, he moved to the floor of Chondrasil's office and began moving much as he had seen Seyloq moving when he had gone to him the other day to talk. He rolled up and down along his spine, his legs pushing up into the air, his arms waving about him, always fluid, always symmetrical. He felt like an energetic dynamo, a self-transforming jewel. Everything was so geometrical. He felt balanced. Empowered. Centered. Open.

Jendru was poised delicately on a point on his spine with his legs straight up in the air and his arms held out to his sides with his fingers spread open when Chondrasil entered his office. The High Maegin stopped abruptly, seeing a novice in his office in such a strange and unusual position. Jendru was suddenly self-conscious and quickly rolled down from his upright stance and hurriedly got to his feet in order to give the High Maegin the required bow of respect. "High Maegin Chondrasil," he said, finishing his bow, but not overlooking the fact that his voice sounded unusually deep and not very much like "Jendru." He also noticed what felt distinctly like an energetic barrier between himself and the High Maegin. It was difficult for Jendru to define or specifically identify, but it seemed clear to him that the High Maegin was "closed," whatever that meant.

"Jendru," said Chondrasil warmly. "You've taken up a new exercise routine?"

"Uh, yes," said Jendru, sounding more like himself now. "Since I was waiting . . ." he said, excusing his use of the High Maegin's office.

"I see . . . A bit unorthodox." He gave Jendru a scrutinizing look, standing there in the doorway for a moment before coming fully inside and taking a seat at his desk. He invited Jendru to come and sit as well. "But tell me, what can I do for you? I understand that Pirfiro wasn't able to find you yesterday. I hope you've been informed - we're going to have an oath-taking ceremony. I very much hoped that you would be ready to take your vows and choose a Maegin-Lu. It's a big day, Jendru. The Darsulans are here, and I'd like them to see how vibrant our tradition is, and our collective commitment to the doctrine. From what I hear, they're something of a rag-tag bunch; men, women, and children, and I'd like them to see the power of our structured hierarchy. I think it would do them good.

"However, back to you, young novice," said Chondrasil, bringing his enthusiastic attention directly to Jendru. "I've heard rumors that you are interested in perhaps Mordoq or Tilvash as your Maegin-Lu. If you are willing, the time to decide has come. Everything is ready for the oath-taking. I just need your decision."

"That's what I've come to talk to you about," said

Jendru.

Chondrasil could tell immediately that there was something wrong. "You don't feel ready? I can't pressure you, Jendru, but from my perspective, there is no longer any need for you to remain a novice. A great future awaits you within the Church. As far as I'm concerned, you are fully ready. Really, I think you've been ready for some time. I don't say this to many novices, Jendru, but you truly are exceptional. Your potential is far beyond anyone else in your class. Personally, I'm eager for you to take your vows and begin ascending within the Church. Who knows how high your star might rise - even High Maegin, someday."

Jendru had known that this would be difficult, but Chondrasil wasn't making it any easier.

"In many ways," Jendru began his response, "you've been like a surrogate father to me." Chondrasil nodded in agreement and smiled. "I want you to know how much that has meant to me. I love my parents, but found that my life lay upon a different path than theirs. They never really understood my decision to come to Azar."

"This I know," said Chondrasil. "When you came here, you were a diamond in the rough, so I took you in. I gave you the guidance and instruction that your parents were not able to provide, and you've grown tremendously. When you first came here, you knew nothing. Now, it's your time to shine."

"Thank you for your praise," said Jendru.

"So what is the problem, for I sense that there is one," said Chondrasil sympathetically. "Have you become displeased with Mordoq or Tilvash? Are you having doubts about finding a proper Maegin-Lu with whom to take your vows?"

Jendru shook his head. "It's not that," he said quietly. He took in a deep breath and looked Chondrasil squarely in the eyes. "To put it bluntly, I've lost my faith. I no longer believe in Azara and the doctrine."

Chondrasil's eyes grew wide and then narrowed. "It's Seyloq Surya, isn't it?" he asked, not really needing an answer. "That's where you were yesterday. With that woman, too, no doubt."

"Yes," said Jendru. "I've been to see Seyloq several times, and his views have affected me."

"He's an apostate and an infidel," said Chondrasil coldly. "As you are only a novice, it has not been within my authority to keep you from seeing that man, but you have made a serious error. This is precisely why we require a five-year novitiate before taking your vows: so that you can be certain in your dedication and show your ability to resist temptation. I cannot begin to tell you how disappointed I am to hear this news, Jendru."

Even now, Jendru could see that Chondrasil was holding himself back, his jaw subtly clenching and tensing. "You've taken his 'medicine,' I presume," he said dispassionately.

"Yes."

Chondrasil let out a sigh meant to communicate his profound sorrow and disappointment. "It is the 'medicine' of a demon, Jendru. He is a demon in human form, sent to test you and lead you astray."

"I don't believe that," said Jendru in his defense.

"Then your beliefs are in error! I'm not as naive as you perhaps think, novice," he said, distancing himself from Jendru. "I knew Seyloq Surya. I was there when he left. I even agreed to take his medicine, out of love for my former friend and a desire to bring him back into the fold. And I can tell you; it is the work of a demon. There is no hope for Seyloq Surya. As he himself will tell you, he's no longer the 'Seyloq' I once knew. That Seyloq is long dead. In his place stands a sweet-talking demon who takes every opportunity to spit upon our holy doctrine and lead impressionable young novices like yourself astray. Though I do not know of your specific interactions with this demon, I can assure you that he is manipulating you for his own ends: nothing more. However you may think that he's helping you, you're wrong. Follow him, and in the eyes of Azara, you will be damned. Is that what you want for yourself, Jendru? Is that the great future you see reflected in his eyes? If not, then look again, because that's all I see."

For a moment, Jendru was shocked and doubt seeped into him. Chondrasil was correct in proclaiming that Jendru assumed him to be naive. He had never considered that Chondrasil himself had tried the toad medicine. The fact that he had, and still rejected Seyloq, was a profound revelation. How could anyone fail to see the truth, he wondered. The medicine was so powerful, he assumed that it must have the same effect on everyone. But apparently this was not the case. He recalled how Seyloq had said that the medicine would never violate someone's free will - that it was always up to the individual what he or she received from the medicine. Then it became clear to him: Chondrasil wasn't ready to accept the fact that he was God. He had chosen Azara over truth, over reality. No doubt he had literally looked Seyloq in the eye while on the medicine and probably seen exactly what he just described - a demon luring him away from Azara. He had seen all his worst fears reflected in the eyes of the man who was a perfectly clear mirror. He had seen and failed to recognize that he was seeing himself, not Seyloq. The irony was almost tragic.

"All you ever see is yourself," said Jendru confidently. "You don't see Seyloq at all, only your own fears and limitations." He could hardly believe that he was speaking this way to the High Maegin, but he continued anyway. "Seyloq is precisely what he says he is. You, however, are not, High Maegin. Seyloq speaks from the clarity of truth. You speak from within the illusions of the ego, from the illusion of separation. I know what I've seen, what I've felt, and you are wrong."

It wasn't so much anger as it was sorrow that showed itself on the High Maegin. Where once he had seen a great and powerful man connected to the sacred, a performer of the most holy of work, Jendru now saw a hollow shell of a man, defeated by his own fears. A man who had seen the truth, but had failed to recognize it. It was so much worse than someone who had never seen, never known. But here he was, the High Maegin, and Jendru *knew* that in his heart, Chondrasil knew the truth. He had been presented with every opportunity to embrace it, yet he had chosen not to. At *some* level, that decision had been conscious, even if Chondrasil couldn't admit it. When faced with the full, awesome - terrible, even -

nature of being, he had backed away. Rather than embracing freedom and liberation, he had chosen his prison, the prison of his church and his role within it. And all the turmoil of that inauthentic decision had been projected out onto Seyloq, whom Chondrasil could only see as a pariah, a demon, an infidel.

"When I look at Seyloq," Jendru continued, "I don't see a demon at all. I see a man who lives in truth and freedom. I see a man who embraces himself for what he is, in all his fullness and complexity. What is more, I see the possibility for myself and my own being. I see my own infinite nature reflected in him, and in his words and actions. There is no demon there, only the self. I see myself. I am Seyloq."

"Then you too are a demon," said Chondrasil with a dramatic sense of finality. It was clear - it was too late for Chondrasil. He had made his choice, and nothing Jendru could ever say or do would change that. If change were to come, it would have to come from within. It would have to be Chondrasil's choice. This wasn't about doctrine, or religion, or anything else. It was about who Chondrasil thought he was, how he had painstakingly constructed his sense of self. Seyloq, and now Jendru, was a challenge to that, and Chondrasil had chosen defensiveness and the protections of religion long ago. If not even the toad medicine could help him break through, then there was nothing Jendru could do. There was nothing anyone could do. Chondrasil was lost. Jendru knew it. And he also knew that even here, in this exchange, Chondrasil was himself. Even in his confusion, he was a perfect reflection. He exactly fulfilled the role that Jendru needed him to. Everything was perfect. It was exactly as it needed to be. Chondrasil may be inauthentically trapped in his ego, but in playing his part, he was entirely authentic for the role he was prepared to allow himself to play. The simple perfection of it all made Jendru smile.

"You think that's funny?" demanded Chondrasil. "You take pride in being possessed by a demon?"

"Demons don't exist," said Jendru. "And neither do lost souls. Not even Azara exists."

"So you're an atheist now, too?" Chondrasil looked

crestfallen.

"No," said Jendru. "But I no longer *believe* in God, because I know that it's me. I *am* God. I see no need to believe in myself, for I exist. I am. To deny God would be equivalent to denying myself - really, there is no difference. There is no separation and there never has been. Only the illusion, and for me, that illusion is no more. I am all things, including you, and including Seyloq Surya. I am."

"So we should worship you?" asked Chondrasil, hostile and incredulous.

Jendru laughed. "No more than I would have you pray to me," he answered. "I'm no more God than you, Chondrasil. Prayer, worship, ritual, all of it. It's all pointless. *We are God.* There is only One. This is how it's always been and always will be. When you pray, you speak to yourself and none other. When you worship, you bow down before a being that you fail to recognize as yourself. Religion is an illusion. All of it, Azara included, right along with the Darsulans. All of reality is a mirror, and you always have the ability to choose what you see. Look clearly, if you dare, and expose your own lies, your own fears, your own half-truths. Seyloq and all that he offers is merely an invitation to wake up and see ourselves for who and what we truly are. I am profoundly grateful I've taken that invitation. It's clear that the invitation was extended to you as well, but you turned your back on the mirror and retreated into your ego, your illusions, your precious doctrine and ritual. Well I'm done with it. I won't be taking my vows - not today, not ever. I refuse to imprison myself here. I had hoped that this could have been easier between you and me, for despite everything, I love you. But I'm done. I will never be a part of your Church."

"Then go," said Chondrasil. "I will not tolerate you here spreading your lies and deceits. If you've chosen the path of damnation, then so be it. Embrace your tragic fate. But here, you are no longer welcome. Take what little belongs to you and go. I have work to do."

At that, Chondrasil turned his attention to some papers lying on his desk, making it clear that he was done and there would be no more to this conversation. While part of him was sad at leaving things this way, Jendru felt jubilant. Though he had no idea what the future would bring, he knew that he was free. He had made his choice and stood by it. Now he was free.

Without saying anything, and without an acknowledging glance from the High Maegin, Jendru, the former star novice of Azara, stood up and left.

Chapter 21

SHAKING THINGS UP

All attention was focused on the soon-to-occur oath-taking ceremony when Jor Alesh returned to Azar. People were gathered in groups in the open courtyards surrounding the Obsidian Temple, dressed even more elaborately than they had been for the prayer ceremony a few nights previous. Jor Alesh felt all the more an outsider here, as though life in Azar was a completely foreign culture, despite the long history between Azar and Jurnda. Visually, everyone looked very impressive in their fine robes of spun gold and intricate geometric designs. It didn't impress her the way it once might have, for she saw it for the show that it was. It seemed so obvious: there was nothing "selfless" about this, despite what the Maegins claimed as truth. No matter what, being a part of the Church was still an expression of identity, still a manifestation of the ego. Yes, a follower got a new hair cut (or lack thereof), a tattoo, and new robes, indicating and expressing the fact that the old identity, the old ego, was being replaced. But that was it, wasn't it? It was merely a replacement. It was a swapping of one ego for another. For all their talk of selfless action and commitment to the holy work that supposedly transcended the individual ego, it just wasn't so. All of this was an elaborate act, a game, a process of make believe where everyone willingly played along. Despite everything, it had no more substance or reality to it than children playing "let's pretend," only no one here seemed able to recognize or admit it.

At least the Darsulans, or Reformed Azarans, as they apparently preferred to be called, gave some of their focus to people's lives and wellbeing and were not exclusively focused on the etheric and transcendent like these Azarans. *This*, above all else regarding these two religions, seemed the most practical to Jor Alesh. The medicines could be used to improve people's lives - help them find better health, better balance within themselves, and, she knew from her work with Seyloq, help individuals discover their true, infinite nature, the greatest gift of all. She had no illusions that any of the Darsulans would see eye-to-eye with Seyloq, but their relaxation of the exclusive focus on reincorporation and all that went with it was an improvement, in her mind, and far more relevant to life in Jurnda than what the Azarans believed themselves to be accomplishing here. What would it take to reform *both religions*, she wondered. Was there a way to divorce the therapeutic and personal growth use of the medicines from the overtly spiritual and religious? Perhaps the underground groups that were using the Darsulans' medicines in Jurnda had already accomplished this. She'd have to ask Seyloq about this and possibly use him as a connection to meet with some of the groups and find out what their practices were.

The more she thought about it, the more it disturbed her that there were groups of people in Jurnda who felt that they needed to keep their practices secret and underground. It was certainly not the self-image that Jurndans had of themselves as a free and open society. Reflecting, Jor Alesh wondered how much of life in Jurnda was a show like what she was seeing here in Azar. What lies were they telling themselves to promote their own self-image and ego writ large in the form of their society? Even there in Jurnda, the religious hegemony of Azara had driven curious seekers underground, afraid of how they would be viewed by others, afraid of losing their positions within society. This wasn't freedom at all. Though there were no laws or regulations, the people were essentially policing themselves. Fear and secrecy were their motivating factors. It wasn't healthy. Changes would have to be made, and she would be the one to spearhead such changes. Yes, she would have to learn more about these underground groups and do what she could to help bring them out into the open.

Ideals such as "tolerance" and "acceptance" were widely promoted in Jurnda, largely inspired by the horrors of the *Great War*, where humanity was divided along religious, political, and ethnic lines. Yet the people were still clearly divided. Despite their points of commonality, the Darsulans and the Azarans were literally physically divided. They had established different communities and were leading different lives. So even here, where there was essentially only one religion with two variations, there were still divisions, still separate identities that conflicted with each other. It was ironic to the extreme - especially considering that both doctrines held out the notion of selflessness and transcending the illusions of the ego and separateness. The religions were creating the very divides they proposed to overcome spiritually, but not in reality, not in the here and now - only in the beyond and the hereafter.

If we're truly all one, by our very natures, Jor Alesh wondered, *then why do we keep separating ourselves?* The answer was clear: it was for the perpetuation of ego illusion and constructed identities. If the truth of being were widely known and accepted by individuals, there would be no pull toward creating these false identities. The result could be social peace and prosperity, not out of some grand ideal of tolerance and acceptance, but grounded in actual reality and the direct experience and knowledge that all was one. It was a reality solution to an ego problem, rather than a social value solution that pandered to ego delusion. The full scope of what Jor Alesh was considering here broke through the immediate and reached into the universal. If everyone knew the truth, religion, war, violence, and social division would be obsolete. People wouldn't have to *try* to get along with each other out of some necessity for "respect" and "tolerance." They could simply live in reality, in the truth that everyone was truly one.

What would it mean for people to work with these powerful tools, these profound medicines, without fear of reprisal or social condemnation? And how might society change if the medicines themselves were freed from the conservative, religious use and context of both Azaran and Darsulan practice? The Reformed Azarans, the Darsulans, had already taken some steps in this direction, but what she was considering here was even more radical and more in line with Seyloq's practices. What would it be like if these medicines were used exclusively for the promotion and discovery of truth and reality, and were no longer bound to any religious, metaphysical, or spiritual view?

It was a complicated question, she knew. It was obvious that these medicines, these tools, could easily contribute to religious belief and experience. If they were let loose in society, maybe they'd see a flowering of new religions, competing ideologies and identities, and none would be better for it. Merely alternate versions of the same old illusions. Really, it was Seyloq's nondual, reality-based approach that seemed simultaneously the most radical and the most applicable to modern life in Jurnda. God without religion; being without belief. These were the greatest gifts Jor Alesh could imagine. To live in truth was liberating, refreshing, radical, and energizing. But how could so many work with the medicines and not see it? It was the strangest paradox. The tools that could bring one to the greatest heights of truth and personal revelation could also be profound tools of willful self-deception and illusion. These tools could either help liberate you from the game, or enmesh you even further into it, as was happening here in Azar with this grand oath-taking ceremony. From what she had experienced, Seyloq had discovered what came closest to a "truth pill" as could be found, but even there, it was all up to individual choice. No one and nothing could make someone who was unwilling or resistant see the truth. What a bizarre paradox!

If the medicines were completely secularized, what then? Artists, philosophers, deep thinkers, creative types - she was sure that they would enjoy unfettered access to the medicines. It was already the case that many such individuals attended communion in the Azaran centers in Jurnda, drawn by the power of the drink, but not desiring to join the Church. What would it mean for them to have access without needing to go through the strictures of Azaran ritual and doctrine? Though it was presented as a necessary safeguard, Jor Alesh suspected that the Azaran insistence on ritual and formality was more an unacknowledged patronizing stance of the ego than anything else. Yes, there was knowledge and experience there, but there was so much focus on "the container" and "the setting" that individuals were also effectively boxed in. The religion itself put limits on people, and also swayed their interpretations of their experiences in subtle, and not so subtle ways. Seyloq, for example, had a genuine breakthrough, and despite all the odds, had found the strength within to stay true to it. Yet from outside, he was marked as a pariah, a demon. It all showed how tightly the reigns of attempted control and hegemony were within the Church. People were only invited to wake up so far, and everything else was anathema. For all the supposed "protection" and "guidance" the Church was providing, it was also objectively holding people back from their greatest, truest potential, and only by breaking free could someone pursue these deeper insights and revelations.

Where was the balance, she wondered. If there was a free-for-all with the medicines, would it incite chaos and social disintegration? Were people *ready* for this? Could all this be managed, somehow, or were such thoughts merely more play of the ego, trying to control things, trying to create a specific outcome? She suspected that this was the case. Why not put the truth out there, the tools out there, and let people decide for themselves? So many questions. What would it look like?

As Alcian, these were all things that she needed to consider, but also, as Alcian, she had no direct control over how such issues would be managed. It was true that in most cases, the advice of the Alcian was followed, unless there were major disagreements. Jurndans trusted their Alcian and the system had worked well for hundreds of years, and Jurnda had flourished as a rebirthing ground for humanity. Perhaps this was the next step, and one that would spell a different future for all of humanity. And as Alcian, Jor Alesh could do her part to help make it a reality. Admittedly, she was excited by the possibilities. Only time would tell what would be.

Scanning the crowd, her thoughts turned once more to Jendru. Now she was thinking personally, not just about the greater good for humanity. She doubted that Seyloq would want to get involved with what was generating in her mind, but Jendru - here was a possibility. Though she knew what her heart, and her body, desired, if Jendru took his vows, maybe he could work on bringing change to the Church from within. Maybe he could help establish more realistic communication with the Darsulans.

What she really wanted was for Jendru to give up his ambitions of becoming a Maegin entirely and join her in Jurnda. Maybe they could be lovers, or even partners. Together, they could work to bring a new openness and self-awareness into Jurndan society. They'd be a dynamic, realized couple, lending their experience and knowledge - especially Jendru, who was far more experienced here than herself. Above all else, they could serve as an example - showing others what was possible - clear mirrors, like Seyloq, but fully enmeshed in society, not removed from it.

Jor Alesh had never wanted a partner before. Of course, there had been suitors, men wanting to join her in her bed and in her life. She had never felt the pull, however. Sex was one thing, but commitment to a life partner hadn't seemed necessary or relevant to her before. But now . . . it was almost silly. Really, she didn't actually *know* Jendru. They only met a few days ago, for goodness sake! Yet energy was energy, and what was transpiring between them was obvious; there was no doubt in her heart - she was drawn to this man, and despite the difficulties of his situation, she knew that he was similarly drawn to her. If he were to take his vows, well, that would be the end of that. If he refused, if he declined to take his vows and left the Church . . . well, then anything was possible, and it gave her hope and a tingling sensation in her heart. At least she knew what *she* wanted.

There was so much color and decoration among the formally dressed that it was hard for her to pick out individuals within the gathering crowd. Many were wearing tall, ceremonial hats, so finding the novices who would take their vows wasn't as easy as it might have otherwise been, as the obvious distinction between haired and shaved heads wasn't as easy to spot. Though she wanted to see Jendru, she definitely didn't want to see him *here*. The disappointment would be crushing.

She mingled amongst the crowd, circling around the base of the great Obsidian Temple. Everyone was abuzz with excitement, eagerly awaiting the arrival of the Darsulans and the upcoming oath-taking. No one paid her any attention as she was obviously not a person of interest for this event - simply another curious onlooker. Eventually, she spotted Chondrasil and approached him, thinking at the very least she would check in with him, though she was sure he would be busy and would probably only spare a moment or two.

Seeing her approach, Chondrasil gave her a sharp look, as did the other men standing with him. *Something's up,* Jor Alesh told herself, bracing for whatever was about to come. Chondrasil was clearly displeased and the pointed look on his face indicated that whatever the displeasure was, he had connected it to her in his mind.

"High Maegin Chondrasil," she greeted him. "It is a momentous day."

"Yes," he responded coldly. "Tell me," he said, "Where were you yesterday?"

"Visiting Seyloq Surya," she answered directly. She could feel the eyes of all the Maegins on her. They weren't happy. That was clear. Why they should be unhappy with her was a mystery. She was perfectly free to meet with whomever she wanted, and in this, the Maegins had no say. Clearly, they felt that they were, or should be, in charge here.

"And who escorted you on this impromptu visit?" Chondrasil was looking flush.

This is about Jendru, Jor Alesh realized. She looked at the Maegins, all staring back at her. *Temptress,* their cold eyes said. Her heart sped up. *Jendru isn't taking his vows! And they think I have something to do with it!*

"The novice, Jendru Amdin, was my escort." This was feeling more and more like an interrogation.

"I see," said Chondrasil. "And did you take Seyloq's medicine along with Jendru?"

"Yes."

Chondrasil narrowed his eyes and stared at Jor Alesh for a few moments, quiet murmurs coming from the other Maegins, shaking their heads and looking askance dismissively.

"Is there a problem?" she asked, playing the innocent, though she knew perfectly well that there was.

"Don't play games with me," said Chondrasil sharply. "I told you what I thought of Seyloq Surya and his ways. If you want to meet with him, well, that's your choice and your folly. I was informed that you specifically sought out Jendru to escort you to the apostate. He makes his own choices as well - he has not yet taken his vows. But I would have hoped for more from you, Ms. Melva. You can see as clearly as anyone else that this is a sensitive and delicate time. The Darsulans are here, for one. And if that weren't enough, now we lose one of our most promising novices to the ways of a heretic!

"Though I have no proof, I strongly feel that your presence and interaction with Jendru has contributed significantly to his recent decision and his falling from the graces of Azara. I hope that you are proud of yourself, Ms. Melva. Jendru Amdin has not spoken of you to me, but I am not blind. I know that you are, in part, at least, responsible. There is a reason we do not allow women into our ranks, and you have helped remind us of the importance of this rule. So perhaps for that we should thank you, especially with the Darsulans here with their fallacious doctrine." He looked at her hard, eyes piercing. "I invited you here as a guest, and for the remainder of your visit, I demand that you not associate yourself with any more of our novices. If you cannot control your weak feminine will, then I will have you removed from the city. With the Darsulans here, we must pay extra attention to being firm in our commitment and dedication, and you are a distraction that I cannot afford to tolerate at this sensitive time."

It was not the response that Chondrasil was looking to garner from her, but Jor Alesh was too excited not to show it. Rather than cowering and showing deference, she seemed to swell. "What are you trying to tell me about Jendru?" she asked, eager for the answer.

"He has left the Church," said Chondrasil with a firm sense of finality. "He has renounced his faith, declined to take his vows, and is exiled from Azar, just as his chosen mentor was before him. My most promising student has fallen into damnation and we have one less future monk. Our ceremonies today will feel the brunt of this sadness and loss rather than be the full celebration and jubilation that they should be. I *know* you had a role in this, and can see by your reaction that you take pleasure in my news. So be it, *temptress*. Understand that you have strained relations between Azar and Jurnda. Is this what you want, at this delicate time?"

"I only want to keep things real," said Jor Alesh, somewhat quixotically. She could see the sense of puzzlement on Chondrasil's face. "And you, High Maegin, could stand to do likewise. You're so wrapped up in what you're doing here, you aren't even aware of what's really going on. Have you even met with the Darsulans yet?" she challenged.

"No," he answered, waiting for Jor Alesh to explain herself further.

"Why do *you* think they're here?" she asked.

"I can only presume that it is because they want to reintegrate with the Church," said Chondrasil confidently. "What else would bring them all this way, and why would they bring so many of them, after so many years of hiding in the far reaches of Lur?"

"You have no idea," said Jor Alesh. "Do you even know what they call themselves?"

His blank stare indicated that he did not.

"They don't call themselves 'Darsulans.' They prefer 'Reformed Azarans,' and they refer to you here as 'Conservative Azarans.' In their mind, your traditions are archaic and out-of-touch with the needs and desires of the people for a more relaxed doctrine. And I must say, from what I have learned, I tend to lean more in their direction than yours, High Maegin. Which isn't to say that I have any particular love for either their doctrine or yours. Out of all of you, Seyloq Surya makes far more sense and is more grounded in reality than you are prepared to recognize. As someone who is not bound to your doctrine and dogma, I can see the value of what he teaches. As far as I am concerned, it is far more relevant for human society and wellbeing than what either of your religions have to offer. But all this is beside the point: the *Reformed Azarans* have most certainly *not* come here to reintegrate back into your church. Even here, you are ignorant. I'd share what I know with you, although, as you seem to have made up your mind about my contribution to this gathering here, I'll leave it to you to figure out on your own. Things are not what they seem, High Maegin Chondrasil, and soon your eyes will be opened, whether you like it or not."

Chondrasil opened his mouth as though about to make a response when he was cut short by the clanging of gongs and cymbals announcing the arrival of the Darsulans, who had at last made their way from the waterfront. Everyone turned to watch. Silence filled the courtyard about the great Obsidian Temple. The crowd opened up to let in the procession. At the front, their matron, "The Mother" and female High Maegin, Meridalthi, was carried on a palanquin by several strong young men. When they reached the center of the courtyard, they set the palanquin down and the large old woman teetered onto her feet, standing confidently with her cane in hand amidst her followers. *You didn't expect that, did you?* thought Jor Alesh, watching the look of realization wash over Chondrasil's face. *That's right - they're led by a woman, so you may have dismissed me, but look who's here now!* Chondrasil and the other Maegins all looked at each other in surprise. Apparently, they had been so busy making preparations for their oath-taking ceremony in their intent to impress the Darsulans that no one had bothered to learn that their highest-ranking representative was a woman. *Good,* thought Jor Alesh. *And they'll be sure to enjoy the further surprises that Darsulans are operating in Jurnda and that it was Seyloq, the demon apostate, who invited them here in the first place. Yes, this will be an interesting day for you, Chondrasil.*

She looked at Chondrasil and smiled. "Enjoy!" she said, turning away with a flourish, dramatically omitting the proper bow she was expected to give the High Maegin and his peers.

And though no one noticed, it was also the moment of the very first tremor, too small to for anyone to register in the excited commotion of the arrival of the Darsulans. Things were just starting to shake up.

Chapter 22

FOLLOW YOUR HEART

Jor Alesh ran into Jendru's friend (and now *former* fellow novitiate), Khalanto, as she made her way hurriedly toward the pyramid that housed the novices' quarters. Hearing the news that Jendru had refused to take his vows, and had been summarily exiled from Azar, she could only assume that he would be gathering whatever belongings he had and going to Seyloq. Where else could he go on such short notice? Perhaps he'd want to return to Jurnda and stay with his parents for a time. For now, he needed someplace close to go and collect his thoughts, she imagined, and where else would that be but Seyloq's? Thankfully, the novices' pyramid was on the side of Azar that opened to the road to Seyloq's, so she didn't have to go running all across the city to get there. Her plan, if she didn't find Jendru at the pyramid, was to continue out to Seyloq's. Even if she didn't find him, she needed time away from the ceremonial proceedings anyway. Chondrasil might cool off later, after the initiates had completed their vows. If not, she'd stick around anyway to continue to develop relations with Meridalthi and the Darsulans. She liked the idea of showing them around Jurnda, and she did want to find out more about the underground communities in her city. It was time for things to change, and she would be a catalyst in any way she could. It wasn't that she wanted to promote "Reformed Azara" - she just wanted the secrecy and self-imposed isolation to end. *A truly free society is an open society*, she told herself.

From the look of him, Khalanto had spoken with Jendru and learned the news of his renunciation. When she first spotted him, he looked sad. Now that he saw who was coming toward him, he looked angry as well. *Great*, thought Jor Alesh, *here comes another anti-woman tirade. Well, nothing to do but get it over with.*

"Jendru's leaving," blurted out Khalanto when they got close to each other.

"I know," said Jor Alesh. "Chondrasil told me. Do you know where he is?"

Khalanto pointed with his head back the way he'd come. "He just left," he said. "As novices, we're not really supposed to own much, so he packed up the few things that were his and headed out of the city. I think we both know where he's going," he added, a taste of bitterness in his words.

Then, unexpectedly, he put his head in his hands and began to cry. "I want to blame Seyloq, and you too," he said between sobs, "but really, I blame myself."

"Why is that?" asked Jor Alesh, attempting a comforting tone and reaching out to put her hand on Khalanto's shoulder. He jerked away and gave her a look that said, "I'm afraid of you."

"Because I taunted him into going to see Seyloq in the first place," he said. "I'm the one who encouraged him and teased him about making Seyloq his Maegin-Lu. It was all a joke! And now . . . it's really happening. Why did I do this? Jendru was like my big brother. He was my family, and now he's gone, and I'll probably never see him again. It's all my fault!"

Jor Alesh couldn't disagree more. "Jendru is responsible for himself, Khalanto. If anything, be happy for your friend. What could be wrong with following your heart?"

Khalanto got angry. "Because 'following your heart,' as you put it, is leading Jendru into damnation! Do you think all of this is a game? That nothing matters? Is the doctrine of Azara completely meaningless to you? You're the Alcian! Do you have no respect at all for our sacred traditions? Or are you happy because you want Jendru for yourself, and you don't care about his immortal soul, or all the beings he could have helped as a monk, or what we do here in Azar? You think our five hundred years of tradition here in Azar have all been a joke that can be tossed off like an old shirt without any consequences?

"The Maegins teach us that the heart is the field of

temptation, especially where women are concerned, and no less with false teachers and false prophets. They lead us astray with sweet promises of happiness, pleasure, and hedonistic, selfish desires. You and Seyloq both are *exactly* what they've warned us about, and Jendru has fallen into the trap you have set for him. And I helped him! Me! I was supposed to be his friend, and look what I've done! I'll be lucky if the Maegins don't come after me. I love this Church! I believe in it! You and Seyloq - you're both demons!"

Jor Alesh didn't know what to say, nor did Khalanto give her a chance. He stormed off in a huff, swishing his robes to show his displeasure. What could she say to him, anyway? He had made up his mind and it was no longer her concern. At least all pretenses were over. *Just keeping it real*, she told herself as she continued on her way out of the city and into the hills to Seyloq's.

This time, she thought she felt the earth shudder beneath her, though she dismissed the sensation as an aftershock of her own nerves. Not even she had the faintest idea how "real" things were about to get for everyone, whether they wanted it or not.

Chapter 23

LAUGHING ALL THE WAY

It was true: there was a little sadness in him. Yet it was only a little. Mostly, he was ecstatic.

Jendru was alive. He was alive and free and full of energy in a way he had never been before. Five years ago, when he left Jurnda and made that initial journey to Azar, he had felt similarly - a young man, heading off to find his life, find his place and his purpose, not only in this world, but the world beyond.

Now, however, it was different, though he recognized the similarities. It had not been all that long ago - one fifth of his life - and he had truly been excited at the time. Yet then, he had been running into the arms of a patriarchal church with a strict doctrine, filled with rules, rituals, and an esoteric philosophy that was little-understood by non-initiates. Admitting it to himself, it had been the esoterica that had truly attracted him to Azara. He had so much *wanted* to be one of those mysterious Maegins who could influence the fates of spirits and souls in the etheric and astral. He had looked up to them as paragons of human activity, wisdom, and selfless commitment. That's how he saw himself in his own development. He wanted to *be* one of them. Realizing this, he knew that really there had been nothing noble or truly selfless in his attraction to the Church. It was only apparently selfless. In supposedly serving the spirits and lost souls, he knew now that he had really only been serving himself, feeding the insatiable hunger of his ego for a sense of self, a sense of purpose, of belonging, of individual worth.

He laughed as he walked through the overgrown jungle, recognizing this truth. He also laughed at the realization that it had all been perfect. From the perspective of being the One, of being God, he saw how he had perfectly orchestrated his life so that it would have just the right amount of tension and attraction to bring him to precisely where he was at this moment. There was the draw of the Church, the almost surrogate fatherhood of Chondrasil, the playful taunting by his friend, Khalanto, and the inexplicable attraction to Seyloq and his teachings. And there was even Jor Alesh, a last-minute addition to his personal drama, arriving, as if on cue, to help build to the final denouement. It was almost absurd how perfectly clear it all was. And all of it, every last bit, had all been himself. The self that he had always assumed was him, this "Jendru," wasn't who or what he was at all! Merely a character in his own drama, his own unfolding tragic comedy. The real self was *all of it. Every last little bit.* And he saw how, despite any appearances to the contrary, it was *all* an act of self-love.

At every stage, the truth of being had been calling him forward, challenging him to step up to the ordeal of genuine self-discovery. It had all been *absolutely perfect in every moment,* and he knew that this was the only way it could ever be, for perfect self-love was the very foundation of reality. If everything was one, as it surely and indisputably was, then there was no part of the self that was not a manifestation of self-love. This love was universal, uncompromising, ruthless, and even fierce. It could create as easily as it could destroy. It could bring unfathomable pleasure as easily as it could bring horrific terror and pain. It was so far beyond any notion of human ethics that the attempts at morality and justice in human cultures and societies could only make Jendru laugh in wild abandon. And the rigid sincerity and devotion of the followers of Azara and their stringent ethical and ritual standards! Absurd! He said it out loud, calling to the jungle, "ABSURD!"

It was a wonder that he was ever a believer, but he also knew that such a judgment was too simplistic. Azara, like other belief systems and cultures, was a sophisticated game, and it offered far more to the ego than most were willing to be aware of, despite all its claims to the contrary. In fact, it was the claims of humble selflessness that made it so devious, so perfectly deceptive. One could spend his entire life in the religion, as so many did, and never see through the veil of illusion, so well had it been drawn. For Jendru, at least, the veil had been lifted. He saw it all for what it was: a mirror. Everything was a mirror. Always, forever, and eternally. If he could maintain his clarity, Jendru felt confident that his image in the mirror would never warp or distort again. From now on, he would see clearly, infinitely, and truthfully.

Now, with giddy excitement, he wandered off into the unknown. Though he had not known what to expect in coming to Azar, he had at least known that the Church would be his home until his dying day. His life was, in essence, laid out for him in the commitment he had intended to make. Walking into that future was nothing like the journey he was currently undertaking. Here, the future was completely open to him. Though Azar may be closed to him, realistically, what he was left with was the entire world. And this time, he was truly entering into it. He had let go of all of his attachments to the beyond, he knew. The etheric, the spiritual, the astral, none of these meant anything to him anymore. There was no longer a pull to the esoteric, the mystical, the transcendent. Life was to be lived right here, right now, in this body, in this world, in this life. He knew without a doubt: *this is it*. Whatever he wanted to get out of life, he would have to find it here, in the world, in his life and his body. There was no beyond. And since he was God and he knew it, there was no longer any spiritual goal to achieve. Oneness simply was. How absurd that he ever could have thought that it was something he needed to achieve through spiritual work and discipline! It was like taking lessons to learn how to breathe!

What people truly needed was training in how to take full responsibility for themselves. If anything was lacking, it was this. How easy it was for the ego to project its ideas and desires outwardly. How easy it was to become attached to what it wanted, thought, and desired. How quickly fear, judgment, and illusion could sweep in and overcome someone. A vast and complex game was being carried out in every moment of every day - a game between God and the ego.

God, of course, always had the upper hand, but it all came down to free will. God could not command the ego to recognize its true nature, because the ego was God as much as God was everything, and the ego was a part of everything. It was impossible for God to command God to do anything, because then God would be violating its own free will. It was a paradox that could not be resolved. So it was up to each and every person, individually, consciously, intentionally, to discover the truth and live by the responsibility that truth required. Here, religion, spirituality, metaphysics - none of it was any real help. Only through the radical encounter with the full nature of the self could any individual hope to come to a realistic sense of what individual responsibility and choice required. Only by directly knowing the truth, and accepting the reality of being, could someone be realized as a responsible, awakened individual.

Though he didn't know how, Jendru knew that this was to be his life. He would help others because *he was them*. His love for himself necessitated that he do what he could for others. And the only way to help them was with truth, and even there, it was one person at a time. Like Seyloq, he would not offer a new religion, a new path to truth or to God. He would simply be himself and love himself fully, in all his manifestations.

He had no idea what this would look like, or what it would mean for his life. He just knew that it was true. In whatever form it would require him to take, he would *be* the truth. It was the only way.

Jendru couldn't help but laugh. He felt so unbelievably free. It was more than a laugh, though. It was more like some vibration had been set off in the fabric of the universe and it was working its way out through his body in the form of a human laugh. At first, it was an almost unnoticeable giggle, released silently to himself. Then he let out a little more and it grew in strength. Letting the laugh release, it overtook all aspects of his being, shaking him to the core. It was the oddest thing - it was both *his* and *not his*. In the most fundamental sense, it was simply something that was happening to him, and he was allowing it. He knew, if he concentrated hard enough, he could bring the riotous laughter to an end and close down the energy that was coursing through him. However, he didn't want to.

He let the laugh rumble up in his belly, shaking his entire body, eventually sending him down to his knees, slapping the ground with his open hand as tears of ecstasy welled up in his eyes and ran down his face. He was done with trying to keep things under control, trying to maintain the facade of his ego and his sense of self. From this point on, he was simply going to be, and if that meant rolling around in the dirt laughing like an idiot, then so be it. He was going to be himself, and it no longer mattered what that looked like, to him or anyone else. So what if someone found him here? Who knows - maybe they would join him, and together they would share in his new-found joy and freedom. Or maybe they would think he was crazy. It no longer mattered. He was free, and it tickled him like he was the universe itself celebrating its freedom. He was at peace with himself.

When the first tremor hit, Jendru was too busy laughing to notice.

Chapter 24

DOING IT IN THE ROAD

It wasn't difficult for Jor Alesh to find Jendru. All she had to do was follow the hysterical laughter and occasional hoots and shouts along the road that led out of Azar to Seyloq's. When she first heard it, she thought it might be a troop of monkeys or baboons and was a little concerned for her safety. There were no such animals in Jurnda, and she had been told that they could be aggressive and territorial around humans, especially the larger apes that made their homes in the forested hills about Azar. And her being a female, well, there was no telling how a large male ape or baboon might react to her presence.

Still, she continued on, drawn by the hope of finding Jendru. There was definitely something *human* about the sounds she heard, but there was more than that. It sounded like the jungle itself were coming alive with the manic laughter with birds, insects, and all manner of creatures responding to the sounds rolling about the hills and cascading along with the rushing waters. The closer she got, the more she could distinguish what she was hearing. There was no doubt - someone was laughing, but he wasn't alone. There was a troop of monkeys or apes that were joining in on the riot, as well as squawking birds and chirping insects. And whatever was going on, it was infectiously funny. She felt a broad smile break out on her face as a few chuckles escaped from her belly. She was drawn by the laughter, as were the other creatures of the forest. There was no doubt - she wanted to join in.

When she found him, Jendru was lying in the middle of the old, overgrown road in the dirt, with his arms and legs all spread out as though he were in the throes of embracing existence. His head was arched back, eyes wide open and teared over, laughing hysterically. Above him, in the trees, medium-sized black and tan monkeys stood on waving branches, shaking the leaves about them as they bobbed up and down while hooting and chattering to each other and to Jendru, the bizarre man laughing on the forest floor. Their antics sent leaves and flower petals falling to the man below, covering him in tree detritus. They obviously didn't know what to make of the scene and would probably start throwing feces if Jendru didn't bring himself under control soon.

Jor Alesh took a moment to take in the tableau. Upon seeing her, the monkeys' attention shifted to her and they momentarily grew silent, leaving Jendru alone with his laughter. It took him a moment to notice. He followed the line of sight of the monkeys above him, eventually bringing his bright gaze directly to Jor Alesh with a turn of his head. He gave her a goofy smile and gestured slightly with his hands and arms, as though to say, "Well, you found me. Here I am in this ridiculous situation. Care to join me?"

She did.

Breaking into a brisk run, she headed for her goal. She wasn't sure what she was going to do upon reaching him. Drawing close, Jendru didn't bother to get up or clean himself off. He lay there, smiling up at her, exposed and vulnerable, almost as though he had been impaled to the forest floor, unable to shift from his awkward repose.

Briming with anticipation, she came to a stop. She was standing over him at his feet, looking down on him. Despite the dirt, leaves, and petals, he looked more beautiful than ever to her. There was an energy about him that was more truly alive than any she had seen. The sparkle in his tear-studded eyes was incomparable. He seemed to radiate love itself. The love didn't have any object. It just was. It was universal, uncompromising, and completely unconditional. It was directed toward nothing in particular. Rather, it embraced all without any exception or qualification.

Part of her wanted that love to be focused on her. She knew that this was only the yearning of her ego, however. She could feel that while she was included in this profound love, it was not meant exclusively for her, and never would be. It was too universal, too all-encompassing for such a narrow, directed focus. This love embraced her and then reached beyond her into the furthest reaches of the universe, including the stars and galaxies, and all that moved beyond the confines of their small planet in an unfathomably vast cosmos. This, she knew, was the love of God. It was self-love. It was eternal and it was complete, with or without her.

If Jendru was self-conscious, he didn't show it. If he intended to interact with her, he didn't show that either. Jor Alesh knew - it was up to her. She knew what she wanted, and she suspected what Jendru personally wanted. At the moment, he seemed too blissed out to take any particular actions. *He*, it seemed obvious, wasn't about to act on personal desire. Wherever his mind was, it wasn't working that way at the moment. In fact, she even wondered if he had consumed some medicine, so enraptured by his experienced he seemed.

She decided to take things into her own hands.

The monkeys were quiet now, as was Jendru. Ceasing their jubilant bobbing up and down in the trees, they settled in, took their seats, and simply watched, curious and expectant.

First, Jor Alesh took off her shoes so that she could feel the cool, moist earth beneath her. Then, stepping forward, she moved herself over Jendru while hiking up her skirt just far enough so that she could straddle him. He merely watched, passive, not reacting either to stop her or encourage her.

Her heart was racing. This was the closest she had been to Jendru, the focus of her unexpected and insistent desire. His eyes just beamed up at her. Whatever resistance or hesitation she might have had melted away and she let herself sink down, bringing her crotch to rest on Jendru's sex. *That* felt good. Though it was subtle, she could distinctly feel his body rise up to meet hers, almost as though some energy field had just embraced her and drew her in. She pushed herself against him as shivers ran up and down her spine. He was stiffening and she could feel his sex pulse against her opening crevice beneath her underclothes.

She reached out and opened his lose shirt, exposing his chest, running her fingers down the center line of his body, feeling his warmth, his sweat, and his pulse beneath his skin.

Energy was running through him and into her - she could feel it distinctly. It tingled and excited her. Though he still said nothing and did not react, it was clear that he had invited her in.

She ran her fingers over his nipples, watching the dark round shapes stiffen as she gave them a little squeeze. His eyes rolled up into his head slightly as he gave out an almost inaudible gasp. He was definitely hard now. There was no doubt about that. She felt him press himself against her more insistently with each tease of his nipples.

Opening his eyes, he looked directly at her and gave her a smile that melted her heart. The look in his eyes said *yes* as his body became alive beneath her. He reached out with his hands and let them run across the smooth, bare skin of her open thighs, slipping beneath the folds of the light fabric of her skirt. Electric tingles shot up her legs and made her vagina convulse in excited expectation. She felt slippery in her underclothes. The muscles in her vagina were contracting, as though attempting to draw him in directly through their clothing. She felt his rock hard sex respond with quick pulses of its own.

Removing his hands from inside her skirt, he placed them around her waist as he lifted his torso up from the ground, leaves and flower petals and bits of bark from the monkeys' shenanigans falling away as he did so. His hands felt strong and smooth. These were the unworn hands of a novice - someone who had spent his time in the pyramids and temples drinking and praying, not the rough hands of someone who had worked the forest, the docks, or other forms of labor. He felt strong, powerful, confident. These were hands that knew what they wanted, and whatever had prevented them from taking what they wanted before was now long gone. These were not the prudish and fearful hands of a monk, but of a passionate lover, full of desire and the strength to take what they wanted and satiate the one to whom they belonged.

Pulling himself up, Jendru's hands moved from her waist up her back, along her spine, eventually caressing the back of her head and then cradling her face as he drew himself close. She could feel his breath as her own breath caught in her throat. She closed her eyes to take in the sensation and then opened them to see Jendru gazing directly at her. The far-away look in his eyes had passed, and all the intensity and focus that was him had zeroed in on her and only her. The forest no longer existed for him, nor did the watching monkeys, the road, the temples and religion he had left behind, or wherever it was that he had been hoping this road would take him to. At this moment, all that existed for him was her, and his eyes told her that he wanted her. And if she allowed it, he would have her.

She shuddered as he drew her face down to his. He watched her, only letting his eyes close as their lips came together, still holding her face and head with his strong hands. Her lips parted and his tongue slipped into her mouth. Electricity shot between the tips of their tongues even before they touched, sending a tingling sensation deep into her core, passing through her heart and finding its home at the tip of her clitoris, which throbbed and swelled as they pressed into each other. His mouth was warm, wet, and fresh, and his tongue came alive inside her. It was like their tongues were caught in a vortex of energy, twirling around each other, diving into each other's mouths. It was vigorous, but not frantic, almost like pulsing music as they played with each other with their tongues. It was more dynamically electric than any kiss Jor Alesh had ever experienced, and she let herself become lost in it. All thoughts of herself melted away and there were only these two tongues, entwined in the most delicious of electric currents, dancing the dance of desire and passion. It was almost like their tongues were the real them, their bodies merely being vehicles in which the strange organ resided and carried itself around, hidden, just waiting to come out and play in precisely this fashion.

The kissing was exquisite, but now she was ready for more.

He could feel it too and slowly withdrew his tongue, relishing the sensation of energy passing between them. Sharp prickles of energy danced back and forth from the tips of their tongues as they each slid back within their respective houses and the two held each other's faces with loving stares.

Without saying anything, Jendru leaned back slightly and shifted his arms so that he was undressing Jor Alesh, pulling her shirt up and over her head. Savoring the sensation, he let his hands run about her exposed skin, taking his time to work his way to her breasts where her pink nipples were swelling in anticipation. First, he caressed the smoothness of her round breasts and spiraled in to her nipples, giving each a firm squeeze. Then, bending down, he took her nipples into his mouth, twirling his tongue over their erect nubs and sucking and biting them, bringing them to full attention. Jor Alesh sighed as she arched back, thrusting her breasts into him, grinding her pelvis down into his. Here again, a strong electric current connected her nipples and his tongue, shooting into her heart and then running down and coalescing at her clitoris, which seemed to be swelling to an impossible size.

After ravishing her breasts this way for some time, Jendru eventually withdrew and Jor Alesh knew that it was her turn to take charge. With her hands, she gently, yet firmly, pushed Jendru back down to the ground as she slowly slid back on his legs, exposing his crotch. The firm bulge of his sex thrust out of the tip of his pants. It was beautiful, and large. She found the shape of its head intoxicating and sublime, the way the rounded head came together just beneath its opening, crowning the top of a firm, veinous shaft that pulsed with blood and life and desire. She reached down and caressed it with her fingertips, smearing the gel that had oozed out from the tip, causing Jendru to quiver beneath her. Sliding further back, she reached down and cupped his testicles in one hand as she maneuvered with the other to undo the tie of his pants.

In one quick move she had his pants off. His penis stood erect before her, like a pillar. He opened his legs for her and she moved in, crouching down on her knees and taking his sex with her hands. It looked large against her small and delicate hands. She could grip with both hands, one on top of the other, and there was still room to spare. Squeezing firmly, the head swelled like a rapidly growing mushroom, turning deep red and purple in the process. The shaft was hairy and covered in thick veins. She couldn't remember when she had last seen anything so beautiful.

Bending down, she kissed it and ran her tongue along the ridge of the head, tasting the saltiness of what had seeped out. Again, it was like an electric current. In moving her tongue over the head of his penis, it was like she were licking her own clitoris, so exactly did the sensation in her own body mirror what she was doing to Jendru. She took it all the way into her mouth and let her tongue flick over the sensitive skin beneath its head, running her tongue up and down and then from side to side. Ever deeper she took his sex into her mouth. She wanted to choke on it, gag on it. She sucked as hard as she could and enveloped him completely. The gag reflex was sweet and was exactly what she wanted. She wanted to fill herself with him in precisely this way and let the gagging shudders run through her body, and when they receded, she took him in deeper.

Slowly at first she moved him in and out, in and out, and then faster while using her hands to massage the shaft and testicles. She didn't want to make him climax - she was saving that - but she did want to bring him to the edge of ecstasy and release. She worked him hard as he groaned with waves of energy moving up and down his body, stopping only when she tasted the first pre-semen seep out of his glorious organ and start to fill her mouth. Slowly, carefully, she withdrew, making sure not to bring him to climax - not yet. She wanted his seed to explode within her, though not in this way.

Sensing that this part of their lovemaking was concluding, Jendru sat up and removed his shirt. He was fully naked now, and for the first time Jor Alesh got to see him in all his vulnerable fullness. He was so beautiful to her that she wanted to melt. *This* was a man. Young, beautiful, and a hard and yearning cock, just for her.

Now it was his turn. He gently, yet decisively, eased Jor Alesh back onto a soft bed of leaves and moss, deftly managing to loosen her skirt as he did so, and in one quick movement, had removed both her skirt and underclothes. Now they were both fully naked, completely exposed and open, and all that either wanted was to continue to enjoy the other. So what if someone came along the road? Let them watch, Jor Alesh told herself. She wasn't about to let anything get in the way of this.

Lying back, Jendru came at her swelling, moist vagina with his mouth. He began by licking her from its base up to her clitoris as waves of ecstatic pleasure rode up and down her lithe and sensuous body. Next he focused on her erect clitoris, teasing it first with his tongue then taking it and the surrounding folds of flesh into his mouth, sucking at her much as he had done with her breasts, rapidly flicking his tongue across the tip of her sensitive organ as he did so. It was wild. Jor Alesh felt her body rising and falling in frenetic waves. The energy was so intense that she found her hands vibrating uncontrollably. She let it happen and chose to receive this intense pleasure without thought or concern. *Yes,* she said to herself. *Eat me alive. Devour me. Leave nothing.*

And that's precisely what he did.

She could feel the inevitable orgasm rising within her, but also knew that it wouldn't release itself until he was inside her. At the precise moment that she reached this conclusion, he moved so that he was on top of her, and with one clean thrust, his rock hard cock slipped effortlessly into her yearning vagina. Instantly, it was like she had just taken a hit of Seyloq's medicine. Her eyes opened and she saw on his face that he felt the same. In fact, it was difficult for her to determine exactly which one of them was the man and which was the woman. They were one and the same - one being with two different bodies. It mattered not which one she personally identified with. Together, they were the act of making love. That was her penis inside his vagina, or the other way around. It didn't matter. All that mattered was this connection, this energy, this experience of absolute unification. And then it dawned on her: this, right here, this act, this experience, was the entire point of creation. God had divided itself and evolved itself into these forms precisely for this purpose: the one being that existed and that was infinitely and eternally alone was, through the act of making love, via the vehicles of its own physical and energetic evolution, truly able to experience connection and unification with another. It was the supreme art of one become many become one yet again, yet still two, still man and woman, still self and other, united in the act of love and ecstatic pleasure. *This was it.* This was what *it was all about.*

Deeper and deeper he thrust into her. Nothing had ever felt so good as his cock pounding into her in a frenzy of love, desire, and mutual exchange of infinite energy. Everything had become thoroughly psychedelic and geometric in her vision. It mattered not if her eyes were open or closed. Everything was pulsing in high-frequency geometric patterns that folded, unfolded, transformed, and morphed into a riot of color and form. Everything was expanding as the energy rose higher and higher, threatening to break apart reality itself in an explosion of unimaginable power. The energy was scaling logarithmically now, rising into the infinite, well beyond what she could measure or hardly even stand.

"Yes!" she heard herself call out. "Fuck me to oblivion!" she cried as she pressed her pelvis into him as hard as she could, his cock reaching into the far and secret depths of her vagina. "Do it!" she commanded. "Come in me. Explode in me! Infinite! Infinite!"

So that's exactly what he did.

In a torrent of ecstatic energy, hunched over her like a wild beast, he exploded all that he had into her. Together, they expanded infinitely. Everything was white light, infinite bliss, and sheer, absolute pleasure and ecstasy. Together, they cried out, waves of bliss overtaking them faster and more powerfully than either could understand or make sense of. It was a frenzy, a cacophony of pleasures, reaching for the infinite where all was one and all was love.

It wasn't until they both finished, lying there, spent in the leaves, moss, and mess of the forest floor, that they noticed that it wasn't only them that was shaking. The tremor that hit just then was far too big for either of them not to notice, and not even they, lying there in the afterglow of their shared ecstasy, could fail to hear the thundering explosion that could only mean one thing: either one or both of the long dormant volcanoes of Ladjup and Nadrasuli had come back to life.

Chapter 25
FIRE DRAGON

The naked couple stood in silence in the middle of the forest road, their clothes strewn about them chaotically, evidence of the passion and desire that had brought them together. The chattering and hooting monkeys were long gone, having swung off deeper into the forest, as was most likely the case with all other animals that could sense what was happening and had the ability to react to it. Though their view was partially obstructed by the dappled foliage of the leaves and upper canopy, the billowing pyroclastic cloud was unmistakeable and undeniable.

"It looks like Ladjup," said Jendru, the first he had spoken since Jor Alesh first came upon him laughing in the middle of the road. Jor Alesh turned, looking away from the growing cloud of dark smoke and lightning to gaze upon her lover. He was still partially erect, his sex standing out before him as it slowly deflated and returned to a flaccid state. Only moments ago he had released years of pent up energy into Jor Alesh, filling her with his milky seed. She had wanted him to linger there, riding on top of her, his back arched like a dominating animal. Yet it was not to be, and they had both risen upon hearing the explosion of the volcano, bringing their lovemaking to a dramatic, and abrupt, conclusion. She could feel him leaking out of her and running down her inner thigh. Almost absentmindedly, she reached down and wiped with her hand, which she then brought to her mouth. She wanted to taste him and didn't want any part of him that he had given her to escape.

The taste was a mixture of both him and her and she liked it. She still wanted him. If the situation had allowed, she would have liked to make love all day until they were both completely spent, but such was not to be the case, not today.

Today, reality had other plans.

"We should see what's happening," she said, beginning to gather up her strewn about clothes, brushing off the leaves and other bits of the forest floor. Looking around, she saw that they were near a small creek running down the hillside toward the Qya River and went to it. There, she crouched down and splashed the cold water on herself, cleaning what remained of their combined fluids. Jendru followed after her, his own clothes in his hands and did the same, as well as splashed some on his face before submerging his whole head in the water, which he brought up with a flourish, sending a spray of fine droplets into the air about them in a perfect arc.

"I'm not going back," said Jendru after they had dressed and stood facing each other. "I'm an exile, and going back . . . well, I doubt Chondrasil would appreciate it."

Jor Alesh frowned. "Who cares what Chondrasil thinks?" she asked. "There are probably people hurt. Who knows what's happening there? We have to go back and see if we can help."

Jendru didn't say anything and only looked around. Finding what he was looking for, he walked over to one of the taller trees with broad limbs. Like a monkey, he quickly ascended the tree, reaching the top after only a few minutes of dextrous climbing.

He called down to Jor Alesh below, "It's definitely Ladjup." And then, "From what I can see here, I don't think that the ash is blowing into Azar. It looks more like it's moving to the southeast, down to the docks and the riverfront."

As he was saying this, another strong trembler hit. Jor Alesh let out a frightened yelp and Jendru clung to the trunk of the tree as it swayed and shook with the rest of the forest. Another thunderous explosion came from down the valley and the pyroclastic cloud seemed to double in size in only a few moments. Whether or not Azar was taking a direct hit, Jendru knew that this was bad. No one had seen anything like this for generations, and from what he knew of their history here on Lur, this was likely to be the most devastating natural disaster they had all endured. He thought of his friends back in Azar and his heart went out to them. He cringed at the thought that some of them might be suffering and dying this very moment. There was nothing he could do, however. They were already an hour out from Azar (far less at a good run), and if there were any immediate danger, they'd have to face it themselves. Beyond that, he no longer felt beholden to Azar and its people in any way. He had been exiled, and it was a resolution that he embraced. There was no place for him there. Really, he didn't care what Chondrasil thought either way. He was done with Azar, and even this wasn't going to bring him back, especially now that he and Jor Alesh had made love. It was like a seal on his departure and his letting go of all that he had left behind. Azar was no longer his world or his concern. He had gone beyond. There was no going back.

He laughed up there in the shaking tree, swaying back and forth. He closed his eyes and listened to the rumbling of the earth and the explosions of the volcano. Deep inside, he accepted that this was merely all part of the process - the process of life, death, change and transformation. *You cannot stop change. Let it all burn and crumble. Everyone there chose to be there for their own reasons, and this is what they've been served by reality. Though my heart goes out to them, it is no longer my concern.*

His treetop revelry was broken by Jor Alesh calling up to him from down below. His laughing was puzzling her. Admittedly, she was a bit concerned that maybe he was a little off-balance after all. A hint of doubt crept into her and she felt the pull of her sense of duty and responsibility to others as Alcian. Here she was in the middle of the jungle with a renegade almost-monk, having just made love in the open - in the middle of the road, of all places! And there he was, clinging to the top branches of a towering tree, laughing at the disaster that was unfolding back in Azar.

"Are you okay?" she called out, wondering how he would respond.

Jendru looked down at her and flashed an exquisite smile. He said something, but she couldn't hear it above the thunder in the distance. "What?" she called out.

"I love you!" he said, loud and clear now. "I love you,

Jor Alesh Melva, Alcian of Jurnda! I love you!"

She closed her eyes and savored the warm explosion in her heart. Her whole body was tingling, still reeling from their passionate lovemaking and slightly off balance from the shaking earth. It was like everything was happening all at once - creation, destruction, love, passion, tragedy, all of it. It was all so beautiful, even with the knowledge that most likely there were people dying and suffering back in Azar.

"I love you, too!" she called back, feeling the truth of the words as she said them. He put his hand over his heart in recognition and then quickly regained his hold on the tree as the earth gave one more good heave.

When the tree stopped shaking, he made his way down. Soon he was standing with her, pressing his body into hers, taking her soft face into his hands. "Go, if you must," he said, "but I am no longer of Azar." Then, looking up the road to Seyloq's, "My life is along a different path, and not even this is going to cause me to backtrack. Not one inch. Azar is my past, not my present, and certainly not my future."

She pressed herself into him, resting her head on his strong chest. "I know," she said softly. Then, pulling back, "I have to go. I wouldn't be much of an Alcian if I didn't. I may not answer to Azar, but back in Jurnda, to ignore this would be considered unconscionable. For now, at least, I am the Alcian, and I've taken on the responsibilities to act as such. My duty is clear: I have to help in any way I can."

"I know," he said, pulling her back into him. Then, after a few moments of silence, save the rumbling volcano in the distance, said, "So go. Go and do what you can. Help where help is needed. Promise me that you'll be careful. From what I saw up there, Azar is probably not in the direct line of the explosions, but you never know. I want you with me, Jor Alesh . . . and I also want you to do what you feel you must. You are your own woman, and as you say, you are the Alcian. So go be Alcian, and when that's done, come find me. You know where I'll be."

Looking up at him, somehow Jor Alesh felt that everything was going to be fine - perfect, even. How could it be any other way? Reality had brought them together, and now their choices were taking them apart, yet it was perfect. Her life was her own, as was his. She knew, without a doubt, that her highest priority was to herself. And right now, she felt the pull of responsibility, and neglecting to act on that would not be true and genuine, as much as she also just wanted to run away with Jendru. If reality would allow it, they would be together. Soon. In her heart, she knew this was only the beginning.

The two shared a long and lingering kiss. When it felt complete, Jor Alesh pulled away, blew Jendru a kiss, and then quickly turned and started out for Azar at a run. Jendru watched her disappear into the forest and then, with a smile on his face, turned back up the road and began to make his way to Seyloq's once more.

Chapter 26

WHO'S EATING WHOM?

It was late afternoon by the time Jendru arrived at Seyloq's. The journey had taken much longer than usual, due to his periodic stopping to survey the scene when the terrain permitted. Ladjup had continued to belch out smoke and ash and all that came with it, but the tremors had largely subsided and the main explosions appeared to be finished. From what Jendru could see, the devastation was sure to be extensive. Still, that didn't draw him back.

The winds were traveling down the valley, headed to the east and thereby the sea, following along the path of the Qya River. Once beyond the volcanic ranges of the Twin Fire Dragons, the alluvial plain along the river was fertile farmland. It was sure to be covered in ash and volcanic stone, and perhaps even lava. In time, it would make the lands fertile and help regenerate the ecology. For now, it was undoubtedly a total disaster.

Though his view was obscured, it looked to Jendru as though Azar had mostly been spared the direct brunt of the volcanic blast and its aftermath, but there was no saying what damage the earthquakes might have caused. It was said that only Azara could bring down the sturdy pyramids, and there was a time that Jendru had believed that. Now, he was not so certain. Most of the pyramids were old and had stood the test of time, but he had never heard of an event like this and guessed that for such, the pyramids were largely untested.

It also looked to him that his original assessment had most likely been correct: the riverfront and dock area looked as though it had been in the direct path of the blast and pyroclastic cloud. That meant that any traffic into or out of Azar would be affected - maybe even rendered impossible, either by land or river. It also meant that the river was likely to experience a die-off in the process. Survivors in Azar would have to turn to the jungle and gardens for food and sustenance, and no supplies or aid would be coming from Jurnda. And Jurndans would probably have problems of their own. Who knows how that city might have been affected by the earthquakes, and surely the ash and smoke was blowing their way.

There was no way around it - it was a catastrophic disaster, and the most dire event to take place on Lur in their five hundred year history of living on the island continent. There was no doubt in Jendru's mind that effects of this event would ripple out through space and time and bring as yet unseen hardship and challenges to everyone. It also meant new possibilities.

The whole thing seemed tragically ironic to Jendru. They had come here to start again and remake human society, in the process yet again dividing humanity, creating subcultures and secret enclaves, religious dissidents, and all the rest. And now, when the two religions of Lur had come to a head with the unprecedented visit of the Darsulans, this happens. Depending on who had survived, it was likely that the Darsulans were trapped in Azar along with everyone else - including Jor Alesh, Jendru reminded himself. Though she wanted to help in Azar, Jendru was certain that she'd want to make her way to Jurnda as soon as possible, given the scope and magnitude of what had occurred. She would be needed there, and expected as well. She was responsible for Jurnda in a way she would never be for Azar. Azar was Chondrasil's problem.

The image of Pirfiro trying to deal with this catastrophe made Jendru laugh. Pirfiro always tried so hard, was so earnest. He wasn't practical, however, and had more of a mind and talent for maintaining appearances than dealing with a crisis or making snap decisions. There, Chondrasil was in his element. Jendru hoped for everyone's sake that Chondrasil hadn't been injured, or worse. Yet if he had been removed from the picture, Jendru couldn't help but imagine Pirfiro stepping in and attempting to take charge - he was just that way - always trying to be helpful and in the center of the wheels of power. It mattered not to him that he was still a Maegin-Lu and not a Maegin proper. He had his charms, Jendru supposed, which was why people tolerated his faux authority. But this would be too much for him to fake his way through. This challenge was real and immediate. They'd need a real leader, not merely someone who *thought* he was a leader. Jendru shrugged. The world was full of surprises. Maybe Pirfiro would be able to rise to the task - but Jendru doubted it.

His real concern was for Jor Alesh and his friends - Davon, Treland, Vico, Sumra, and Khalanto. With the volcano exploding, they were all in harm's way, not to mention that his friends were devoted to a belief system he could no longer support or give any credence to. He wished he could take them with him on this new journey he was embarking upon. If only they would be open to seeing and learning the truth. Yet he knew that it was only possible to find this truth within and to know it for oneself. He hadn't thought to try and persuade them, for he knew such was futile. They would have to come to the truth the same way he had - on their own and under their own motivation. As much as he wanted to take them along, he couldn't.

Jor Alesh was another matter entirely. She had chosen to return to Azar, so they couldn't be together right at this moment, but Jendru saw no reason why they couldn't be together when this disaster got sorted out, provided she made it through unharmed. She would return to Jurnda, no doubt, and perhaps he should too. He had nowhere else to go. It seemed unlikely that Seyloq would be interested in having an extended houseguest, regardless of how much Jendru could stand to learn from him. He was no Maegin-Lu, and he certainly wasn't running a monastery. So maybe returning to Jurnda with Jor Alesh was the answer. *Whatever,* Jendru told himself. His mind was racing with possibilities. This was nothing that he needed to resolve right now. For the time being, he had made it to Seyloq's, Jor Alesh was helping in

Azar, and the disaster was whatever it was. At the moment, his main concern was to see if he could stay with Seyloq, at least for a little while, and even more importantly, get something to eat.

Jendru had snacked on fruits on his way to Seyloq's, but making love with Jor Alesh had been quite the vigorous (and sublime!) activity, and he needed nourishment. It was like releasing himself inside her had somehow turned him inside out - drawing energy from deep within his core and pulling him along with it. It had been an absolutely ecstatic experience, and quite unlike any previous time he had made love with a woman. The last time had been with a girl named Sarran Gaimil when he was nineteen back in Jurnda. That had been sweet, but this had been cosmic. And reaffirming. There was no doubt in Jendru's mind that they had both experienced themselves as one unified being during their lovemaking, and there had been no energetic barriers between them. In fact, the opposite was true. Their energies had been completely open to each other at the deepest, most profoundly intimate levels. The electric current between them was undeniable and more than palpable. It was like taking the medicine, but being right there together with no separation. Two bodies, but only one being, and that one being was madly in love with itself. But the act had taken its energetic toll and Jendru was hungry beyond belief, as though he hadn't eaten in years. The small amount of chocolate he had with him had helped with the drained sensation in the immediate aftermath, and the fruits he found along the path had helped sustain him on the uphill climb to Seyloq's. Now he was famished, and shoveling more sweet fruit in wasn't going to do it for Jendru. He needed something heavier and more substantial.

Even his hunger made him smile and spoke to his freedom. What he really wanted was meat. Despite Azarans being vegetarians (it wasn't good for the soul to eat meat and created bad energy for future incarnations), he couldn't help the overwhelming feeling that a piece of charred meat would really hit the spot. It had been five years since he had last eaten meat in a meal with his parents before making his way upriver to Azar and beginning his novitiate. They insisted he share a final meal with them and took him to an artists' hangout by the beach where they ate steak with fried calamari, caught fresh only minutes before they arrived. At the time, he had been weaning himself from all forms of meat in preparation for his life in Azar. It wasn't his first choice to take this meal with his parents, though he chose to humor them. Recalling the meal, he thought of how he would savor every bite were it in front of him now.

What if they're not wrong about everything? The question echoed through Jendru's mind. What if, despite their other delusions, there was something to the Azarans' belief that eating meat was wrong? After all, it *seemed* reasonable that there was something at least ethical about not eating other beings. But then why did he *want* meat? There was a disconnect between what he felt and what he thought. It was strange how the effects of his training lingered. *I've been taught how to think,* he told himself. He supposed these patterns would repeat themselves and gradually lessen over time. He had only left Azar this morning, after all.

It was with such thoughts in his mind that Jendru eventually emerged out of the jungle and came to Seyloq, who, apparently, had been of a similar inspiration and was standing outside roasting a small boar on a spit in front of his house, watching the smoke from the volcano billow in the distance. The smell was divine and it made Jendru's mouth water. It was a smell one might encounter down by the docks among the laypeople and tradesmen who came from Jurnda, but never in Azar, where strict vegetarianism ruled as a matter of doctrine and ethical purity. Obviously, Seyloq thought otherwise. *Too perfect,* Jendru commented to himself.

"I see you're not dead," Seyloq called out upon seeing Jendru approach. He had a funny look on his face showing that he hadn't expected Jendru to stumble out of the jungle at this time. "Are you hungry?" he asked, gesturing to the roasting boar. "The forest people brought me this today, and what with the volcano, it seemed like a good day for some roasted meat," he said with an ironic smile.

Jendru didn't say anything. He felt slightly in a daze. Now that he had reached his destination, the magnitude of everything that had transpired this day overwhelmed him. All he could do was stumble up to Seyloq's side and plop down in a simple lawn chair next to the old man. Seeing his state, Seyloq didn't press him for answers. He retrieved another chair from under a nearby tree and brought it next to Jendru, sitting beside him in silence, slowly turning the boar. They sat there for some time with the sound of the fire, the crackling juices of the boar, and the ever-present sound of both the toads and the distant rumble of the volcano.

After a while, Seyloq spoke to Jendru. "Turn this," he said, indicating the spit. He got up and went inside, returning a few moments later with drinks, bread, and some cheese, along with various fruits. He set up a little table between them and placed the tray with the food down, gesturing for Jendru to eat and drink. He eagerly dove in, not needing to be invited a second time. Soon the boar was ready. Jendru devoured a healthy portion of it. Seyloq ate a little, but mostly just watched.

The sun was getting low behind them, turning the eastern sky deep reds, oranges, and magentas, refracting through the volcanic smoke and ash, casting an errie glow about the valley of Azar. The winds were still blowing to the east down the valley, as was most common, so none of the smoke or ash had made it their way. Here, the air was clean and fresh, and smelled of distant rain. Now that it was getting dark, crickets were joining their calls to the other sounds of the forest and lightning bugs flitted about in the clearing around Seyloq's house with their yellow-green bioluminescent bodies blinking on and off.

The scene of the volcano became even more dramatic now that the light was growing darker. Lightning, which had been largely unseen during the light of day, flashed in the dark billowing smoke that continued to belch up from the caldera. Blue and white crackles of electricity could be seen dancing about the cloud that reached high into the evening sky, blotting out the emerging stars and stretching far to the east, no doubt reaching to the coast and beyond, drifting out over the ocean. If the winds were right, the ash would make it to the mainland eventually, traveling all the way back to *The*

World. Even that seemed strangely ironic and meaningful.

"So, do you want to talk about what you're doing here?" asked Seyloq after Jendru had satiated himself. He took some dried leaves and flowers and rolled them up in a small paper, making something of a wand, which he lit from the fire and started smoking. After taking a few drags, he offered it to Jendru, saying (while still attempting to keep the smoke in his lungs), "Try some of this, if you like. The forest people smoke it. It's mild and relaxing. I think you'll enjoy it. We had some the other day with the medicine, but you probably didn't even notice it."

Jendru took it from him. It had a pungent taste and he found that he did like it. He took the smoke deep into his lungs and held it there, following Seyloq's lead. It was almost like the toad medicine, but far milder and nowhere near as explosive. He felt his body relaxing, allowing various energy currents to run their course through his being. Despite the warm embrace of the humid evening air, he got the chills for a few moments, causing his teeth to chatter.

"You've got some energy working out," commented Seyloq, intended as both an observation and as a way of saying, *Just let it happen.* Jendru found himself making odd purring noises as the energy moved up into his throat. Working with his breath, just allowing, he found his body opening up and releasing, finishing with a few gags that seemed to expel any energetic residue from whatever it was that was working through him.

By this time, Seyloq had almost finished the smoke. He passed the remainder back to Jendru. His energy felt smooth and calm now. He still felt like this plant was a shallow imitation of the toad medicine, but far gentler. Looking out at the volcano, he thought of how much the toad medicine was like an immediate internal volcano itself when it exploded into one's being. By comparison, this flower they were smoking was more of a gentle lifting, though still subtly powerful. He liked it.

Seyloq took the very last of the smoke from Jendru and then flicked the butt into the fire, to which he also added some logs - more for light than for warmth. When the fire blazed, it obscured their view of the valley and the evening sank into darkness beyond the orange and yellow glow of the fire.

Finally answering Seyloq's question, Jendru spoke at last. "I refused to take my vows today, so Chondrasil sent me away. He wanted to make a big show for the Darsulans, who arrived when Jor Alesh and I were out here yesterday. I couldn't do it – take my vows. I'm not one of them anymore - thanks to you."

"No," said Seyloq. "Thanks to *you*. Don't try to give me any credit for your own decisions and realizations. I'm only a mirror. You are responsible for your own life, not me, not from over here in this body. Each version of the self is fully responsible for itself."

"I know," said Jendru. "I didn't mean it that way. I only meant that if I hadn't started coming out here to talk with you and share your medicine, none of this would have happened. I would have been there with everyone else, taking my vows today and securing my place in Azara for the remainder of my life."

"Maybe," said Seyloq. "Things are what they are, and there's not much point in speculating about how things might have been otherwise were they different, because they aren't. All that really matters is that you had the opportunity to take your vows and you didn't, and so now you're here. And who knows? If you had taken your vows, maybe you'd be dead, or injured. From up here, it looks like things might be pretty serious in Azar. Many people are suffering, no doubt. I would think you might be grateful for having gotten out just in time."

Jendru nodded in agreement.

"What about your girlfriend?" Seyloq asked.

Jendru was a little taken aback. "Jor Alesh?"

"Sure."

"We were making love in the forest in the middle of the road. The volcano erupted right as we were climaxing."

Seyloq let out a riotous laugh.

"You don't think we somehow caused this, do you?" Jendru asked, finally voicing a thought that had been bouncing around in his head ever since the volcano first exploded earlier that day.

Seyloq only laughed harder. "Don't confuse correlation with causation," he said at last, after getting his laughter under control. "As an individual vehicle for the One, you have control and responsibility for various aspects of your being right here in this body, but not much else. When you're clear, and in the flow of the energy that is reality, you'll see all kinds of strange synchronicities, but it's only the ego that wants to take responsibility for them or apply its own particular meaning and interpretation to the event. So the volcano exploded at the same time you did - so what? It's cute, in its own way, but I wouldn't read too much into it. It's simply what's happening. Every vehicle, every perspective, is free to put its own spin on the event. Take your girlfriend, for example. What does she think of all this? Or Chondrasil? For him, I'm sure this is full of all kinds of divine portents and signs. And what do the Darsulans think? Maybe they all think they caused this somehow, or that it is a sign from Azara, or God, or whatever. Or maybe, this is simply how reality works, and it is what it is. In the end, we vehicles are just along for the ride, and it has its various thrills, disasters, and sublime joys along the way. Looking for *meaning* is a fool's game, and one that I personally choose not to play."

Jendru didn't respond directly. His mind had turned to Jor Alesh. "She's down there," he said, thankful that there hadn't been any further major explosions from the volcano. He felt somewhat confident that she was probably okay.

"She's the Alcian," said Seyloq as a matter-of-fact. Jendru nodded.

"You don't feel the need to help?" Jendru asked, turning to Seyloq.

The older man laughed. "No," he said without any hesitation. "The world is a big place, and there's *lots* of suffering out there. I've chosen to help people in my own way by assisting them in discovering the truth about themselves. I've taken that on as my personal responsibility because I know the truth and know that I can help others with this. Beyond that, well, everyone is on his or her own, at least as far as I'm concerned from this body right here. We all make our choices, and this is mine. I do what I can, according to what feels authentic and genuine for me. I'm not a do-gooder and I don't go where I'm not invited. I'm sure Chondrasil would be no more happy to see me down there than he would be to see you. Now, that's his own problem, not mine - or yours, for that matter. So that isn't what keeps me from going down there. I'm not motivated by concern for others the way that people who are trapped in their egos are. In the end, always remember that there's only one being and we're all merely versions of that being. Take a look around you. Reality is a challenging place. In the end, everyone dies, everyone suffers, everyone encounters tragedy and difficulty. None of us can stop these things from happening, and when it comes down to it, every version of the self is perfectly expendable – we all die, eventually. Reality goes on. Life goes on. The process continues. That's the important thing."

"So it doesn't matter if we help others or not?"

"Not in any grand cosmic sense. No, not really. If you're motivated to help, then do it. If not, don't. It's up to you. As a fully actualized version of the One, it's up to you. Personal choice. That's all."

"Like eating meat?" Jendru asked.

Seyloq laughed. "Like eating meat, sure. Who's eating whom, in the end? Who's killing whom? Who's fucking whom? Who's giving birth to whom? Who's exploding volcanoes on whom? It's all One. There is no moral or ethical system to the universe. Things are what they are. It's only us vehicles that tend to take things personally - especially us human vehicles. Everyone wants to be a good person and wants to be liked, loved, and accepted. Everyone wants to fit in and find their place in society and in relationship to others. The only real relationship that counts is your relationship to yourself. Everything we experience on the *outside* is merely a reflection of our relationship on the *inside*.

"Take your girlfriend, for example. Both of you have truly opened up to yourselves and are learning to love yourselves and accept yourselves without qualification. And now, because you're both going through this at the same time, you can be mirrors for each other and help reflect each other, and in the end, serve each other's purposes. You're fulfilling her and she's fulfilling you because your energy is compatible in that way. Like magnets, you find yourselves mysteriously drawn together and expressing your ecstatic love with one another. Well that's what it's all about, isn't it? It's true. It's genuine, and you're both open to it, so that's what's happening. Nothing but mirrors. It's not about right or wrong, should or shouldn't; it's about being true to what is - like the tasty boar.

"Believe me - I know about the whole vegetarian thing. As if plants weren't alive! Sure, animals are more personally sentient than plants, but *everything* is alive in its own way. Telling yourself that you're being a moral or ethical or *spiritual* person by not eating meat is a form of self-delusion. The universe doesn't give a fuck! That's just the fact of the matter. Humans are free to care about it, if they want, but that doesn't make it any kind of grand gesture, and doesn't *do* anything for anyone. If you're hungry and want to eat some meat, do it. If you don't, don't. It's only the ego that wants to turn it into something that *means* something or has some particular value or purpose. It's the same for sex - if you feel it and want it, go for it. Celibacy is a fool's game and has zero relevance for your inherent, natural divinity. Actually, I'd say it's the other way around. How else is the One supposed to evolve and propagate itself if people don't have sex? Imagine if *everyone* were an Azaran! Humanity would die off in a generation. What good would that do the One? We humans are the *entire point* of this whole evolution game - self-aware versions of the One freely expressing and enjoying themselves. What could be more meaningful than that?"

Seyloq turned to Jendru. He had been staring at the fire while talking. It was clear that the younger man was hanging on his words and wanted him to continue, with nothing of his own to contribute.

"I'll tell you a story," said Seyloq. He rolled another wand of flowers, lit it up, and then said, "It's the story of the One."

Chapter 27

THE STORY OF THE ONE

A long time ago, so long ago, in fact, that it was a time before time as we know and experience it existed, there was a being.

This one awoke to the reality of its own being, its own existence.

In awakening to itself, this being knew that it was immortal, eternal, and infinite. This being was the only being to exist. There was nothing beyond it or outside of it or separate from it in any way, because there was no beyond or outside. This one being was reality itself.

This being was the One, and there was no other.

This being, this One, was not like the physical, living beings that we can see around us here, in space and time, for this being was the potential for all *things* and all *individual beings*. Just as the tiniest seed contains the potential for the greatest tree, so was the potential of all things contained within the essence and very nature of the One. But in this time before time, there was only the One, and the potential that was contained in its essence and being was as yet unrealized and unexpressed.

Knowing this of its own nature, the One also knew that it had a choice. The choice was to be itself, and in doing so, give birth to all things, or not be itself, and there would be nothing.

Really, it wasn't a choice.

It wasn't a choice because this One had supreme knowledge of itself and it was incapable of lying to itself or deceiving itself because there was no *other*. There was no one to lie to, no one to deceive. Only the self. Nothing more, and nothing less.

So even though it was a choice, it really wasn't a choice. The one knew that it was reality itself, and if it didn't allow itself to be itself, then nothing else would be. There would only be potential, and nothing actual would ever occur.

And the One knew that if it chose not to be itself, it would be alone, forever, and for eternity.

Now, this One being loved itself fully and completely without reservations or limits, for there was nothing that was not itself. There was nothing to fear, nothing to judge, nothing to withhold, for only the self existed and nothing else. Love, in fact, was the very nature, very essence of the being, for love is the acceptance of all possibilities and the recognition of the true nature of the self. Infinite love was the very nature of the being, and this was its energy, its essence, its nature. It was what was.

Because this being loved itself infinitely, as was true to its nature, it could do no less than be authentic to itself and express itself fully in its infinite love. For it was all or nothing, you see. The choice wasn't really a choice.

But the One was alone in its love, for there was no other. There was only the self. And while it loved itself, that love would never be returned, never be shared, never be experienced by anyone, for the One was all and beyond it was nothingness, non-existence - not even a void or an emptiness, so really there was no beyond. All that was, was the self.

In order for the One to be itself, to express its love and to give birth to the possibilities that existed inside itself, it had to divide itself. It had to create limits. It had to divide its infinite energy of love into spectrums of energy that could interact and exchange with each other. Now, it was still all the One, but this division would allow for change, growth, and transformation. This division would make the container of reality possible, the container of space and time, the matrix in which all transformations take place. Without division, no space and time. Without space and time, no change, no becoming, no growth, no evolution.

So this One made the decision to commit fully to being itself without reservation. It chose to let its energy divide, as it wanted to do, and give birth to actuality, to reality, to what is.

From our perspective, if we could have been there, which of course no one and no thing was, for nothing else existed, but if we could have been there, it would have appeared to us as though nothing had suddenly and inexplicably transformed into something. From absolutely nowhere in particular, for there was not any *where*, the energies that form and structure our reality burst forth into being.

It was violent and chaotic, a mad rush of non-being becoming being. In those first moments, in that crucial time of transformation from infinite non-being to infinite, yet divided, being, all was pure energy, for this was the very nature and essence of the One.

It was then that space and time as we experience them came into being, for prior to this moment, they only existed as potential, as what might be, but not what was, for there was nothing.

From this nowhere, the energy of the One radiated in all directions simultaneously, and with this radiation came the structure of spacetime. Within it, the energy that had been One and still was one but was now divided, was able to form into different spectrums, different vibrations, and different expressions of the one energy of reality, which is love. Suddenly, there was apparent multiplicity, though all was still one. This was when difference came into being, and it was difference that made everything else that followed possible.

As spacetime grew and expanded, the spectrums of energy grew more distinct from each other, each taking on their own characteristics, each expressing their own possibilities. But in reality, the One could never actually divide itself, for it was still the only thing that truly existed. All these spectrums were variations and expressions of the One, and they were never separate from the One. The divisions of the One did not create *another;* only diversity of the manifestations of the One. The One was still and forever after only One.

And the One knew - this was its life. This was its being. This was itself. This, what we call reality, was what the One loving itself fully looked and felt like.

So the One continued to transform itself in every way that it could, because it was the only way reality could be. Things were the way they were because they had to be. This was truth. This was reality.

And from the original chaos came form, order, regularity, and structure – fractal patterns of energy and geometry that structured and gave shape and form to all things. Yet nothing was ever permanent, for all things eventually transformed into all other things, so all order and structure was merely temporary expressions of the One - endlessly transforming patterns of energy. Within the multitude, nothing was given preference, for all was the One equally and fully, and only by being so could the project of reality continue. The only true constant was continual transformation, which took the form of creation, process, exchange, and destruction. This was what the process looked like. The process was the *thing*, and not the temporary configurations produced by the process.

The process took place across all levels simultaneously, from the infinitely small to the infinitely big. Structures organized at every level, each with their own rules for interaction, transformation, and exchange. It was all energy. It was all the One. But now there was true diversity, true difference, at an energetic level. Waves coalesced into particles, and particles interacted and joined to create elements, and elements coalesced and transformed to become substance, and substance collected into objects, and eventually, the pure energy that was the One had transformed itself, evolved itself, into stars, planets, nebulae, galaxies, singularities, and everything in between. It became what we know as the universe. And it was still the One.

Yet this was not the fulfillment of the potential and possibilities that were the essence of the One. There was more, much more.

There was life.

All that yet existed was beautiful and complete, but that which existed was confined and limited by its energetic form. Stars could only be stars. Planets could only be planets. Atoms could only be atoms. At each level, all the One could be was true to itself, and the limits and divisions it had enacted within itself were the limits of reality. The One knew *this* was not the full and complete expression of itself, for it was alive, conscious, aware, and had will, had choice, and the need to express and manifest that choice and will.

Thus what we now know of as *life* was the next stage of the process. And it too, like everything that came before it, was made possible by transformations of fractal patterns of energy that grew and changed over time.

From our perspective, the process began on one small planet in an infinite cosmos. Maybe it happened elsewhere - we don't know. But we do know that it happened here, because we are here - this is where we find ourselves, so this we can know.

It was all a question of probability and possibility. Life, as we experience it, was the goal, the purpose, so to speak, of the universe coming into being. Living beings couldn't just pop into existence out of nowhere the way that the universe itself did, however. Life required structure, form, stability, and regular exchanges of different spectrums of energy. And for that, life needed the right mix of elements and energies in order to come into being. And for the right mix of elements and energies to come into being, it took an entire universe of expression of possibilities to give rise to even one planet that had what was necessary. It took all of this to bring this one possibility into actuality.

It was here that conditions were exactly right. With the right mix of energies and physical substances, the potentials for biological life that resided within the One were able to express themselves and begin their evolutionary process. It began simply, and by appearances, individual beings came to be. At first, they were terribly simple, but they were, unlike inorganic reality, vehicles through which the One could experience itself in a new way, in a way that allowed for greater expression of will, greater detail and nuance of experience, and greater realization of self. Life became the medium through which the One could enjoy itself simultaneously as both subject and object, as the experiencer and that which is experienced. And from the perspectives of the individual vehicles, *this was reality:*

subject and object. The divisions within the One became open to direct experience and observation in a way that had not been previously possible.

Life flourished and transformed. From simplicity came ever-greater complexity, ever-greater specialization with ever more finely tuned structures and mechanisms. It was all an energetic process, so it had to follow all the rules and requirements of energetic reality. It occurred the only way it could - through what we know as biological evolution.

As a being of energy embodied in individual bodies, or vehicles, all aspects of living beings function according to energetic reality. All life processes energy. All life must take in energy from outside its physical self and transform it internally. Everything that living beings know of themselves and their environment is based on how the structures of that being are able to perceive, experience, and interpret the energies of their reality, both internally and externally. So in this way, living beings are direct expressions of the One, for they are living energy, just as is the One, and in truth, they are the One, but in divided, embodied form.

In this way, the One was able to shape itself into multiple forms simultaneously, each with its own particular perspective and experience. Yet within this mix of multiplicity, no one manifestation was given any preference over any other, for all are equally autonomous versions of the One. Each is fully capable of following its own interest. This is itself a reflection of the One's uncompromising self-love. The One does not play favorites with any version of itself. All are equally self-responsible. Sometimes, this manifests as competition between living beings. Sometimes, this manifests as symbiosis and cooperation. Other times it is parasitic and manipulative. It is all the expression, ultimately, of self-interest, and this is an expression of universal love, the foundational energy of reality.

Since there is no true *other*, all living beings must rely on other living beings for their individual existence and continuance, and as a result, must kill and eat apparently other versions of the self in order to survive and thrive. *All life feeds on life*, and there is no moral or ethical guide or standard for this process within reality. It is simply how things are. From the individual perspective, this may seem cruel or even horrific, but from the unitary perspective, it is necessary and holds no moral or ethical import. It is, after all, only one being that is doing this to itself, and no matter how it looks or appears to any one given individual, or even collections of individuals, it is the manifestation and expression of love.

This is the reality of embodied life.

Without physical bodies to hold the energy together, there are no individual perspectives or experiences. The universal consciousness and awareness of the One requires individual vehicles in order to have immediate experience and perspective. The only individual vehicles that exist are physical in nature, and all are equally enmeshed in the larger structures of the physical universe and the energetic constructs of spacetime. This is what allows the One to experience multiple perspectives simultaneously and experience apparent difference. Through this process, the One was able to create itself in diverse forms and though it was still, in truth, completely alone and utterly solitary in existence, it no longer *seemed* that way.

As with inorganic reality, it took a great deal of time and countless transformations of energy to evolve ever more sophisticated reality enjoyment vehicles. And somewhere along the way, after countless eons of evolution, something completely new happened - the beings the One was evolving itself into became self-aware and realized that they existed. These beings woke up from the dream of the universe and started to dream their own dreams and said, "I am here!" and with that came the questions: "What am I? Who am I? Where did I come from? Where am I going? Is there anything more, or is this it?"

This was a grand achievement for the One, for with this self-awareness came great freedom. *These* vehicles could truly enact their own will. Though they were limited in their physical form, as are all physical beings, they were not limited in their thought, in their imagination, and in their ability to enact their will within reality. Of all the creatures that had come into being, these were the fullest and most complete expression of the One because they had the power of thought, of understanding, and they were able to know that they existed.

However, they didn't know who they were. They knew themselves as creatures, as individuals, but not as embodiments of the One. They did not know themselves because they had a sense of self, of ego, of being *different, separate, and unique.* And because they had free will, they were able to conceive of themselves and the world they found themselves in according to their own minds and ideas. In asking questions of their identity, they were free to invent any answer they wanted.

Paradoxically, this propensity for self-delusion served these creatures well. It gave birth not only to personal identity, but to collective identity as well. It gave rise to religions, cultures, politics, and all manner of human expression, creativity, thought and imagination. This allowed these self-aware creatures to act collectively in groups, not out of instinct and inherent energy, as was the case for their fellow creatures, but out of conscious choice. Thus they were able to achieve things that were impossible for other creatures. They created art and cities and technology, and they also created belief systems and religions and dogmas. They came to understand symbols and how to manipulate and use them. They learned how to communicate in sophisticated and nuanced ways, and from this came human language.

In many ways, these creatures became unbound, and both individually and collectively, they explored every possibility in every possible way. In this, a new phase of evolution had begun. No longer was the One limited to the gradual and mechanical transformations of energy that had made evolution and being possible. Now, through these glorious reality enjoyment vehicles, evolution could proceed from idea to concrete reality in a way that had never before been possible, for these creatures could make their thoughts become reality. This was nothing magical, for it still required that these creatures operate within the limits of energetic reality, but *they* could exert their will and change reality through the manipulations of energy that were made possible by their bodies.

Now it was possible for things that had never existed except as a possibility to suddenly pop into existence, almost as if from nowhere. Someone, somewhere, wrote the first word, and written language came into existence. Someone, somewhere, built the first home, and architecture came into being. Everything that we can see in the human world started with thought and became reality through the choices and actions of humans. No other creatures could function this way, for no other beings were truly self-aware or had the ability to understand and manipulate their environment in anything close to a comparable manner. In this way, humans were fundamentally unique. They had the mental capacity and physical means to both understand and shape their world. And their languages, cultures, and symbol systems made it possible for them to accumulate vast stores of ideas and knowledge so that every future generation could benefit from what was learned and accomplished before. Whereas every other creature could only know what they needed to know to survive and continue their life cycles, humans and their knowledge and creations transcended well beyond the merely necessary into the exploration of the possible in search of answers and understanding. As living beings, they were marvelous and sublime.

So they imagined and they created. Some of what they created benefited them. Some of it didn't. The drive to explore, create, and understand was always there. Over time, they progressed and their creations became ever-more sophisticated, though now this process of evolution was occurring at a much faster rate, for the previous limits of reality had effectively been transcended.

Yet still these creatures did not know who they were. In creating their identities, and their understandings of themselves and their world, they divided themselves. They made arbitrary distinctions. And when these arbitrary distinctions were exposed, they became uncomfortable. They found that other humans that did not fit their pre-conceived notions and beliefs threatened them, and made them question their own identity. This gave rise to fear, hate, jealousy, rage.

Identities clashed. Some people had the wrong color skin. Others believed in the wrong god. Some people dressed wrong, or thought wrong. Groups of identities competed for power, for prominence, for security. Illusions clashed and time after time, these humans proved again and again that they were willing to kill and die for their beliefs. And not only that, they were willing to compromise what they felt and experienced in their very bodies out of allegiance to their ideas, which were not reality. They convinced themselves that all kinds of things that weren't true, were, and then went around behaving as though those assumptions and beliefs were reality. They told themselves lies, and they believed the lies. Without even realizing it, they committed themselves to playing games of make-believe and lived their lives as though it were the games that really mattered.

Eventually, these creatures, these versions of the One, decided that they were going to fight it out until the bitter end, each protecting and projecting their own illusions, all based on the lack of awareness of the true nature of the self. Rather than living in universal love and truth, they existed in countless projections and illusions, all competing for dominance. What once served these creatures, their egos, became the source of their own undoing and destruction. And they had no one to blame but themselves.

Yet it is a willful and conscious self-deception. The many versions of the One have all agreed to *believe* that they are separate, unique, and divided. Otherwise, there is a vast existential loneliness, and the game isn't nearly as much fun. It would be like trying to play a game with yourself, but consciously and knowingly playing both sides of the game board. It can't be done. Both players have to be fully invested in playing and winning the game, and they can't do that if they know they are actually the same being. They have to believe themselves to be separate and behave accordingly. That's what makes the game fun and provides the thrill for the players. Otherwise, the game is unplayable, unwinnable, and there is no motivation. The trick is a necessary one.

But no longer. The trick was a necessary evolutionary stage, but it is no longer needed, and in fact, has become counter-productive. As a species, it is time for humanity to evolve and wake up to its true nature: One Being, One Life, embodied in multiple forms, but not separate, not divided. The imaginary beliefs that drove our cultural evolution brought humanity to the brink of total destruction. And now, in the aftermath, we are repeating many of the same errors we made before. Even with the use of the medicines, those precious crystalline substances that hold the potential for enabling us to perceive and experience our true nature, we still cling to our illusions.

So the energy of the One has shifted. The game was once the thing, but no longer. It's time to grow up and play a new game, a conscious game, a game that is not enshrouded in and obfuscated by illusion, deception, and the projection of false identities. The time has simply come. The evolution of the universe is moving on, and it is moving on because it must. It's time to wake up. The time of illusion is over.

After the *Great War*, many like-minded versions of the One gathered on this small island continent called Lur. They brought with them a powerful medicine, one that had the capacity to wake these versions of the One up to who they really were. Yet that wasn't what happened, because it is always a matter of choice, and individuals must choose truth over illusion. No medicine, no matter how powerful, can make that choice for anyone. Thus, rather than breaking down illusions, this use of the medicine served to strengthen illusions and false beliefs, and people became divided again. Some went to form their own society that was not couched in fantastic beliefs and esoteric practices, yet still they did not know who they were. It was a step, but only a step. Then, another opening came when the doctrine was challenged and reformed. Yet here again, rather than integrate this new understanding, a new divide was chosen by the people, and humanity split yet again. Though the movement was toward awakening and self-realization, beliefs and identities still held more power than truth.

And then at last, one person did wake up completely. This awakening came with a complete personal transformation, and the man who had been, in some ways, died, and another, more universal consciousness took his place. For this one man, all the illusions were shattered and reality was seen for what it is: one unified being of energy that is all beings and all things with nothing beyond, no *other*. So this man knew - the story of the One was *his* story, and the pages of this story could be seen in all of existence.

This is reality. There is nothing beyond. There is no great goal, no great plan, no transcendent realm, no reward, and no punishment. This is it. And the time for us to live fully and completely in reality has arrived. We had our time to play, but we're growing up, whether we want to or not. Reality demands it. The time for religion and belief is over. It is a remnant of our past. The future we move toward is one of knowledge, not belief. It is knowledge of the self, knowledge of the One, knowledge of who and what we are so that we can make our decisions based on reality, not speculation, wishes, and dreams. And in stepping into what we have always been, the problems that divide and plague us as humans, as vehicles for the One, will evaporate. Other creatures don't hate. Other creatures don't go to war. Other creatures don't ostracize those who think the wrong thoughts, or wear the wrong clothes, or listen to the wrong music, or anything else. They are what they are and do what they do. Humans, while more sophisticated, need not be any different. We are free to be ourselves, and to do that, we must know who and what we are. For how could we be ourselves in ignorance and self-deception? True freedom, true liberation, true love, requires truth. Nothing less will do.

So here we now sit, two versions of the One, understanding our true nature and our place within the process that is occurring. Energy always follows the path of least resistance, and that is what it has found in you, and in me, and in Jor Alesh. We are the vanguard of the new evolution. Volcanoes release energy when and where they can. Lightning strikes where and when it can. Transformation comes when and where it can. It is the nature of energy, the nature of being. From our embodied perspectives, we do not control it. We give it our assent, for we acknowledge the truth. That is all we can do. For those who are willing to be ready, the time is now. For those who are unwilling to be ready, the time is still now. There is nothing that any of us can do about it, aside from finding the clarity within ourselves to allow us to be ourselves fully, completely, and without hesitation or reservation. It's up to each one of us to accept the truth and discover it within ourselves, for ourselves. No one can do it for us. Azara won't do it for us. The Maegins won't do it for us. The Darsulans won't do it for us. We are all fully responsible for ourselves. Looking outside the self for truth is a fool's errand, and the time to set that errand aside has come. It's what's happening, and it has already begun. We are past the point of no return.

To continue, we must continue in truth. Divine moments of truth may be hard to come by, but it is the only way. It's up to each individual to wake up and become the fullness of his or her potential in every moment.

This is why we have the medicine, and why we have it now.

It's why I woke up to my true nature. It's why you came to me. It's why you and Jor Alesh found each other. It's why all that is happening right now is happening the way it is. It is the path of least resistance. Energy, the truth of being, will always find a way, because it must.

End of story . . .

Chapter 28

CHAOS

All was chaos and confusion when Jor Alesh got back to Azar. The volcano of Ladjup was still rumbling and belching, threatening a new explosion at any moment. The ground still shook and trembled beneath them. People were running about in all directions, calling out for their loved ones, trying desperately to alleviate their fears that someone close to them had been hurt, or worse, killed. Jor Alesh looked around for someone in a position of authority, but there didn't seem to be anyone in charge of things here at the western edge of the city, and there wasn't anywhere in particular for her to focus her attention or offer help.

Surverying the pyramid city, it appeared that it had mostly withstood the tremors and had definitely avoided the brunt of the blast from the volcano. Jendru had been correct - from what she could see, the bulk of the explosion of the pyroclastic cloud had been directed toward the docks and waterfront. Jor Alesh wondered how many people had instantly died when it hit. Not nearly as many had the explosion come directly to the city, but the death toll would still be significant - at least several hundred, she guessed.

The pyramids and other structures of the city had not been unaffected, however. Archways and terraces lining the streets had collapsed and there were many places where bricks from the pyramids had come loose and crashed to the ground, making travel and movement about the city difficult. Since the pyramids were mostly made of stone, fire was at a minimum, but not everything in Azar was stonework, and small fires were scattered about here and there. Trees had also fallen, some blocking the pathways, others having crashed into pyramids. The glass coverings of many of the walkways were shattered and broken.

The further she moved into the city, the worse the destruction and damage seemed to become. It occurred to her that the epicenter of the quakes might have been right here, in the center of Azar. She came across a group of people, monks, novices, and laypersons alike, struggling to remove fallen bricks and stones from a large pile of rubble where the sides of one of the pyramids had collapsed. People were shouting and crying, passing bricks from one person to the next. Not sure what was happening, Jor Alesh rushed over and before she knew it, someone was handing her large stones. She could hear cries coming from underneath the rubble, and before long, a grasping hand was uncovered as more bricks were moved away. Everyone worked faster, digging out the person or persons trapped within. Bricks were coming covered in blood, as though the red stones had been covered in a paint of matching color. Working frantically, they were finally able to pull the person out - by his look, he was a Maegin or Maegin-Lu, though Jor Alesh didn't recognize him or know his name. They could see other body parts deeper within the rubble, but there were no more cries for help and no more movement.

Jor Alesh had to excuse herself and go throw up. She wasn't the only one.

Everyone seemed to be in a daze, including Jor Alesh. Some people were stumbling around without any direction or purpose. Many had cuts and bruises, as though something had either fallen on them, or they had fallen into something during the tremors. Everything was a mess. It was such a dramatic contrast to how Azar had looked only a few hours ago that it was hard for Jor Alesh to process the reality of what had occurred. Though the city was still standing, it was severely damaged. The number of injured seemed to exceed those fortunate ones who had made it through unharmed. That morning, it had been a beautiful and ordered temple city - now it was something else entirely.

Pulling herself together, and fighting the urge to give help and assistance at every turn, she decided to head directly for the center of the city and the Obsidian Temple. In all likelihood, this was where the majority of the population had been at the time the volcano blew, as this was where the oath-taking ceremony was to have taken place. All the Darsulans, novices, and monks would have been gathered there. She imagined the volcano must have gone off just as they were holding their ceremony. Her hope was that the magnificent temple, the centerpiece of the city, had been built strong enough to withstand the quakes. As she made her way, she hoped to catch a reassuring glimpse of the large black pyramid, but she kept getting confused and turned around. The streets and pathways of Azar weren't laid out in long, straight streets as they were in Jurnda. Here everything was fractal and geometric patterns, and the only way to make one's way through the city was to wind through it like some kind of immense labyrinth. She had thought she had been getting the hang of it, but now it was confusing. The result was that it seemed like an eternity before her view finally opened up onto the great pyramid.

The scene was simultaneously ominous and reassuring. The temple still stood with no visible exterior damage. *Good,* thought Jor Alesh. Yet it was framed in the background by the billowing plumes of toxic smoke and ash from Ladjup, casting a dark pall over the scene, a clear reminder that even though the main temple still stood, destruction and chaos swirled around it.

Most of the population was gathering here at the center of the city. It was Pirfiro who noticed Jor Alesh first. He was on his way running from somewhere to somewhere else, his large belly jiggling as he bounced along. "My lady!" he called out upon seeing her. He looked worried, running up to her. "Are you hurt?"

It was then that Jor Alesh realized that she had blood on her hands and clothes from the rescue she participated in at the outskirts of the city. "I'm fine," she answered. "This belongs to someone else," she said, indicating the blood.

"I'm so happy to hear that," said Pirfiro, forcing a smile. "It would have been a great tragedy if you had been injured as well. There's enough destruction here as it is without us losing the Alcian." There were tears in his eyes.

"Where's Chondrasil?" Jor Alesh asked.

"Down there," said Pirfiro, indicating with his head the

Obsidian Temple.

"Is he okay?"

"He's hurt," said Pirfiro, "but he'll be alright. For many others . . ."

She wanted to ask him more, but seeing that Jor Alesh didn't need his help, he excused himself and continued on his way to wherever it was he had originally been going. Jor Alesh made her way to the temple to see if she could find Chondrasil and figure out how she could be most helpful.

A group of Maegins outside the temple informed Jor Alesh that she should find Chondrasil inside. She started to make her way to the steps leading into the massive pyramid when people emerged from the top of the stairs, attempting to make their way down. It was then that Jor Alesh realized that while the temple might look sound from the outside, things inside must be a different matter. The people were carrying bodies.

Everyone gathered outside started to notice and silence overcame the crowd. First one body, and then many more, were brought out from the temple, which seemed more of a tomb than a place of religious ceremony. The bodies were mixed - some were novices, others monks, and some were clearly from among the Darsulans. Jor Alesh wondered what had happened and was itching to get inside and find out for herself. In the meantime, she had to wait for the procession of corpses. Many of them appeared to be crushed with large portions of their bodies flattened out and utterly destroyed. Some bodies were no more than piles of flesh and bone. The scene was utterly horrifying. Jor Alesh fought back the gags welling up within her. Several of the people standing by her were not as controlled, and many sobbed between retches.

Standing there watching, she suddenly realized that she recognized one of the bodies. It was Jendru's friend - she thought his name was Sumra, but wasn't sure. And there was another one. That was Davon? The next one she was sure of. That was Khalanto, without a doubt. It was then that it dawned on Jor Alesh - the novices and those who were taking their vows had been crushed by something, along with their Maegin-Lus and some of the Darsulans. Her heart leapt in her chest. If Jendru had been there . . .

It was the next body that made her realize how bad the situation really was. Wails and cries emerged from the small group of Darsulans who had gathered outside at the base of the pyramid. The body of an older, and somewhat overweight, woman was being carried down by several strong young men. The head looked completely crushed - just a mash of skull and brains. It was horrific to look upon. Jor Alesh didn't have any doubts. It was Meridalthi Vitri, the High Maegin of the Darsulans, the Reformed Azarans. She had come all this way at Seyloq's invitation only to encounter her death in the very heart of the world of Azara, here in the center of the ceremonial city in the very pyramid that housed their faith. If it were possible for fate to be more ironic, Jor Alesh couldn't see how.

At last the parade of mangled bodies ended. Jor Alesh hurried up the steps, surmounted them, and descended into the interior of the great pyramid. It all became clear what had happened. There, on the floor of the pyramid, were remnants of the Flower of Azara, the large and complex geometrical form that had graced the center of the pyramid's ceiling at the very apex of the interior. The irony level jumped up a few notches for Jor Alesh.

Chondrasil was trying to wave off those who were attempting to help him. He had a large gash across his face and was bleeding profusely down his front, though he appeared to be ignoring it and was not appreciative of the attention. "Go tend to someone who really needs it," he barked at those around him, putting a cloth up to his face to try and clean himself up some. He tried to stand when he saw Jor Alesh approaching, but tumbled back into the chair he was sitting in, clearly having trouble finding his balance. He was alive, but the seriousness of his wound and his age made Jor Alesh wonder for how long.

Chondrasil looked at her, glancing over her body. "I presume that's not yours," he said in reference to the blood on her hands and clothing. "You don't look hurt."

"No, I'm fine," she responded.

He looked disconsolate and crestfallen. He shook his

head and gestured meekly to the devastation in the center of the ceremonial hall. "Look what that demon brought upon us," he said angrily.

His meaning was clear. Chondrasil had concluded that Seyloq was to blame for this.

"Azara has punished us for allowing the Darsulans into our sanctuary, and the Mother/Father has punished the Darsulans as well, killing their leader along with our novices who were finishing reciting their vows. The judgment of God is upon us all, and it's that demon's doing. *He* invited them here. *He* is the cause of this."

Jor Alesh didn't know what to say, though the look upon her face probably said it all for her: *you poor, deluded man.* Chondrasil was too busy looking at the fallen Flower of Azara to notice.

It was then that a huffing and puffing Pirfiro reappeared. Chondrasil turned and looked up at him, bracing himself for whatever it was the lesser monk had to say. Pirfiro hesitated. "Out with it," commanded the High Maegin.

"It's worse than we feared," said the Maegin-Lu.

"How?"

"The waterfront is completely destroyed, as we expected," said Pirfiro.

"And . . . ?" asked Chondrasil in dreaded anticipation.

"And there's lava flowing from Ladjup."

Chondrasil's eyes widened. "It's not coming to the city, is it?" he asked, the sound of near panic in his voice.

"No," said Pirfiro, "but it might as well be."

"What do you mean?" asked Jor Alesh.

"It's headed for the river," he answered.

Jor Alesh didn't understand, but Chondrasil did. "It will block the river." Pirfiro nodded. "And then the valley will flood." Chondrasil put his head in his hands. He was crying now, though he tried not to show it. "We were spared the fire, and now water will get us, in the end."

Regaining some composure, he issued an order.

"Have as much water diverted into the aqueducts as possible - as much as they can hold. It won't stop the coming flood, but that will buy us some time."

Pirfiro turned to rush off. Chondrasil reached out and grabbed his robe, preventing him. "And have our engineers watch the lava. Have them calculate how long we have and decide where in the city we might be able to relocate the wounded that will stay above water, and then start moving people. I doubt any of the pyramids will be entirely submerged by rising waters, and we can always use the upper levels, but I want to know what they think. Fast!"

It was a good idea, diverting the water into the aqueducts. Jor Alesh had seen them on her own journey into Azar when she came up river from Jurnda. They started at the western end of the valley where the river was higher in altitude and then carried water off to the fertile lands of the open plains before the sea. Fortunately, they were on the Nadrasuli side of the valley, opposite from where the volcano had blown out. If they hadn't cracked and crumbled in the earthquakes, they might be able to significantly affect the flow of water backing up behind the growing wall of cooling lava. There would still be a flood, but at least it wouldn't be a flash flood. And it was true that they would most likely still be able to use the upper floors of the pyramids, though this would isolate them into virtual islands, making caring for the injured all the more problematic.

"We're trapped here," said Chondrasil, as much to the air as to Jor Alesh. He put his face in his hands. He was disconsolate.

He was right. High mountains bordered the valley of Azar on both sides. The only way in or out of the valley was the river, which was now rendered impassible. Jor Alesh knew what this meant - help from Jurnda would not be forthcoming - at least, not any time soon. They'd have to find a way around, or wait until the lava had stopped and cooled and the volcano relaxed before attempting to come up the river. Even then, they'd have a difficult time bringing supplies or getting injured people out. This truly was a disaster. How were they going to manage?

"You need to set up a triage center," said Jor Alesh, calling Chondrasil out of his despair. "Do any of your pyramids serve as hospitals? Do you have any doctors or medical equipment?"

"Samudje was our only doctor," said Chondrasil.

"Was?"

Chondrasil nodded. "He was also a Maegin-Lu. He was seated with the others when the Flower of Azara came down. Most of us can function as healers," he added, "but we don't serve wounds of this kind. There used to be a medical center at the waterfront where doctors from Jurnda would visit and tend to the sick. Those who were in greatest need would be brought back to Jurnda. Our focus here has always been on the spirit, not the body."

This last truth was relevant in more than one way. While the pursuit of technological development and medical science was normal in Jurnda, here in Azar, technology had mostly been foresworn for a more austere and primal life. They had no communications technology, no powered vehicles, none of the conveniences that Jor Alesh and her fellow Jurndans took for granted and expected to be part of everyday life. For some, this was part of the appeal of life in Azar. It was comparatively rustic and anachronistic - the way the Azarans wanted it. They had their traditions, their pyramids, their drink, and their doctrine - that was enough. Everything else was considered a distraction and temptation of the secular and material world. Their disdain for the material was apparently going to make this an even greater challenge than it might have been.

"What about the lay community?" asked Jor Alesh. "Surely they have doctors, or at least midwives."

Chondrasil brightened, slightly. "Yes, they do have some. Their resources are even cruder than ours, but they may be of some help . . . if they haven't all run off into the jungle already . . ."

Clearly this wasn't going to be easy. "Who can I talk to?" asked Jor Alesh. "Let me take care of this. It's the least I can do."

"Katudrup . . . talk to Maegin Katudrup. He'll help you."

After that, Chondrasil just stared at the wreckage before him. It was as though all his dreams had been shattered by the horrific event. Jor Alesh could only imagine what was taking place in his mind right now. For him, this was judgment passed down from on high by Azara. They had been punished. This wasn't just a natural disaster: this was personal, and it was a message intended for him. She could tell by the look on his face. He had failed as High Maegin. He had allowed heretics into their sacred sanctuary, and Azara had rendered judgment upon them all, killing infidels and would-be monks alike. Yet he had survived - wounded, but still alive. Left as a witness to his own folly and downfall. Whatever inner equanimity he had cultivated as a monk was left shaken to its very foundations. Whatever he had imagined would accompany the arrival of the Darsulans, *this* was not it.

Without saying more, Jor Alesh left Chondrasil, bleeding and overcome with sorrow. In her wake, others stepped in to try to console the High Maegin - gestures of support that were dismissed with angry waves of his hands. Even those who tried to attend to the wound on his face were sent away. For his own reasons, he wanted to suffer. "Make yourselves useful!" Jor Alesh heard him shout as she began her descent to the base of the exterior of the pyramid where the wounded and injured had been collected. She glanced back and saw everyone else withdraw as well, aside from those who were doing their best to clean up the wreckage in the center of the ritual room. It was a sad scene. Secretly, Jor Alesh also understood that it marked the possibility for change. Destruction of the old always made way for something new . . .

It took her some time to find Maegin Katudrup. Jor Alesh found him helpful, and several hours later, they had managed to set up a recovery center in one of the pyramids at the far western end of the valley, farthest away from the initial disaster and the rising floodwaters of the Qya. It was in the shuffling of people back and forth from one end of the valley to the other that Jor Alesh realized that it wasn't so much of a valley as it was a series of plateaus. *This has happened many times before*, she told herself as she surveyed the geological reality around her. How many times had lava burst forth from the volcanic ranges, dammed the river, created a flood plain, and then the water had broken through? The whole layout of the valley indicated that the answer was many times. In geologic time, this was a constantly shifting and changing environment - one marked by fire and water in continual cycles. *We could have seen this coming.* Human time, by comparison to geologic time, was the blink of an eye. Failure to think in the truly long term had contributed to many of the tensions of the *Great War* - changing climate, overuse of resources, deforestation - all these added to the already volatile mix of ethnic, cultural, religious, and political rivalry that had spurred the war on. Humans needed to think in the long term. Most never saw past the boundaries of their own ego-generated illusions. Was it foolish pride that had inspired those original Azarans to build their temple city here? Whatever it was, they were paying for it now.

Exhausted at the end of the day, Jor Alesh met with Chondrasil once more. Much of the lower valley had already flooded. As Chondrasil had predicted, the diversion of water into the aqueducts had bought them time and not much more. The lower third of the valley was flooded and waters were still rising. Based on estimates of the engineers, a full three quarters of the valley would be underwater by tomorrow morning. The water was expected to crest around midday - provided that more lava didn't pile on top of what was already blocking the river from its usual course. At that point, the new lake would begin to pour over the fresh lava creating a new waterfall where the waterfront once was. It would take a massive effort to break apart the new dam. It would also require the aid of Jurnda, as the Azarans had long ago relinquished all of their mining equipment after the final pyramid had been completed hundreds of years ago.

"I have to get back to Jurnda," Jor Alesh said to the now bandaged and obviously exhausted High Maegin. Though still hurting, Azar was at least stable for the time being. The triage center was up and running - mostly relying on the expertise of lay healers - but functional, nonetheless. Grudgingly, the Darsulans had been given a residence pyramid of their own above the rising floodwaters where they were mostly keeping to themselves and mourning the loss of their beloved matron, Meridalthi. Others had organized efforts to coordinate food and supplies. Everyone had gone into survival mode and was helping in whatever way possible. There wasn't much more that Jor Alesh could do from here, and thus her priority had shifted to finding a way back to Jurnda. At the very least, she knew that she would be needed and expected there, and once in Jurnda, she could help coordinate the relief efforts for Azar. First, though, she needed to get home. "There's got to be another way out of here."

Chondrasil thought for a moment as a displeased look passed over his face. "In the old days, when we were still working the mines, there were roads through the mountains. You've visited with the demon, so you know the roads. Go ask him. If anyone knows a way over the mountains, it would be him." Clearly, he wasn't fond of the idea of Seyloq - they very man Chondrasil blamed for what had occurred - becoming involved in the disaster, even in a minor way. It had been Seyloq who duplicitously invited the Darsulans in the first place and brought the wrath of Azara down upon them all. A smile crossed his face. "But if there's any justice, Azara will have brought his demon house down upon his head and buried him there in the wild just like he deserves."

Jor Alesh ignored this comment. What she wanted to say was that the true fault lay with the founders of Azar for having chosen this geologically volatile location for their sacred city in the first place. They had wanted an isolated refuge, secreted away from the distractions and temptations of the world, a refuge for their divine work. From what she understood, the symbol of the Twin Fire Dragons as protectors of the Flower of Azara was an ancient myth that originated from the time when the Azarans had lived back in *The World*. It was said that in the heavenly ascent of the first Azaran Maegin, *The Nameless One*, (Was he nameless because his personal identity was insignificant, or was he nameless because he was simply a mythological figure with no historical reference?) had to pass beyond two dragons (sometimes also called "serpents") on his way to commune with Azara in the form of the complex geometric "flower." To pass beyond them, according to the story, *The Nameless One* had to speak the dragons' true names, Ladjup and Nadrasuli. If he had failed, his soul would have been eaten by the dragons, after they incinerated his physical body. By all accounts, *The Nameless One* had been successful and thereby created the religion of Azara. How long ago that might have been - a thousand years . . . ten thousand - Jor Alesh had no idea. It was a story that was still taught in schools in Jurnda and was used to explain why the Azarans felt that they had reached the promised land. Apparently, the founders' interpretation of the local geography had been too auspicious to pass up, despite the dangers. It was ironic to the extreme that the very features they had deemed protective in nature would cause the disaster they faced today. For Jor Alesh, it was another lesson in how the delusional imposition of beliefs onto reality clouded the judgment of individuals and collectives alike. And it was still happening with Chondrasil's assessment that Seyloq was to blame. Beliefs, ultimately, helped people avoid responsibility for their own choices and only served to wrap them in a narrative of fantasy, projection, and illusion.

Knowing that it would be fruitless to challenge Chondrasil - you could only awaken those who wanted to be awakened, for facing the true complexity of reality was always a personal choice - Jor Alesh offered no critique and instead chose to focus on the practical. "Good," she said. "I'll head out tomorrow morning. If you had communication equipment here, this would be much easier, but since you don't, I'll have to travel to Jurnda personally. For tonight, I'll gather as much information about the disaster and the conditions of those who have been killed or injured and take that with me. I'd also like to speak with your engineers so we can try and address the issue of the dammed river, and what can be done to relieve the flooding of the city. And I need to know how many Darsulans are here, and what you intend to do with them."

Chondrasil sighed. "They should go. They're not welcome here."

"Be that as it may," said Jor Alesh, "many of them are injured, and they have their own dead to attend to. I would think it profoundly lacking in compassion of you to try and send them away at this time, no matter what you think Azara wants or doesn't want. Help and assistance from Jurnda is going to be for everyone - Azarans, Darsulans, laypeople, and even the people of the forest, if they need it. I will do what I can to coordinate rescue and relief efforts for everyone. In the meantime, I expect you to treat your guests well. Anything less will seriously strain relationships between Jurnda and Azar."

Chondrasil gave her a sharp look. "You don't rule here. We don't recognize your authority."

"No," she responded. "You are High Maegin and this is your city. I'm informing you of what *I* expect if you want *our* help. For now, I expect the Darsulans to be treated well, and given the attention and hospitality they need. Their leader lost her life in this tragedy, along with several others from their group. They probably have their own religious interpretation of this event. What I *don't* want to find when I return to Azar is some kind of holy war or scapegoating. We're all in this together, Chondrasil. Despite whatever you believe, this is a time for us to work together - like everyone is doing now. And if you insist upon it, your followers will listen to you and follow your example. If you go around expressing your belief that the Darsulans are somehow at fault, it won't take long for the situation to become far worse than it already is. Now is the time for diplomacy and compassion, not further divisions along lines of religious identity."

"They will be well treated," said Chondrasil. "You have my word. Now go and do what you have to do. I don't need to be lectured, and I don't need your advice. Go and be Alcian. I'll take care of Azar."

With that, Jor Alesh left Chondrasil and began the long task of collecting as many details about the disaster as possible, working late into the night. In the morning, she would find her way home.

Chapter 29

MUSHROOMS?

It was late when Jendru and Seyloq finally turned in for the night. They had sat out under the stars talking, smoking, and enjoying each other's company while they reflected on the day's events and speculated about what might be taking place back in Azar. Seyloq had readied a spare room for Jendru, informing him that he was welcome to stay as long as he liked or deemed necessary. "And the bed's big enough if your girlfriend shows up too," he had added with a knowing smile.

Going to sleep had been an interesting phenomenon for Jendru. As soon as he closed his eyes, the colorful geometry started, filling his inner vision as though he had taken a large glass of the communion drink. For a time, he wondered if he would ever sleep again. *Is this what Seyloq goes through every night,* he pondered. There wasn't any particular content to his visions - just endless transformations of infinite geometric patterns and matrices, continually turning on themselves, expanding, contracting, and shifting in color and form. It was beautiful, but didn't make for restful sleep. It felt good, however, so he accepted his condition and let the play of forms do their thing. Eventually, sleep found him.

When he woke in the morning, the sun was already high in the sky, streaming in through the open windows of his room, along with the perpetual sounds of the jungle. Jendru lay in bed for a few moments, listening and feeling. Neither the ground appeared to be shaking nor did he hear the distant rumble of a volcano. It appeared that the brunt of the disaster had completed its cycle and whatever was occurring in Azar now was merely the aftermath of yesterday's unexpected turn of events.

Jendru found that he felt truly excellent. Despite his difficulty going to sleep, he was still enthused with a fervor and zest for life - his life - that he had never truly known before. He felt full of energy and an eagerness to explore his new life. Whatever was to come next, he felt ready.

He got out of bed and threw on a light pair of pants that Seyloq had left out for him. In fact, Seyloq had provided him with several clothing options. It seemed clear to Jendru what the message was: you're no longer a novice or follower of Azara, and it is time to dress accordingly. Jendru reflected on how much of personal identity was tied up with appearances, attire, and personal style and accoutrement. Seyloq had always dressed inconspicuously and casually. There was none of the pomp and explicit symbolism on his body that was so prominent among the Azarans, where everyone's identity was clearly marked by their clothes, hair (or lack of it), and tattoos. They were all so busy fitting into the structures of Azaran belief that no one was truly being himself - they were too focused on being members of the religion and indicating their status in the strict hierarchy. For many, it seemed to provide them with a satisfactory sense of personal identity and purpose. Yet Jendru knew that it simply wasn't authentic. They may have left their secular identities behind, but they were still overtly structured by the dogmatic identities imposed upon them by the Church. It was still ego - just reformulated and made sacred, but still ego nonetheless, even if they didn't see it that way. What a game!

Jendru gathered up his old clothes, intending to take them outside and burn them in Seyloq's fire pit. As he was doing so, he also took a few moments to look around his room. Something surprising caught his attention. There, on the wall above the bed he had spent the night in, was a fabulous piece of art. It was an abstract piece with strong bilateral symmetry, like a matrix of energy that divided directly down the middle, each side mirroring the other. It was complex and almost seemed to move, causing Jendru to wonder if he was in some permanent state of experiencing the medicines without having to consume them. He recognized that the art reflected Seyloq's emphasis on bilateral symmetry in the body and its relationship to authentic energy, as opposed to the asymmetrical manipulations of the ego in the body and its attempt to control the infinite flow of authentic energy that welled up within each individual. But what was more, he recognized the art for what it truly was, for the style was unmistakable. This art was created by Jendru's parents, Sila and Jeresh.

Jendru sat down on a chair opposite the bed and stared at the painting. He recalled how, not too long before he made his decision to go to Azar and commit himself to the religion, his parents' art had gone through a transformation. This theme of bilateral symmetry had suddenly invaded everything they produced, especially the pieces that they worked on together, such as this painting here. At the time, Jendru hadn't thought much of it, and in fact, had been somewhat dismissive. He had become enamored with Azaran symbolism and artistic expression as his enthusiasm for Azara grew. Azaran art tended to exhibit radial symmetry, like in the Flower of Azara, and Jendru's affinity for this style led him to dismiss the "secular" art of his parents as being uninteresting. Now he saw it in a new light, and he reached a startling conclusion about his parents: they knew Seyloq. That would explain their lack of enthusiasm for his decision to join the Azaran religion. It had been peculiar to Jendru at the time. They had always supported and encouraged him in all that he did, but when he had informed them of his desire to become a monk, they had seemed disappointed, though they tried not to let it show. He had known that despite their words, in their hearts, they had wished for something different for him.

Yet they had said nothing, and instead had decided to let him follow his own path to discover the truth for himself. He found that an overwhelming sense of love was welling up within him for his parents, knowing that they had served him precisely as he had needed to be served. Though his ego had wanted their approval, and nominally, they had given it to him, he had always known, there in the back of his mind, that there was something amiss - something they weren't really saying to him. But if they had said it then, most likely it would have only served to drive a wedge between them. He had been so fervent in his desire to become a monk, and so self-righteous in his commitment to what he then believed to be transcendent truth, that he never would have heard them. And if they had told him of Seyloq then, perhaps he would have developed an inner resentment and judgment of the one who had helped to liberate him before he ever encountered Seyloq. And if that had happened, he probably would have been inside the Obsidian Temple yesterday taking his vows along with the others. It was all speculation, of course. But this alternate path seemed clear to Jendru, and he realized how close he had been to having all the excuses he would have needed to never discover his true nature. Yet things had happened as they had, and he had discovered what he had, and now all he found was infinite love in his heart - and not only for his parents, but for everyone and everything. There was simply no limit. It was unconditional and universal. Love, for Jendru, was simply reality.

Jendru emerged from his room full of questions, ready to talk to Seyloq about his connection to his parents and how they had come to work with him, for he felt sure that this was the case - his parents had taken the medicine with Seyloq, completely unknown to him. Their view of the world and of themselves had been transformed at the hands of this man who had altered his own world, and he wanted to find out more. It was exciting to think that he had this unexpected connection to his parents. It gave him the confidence he needed that he could share everything with them, and that they would fully understand, and even congratulate him, on his decision to leave the Church. He also knew that he didn't *need* this understanding from them, or anybody else. But this didn't change the fact that he *wanted* it. They were his parents, after all, and he loved them. The hope that they could fully live in reality, all of them awakened to their true nature, filled him with an exciting and fluttering energy. Above all, it meant that he wouldn't be alone in his newfound self-awareness. Though he had rejected the family of the Church, he still had his true family.

Jendru searched about the house and looked around outside. Seyloq was nowhere to be found. In his place, Jendru discovered a bowl set out on a low table in the front room. Inside were several dried mushrooms. They had shrunken, golden caps, with white stems that were stained blue in places. They were unfamiliar to Jendru. He picked one up and sniffed it. He couldn't say it smelled all that good. If these were meant to be culinary mushrooms, one would have to have a taste for manure to enjoy them. Setting the mushroom back in the bowl, he noticed that beneath the collection of dried fungi was a note.

It read: *I've gone to take a look at Azar and see how things are there. I should be back by nightfall. Make yourself at home and enjoy these gifts of Darsulan medicine. When in doubt, remember: Stay symmetrical! - Seyloq*

And that was all. No instructions. No comments about how strong these medicinal mushrooms might be, how long they would last, or what kinds of effects he might expect from them - just the universal command of "stay symmetrical!" Jendru smiled. He didn't have any other plans for the day, so why not?

He was hungry, though, so first he went about preparing some food to break his fast. After, he gathered up his old Church clothes and made a small fire outside. One by one, he burned the items of his ceremonial attire, feeling ever more free and liberated as he did so. When it was all completed, it was midday, and some light rains were moving in, bringing warm, humid air with them. Jendru got out a blanket and placed it on the grass in front of Seyloq's home. He brought out the bowl of mushrooms, along with some water to help wash them down. He suspected they weren't going to taste so great. If he could drink Azara, he was confident that he could get these strange smelling fungi down.

His prediction that they would taste like shit proved correct. It wasn't so bad, though there was an earthy, decomposing taste to them. He found that the more he chewed, the less the taste mattered. In comparison to Azara, they weren't that bad at all. They crunched in his mouth at first, and then swelled with the addition of his saliva like rehydrating crackers. It took him some time to chew them all up and get all the small fragments that had lodged themselves in his teeth and gums down. Eventually, the bowl was empty and all the mushrooms were in his gut, which he could feel begin to react to what he had ingested.   Now there was nothing to do but wait.

Jendru lay back on the blanket, looking up into the leaves and branches of the tree above him.   He was immediately struck by how the twisting branches and patterns of veins in the leaves were, in essence, identical to the geometric formations that he had seen the previous night while lying in bed, which were themselves identical to patterns he had seen many times while drinking Azara. It was obvious that *everything* that existed was an expression and manifestation of the same fundamental and universal patterns of energy. It didn't matter if it were a tree, a mountain range, a cloud drifting through the sky, the veins in his body, or the patterns of thoughts in his mind - it was all basically the same. There truly was no separation. Everything was an expression of the same thing, the same energetic process.

Waves of energy started working through Jendru's body as the mushrooms began to do their work. He felt himself alternate between warm sleepiness and jittery, vibrating cold waves that passed over the surface of his body. It was both similar to Azara and also different.   He speculated that whatever the active ingredient of these mushrooms was, it must be similar to that found in Azara. It occurred to him that *someone* ought to figure out what these ingredients were. The contents of the Azara drink were a carefully guarded secret within the Church - a secret he knew (Though technically, this was something that was supposedly only revealed to those who had taken their vows. It had been Chondrasil himself who had exposed the secret to Jendru. He knew exactly which kind of vine and which kind of leaf was used to make the communion drink - and that the truly active ingredient was in the leaf, not the vine, which only served to activate it and catalyze it in the human digestive tract). It wasn't much of a wonder that his fellow novitiates had called him "Chondrasil's pet," given the High Maegin's willingness to bend the rules where he was concerned. Whatever high hopes Chondrasil might have had for Jendru in revealing these divine secrets prematurely, they were surely dashed now.   Never again would he be Chondrasil's pet.

Feeling the waves of the mushroom energy wash over him as his heart and mind began to open, Jendru let all concerns for active ingredients and Chondrasil and the Church and everything else slip away. He lay on the ground, symmetrical and open, as Seyloq had taught him. He closed his eyes, letting the inner theater of the medicine unfold and transform before him.

At first, there was only the light of the sky and sun, as filtered through the dappled leaves of the tree above him, playing against his eyelids, seen as red and gold spectrums of light. Gradually, subtle geometric forms started to take shape in the expanding sea of color, slowly moving and breathing. As they grew in intensity, a sharp, almost electric blue that was tinged with white edges started creeping in at the edges of his vision. The electric blue contracted into the center of his vision, almost seeming to eat or consume the reds and golds, leaving only stark, empty blackness in its wake. When the electric blue reached the center, nothing was left - only pure, impenetrable darkness.

Then, as if someone were turning on small pinpointed lights one by one, the blackness began to take on the look of an infinite, starry sky. First there was one small point of white light, then another, and then another. Faster they came until all the blackness was filled with starry brilliance. Jendru found himself at the very center of the cosmos, and infinity stretched out in every direction.

One star, which appeared to be in the very center of Jendru's vision, began to glow brighter than the others. When it did, it illuminated a subtle geometric matrix that suddenly and unexpectedly revealed that the apparent randomness of the placement of the stars wasn't random at all - it was only the effect of their relative brightness. When the matrix was lit up, Jendru could see that in fact each star was located somewhere on a grid of interpenetrating and repeating geometric forms across various levels simultaneously. Everything, every star, had its place within the matrix, and despite any appearances, absolutely nothing was random or chaotic. The matrix itself was made of subtle blues and reds that ebbed and flowed following Jendru's own pulse and breath. As the star in the center grew brighter, Jendru began to understand that he was showing himself himself - he, as Jendru, was that star, but he was also the entire matrix and all the stars within it - he was both Jendru and everything that was not Jendru. His true identity was *everything*.

As the star that he identified as Jendru grew in intensity, he saw that the stars that were in the most immediate proximity to this central star (which were themselves located at the outer points of the geometric star pattern that encompassed the central star), began to shine more brightly as well, though not as bright as the central star. Once these lit up, the matrix shifted so that now these stars were no longer on the points of the geometric grid, but were themselves center points of their own starry grids. Then the subsidiary stars about them began to glow brighter, and as they did, the increasing intensity of brightness expanded ever-outwards, with more and more stars bursting into full illumination. The message to Jendru seemed clear: his own awakening to the truth of being would galvanize those he had immediate contact with, and they in turn would galvanize others, spreading out across the entire grid until every star, every individual, would shine with the full force of their genuine inner light. It was precisely like what had happened between Seyloq and Jendru and Jor Alesh. Then, Seyloq had been the central star and they the periphery. Now, they were their own central stars, and those who surrounded them would be similarly awakened to the truth. This was how it worked, how the process would proceed: one individual at a time. And given enough time, the energy of awakening would sweep across the fabric of reality. It would be a universal awakening, accomplished one person at a time.

Once all the stars were lit, still with his "own" shining the brightest in the very center of the vision, the matrix that bound them all together faded from view. Once more it appeared as bright stars in a black, universal emptiness. Then it began to shift, as though his perspective was receding from the stars, or vice versa. He went so far out from the stars that they began to collect together in an undifferentiated whiteness. Jendru realized he was looking at a galaxy from a point that was far removed in space, as though he were looking through one of the high-powered telescopes in one of the research universities back in Jurnda. For all intents and purposes, he seemed to be staring out into deep space.

Momentarily, the view gave him a feeling of vertigo. He noticed a sudden urge to open his eyes and adjust his body, which once more came into his consciousness. He remembered that he was lying on the grass outside beneath the tree, and was not, in fact, floating disembodied in the deep reaches of outer space. He took a couple breaths, felt some fluttering energy in his abdomen, and let his shoulders and back relax, checking internally to make sure he still maintained his open, surrendered, and symmetrical posture. *Everything is perfect,* he found himself saying internally. *Let the vision continue.*

And so it did.

The galaxy was still there, and his perspective was still floating out there in space, but now there was something moving inside the image of the galaxy. Something was coming *toward* him. At first, it was only an indistinct dot of color in the vision, but as it drew closer, more details came into focus. Of all the odd things, it was an eagle flying through space. It wasn't like any eagle Jendru had ever seen, however. In shape, it resembled the large grey eagles of the jungle that preyed on monkey and sloth. But unlike those actual eagles, this visionary eagle was rainbow colored in its plumage - and not just rainbow colored, but vividly so. It was breathtaking and majestic in appearance, and though he had nothing to judge its size from, Jendru intuited that it was enormous. It flew directly up to the place of Jendru's perspective and landed (on what?), facing him directly, staring deep into his eyes (if he even had eyes in this seemingly disembodied perspective).

Jendru and the rainbow eagle studied each other intently for some time. Jendru marveled at the bird's beauty. He could only love it. It was so exquisite. Internally, he was about to ask the question, "Who are you?" when the truth dawned on him: he was looking into a mirror. *I am the eagle.*

It was too obvious! Laughter and joy rippled through the fabric of the vision, revealing its artificiality. *I am the eagle!* It was even in his name! Jendru was a variation of the word *jendruli,* which meant "one who sees" or "seer" - a common word used for eagles, given their exceptional sight and ability to discern fine details, even from very far away.

With this realization, the eagle suddenly took flight once more, but rather than seeing the eagle as exterior to his own perspective, Jendru knew that he was looking through the eyes of the great rainbow bird. He could feel the beat and pulse of its massive wings as it plunged into the sea of stars that was the distant galaxy, which was looming ever larger within his vision. The closer he came, the more distinct individual stars became. Once more, he could see the geometric matrix that bound them all together. The matrix began to resemble the Flower of Azara, as though he were looking down on it. It was twisting, the way spiral galaxies do, and he was being drawn into it, through the center. He could feel himself moving through layers and layers of energy, all parceled out in various spectrums, like traveling through some rainbow matrix. The Flower was spinning faster now as he drew ever closer and then suddenly shot through the very middle and found himself on the other side.

The visionary scene was totally different. Rather than images of space and cosmos, Jendru found that he was looking at some kind of religious gathering. There was a temple, shrouded in shadows, but still rendered visible by the ambient torchlight that surrounded it. Jendru could make out that it was shaped as an enormous jaguar. People were moving into the temple through the left front paw of the great beast. They were robed in red, and through the doorway and hall that was the foreleg, he could see that there were many more people inside, circumambulating about, dancing and swaying. The temple itself appeared made of gold. It was strange and completely unfamiliar. Jendru had no idea why he was seeing this, or what it might mean.

Then the vision shifted again. Now he was seeing what appeared to be enormous statues or works of art, one after another, all in amazingly intricate detail. From his perspective as an eagle (or once again a disembodied point of view - he wasn't sure which, and it didn't matter anyway), he was able to fly all about them and inspect them from all angles. Each statue was made of four faces or sides, and each face exhibited perfect bilateral symmetry. The first was made of four eagles, facing outwards, the tips of their outstretched wings touching. Another was what Jendru knew to be made of bears (though he had never seen a living bear himself as they weren't indigenous to Lur). Others were animals that he couldn't recognize, but they were all equally beautiful and powerful in appearance. And like the earlier jaguar temple, they were all made of gold and encrusted with sparkling jewels and gems. He had never seen anything like them. He wondered if they were from the past, the future, or the present. Was he seeing something that was, or something that might be? He had no idea. All he knew was that they were beautiful. The level of intricate and astounding detail was phenomenal - he could clearly see every constituent bit of their composition down to the very molecules themselves. Everything was perfectly ordered, like billions of tiny puzzle pieces that all fit together in one vast and complex symphony of form.

The last statue he came to in his vision was that of a human being. Like himself, it was male and looked vaguely like him, though it also seemed simultaneously generic and non-specific - it could have been anyone. Although it was standing, the posture reminded him of what he must look like after taking a hit of the toad medicine and lying on his back with his arms open, head reaching back, and eyes looking upward, slightly rolled up into the head, with the edges of the retinas barely visible. It was clear - this was a person in a state of ecstasy and full energetic opening and release. *A posture of universal embrace,* Jendru told himself. Similar to all else he had seen, the statue was made of extremely fine gold work with inlaid jewels that scintillated in the hyper-defined light of the vision. The surface of the statue was shaped with intricate, interlaced geometric designs, as was everything else in the vision. At the breast, over the heart of the statue, was a radial design that was reminiscent of the Flower of Azara, similar to what he had seen earlier when the galaxy had transformed into pure geometry. There was another variation of the same theme on the center of the forehead, above the eyes, and a third at the statue's golden sex. A subtle line ran down the very center of the statue, dividing the entire image into two mirrored, symmetrical sides with fractal patterns radiating out in subtle movements and flows in either direction.

Though Jendru had little awareness of his body right then, it occurred to him that he was still lying in the grass outside of Seyloq's house in a posture that mirrored what he was witnessing before him. *It's all a mirror*, he said to himself, feeling the truth of this statement saturate his being. *All observation is observation of the self, for there is nothing else.*

Suddenly, as if in response to his inner knowing, the vision of the statue shifted. Torus-shaped torrents of energy were exploding from the male form from the three primary energy centers of the body: heart, mind, and sex. The largest energy vortex, by far, emanated from the heart center, bringing the others into its universal flow of energy. Subtle shifts of rainbow colors of lights in amazingly complex forms coruscated about the image of the man, making the once inert image appear alive with vital energy and being. Jendru marveled at the beauty of what he saw. His fascination drew him into the image, passing beneath the surface to witness the subtle inner workings of the human form.

He saw organs, systems within the body, energy flows, complex networks of fibers and nerves and veins. Everything was laid out before him. It was as though the human form were being deconstructed and broken down into all its component parts, revealing the intricate geometry and structure within. It drew him so far within that the very molecular structure seemed to be revealed, appearing much like the images of stars and cosmos that he had seen earlier. *The human body is the supreme interface*, he realized. *It is the ultimate reality enjoyment vehicle. It is perfectly poised between the extremes of the minute and the immense, finely tuned to receive and process energetic systems across all levels simultaneously, both within and without. It is complex enough to process high-level thought and self-awareness, while also allowing maximum personal expression and choice. It is the supreme nexus of the universal body of the One. Every person is a full expression and embodiment of the One. We are all God in human form. We are divine.*

Abruptly, the vision shifted again. Now, the inner

workings of the body appeared to Jendru not as a cosmos, but as a sophisticated network of circuitry and electrical activity. He could no longer tell if he was looking at something biological or technological, organic or inorganic. Vast webs of information locked together across detailed circuit boards and microscopic processors. Yet even here, everything was fractal and symmetrical, just as the original image of the body had been. The message was clear: the human body was a technological marvel, and the human propensity to create technology was an extension of this truth of being. Rather than the largely anti-technology bent of the Azaran religion, he found that his true inner essence embraced and loved technology as a genuine expression of being. *This*, to Jendru, seemed the true expression of knowledge and self-awareness. Technology was made possible by genuine knowledge and discovery. It was not dependent on belief, ritual, symbolism, dogma, or doctrine. Technology, and the science it sprang from, was true because it was a reflection of the energetic and mathematical/geometric nature of reality, as was the human body and all lifeforms. Human science and technology seemed God-like because *it was.* There was no magic and slight-of-hand involved - only observation, understanding, and innovation. This was what the whole human evolution project was primed for. This was the full expression of God in embodied form - mastery of the elements of creation and their transformation for human use, the ultimate God vehicles.

Seeing and understanding all this, Jendru's awareness shifted to the *Great War* that had so devastated humanity and the precious planet they depended on for their life. He knew that this had all been part of the birth pangs of a greater human reality, a new evolution that was reaching out from deep within humanity. When illusory belief and false identity, created and projected by the ego, wrapped in symbols and patterns of religion, culture, and politics, had developed the weapons of mass destruction, their delusions had nearly brought humanity, and all life on the planet, to an end. They were like little children, not realizing the tremendous potential of what they had created through their sciences and technologies. Rather than using these evolutionary masterpieces to their advantage and liberation, they had turned against each other and used every means available to annihilate each other in an apocalyptic bloodbath. The answer, Jendru knew, was not to outlaw religion, as had happened back in *The World,* or to reject technology, as had happened in Azar, but to overcome the false beliefs and projections and embrace the fullness of human reality. The only way forward was true knowledge - knowledge of the fundamental nature of the self through inner knowing, and knowledge of the fundamental nature of reality through scientific observation and measurement. Only through knowing the inner and the outer with complete clarity and self-awareness could the destructive and delusional nature of human society and expression be overcome.

From the center, all things are clear.

Jendru felt himself at the vanguard of a new evolution, a new humanity, and ultimately, a new world. The old taboos and fears could be overcome and left behind. Religion, fear, and dogma were obsolete. Illusory boundaries of separation and isolation, those products of the ego, were similarly obsolete. The future of humanity was one liberated from the need for religion, spirituality, and fantasy-based systems of thought and behavior. It was one of integration with technology and scientific development. It was God's gift to humanity - the capacity to truly know the self and master the energetic environment to humanity's fullest potential as creative and expressive beings. And with clarity and genuine self-knowledge, balance could always be maintained. It was the ego and its workings that brought humanity into such perilous, asymmetrical relationships and energetic exchanges. From the clarity of the center, all things were in perfect balance and symmetry. And humanity was ready. He knew it. If it weren't, he wouldn't know what he did. Seyloq never would have awakened, nor awakened Jendru and Jor Alesh, and who knows how many others in turn. It was simply time.

Energy always follows the path of least resistance.

Jendru marveled at the complexity of it all, and the impartial nature through which evolution proceeded. There were no favorites, no preferences given. God, as humanity, had been willing to nearly destroy itself to make this current reality possible. The One did what it needed to do, never taking sides, never coddling or pandering to any part of itself. It had *all* been necessary, somehow - the war, the exodus of the Azarans, the founding of Azar and Jurnda, the exile of the Darsulans, Seyloq's excommunication, and Jendru's own stumbling into the toad medicine just as Jor Alesh crossed his path. It was the most marvelous drama, comical and tragic, that he could possibly imagine. *Everything is part of the process. It cannot be any other way.* Microcosm and macrocosm, individual and collective, self and other, it was all the same. And in the end, it was all absolute, unconditional, ruthlessly fierce love. All versions of the self were expendable - all were only temporary. It was the process, the evolution; that was the thing. And no matter what, all individuals served this process, this great, universal becoming. They served it either consciously and willingly, or unconsciously and unwillingly - it made little difference in the end for the process. Yet it made all the difference for the individual. *Sleepwalkers will always suffer,* Jendru told himself. Yet he knew that awakening was not the end of suffering, either. Surely he, like everyone else, would die. He was awakened, but he was no miracle worker. He wasn't a saint or some ascended master, working great mysteries and wonders. He, like everyone else, was only a human being - a living embodiment of the One. But this knowledge gave him strength and empowered him from his very core. He had let go of his fears, his need for personal identity, his grasping at meaning, at purpose, at specious truth. All he wanted was to live in reality, whatever joys or pains it brought him. For him, the time of illusion and false belief was over. He was liberated. He was free.

And he knew he would share this understanding with anyone who was willing to listen and do the difficult work of genuine self-discovery. There was no mystery here - it was an energetic reality. The ego, as a collection of energetic constructs and patterns, limited the individual from the full energetic expansion and awareness that was each person's birthright and fundamental nature. It was not a religious or spiritual problem. It was not an existential separation. It was not something that could be legislated away, or engineered into society by rational rulers. It was a truth that had to be discovered within, and the surest route to this discovery was direct and immediate experience, as afforded by the medicines. There really wasn't anything else to it - it was just that simple.

The medicines, freed from their restrictive and dogmatic use within pre-existing religious structures, were the ultimate tools. They went right to the heart of the matter: the false energetic boundaries and holdings created by the individual ego through a long process of choice and conscious self-definition. The medicines worked because they acted on the biological and energetic structures of the human body. It was so simple! Everything was energy, and these medicines made the full energetic nature of the self open to observation and self-knowledge. There was no mysticism or arcane knowledge involved whatsoever. It wasn't much different from technology, Jendru realized. In order for technological creations to work, they needed a source of energy. The human body, the ultimate reality enjoyment vehicle of God, was no different. The ego might naturally and habitually obscure the true nature of the self, but reality also came complete with the tools necessary to transcend that habit of illusion and separation. Reality had supplied both the problem and the solution. No prayer or ritual or doctrine was necessary to experience this truth and make use of the tools that had been provided. Anyone who wanted, and who was willing to undergo the energetic rigors of the work, could discover his or her true nature for him or herself, directly and immediately.

Though he couldn't know what it would look like, Jendru was convinced that if more people knew, if everyone knew, it would be a completely different world. It would be a world without religion, without politics, without arbitrary separations and competing identities. People would live for their own maximum expression and self-fulfillment, fully embodying the reality of God's self-love. And through doing so, all the constituent parts would mesh together in perfect balance and harmony. Violence and war would be a relic of the past, as would persecution, judgment, fear, and envy. Technology would serve humanity and the planet, rather than serving death and destruction. The weight of existential questions would evaporate. Metaphysics and speculation would dissolve away in the face of truth and genuine knowledge. It was all so perfect. It was *exactly* what the inevitable process of evolution was heading toward. *This is the process.*

Just imagine . . .

It was time for the world to know the truth.

Jendru knew the only way for him to be authentic and genuine with himself was to share this truth. Though he had a choice, he didn't really have a choice, for the time of hiding from his true nature and avoiding the commitment that it demanded of him was done. He had seen through the guise of his ego and all that it had brought him in his life, and he knew: no more. Though he didn't know how he would do it, or what it would look like, his commitment was clear. He would share the truth with others by being completely and utterly authentic with himself at all times. He would share the truth by being the truth, like Seyloq. Yet he also knew that for him, that didn't mean living up in the hills, removed from the workings of society. He wouldn't be a beacon in the wilderness, as was Seyloq. He felt himself drawn deep into the heart of society. It was this very drive that had brought him to Azar with dreams of one day becoming High Maegin, and now this drive was sending him forth into a new world. As much as he might like it to be so, he knew in his heart that he would not be satisfied here on the outskirts of human activity. He needed to be in the center of things, where he could feel the pulse of the world and apply pressure or assist in release as required. He had been on the sidelines for long enough. Not any more. No longer would he recluse himself, walled off from the world. It was time to dive in head first, confident in his own being and self-knowledge that he could freely follow his heart, and would be able to meet whatever challenges and difficulties might come his way as a result of embracing that choice.

It is time.

Jendru knew he wasn't a prophet for a new religion. He

was the truth, embodied, alive, and conscious. His only commitment was to being himself, fully, completely, and without reservation. The infinite could not be communicated in words. It was not something that could be understood conceptually, and it could not be an object of belief, worship, or praise. It was only something that could be experienced directly, and the only way to share it with others was to embody it - to live it. It was the only way.

The final series of images that Jendru saw in his vision centered on a book. Out of the fundamental geometric matrix of the vision, two disembodied hands held out a book with a worked leather cover. The hands opened the book before him. The pages were translucent and on them were abstract geometrical designs in black ink. Each design was bilateral in symmetry, like butterflies spread out upon the pages. The designs were beautiful, but otherwise seemed without meaning or specific intent - just abstract forms. Yet before Jendru could study the images carefully, the two visionary hands shoved the book at Jendru, seeming to push the book into his heart. With that, the vision disappeared.

Unexpectedly, Jendru's eyes suddenly popped open. It was late afternoon, the sunlight slanting through the trees at a sharp angle. Awareness of the world around him flooded into his senses. Everything was so alive! The warm, moist wind caressed his skin. It felt perfect, sublime. Birds chirped as they flitted about from tree to tree, and the toads were singing in the background. High overheard, a large eagle circled, passing between the bulbous, drifting clouds that let out a soft rain that didn't quite reach the earth, evaporating in the air. Jendru followed the grey eagle with his eyes until it disappeared into the clouds. One last burst of energy ran through his body, giving him the shivers momentarily, and then quickly balanced out.

The mushrooms were done. They had run their course. He could still taste them in his mouth, which was mucky and needed water. Jendru also noticed a somewhat uncomfortable sensation of gas in his gut - a product of the mushrooms, no doubt. He could feel it moving through him. He passed gas loudly while also belching. It made him giggle as he thought of how he would have received disapproving looks had he been in a ceremony in Azar and made such rude noises, as though it were possible to offend God.　He farted again - long and slow and very satisfying as a broad grin passed over his face. "Human bodies sure can be disgusting!" he said with a tone of absolute love and joy - which surprised him, as he realized that he sounded like Seyloq when he was speaking in the God voice - low, deep, and richly resonant.　He flopped back down on his back and relished his beautifully disgusting embodied nature.

It was good to be alive.

Chapter 30

HI THERE, BEAUTIFUL

Somehow, Jendru fell asleep there in the grass in the warm afterglow of the fantastic mushroom experience. When he awoke, he looked up to see a stunningly beautiful woman standing over him, face framed by the brilliant colors of sunset and looking down on him lovingly. She smiled and he felt his heart flood with warmth.

"Hi there, Beautiful," he said, still sounding deep and resonant.

"Hi there, Lover," she said back as she slid down on top of him, bringing her sex to rest on top of his, which immediately responded by swelling and hardening. They kissed. A delicious energy passed between them, reminiscent of their lovemaking the day before.

Jendru stopped them briefly, asking, "Is Seyloq with you?"

Slyly she shook her head as she licked her lips and started undoing her shirt. "He's with the forest people," she said. "He'll be back in a couple more hours. We've got plenty of time."

With that, they both let themselves go, allowing their bodies to do what they wanted with each other in an ecstatic exchange of energy and sublime release. It was perfect. It was eternal.

It was love.

Chapter 31

AZARA'S WRATH

Seyloq showed up a couple hours later. Jendru and Jor Alesh were sitting outside by the fire, eating some food they found inside and enjoying each other's company. Jendru was glad to see the older man. Admittedly, he had some worries that if he were found sneaking around Azar, he would be snatched up by Chondrasil and others in an attempt to make a scapegoat of him. Thankfully, that wasn't the case, and if he had been hassled, it didn't show.

Jendru and Jor Alesh hadn't had too much time to talk in Seyloq's absence - they had mostly been busy enjoying each other in other ways. Thus, when Seyloq joined them, they all recounted recent events together and took stock of what had occurred, and what was to be done about it. Seyloq rolled a smoke for himself and shared with the two lovers, bringing them all into a relaxed, yet still energized state.

"I don't know if Azar will ever recover fully," said Seyloq, letting the smoke drift out in lazy blue clouds from his nostrils. "The flooding is bad, and the lava dam on the river is large and thick. I'd be amazed if they'll be able to break through it and get the floodwaters to recede."

"We'll have to try," said Jor Alesh. "That's why I need to get back to Jurnda and coordinate from there. We can help."

Seyloq shrugged. "It might not be enough."

"Did many die?" asked Jendru.

Jor Alesh gave him a sympathetic look. She hadn't yet shared what she knew with him.

"Enough," quipped Seyloq. "Enough for them to call it 'the wrath of Azara,'" he said while shaking his head.

"Many are hurt," said Jor Alesh, "and some of your friends . . ."

Jendru only nodded, not bothering to ask for clarification. It was clear by Jor Alesh's look that people he knew and cared for had died. It didn't really matter, he supposed. That was no longer his world and there wasn't anything he could do about it anyway. Everyone died, in the end. The One continued on. That was the way of things.

"Chondrasil?" he asked.

Seyloq laughed. "It will take more than a volcano and some lava to stop that one!"

"He's hurt, but otherwise alive," said Jor Alesh. "Things are a mess down there, so he has his work cut out for him. He could use help. I need to get back to Jurnda."

"You can leave tomorrow," said Seyloq. "The old mining roads go over the mountains up past my house. I've kept them reasonably clear. They're in pretty bad shape on this side, but once you get on the other side, they're in much better condition. I've got a vehicle stashed over there. You can use that to get back to Jurnda."

"You have a vehicle?" asked Jendru, unbelieving.

"How do you think I travel back and forth to Jurnda?" Seyloq asked. "I can't very well walk, and traveling via the waterfront in Azar isn't open to me. So I found my own way. I go back and forth from Jurnda more than either of you probably realize - that's how I know your parents, for example, Jendru."

"So you do know them!" he blurted. "I saw the painting. Why didn't you tell me you knew them?"

"I just did."

"Earlier, I mean?"

"And that would have helped your work here with me how?" asked Seyloq.

Jendru thought for a moment. He realized that it didn't matter. His work with Seyloq was his own, and that was the way it needed to be. Seyloq's connection with his parents was irrelevant. He had had to find his own way to the truth.

"I suppose it wouldn't have," he said.

"Do you want to see them?" asked Jor Alesh.

Jendru nodded. "Yes. I'd like that."

She reached out and took his hand, looking deep into his

eyes. "Then come with me tomorrow," she said. "Let's go back to Jurnda together. Go see your parents, then come and help me with the relief efforts. You could be my special liaison to Azar. Chondrasil might not like it, but I can't think of anyone who would be more qualified. You know the city and how it works and what their concerns are. You'd be perfect. And if you need a place to stay . . ."

"Ah, the truth comes out!" exclaimed Seyloq. Jor Alesh blushed in the firelight. "Put him to work, yes, but don't try and cover over what you two feel. Shit - live it up!"

Jor Alesh smiled. "Yes, Jendru," she said. "I do want you with me."

"And I want you with me," he said. "I'd like very much to come with you. And perhaps I can help you with Azar. I have the feeling that this is only the beginning. There will be plenty of challenges ahead, and this is only one of them. I don't yet know what I'm going to do, but I'm going to do something."

Seyloq nodded, understanding Jendru's passion. "Tell people the truth," he said. "Show them. Help them find it themselves. I'm old, and I can't keep doing all this back and forth. Besides, my place is here. But you two - you two are perfect. You're young, intelligent, and have access to all that you'll need to make a difference. If you answer the challenge, you'll both have a lot of work to do."

"I've been thinking about that," said Jendru, suddenly realizing that he already had an idea. It was a simple idea, but it was a place for him to start. "I think I want to tell people a story - our story. I want to write about what's happened here and what I've learned. I want to tell them about the medicine, and about you, Seyloq, and you, Jor Alesh, and how I've come to know and understand myself. I don't know what people will think, but it feels like a good place to start - at least, in writing all this down, I'll come to an understanding of what's changed for me and why. And most importantly, who I am - who we are - now."

Jor Alesh smiled and squeezed his hand. "As long as I get some of your time and attention, that sounds good to me."

"Good," said Seyloq, taking one last drag from his

smoke and flicking the butt into the dwindling fire. "You've gone beyond Azara. Now go home. Go home and be yourselves. In the end, that's all there is to do. If you need me, you know where to find me," he added, opening his arms to indicate that he'd be right there.

"Thank you," said Jendru. "For everything you've done for me, for us."

"Yes," agreed Jor Alesh.

Seyloq shrugged. "I am you, and I love myself completely and without reservation. Everything I've done for you or anyone else has been for myself, and that's the way it will always be. End of story."

"Yes," said Jendru, gazing into Jor Alesh's eyes, who returned his passion and love in equal measure. "End of story."

And so it was.

Chapter 32
DOWN PATHS
UNKNOWN

The next morning, Jendru and Jor Alesh set out together for Jurnda and the new life that awaited them both, heading down a road that neither had yet traveled, confident that with each other, and the clarity of their knowledge within, they would find their way . . .

ALSO BY MARTIN W. BALL:

TALES OF AURDUIN

PREVIEW:

OROBAI'S VISION

CHAPTER 1

The Jewel

Tired. So very tired. Even here in Jeaniaurduin Orobai could feel his strength and vitality leaving him. *It won't be long now.* Not yet, but soon he would lay himself down to sleep his dreamless sleep of death, only to be reborn from the body of the world, Eyar. For over 23,000 years it had been the same. Every one hundred and thirty years or so Orobai would "die" and be reborn again. He could feel it now. Soon the process would happen again, but he still had a little strength left in him.

Orobai pushed the weariness back from his mind and tried to cast it from his body. Closing his eyes, he struggled to recall the dreams. They had started coming to him not long ago. Images he couldn't recognize. Strange shapes and machines that he had never seen before filled his mind with visions of metal and suffering. Digging, tearing at the earth, odd metal bodies stirred up death and destruction, poisoning Aurduin.

People were suffering. They seemed to be from many cultures of far and distant lands in Aurduin. They were forced to work against their will. *Slaves.* There was so much he didn't understand in the dreams. *What can they mean?* Never before had his dreams been filled with so much darkness.

Orobai had come here to Jeaniaurduin, the Heart of the Sacred Land, to rest through the cold winter. Even now, in late winter, the lush and verdant lands of Jeaniaurduin seemed to teem with the life and energy of perpetual spring. Clear, life-giving waters bubbled up from deep underground springs, fed by the far away abyss of the Goarnaltrai near Norgath. Orobai always felt perfectly at home here, lost among the twisted branches of oaks and the soft murmuring of leaves in the characteristically pleasant breeze, accompanied by the songs of birds and babble of brooks with water lapping on stones.

But none of this comforted Orobai now. The dreams had only become more frequent. The rest he so badly needed only seemed to drift further away from his reach. Instead, he was filled with dark visions and an anxious heart.

Something was changing in the world. Orobai could feel it. He knew it. The dreams were only the beginning. Something profound was happening.

Orobai had long been one to dream. The Arnyar had always emphasized the significance of dreams to him and he had learned that much of value was revealed to the sleeping mind. Sometimes the meaning was immediate and obvious. Other times meanings were hidden deep within esoteric and cryptic symbolism and vague and shadowy images. There were techniques that would help to reveal such hidden meanings through meditation, even while sleeping. These recent dreams, however, had impressed Orobai with a firm sense of reality, as though the surface of the dream was reflecting actual events in the world. Something terribly disturbing, something that had never happened before, was now taking place somewhere in Jeaniaurduin. He knew he had to see for himself. Perhaps then the dreams would lose their anxious power.   He was apprehensive about what he might find.

Orobai waited until Urya was a quarter of the way through the sky before starting out to the southwest, where Jeaniaurduin met the great plains of Nulthali. Orobai had been camped at one of his favorite spots on Lilgurinlth, Clear Water Creek. Here the oaks were ancient and wise and all the land, air, and water were clean and pure. Orobai had come here often through his many lives simply to meditate and be with the creatures of the oak forest – the foxes, wildcats, raccoons, squirrels, and all the many birds who made their homes here. He would sit by the clear running water and listen to the songs of the birds in the early morning and late evening, watching the rising and setting of the sun and moon. It was peaceful here and was a place of eternal spring, for even in the dead of winter the grass was still green and many plants continually gave flowers. It was as though a perfect balance of natural elements existed here so that life could eternally flourish. But now something was changing and its effects reached even here, into this sanctuary. The peace and tranquility was threatened, but by what?

The sun was high enough now to break through the twisting canopy of the towering oak trees. Orobai climbed to the top of a small outlook above Lilgurinlth and "sang" the rest of his belongings home to Golgath. Long ago, really as far back as he could remember, Orobai had learned how to use the Altfein to temporarily collapse spatial distances. He was never exactly sure how he was able to accomplish this, but he knew that when producing the proper combination of tones while blowing on an object he could direct it to far away locations.   It did not matter much to Orobai how this happened, only that it did, and that it was exceedingly convenient. In this manner he could quickly deliver whatever he wanted to his home in the north and all would be waiting for him, just as he had prepared it, when he returned. Now he sent back a final collection of stones, clays, and dried herbs and plants he had collected in Jeaniaurduin. Once everything was gone, he quickly performed one of his many shape shifting transformations and in an instant was circling up on the warming morning air as a jet-black raven.

In his natural form Orobai was a rather unusual looking creature. His most distinguishing characteristic was his pure black color that rivaled the darkness of the night sky or even Norgath, the Black Mountain. Upon his face was an inordinately large nose that protruded like a large beak and contrasted sharply with his dark, penetrating eyes. Stooped over by a severely hunched back, he carried himself about with a staff. From his head fell long strands of matted and tangled black hair, giving him a wild and untamed appearance. Though he did his best to hide his unusual form under a heavy black cloak, Orobai was clearly unique. There was no other like him.

Though Orobai had the ability to transform himself into any kind of being, albeit temporarily, he found the form of the raven to be most suiting to his "natural" form. Like himself, the raven was black, had a large "nose," and had the ability to produce impressive vocalizations from the common squawk to intricate gurgles and trills, which Orobai likened to his own singing ability of being able to produce rich vocalizations of multiple tones simultaneously from a deep drone to high-pitched soaring whistles. What was perhaps even more fitting was that Orobai had learned long ago that like him, ravens had a proclivity for finding and collecting bright and beautiful objects. They too found shimmering jewels nearly irresistible.

If he wanted, he could be a majestic eagle, but then he'd have to worry about someone trying to get his feathers. Or he could be a graceful waterfowl, but then someone might try and eat him. These other forms just did not feel right anyway. The raven simply fit.

Dressed in black feathers, Orobai took to the wind. Urya was warm and bright, the land below was green. If it weren't for his dreams, Orobai would have thought all was well in Aurduin. To the north Orobai could see distant clouds that threatened snow, and on the mountains to the west he could see the white tips of far-off peaks. To the southwest the land sloped away to the great plain of Nulthali where many of the waters of Jeaniaurduin that bubbled up from its natural springs ran and the great herds of grazing animals roamed. From there the waters flowed into the sea among the many islands and reefs beyond the horizon in the western archipelago.

Looking out to the west and imagining the flowing of the water to the ocean in his mind, Orobai thought of how long it had been since he had traveled to the far west. Aurduin was a vast place, and though Orobai traveled about it regularly, he gravitated more towards some areas and peoples than others. Recently, which for Orobai meant the past several hundred years, he had passed much of his time with the Yamné in the north and the Ulusi-Rata in the east. He had found a place among these peoples and was happy to have their company and share in their joys and tragedies.

From the lands of the Yamné and the Ulusi-Rata the west coast seemed far indeed and it had been many generations since Orobai had spent any time among the peoples of the west. In fact, it had been so long now that Orobai supposed there had probably been great changes in their cultures, languages, and customs. Perhaps he would have to learn them all anew. Maybe in his next life he could concentrate some time and energy on getting to know these peoples again, Orobai thought to himself. Perhaps in his "old age" he had gotten too sedentary, too accustomed to old friends and old habits.

After a couple days of flying, Orobai finally arrived where he felt his dreams had been pointing him. Circling about in the air, Orobai's attention was called back from his mental wandering to the view below him. Something seemed amiss in Nulthali. Usually he could see some of the grazing animals on the great plain, but even from his vantage point high in the air, he could see none. As he looked closer he saw that even the small birds seemed to be absent and all below him was quiet.

Yet there was something far more disturbing. Just as in his dream, in some areas it seemed as if some great beast had dug at the earth with enormous claws and raked the land clear of all living things, leaving barren, gaping holes in the landscape with dark tunnels leading deep into the ground. Indeed, it had been many years now since he had come to the edge of Nulthali, but he could never remember seeing this before. There was no doubt in his mind that this was not a natural phenomenon, and certainly was not the result of any creature that he had ever encountered.

Almost fearful of what he might find, the raven flew down for a closer look, settling into a circular pattern drifting over the damaged terrain on gentle currents of air. It was clear that the waters that flowed through and around these damaged areas were not pure and clean as they once had been. There was an odd color to the water and nothing living remained on the banks of the creeks and streams. All was dead and desolate. And in the dust and dirt left over from the excavations were strange tracks that were not of any animal. Mixed in with these odd tracks were the footprints of many people, all leading off to the west on distant roads that passed beyond the horizon. *What could all this be?* Orobai wondered to himself.

Orobai began to think of his home. Though it would be very cold to the north, he longed to sit by the fire and rest his weary body. Besides, the Yamné would be coming soon, looking for their sacrament, and no doubt wanting him to join them in their annual winter ceremony. Yes, he could go home, despite the unusual marks on the land below. He would continue to sort through the strange images of his dreams. The answer would come, in time. There was always more time, and as curious as he was, this was a mystery that could wait.

Just at the moment when the old one circled to the north, about to make a direct line toward his home, something caught his eye. Down below in one of the excavated areas something flashed in the now-waning sunlight. Orobai knew the glint and flash of all of the gems of the world and could easily identify them in an instant, even with his raven eyes. But this was new. Something different. Something he had not seen before. And that got his attention.

Quickly he swooped down. Still in the form of a raven, he hopped close to where he had seen the glittering jewel. He kept his raven form as he felt very ill at ease here in this desolate area and thought it best to be prepared for a quick flight, if necessary. Though he told himself that he had not seen anyone, he could not shake the feeling that something here just was not right and thought it best to be on his guard. A nervous raven, he hopped about cautiously, turning his head from side to side and pausing every few moments as he sought out the shimmering object he had seen from above.

Hopping up on a small mound of dirt, Orobai could see that the jewel that had caught his raven eye was in the center of a small lake that had been drained in the course of the strange excavation that had gone on in the area. Why no one else had seen such a radiant gem seemed puzzling, but for whatever reason, it had been completely overlooked.

But how could anyone miss this? What a jewel!

It was large, for one, easily requiring two hands to simply hold it. *And its light!* It shimmered in pure and translucent white light that seemed not only to reflect the light around it, but seemed to actually emanate from its own depths, from somewhere deep within its core.

It certainly was not one of the Altfein. Those were not nearly so large, and they came in pairs with the Sarnfein being sharp and angular and the Alkeinfein being rounded and smooth. This was neither, however, and it was alone. This jewel was rounded, oblong and somewhat egg-shaped, but cut at clear and precise angles, much like a large, expertly cut diamond. It was unlike a diamond, however, for the pure white radiance that emanated from within it was unlike any ordinary stone. And what was more, as he came closer to it, hopping cautiously across the bed of the now dry lake, it seemed to hum and resonate in a soft and beautiful tone. Never had Orobai encountered such a singing stone as this.

What, in all of Aurduin, could this possibly be?

Orobai hopped all around the gem, inspecting it from all angles, cocking his head this way and that, listening intently to its soft song. It was utterly magnificent. No imperfections or blemishes of any kind were apparent. And its sound! *How enchanting!* It would be just the thing to give him something beautiful and mysterious to ponder through the long winter nights that lay ahead as he awaited the spring. Something this attractive might even help him forget the disturbing images of his dreams.

He decided to take the mysterious gem.

Orobai quickly transformed himself into his natural form, after having taken one last brief look around to make sure he was still alone. The gem came easily from the dry lakebed with the dirt quickly falling away, revealing a perfectly formed and unblemished stone. It was heavy, yet sat comfortably in his hands. It had a good solid feeling to it, though it also felt paradoxically light, almost buoyant in his hands. He turned it over several times, getting a good look at it and assessing it with his lifetimes of experience with gems. "Truly unique!" he pronounced to himself with satisfaction. This would be the find of a lifetime, or even many. Finding something new and yet unseen was always a great, and now exceedingly rare, occurrence for Orobai, and this was rare indeed. *Perhaps the Arnyar might have something to say about this,* he thought to himself. He took one more loving glance at the mysterious gem and quickly sang it back to his home where he would find it waiting for him among all the other things he had already sent back from this journey to Jeaniaurduin. "The trip to Nulthali has certainly been worth it," he concluded, speaking to himself.

Turning back into his raven form, Orobai began the long journey north to his home at the foot of Golgath as Urya sank beneath the western horizon and Ranya began to peak over the hills to the east. His wings felt propelled by his growing fascination and wonder for the strange gem. Now if only the weight of the disturbing dreams could be left behind, then he'd truly feel young again.

ABOUT THE AUTHOR

Martin W. Ball, Ph.D. is a novelist, independent entheogenic researcher, professor of Religion and Native American Studies, and musician. In addition to *Beyond Azara,* his novels include the *Tales of Aurduin* fantasy series. His most recent writings on entheogens and nondualism/mysticism are *Being Human: An Entheological Guide to God, Evolution, and the Fractal, Energetic Nature of Reality* and *The Entheological Paradigm: Essays on the DMT and 5-MeO-DMT Experience and the Meaning of it All.* Martin currently lives in Ashland, Oregon with his wife, Jessalynn, and dog, Moxi. His books, music, and art can be found at his website, www.martinball.net and other online outlets.

Made in the USA
San Bernardino, CA
21 January 2013